PANU

PANU

ELYSIUM'S MULTIVERSE | BOOK 2

Ranyhin1

Podium

Copyright © 2024 by Trent Boehm

Cover design by Jason Nathaniel Artuz

ISBN: 978-1-0394-5251-0

Published in 2024 by Podium Publishing
www.podiumaudio.com

Podium

PANU

CHAPTER 1

Boom!

The door to Allie's left shattered in a cloud of splintered wood, and the roar of battle could be heard all around her.

She ducked and wove in the dying light of day, shredding a man in a spray of viscera with a black arc of light from her wand. Granite exploded amid a hail of holy lightning smites that fractured the building around her, and dozens of skeletons poured forth through the courtyard to meet a charging horde of men and women wielding maces, baseball bats, shields, guns, and swords.

Priests in the back lines frantically healed the front-line warriors of the chapel's defense, using the powers of their newfound holy book to quickly mend the flesh of their comrades in flashes of white light whenever bone claws and teeth tore at their bodies.

She blurred across the far wall of the outer courtyard and into a side building, her hand tearing through the throat of a woman just as she opened the door. Blood sprayed across the worn paint, and Allie launched herself through another window to hit the ground and roll amid the spray of bullets, taking one of them to the skull where her bone mask deflected it.

Her hand gestures blurred, producing a spell of black and neon-teal death energy that crashed into the bloodstained grass in front of her like a freight train. Forming rapidly, a spire created from mana ripped out of the ground— Unholy symbols etched into its body that radiated a curse to apply a weakening effect on all living creatures within its zone. The area around them darkened for hundreds of feet in all directions despite the sun remaining on the horizon. The men and women fighting her small army noticeably slowed, already exhausted from the drain of the battle, and the undead began to push forward with more brutality.

Out of the alley between buildings behind her, a series of death balls rocketed overhead and slammed into one of the towers overlooking the courtyard.

Screams were heard from overhead, and the tower began to crumble and crash to the ground while more of the undead poured in.

Allie turned and ran over to where the attacks had come from, seeing her subordinates slowly walking toward her. There were three of them, all souls she'd saved from Chalgathi's trials, all loyal to her despite not being her minions. Rather than that, they were all independent undead that had chosen to serve her for the grace she'd shown them. And in turn, they all had their own minions to add to Allie's for this assault.

Each was a low-level necromancer just like herself, though instead of being vampires like her, one was a ghoul and two of them were called skresh. Each of them also had a different type of necromancer specialty class, which made their inherent pathways to power a lot different than one would think, considering they were all necromancers.

As for what skresh were: skresh were a form of living skeleton, though they certainly weren't mindless like the creatures charging the compound. They were also a lot thicker in terms of basic body mass when compared to normal skeletons and were able to modify their own bodies by collecting new materials that made them rather intimidating to look at. Undead anatomy was a bit complicated, and there were still rules to abide by if one wanted to maintain stability within one's undead race. But because these skresh were just now starting to level up and grow after being trapped in stasis for so long, they hadn't had the time or power to incorporate anything other than more reinforcing bones along their basic humanoid skeletons. Each arm and leg had multiple long bones along their shafts, fused together with death mana, and their eyes would start radiating neon-teal light whenever they activated their mana channels. Instead of a hollow interior underneath the rib cage and along the spine, there were interwoven cords of mana strapping a cage of further reinforced bones onto one another as well.

"Mistress . . ." The hooded ghoul necromancer by the name of Mara bowed at the waist, followed by the other two hooded and more skeletal figures of Nin and Vin. "We destroyed the messengers sent for aid. The prophet will likely not know of this attack until the morrow. I have also stationed some of my raven familiars along the rooftops overlooking the more prominent paths through the city; if the prophet does manage to send troops, we will see them coming."

Allie silently nodded, examining the ghoul. Mara was rather pretty, with long raven hair that trailed down her breasts and a patchwork of stitched flesh melded together from pieces of females she'd killed that Mara found attractive. Incorporating them into herself and stabilizing their flesh with necromantic powers, Mara had managed to become quite the beauty—with the exception of her dead, milky eyes. She'd evolved her necromancer class into something called a Novice Black Summoner. It allowed Mara to see into the void that permeated reality around them, and she could bind shadow familiars in place of undead creations or even fuse the two types together to create a shadow-undead hybrid—but fusions cost three times the normal minion slot requirement, so it was reserved only for the personal guards she created. Of which, two pitch-black skeletons holding long daggers blended in and out of the shadows of another doorway off to her left.

Allie had actually had this class presented to her as an option as well, though she'd opted to take the Novice Swarm Necromancer instead, which boosted her up to a staggering two hundred basic undead minion slots and two captain undead minion slots. The captains, which she hadn't successfully created just yet, were supposed to be intelligent and could control the other undead she commanded, giving her swarm a command stat buff whenever they were nearby. However, she'd failed every time she'd tried to create a captain-type undead, as it required the soul to remain completely intact while simultaneously controlling them.

Allie's current minions were all just soul shards rather than entire souls. They were merely fragments of the souls they'd once been, used to manipulate the skeletons she was sending in waves at the chapel ahead of her, and neither she nor any of the other three necromancers she'd befriended had figured out how to completely control an intact soul yet.

This was also why she'd been unable to save Jose. The day he'd died, she'd tried to keep his soul here in the physical realm—but it'd slipped through her fingers despite all the power and knowledge she'd acquired. He'd died bleeding out in her arms as she wept uncontrollably, and she'd vowed vengeance on the people who'd so eagerly cut him down just for being in the wrong place at the wrong time.

For not wanting to accept their bogus new religion.

"Good job on hunting down their messengers." Allie gave an approving nod as Mara smiled brightly up at her with her milky-white eyes. "Nin? Vin? Did you plant the bombs?"

Each of the skeletal skresh cackled delightedly, eagerly nodding with Nin on the right side rubbing his bony hands together. "It is done! Time to rake in more bodies and materials for us to use!"

Allie grinned maliciously underneath the skull mask she wore. Nin and Vin had actually been brothers in their past lives; they'd ended up learning a bit of necromancy before they'd died, though they'd progressed farther following her than they had before their first deaths. They followed each other's footsteps and paths to power to a tee, basically copying one another as long as the system would allow it, and were both a type of necromancer that specialized in plagues. They were called Novice Deathbringers, which severely limited the number of undead they could have but enabled them to imbue their minions with various types of plague resonating with death magic. One of their abilities, called

Corpse Bomb, allowed them to create zombies with built-in bombs. They were essentially suicide bombers, and when triggered, they'd blast an area with death mana and simultaneously release a wave of cursed plague that spread many times farther than the actual blast radius. It rapidly caused people to decay and necrose, resulting in a painful and horrible death, and would literally peel flesh off bone. The plague was contagious as well, though it often killed people far too fast to spread much.

And as of right now, those suicide zombies were positioned along the perimeter of the opposite side of the chapel, where more of Allie's minions stood in hiding. Now, with the front of the chapel and courtyard under heavy siege, it was time to come in through the back. They'd piled bodies upon bodies in various positions around the chapel in preparation for the siege, and with each new minion cut down by the prophet's forces, more of them were raised up and sent in. In total Allie and her three subordinates had collected well over a thousand bodies in nearby buildings along the ruined city, meaning that the chapel defenders—who only numbered in the couple hundred—would each need to do some heavy lifting in order to offset the number disadvantage.

Allie gave an affirmative nod, clasped her hands behind her back, and waited for it to begin. Within ten seconds, a flare of holy light enveloped the chapel, likely a reaction to the subsequent blasts of black and teal mana that rocked the ground she stood on. Screams from within the chapel echoed out amid the clatter of weapons and battle within, and the holy shield abruptly shattered when three more blasts ripped through the stone walls on the opposite side.

With a mental command, the shrieks and clattering of undead rose like a hurricane, and her minions rushed in through the back of the compound. With the majority of the defenders at the front end and those akin to civilians in the back, her creations tore through them like a wrecking ball. The flank had been incorporated spectacularly, and soon the primary fighters would be pinched on two sides.

The battle was over, and Allie had won.

The words of warning from Negrada haunted Riven's sleep that night as he slept in the makeshift bunker he and his two demonic minions had created earlier that week as a safe haven. It was located in one of the cellars of the ruins, but this would likely be the very last night he slept here.

He'd be hunted just for what he was?

Because he was a vampire now?

Then again, he'd murdered Ben in cold blood without even realizing what he was doing until it was already too late. His insane hunger and crazed state of mind had led him to literally eat the poor guy in a disgusting act of cruelty, and the knowledge of this was gnawing at Riven's guilty conscience at a constant rate.

But he couldn't just avoid human society. It simply wasn't an option for him. Allie, his little sister, and his best friend, Jose, were both human. As long as they'd all survived, they'd probably be waiting for him. The system had told him right before starting Chalgathi's trials that he'd have the opportunity to make it back to them as long as he survived. There was no way he could drag them into a den of creatures like himself.

And he wasn't even going to entertain the thought of how they possibly could have died. No, that wasn't an option. They were alive, and he needed to get back to them soon.

The small rectangular room was devoid of all light, with wreckage from an age past piled in front of the door as he hid in a closet in the back corner, using the sack of Jalel's old belongings as a pillow. He tossed and turned as the howls of demons and undead alike echoed through the ancient hellscape, and even after waking up the next morning he still found himself mentally exhausted, with little appreciation for the minimal sleep that he had managed to get.

He stared at the ceiling for a few hours, listening to the echoing cries throughout the city, until his minions eventually appeared another eight hours after he'd woken up.

"We were watching the entire thing from the nether realms! That was so brutal!" Athela squealed with excitement as the arachnid promptly exited her portal from the nether realm and rushed over to his side. She began violently and excitedly whacking his forehead as he blankly stared back at her, and her giddy, chittering laugh echoed throughout the room as Azmoth stepped through a fiery portal of his own. "Oh my gawddd! Riven, you beast you! Why didn't you tell me you had an ancient vampiric bloodline?! Oh *mur gawd*, you're so buff now, too! And handsome! Riven, you should have stayed ugly. Now I'm going to have to fight off all the succubi who want to contact you for a new contract."

CHAPTER 2

Riven couldn't help but smirk at that one, and he began to feel a little bit better having his friends back so he could talk about what happened. "Succubi, huh?"

"Yes!" Athela whacked him again and sat her big thorax down on his lap with a prompt humph. "Though you should really wait awhile before you even attempt to bind one. I assume they've already started knocking on the door in your mind?"

Riven blinked, then nodded. He could feel numerous otherworldly creatures, their auras, pressing up against his consciousness—inviting him to come speak with them. "Only a handful, but yes."

"Well, ignore them for now."

"Why?"

"Because the longer you wait, the more time they'll have to discover you. Don't commit to one until you have more options. Plus, you can't bind them until level 35 anyways, right?"

"Right."

Athela nodded vigorously. "Yes, yes! I'd say wait at least a month! Despite your fast progression, binding demonic familiars and acquiring new contract slots is very hard to do most of the time and is not to be taken lightly. Wait awhile and then decide—don't even try to talk to them now. Oh, and that poor Ben guy, such a shame! Was he at least tasty?!"

Riven's eyes narrowed at the chipper spider in the dark, ancient cellar, and he didn't bother to reply.

Athela quickly caught the hint, and her usually buoyant demeanor faltered under his angry gaze. "Sorry. I forget you're a little nicer than most warlocks I've heard of, or vampires, for that matter. You probably felt bad about accidentally eating him. That's it, isn't it?"

"Don't feel bad," Azmoth stated in a deep, rumbling voice as the huge demon approached the other two and slid down the wall with a grating sound of his metal plates against stone until he came to an abrupt stop. The Hellscape Brutalisk placed a clawed hand on Riven's shoulder and shook his head. "Not your fault."

Riven gave Azmoth an appreciative nod. "Thanks, man. Yeah, it made me feel shitty, that's for sure. What's worse is that I was trying to save him. I'll figure my thoughts out eventually . . . but onto more important things. Now that I've killed a miniboss, I can exit the dungeon at any time and end the tutorial if I focus on the command Exit Dungeon, but first I'd like to evolve you two. You both have pending evolutions, right?"

Azmoth grinned widely, and Athela shrieked with delight.

"Yes! We have our very own evolutions!" Athela began dancing up and down on her four hind legs but abruptly stopped to look down at Riven skeptically. "I'm not sure you can afford them yet, though."

"What do you mean?"

"How much Willpower do you have? Have you checked out what our available evolutions are yet? This is another reason why you need to wait on the new familiar—each additional familiar will cost more Willpower, and every familiar you have will take up more Willpower with each of their evolutions. If you're not careful, you could contract too many and stunt your own growth due to Willpower being more of a priority to Intelligence."

Truthfully, Riven had been so caught up in his own changes and the events that'd happened that he hadn't checked his minions' status pages yet, but Athela did him the favor of pulling them up for him. Each evolution would cost the master a certain number of Willpower stat points, otherwise the evolution couldn't proceed. He also quickly realized that the evolutions were slightly different in terms of what they offered: Athela had actual race evolutions, while Azmoth had bodily modification evolutions but kept his race the same.

[Available Evolutions for Athela:
- **Dryder: Your Blood Weaver will evolve into a Dryder, a half woman, half giant spider demon that gains a large bonus to magical damage and mana regeneration. Comes with one randomized offensive spell designated by the system. COST: 11 additional Willpower.**
- **Abyssal Trapper: Your Blood Weaver will evolve into an Abyssal Trapper. This demon has a set of six legs and two large scythes, along with numerous appendages along its back that are utilized for snaring enemies with webbing or injecting poisons. This evolution trades the speed of the Blood Weaver for a slow-moving and tanky evolution, but the utility and damage output are drastically increased. COST: 18 additional Willpower.**

- Arshakai: Your Blood Weaver will evolve into an Arshakai. Arshakai are humanoids with spiderlike attributes, specializing in assassination with their high speed and Agility and utilizing their minor shape-shifting abilities to infiltrate enemy establishments. Shape-shifting abilities are limited to both spider and humanoid forms. COST: 12 additional Willpower.]

[Available Evolutions for Azmoth:
- Tail: Your Hellscape Brutalisk will gain a tail, increasing the Agility per level as well as balance and acrobatic ability. Your brutalisk will become faster and more nimble. COST: 7 additional Willpower.]

Riven quickly reviewed his own status page after reviewing the potential evolutions.

[Riven Thane's Status Page:
- Level 18
- Pillar Orientations: Unholy Foundation, Blood Specialty, Infernal, Shadow
- Core of Original Sin—Gluttony: (Under Construction) (???)
- Traits: Race: Pure-blooded Vampire (Extreme Darkness Regeneration) (Sunlight Decay) (Extreme weakness to silver weapons, Sun pillar, and Light pillar attacks), Class: Warlock Adept, Adrenaline Junkie (Blood) (+15% to Agility)
- Abilities: Blessing of the Crow (Unholy), Wretched Snare (Unholy), Bloody Razors (Blood), Crimson Ice (Blood), Blood Lance (Blood) (Tier 2), Hell's Armor (Infernal), Riftwalk (Shadow)
- Stats: 50 Strength, 98 Sturdiness, 188 Intelligence, 98 Agility, 1 Luck, -308 Charisma, 155 Vampiric Perception, 59 Willpower, 9 Faith
- Free Stat Points: 14
- Minions: Athela, Level 13 Blood Weaver [14 Willpower Requirement]. Azmoth, Level 9 Hellscape Brutalisk [20 Willpower Requirement].
- Equipped Items: Crude Cultist's Robes (1 def), Black Redemption (74 shadow dmg, 68% mana regen, shadow dmg +27%, Black Lightning), Chalgathi Cultist Amulet (???), Leather Boots (1 def), Backpack of Supplies (Guild Hall: Stone Manor), Witch's Ring of Grand Casting (+26 Intelligence), Cloak of the

Tundra (22 def, +56 bonus def vs frost), Breath of Valgeshia (48 def, +13 dmg & +9% mana output dmg for blood dmg, 6% mana regen)]

So he had thirty-four Willpower already utilized to contain their contracts. He had fifty-nine currently, which was twenty-five free points already applied. That was just barely enough to both get Azmoth his tail and pick any one of the upgrades for Athela—including the most expensive one at an eighteen Willpower cost.

"Which were you thinking you wanted?" Riven asked curiously, looking up from the hologram in front of him that portrayed his stats.

Athela immediately let out a long, exaggerated sigh. "I was talking to my mother about this back in the void. She's got a load of her own opinions . . . but she said to go with my heart. I think I'll take Arshakai. It'll take some adjusting with the new body, but my fighting style and trait are Agility based, and I don't see myself changing that. Plus, the infiltrating stuff would be so neat, and I can switch back into a spider whenever I need to! Hee-hee-hee!!!"

The spider rubbed her two front paws together mischievously, causing Riven to grin.

"Fine. Let me apply my points, and I'll start the upgrade process now. Is there anything I need to know about these evolutions before we proceed?"

He looked from Athela to Azmoth, but both shook their heads and remained in quiet excitement. It was palpable for both of them, Riven could feel it, and he quietly assigned all fourteen of his free points to Willpower. Though he didn't need all of them for the evolutions, the additional few points would help for whatever evolutions or minions came next.

But upon selecting the evolutions for his minions, the changes were a lot more violent than he'd expected. At least in Athela's case.

"AAAAAAAAHHAHHHHHHH!!!!" Athela screamed in both excitement and incredible pain as her body shifted, limbs snapped, and parts of her innards began to bulge and split her carapace. Inky, smooth, pitch-black skin then started replacing her harder exterior. She belched ichor and writhed on the floor while hiccuping the nasty stuff out of her mouth every couple seconds during sudden, abrupt movements as her body expanded.

Meanwhile, Azmoth looked back over his shoulder with a "tee-hee-hee" chuckle as his lower back exploded—and out of it came a long, thick tail. It was spiked, covered in plate armor just like the rest of him, and easily doubled the length of his body from the tip of his head to the tip of his new appendage. Sinewy, muscular flesh underneath and between the spikes and obsidian plates flexed as he waved it around in the air, and the demon looked rather proud of himself as he spun excitedly around to show Riven. Sometimes Riven forgot that Azmoth was still a baby in the eyes of demonkind, but moments like this gave him pause to remember, and he celebrated with the large demon with a thumbs-up and a laugh.

SNAP-CRACK-POP

"Ow, this hurts!" Athela groaned and rolled around on the floor, finally coming into the final stages of her evolution as her body's features began to shape themselves from the writhing mass of flesh and muscle. Calf muscles, thighs, abdominals, and arms quickly took shape while ichor poured onto the floor after being purged from her body.

Riven's eyebrows rose in surprise upon her final completion, and as Athela stood up in the darkness of the cellar they resided in—Riven couldn't help think that she was actually quite pretty. He would never, ever tell her that—hell, he'd go to the grave with it so that she didn't get a big head or make fun of him for the rest of his life—but even as weird as it was to admit it to himself, he had to acknowledge it. It was very much a surprise, considering he had been expecting something more along the lines of thin and wiry, with more spiderlike features, but she looked more human that she did arachnid now, with a very demonic twist.

She now resembled a young woman, with silky black hair that trailed down to her lower back. Her skin was a mixture of white and pitch-black, as black as the void, and it almost glinted in the light of Azmoth's flames when the brutalisk flared up slightly to look at the tail he'd acquired. Athela was stark naked and had prominent womanly curves and features, the body of an Olympian and a perfectly symmetrical face with a strong but very feminine jawline.

Then came the demonic touch: she had the same two brilliantly red eyes. A long, black tongue briefly whipped around the room at a length well over twenty feet as she stretched it—cutting through the far stone wall like a knife through butter before she withdrew the tongue to zip it back into her mouth. She gave Riven a perfect, pearly-white smile. She had six arachnid legs protruding from her back as well, each of them far sharper, longer, and larger than the ones she'd had in the past, and she was easily able to climb up the wall using them—or even just her humanoid limbs, which appeared to stick to smooth vertical surfaces without a problem. The extra legs were essentially blades coming out of her back and were no doubt meant to be used as weapons. On top of that, every movement she made was utterly silent . . . Riven was pretty sure that it had to be a perk of some kind, because she made literally no noise walking up the wall until she began to test it herself. She tapped the ceiling up above once as it made no sound, then tapped it again with the same spider leg with a resultant sound.

CHAPTER 3

She'd gained a new silencing ability or trait concerning the movements of her body, in addition to the elongating razor-sharp tongue she could now use as a weapon.

As Riven silently admired her new look, she dropped from the ceiling and sputtered a cough of irritation.

"Ugh! I can't seem to get this shape-shifting thing under control!"

Riven watched as she furrowed her brows in concentration and saw her nose began to shift slightly—but then it quickly reverted back to the normal, symmetrical features she originally had a second later. "I'm sure you'll get it under control soon enough. How do you like the changes?"

Athela brushed the silky black hair out of her eyes, hissing in irritation at the failure of her shape-shifting, and stood to her full height while looking her new body up and down with her glowing red eyes. She turned around, looked at her backside, felt up her bare muscles, and seductively wiggled her eyebrows Riven's way. "How do *you* like them?!"

"Oh, shut up!" Riven laughed and threw his cloak to nail Athela in the face, knocking her over as she screeched in protest. It was obvious she was going to have a lot of coordination training to do before she got control of her new body, as a simple act like that would never have knocked her over while she'd still been a full-blown spider. "Put that on and stop playing around. We have to get out of the dungeon, and I'm truly tired of being here."

"Indeed!" Athela spluttered as she spun a cord of blood webbing from her fingertips and launched them at Azmoth with a splat. "*Yus*! I still got it, baby! You can keep the robe, too; I don't want it. I'm a free spirit! Your mortal clothes can't hold me down! Oh, and Azmoth—I like the tail!"

"Thanks, Athela. You look pretty."

"How sweet of you to think so, Azmoth! I wish I got compliments like that from our master, but he's too busy eating people to realize perfection when he sees it!"

Riven stared blankly back at them, then sighed and shook his head. Despite her shenanigans, he was really glad to have her back. Same with Azmoth. He'd missed them both, and he was looking forward to introducing them to his sister. He hadn't told Azmoth or Athela about Allie just yet, but he was sure that they'd get along.

"Exit Dungeon."

Light bloomed overhead and directly in front of him as he spoke the words aloud.

The portal erupted before them in the form of a set of translucent stairs leading up to a spinning vortex a couple yards above them.

This was it. He was finally getting out of here.

Meanwhile, Athela cackled with delight and playfully nudged Azmoth before whispering something into his ear. Riven stared up at the spinning lights, pondering what was awaiting him in the next step of this strange adventure his life had become, before the two demons abruptly picked Riven up and flung him into the portal headfirst, despite the profanities he threw their way before he was tossed unceremoniously upward.

[Pretutorial and Tutorial trials have been completed. Dao advancement is now possible.]

[You have exited Dungeon Negrada. You have completed your modified Tutorial and are now embarking on the beginnings of your new life on a newly created planet. Earth has been merged with worlds Zazir and Elhisterii to form the new world of Panu. Of the fifty-three billion original participants from these three worlds, thirty-two billion participants still remain. Of the thirty-two billion remaining participants, twenty-eight billion have finished their tutorials, while four billion are still finishing up. Do not be concerned, as this is within normal parameters for early integration death rates for tutorials.]

[All identification information prior to this point was previously enhanced by the system due to the Tutorial parameters, resulting in low-tier identifier-class level information on all items. Identification information parameters returning to normal. To acquire more information on your surroundings: obtain the identifier class, obtain an equivalent class, or utilize someone who has such a class.]

[New Quest: Finding Your Family—As promised by the administrator, your completion of Chalgathi's Trials and the Tutorial Trials
have brought you together in close proximity with your family and
friends. Allie has survived her trials and continues to live. Once per
day, you will receive a ping on Allie's general location to let you
know which way to go. Finding her and completing this quest will
grant you XP.]

The portal created by the system erupted into the new world, violently
expelling Riven and his two demonic minions from a height of six feet in the air
and landing them on a wet, grassy hilltop.

Landing with a thud, Riven scowled and rubbed his head. He was still covered in blood, completely disoriented after the transition with a mix of warring
emotions. On one hand, he was delighted to hear that his sister was alive. By
God, did that make him happy. But on the other hand, the system had told him
he'd be reunited after the trials were done . . . So basically, he'd been cheated, as
they were just "nearby" and he still had to find them.

Frankly, the bastard system had lied to him. Or at the very least, it'd only
given him a half-truth. And why had it only talked about Allie? It hadn't mentioned Jose at all.

Sitting up and letting his eyes adjust to the dim light, he noticed how much
more comfortable his vision was when staring into the darker places across the
landscape surrounding them—as opposed to when he looked up to the patches
and rays of sunlight streaming down from the cloud-covered gray heavens. It
wasn't that he couldn't look that way, but it definitely wasn't comfortable.

A light drizzle of raindrops was pouring down onto a temperate forest along
the base of the mountain they stood on, and a valley was a little farther down
from their position. In that valley was what looked like a small city or large town,
depending on personal definition, but it was at least a couple miles away and
hard to make out due to the rain.

Cranking his neck left and feeling it crack, he sighed with relief and watched
as the rainwater cleansed his bloodstained, dirty skin. The blood began to fall off
in coagulated clumps, and soon it revealed the ivory complexion underneath.

Startled at the change, he looked closer. His skin had always been mildly
olive—still white, but he'd definitely had a touch of olive complexion. Now it
wasn't even close; he was very pale white, and the skin was devoid of any blem-
ishes. Hadn't he only been just slightly pale the last time he saw his reflection in
Negrada's sacrificial chamber? He'd changed even more over the past day. His jaw
dropped slightly, and he stood up to walk over to a pool of water collecting in a
divot along the hillside. There, in the dim reflection of the puddle, was his face
staring right back. He thought about stories he'd heard where vampires didn't

have reflections and was thankful that wasn't the case. It would have creeped him out.

Despite the ripples that the drizzle poured on, he could still easily make out his features—and just as Athela had said, he looked startlingly good. His cheekbones had come up slightly, his chin smoothed out, and it had the same ivory look to his skin as his hands. His brown hair was the same, but he looked like a model . . . and his eyes were now a bright red that gave off a very faint glow. Touching his face and feeling out his new features, he just shook his head as the rainwater washed off the majority of the blood.

"Told you! You look pretty!" Athela stated happily as she joined him to look down at Riven's reflection. Her dark hair drifted over her own red eyes as her long black tongue snaked out and latched onto a nearby cricket before tearing it back into her mouth to chomp down on. "Er—handsome. I can still tell it's you, though. Azmoth, you okay over there?"

Riven and Athela both turned to look back at the huge fire-attuned demon, who was picking himself up off the ground and looking absolutely miserable in the downpour. He looked *so* miserable, in fact, that Riven thought he was going to have a mental breakdown at any second. With the way Azmoth's large, armored body shook with disgust as he spat repetitively, Riven couldn't help but snicker loudly.

"You'll be fine," Riven said with a laugh, waving a hand at Azmoth as if to tell the huge brute to get over it. "It's just rainwater."

"AZMOTH DOES NOT LIKE RAINWATER!"

The flustered infant demon bellowed a roar to the heavens with all four obsidian sets of claws stretched out, and a blast of flame tore skyward off his armored body. His immense muscles, completely devoid of skin between fused metal plates, tensed and rippled in the exertion as he screamed an angry tantrum upward into the shimmering sky of rain and storm clouds.

"Oh, don't be so dramatic!" Athela crowed with amusement, extending her four long spider legs to prop her up and hoist her over the ground with stunning speed to tower over the more brutish demon for just a minute. "Just flare up or something—it'll evaporate. You're hotheaded as it is already and no doubt you shan't have a problem purging some itty-bitty droplets!"

Athela cackled and avoided a swipe from one of Azmoth's claws, and she glanced over her shoulder to catch Riven staring. She raised an eyebrow teasingly. "What are you staring at? Did I do something wrong?"

Riven shook his head, unblinkingly, and he slowly stood up with his gnarled black staff in his hand. "I'm not staring at you . . . I'm staring at that."

Athela and Azmoth both turned to where Riven had nodded, and a moment later they wore the same expression as Riven. There, only a dozen yards off, was an overgrown gas station.

The structure looked like it'd been torn out of the earth along with half of the connected parking lot, then had been transplanted to land smack-dab in the middle of nowhere while leaning at a slant along the hill's side. The glass door had been ripped off its hinges and thrown to the left, and a couple of the windows were shattered—showing a dark interior that Riven's eyes could now easily penetrate.

There were shelves that'd once held food, now all empty. A cashier's station had been hammered with a club or baseball bat, leaving dents and bent metal along the counter. The lights on the ceiling all lacked power, and as Riven came closer he saw there were two half-eaten human bodies on the floor.

The sight was gruesome; the remains were starting to decay with a swarm of flies circling the corpses. Riven bent down a few feet from the bodies, evaluating the shredded T-shirt on one and the half-torn jeans on the other. Both were young men and had obviously had some very violent last moments. Whatever had eaten them was very big, given the size of the bite marks on what remained.

"Brutal." Riven stated glumly. "I'm really hoping this place isn't as bad as the dungeon we . . ."

His voice trailed off as an unfamiliar scent hit his nostrils like a tidal wave. It smelled like wet dog and came in conjunction with the sound of a beating heart that was growing faster and faster in pace. Riven's new vampiric senses also picked up the crunching of leaves from the tree line a little ways away, and his red eyes slowly rose to peer into the forest from over the border of his runic mask.

It likely didn't know he could see it at this distance and kept to the shadows, hulking down between two bushes and readying itself to spring forward. It was something like a cross between a gigantic wolf and a bear—but was neither: too large to be a wolf, too elongated to be a bear. It was covered in brown fur and had small tufts of darker black fur coursing down its back.

[Mountain Warg]

CHAPTER 4

Ah. So that's what it was. Riven had read about creatures like this in fantasy novels, though he'd never thought them to be real up until now. He supposed it shouldn't surprise him, though, considering what he'd been through over the last little while.

Wait, why didn't his identification give any more than a name? Wasn't it supposed to come with levels, or at least question marks afterward? It didn't give him any indication of power level at all.

Was this what the system notification upon leaving the dungeon had meant concerning identification going back to "normal"?

He motioned for the others to come in closer and planted his staff into the ground while pretending not to have noticed the creature at all—whispering to his demons to keep quiet and remain nonconfrontational. This was a perfect opportunity to experiment.

He grinned as Athela and Azmoth came up behind him, and he gripped his weapon more firmly. "Let's see what this bad boy can do, yeah?"

Channeling into the staff felt like slowly pouring a pitcher of water into an immense vacuum in space. The staff sucked up the given mana like it had been starved for millennia, and Black Lightning began to crackle down its surface as the simmering dark wood palpably begged him for more.

So he gave it more. The item description said it would passively charge this item over time, but he didn't have time to wait if he wanted to field-test this little experiment. He continued to actively charge the staff with his own mana over the next couple seconds while warily keeping a peripheral watch on the warg, just as eager as the staff to see what exactly his new weapon could do. It even began to give him a migraine by the end of his distribution.

But that migraine still wasn't enough to slow his reflexes down as the incoming warg made its move. The large beast sprang into motion, silently rushing them from behind with muscles rippling along its back and limbs. No doubt it thought itself the apex predator of this part of the mountain, but it was sorely mistaken.

Riven simultaneously turned his heel, pushing past Athela and raising his new staff directly at the sprinting warg. Black sparks of lightning rippled across the polished wood as the item began to activate, and with a thought the power erupted out of the tip of the weapon.

A torrent of magic roared into life, sending a chaotic beam of pitch-black electricity as thick as his thigh out to crush the incoming enemy, ripping the warg apart as the animal let out an abrupt screech that cut off just as quickly as it'd come. The magic bloomed and exploded through the large beast to discharge into the trees beyond.

CRASH

The blast had left scorched earth in its wake, a long, jagged line carved into the ground with ripples of power still sparking along the dirt as an aftereffect. Trees in the background had caught fire under the rain of the storm clouds, and pieces of the animal's body had been violently flung in various directions.

[**You have killed one enemy. Your battle has ended. You have acquired forty-eight Elysium coins. You have gained XP.**]

Riven gawked.

"What the hell was that?!" Athela exclaimed as she got up from the floor with an open mouth. "And what did you just kill?! Was that a wolf?! How did you see it and I couldn't?! This is bullshit! Give me your vampiric powers, you dirty, good-for-nothing peasant!"

"Quiet, spider woman! Do not speak to Master that way!" Azmoth aggressively smacked the demoness along the back side of her head and sent her face-planting into the wet ground with an ***UMPH***, then he chuckled as she glared back up at him from where she lay covered in mud.

Riven eyed the downed woman with a raised eyebrow. "Azmoth, smack her like that every time she smack talks me from now on. Anyways, that was my staff's inherent ability: Black Lightning. Really a kicker, right? And that creature was a warg."

Athela raised her own muddy eyebrow at the scattered remnants of the monster. "Oh. Didn't think those were real, but I guess I'm not surprised."

"How did you not know wargs were real?! Aren't you supposed to be the knowledge guru of our group?!"

Athela threw up her hands defensively between wiping the mud off her athletic, feminine body that shimmered black in the dim light of the midday storm. "I could only study so much before coming out of the nether realms! Sheesh! This is my first time out and about, you know!"

Riven saw the long-cooldown insignia concerning his staff's Black Lightning ability in the top-right corner of his vision after casting. He'd noticed them before with other abilities, but this one was going down much more slowly than any of the others. He didn't know the exact time, as it was represented by a circle slowly starting to disappear in a clockwise fashion, but if he had to guess just by staring at it over the past ten seconds, it would likely be a couple of minutes before he could use it again. Nothing to complain about if he got to use a high-impact spell like that, though, as long as he let the staff charge it up on its own.

He was also slightly surprised it'd created a cooldown in the first attempt at using the staff's inherent spell, because most of his other spells often completely overlooked their cooldowns unless he got unlucky. Cooldowns didn't always activate, and according to the magical theory texts he'd read in Chalgathi's trials, when cooldowns would activate was usually random. More accurately, it just involved a lot of different factors, but because he had such high affinities for the magics he used, he experienced a lot fewer cooldown periods than other casters usually would.

With great power come great cooldown times.

"Well, let's try to get some sleep. We have some exploring to do in the morning, and that teleportation out of the dungeon has me feeling really queasy."

Unfortunately Riven wouldn't get much sleep that night, and neither would Athela or Azmoth. The new vampiric changes to his body were still causing slight physical adjustments here or there, with a random snap of tendon or crunch of bone that would elicit a scream from the exhausted man. His previously green eyes would revert to their original form for just a moment before appearing bright red again; his fangs would sprout out and then retract rapidly and then settle back down again. His senses would fade in and out, and it made him feel absolutely nauseous. Originally they'd been absolutely exhausted and decided on picking up the trail for Riven's sister and his friend Jose the next morning, but instead Athela found herself comforting Riven as best she could while Azmoth patrolled the surrounding areas to relieve his boredom.

Stunning orange, red, and yellow hues scattered across the horizon that, in terms of beauty, dwarfed anything any painting could truly capture. The storm was gone, replaced with scattered tufts of clouds that reflected the brilliant colors of the sunrise.

Riven stood on the hill after having practiced his newest acquired spell: Riftwalk many times over. Riftwalk was definitely an interesting ability, where he could cut open a linear black rift in space by thought alone, get sucked through it, and literally vanish from one location to the next at any point within about twenty or twenty-five yards, with a silent black rift opening up at the point of exit, too. Even more interesting was that his demons could go through the rift, too, though maintaining it for more than a couple seconds was very mana-heavy—and if he tried to extend the normal range of the ability, it was still doable but even more costly. Currently he was able to max out the distance at a little over one hundred yards, but mana cost climbed exponentially as he improved the range, and the maximum range drained his entire mana pool. The skill would certainly be useful to have, considering he was currently going for a highly mobile mage-type build.

Intentionally defying his new body's discomfort, he stood looking out toward the oncoming sunlight. He could feel himself weakening as he looked directly at it, and in some ways that made him very sad. He'd spent his entire life cooped up inside while living in Dallas, kept away from the outdoors all those years like so many people in the newer generations did—only to arrive in a refreshed world of magic with an aversion to being outside in the life-giving light of the sun.

He couldn't complain too much, though. Without his newfound power, he would be long dead . . . and although it was a bit uncomfortable watching the sun rise, it was bearable. Definitely worth it to bask in the beauty of the morning, in his opinion, even as his stamina and mana very slowly ticked down. At the very least, he was getting an idea for how long it'd take to reach a point that was painful, and from what he could tell, he guessed he'd be able to withstand direct sunlight touching his skin for about an hour before serious repercussions set in.

He also learned through trial and error that pulling down his hood, putting his hands inside sleeves or pockets, and covering his skin from direct rays of sunlight meant the debuff would stop accumulating.

He needed to get some gloves, and maybe even some sunglasses.

Maybe sunscreen would work?

Nah, it couldn't be that easy. And even if it was, where would he get some?

He thought about it some more. It was also rather interesting that utilizing Riftwalk did give him some relief from the sun's rays. It didn't necessarily replenish any stamina or mana that the sun had drained away, but it kind of reset the wear on his mind.

Athela was still asleep, as was Azmoth, but he could hear their heartbeats from here if he focused hard enough. The dull thuds echoed in his ears until he somehow was able to transition that focus elsewhere through nothing but his own Willpower. His new vampiric perception even enabled him to sift through the sounds of the surrounding forest, and he could make out the locations of small chipmunks from farther into the trees in front of him—versus the owl fast asleep in its nest behind him. Most of these creatures he could only sense in terms of their actual heartbeats, though, and he wasn't able to tell exactly what they were until he made visual confirmation. Still, he was able to generally tell how big they were based on their heartbeats—so that was something he could probably utilize in the future.

Songbirds of the early morning chirped in the treetops, a frog off to his left ribbited, and wind rustled the surrounding foliage with a chill breeze.

Turning his gaze to the south, he gave himself a break from the debuff and kept his hood up, immediately beginning to feel better as he turned away from the sun. It was as if a pressure had been lifted off his shoulders and a fog had cleared from his mind. He continued pondering his current situation as his sunlight debuff slowly fizzled away while he kept his skin hidden from the light underneath his cloak, but over time he was beginning to grow restless. He'd been thinking about it all night, and the anxiety was getting to him.

He needed blood.

CHAPTER 5

The thoughts that had repulsed him after he'd killed that man in the dungeon now swept through his mind like a tidal wave of hunger. Killing had satiated him then, and he didn't feel crazed like he had in that moment of blood starvation, but he could still feel the wanting. It'd been a little over two days since he'd fed, and he was getting hungry.

His red eyes cast over the corpse of a nearby bird, and he frowned. Animals did not satiate his hunger. The words of the system spelled it out for him well enough—he needed the blood of mortals. Humanoids.

And yet . . . he did not feel disgust any longer.

Disgust had been replaced by cravings.

The trek to the town was much longer than they'd anticipated due to a steep drop-off down the side of the mountain that they had to navigate around. The sun was already starting to set, and they'd walked all day with a couple breaks here and there to explore the area. They also crossed paths with a couple of very weak monsters that, despite the power discrepancy, attacked them like rabid animals.

There were horned rabbits and a couple of smaller wargs, the latter usually coming in pairs or trios, but none of them were nearly as large as the one that Riven had blasted the day before. The bloodthirsty wargs were usually about the size of wolves and would have given any normal human that hadn't been subject to recent continuous combat a run for their money and lives . . . but they were all left very dead in the wake of Riven's small group. It was so easy for the mageling and his two summons that Riven, Athela, and Azmoth often didn't even pause in their trek toward the distant town other than to pick up the bags of Elysium coins that the system dropped after kills. He moved the coins to his backpack, and the small sacks they started in disappeared soon after collection.

"Do you think monsters are spawning all over the world like this?" Riven eventually asked as he stepped over the mutilated corpse of a warg that'd gotten a little too close for comfort. "And why only wargs and horned rabbits?"

The demons both shrugged in unison and proceeded through the trees farther down the mountain toward the valley.

"We don't question the system." Athela eventually said as her extended arachnoid legs kept her more humanoid legs and body up in the air—gracefully guiding her across the forest floor at an elevated height. "None of it ever made sense to me, and half the things it does won't ever have answers. There are theories about why it does the things it does, but it wasn't an area of interest or study for me."

Azmoth just grunted in affirmation as a heavy, plated leg smashed through the wet undergrowth with indifference to what was in his way. Toppling a small tree over with an irritated flick of his hand, the large demon plowed ahead to clear a path for the other two.

Riven's stomach growled loudly, and the knot inside his gut began to churn. Both Athela and Azmoth looked back at their master with curious glances, but Riven could only shrug helplessly and hold up his free hand in a gesture of helplessness.

"Sorry."

"Didn't you already eat part of that warg you killed? That wasn't enough?"

"Eh . . . no. I think I'll need what the system considers mortal blood to fill me up all the way. Other food seems to help just a little bit, but I can't get the edge off."

"Oh! Right. You need the blood of mortals, otherwise you'll go insane like you did a couple days ago!" Athela gave him a wicked grin that earned her a scowl, but she brushed it off with a flick of her long black hair. "I thought you were rather dashing, the way you ate him. It made me want to join in as well!"

He paused their trek, turning around fully to gaze at his minion. True anger toward her, something he hadn't experienced much since meeting the demoness, surged forward, and he jabbed a finger into her chest. "Athela, shut up."

The tone he used was obviously not playful, and for the first time ever, Athela was taken aback. Her eyes went wide, she opened her mouth to speak, and then she glanced shamefully at the floor. "Did I go too far?"

"Yes, and it's fucking pissing me off." Riven pushed his finger off her chest with a little bit of force, but it wasn't enough to shove her. He took a step back, calmed himself, and met her eyes as she stared back at him like a kicked puppy dog. "Honestly, I'm tired of the disrespect. I told you that was a touchy subject, and I've been lenient in how I've handled you because you've been a great help. But you need to fucking know when you've crossed the line, and you just crossed it. I fucking *murdered* someone who didn't deserve it, Athela, someone I didn't want to hurt and had no control over. It's not like the others; he was innocent, and it isn't fucking funny. Got it?"

She clasped her hands in front of her and gave a sheepish nod. "Yes, Master."

"Good. Don't fucking forget it."

He was about to turn around when she hesitantly reached out to grab his sleeve. Turning back around, he was surprised to see her tearing up.

"I . . . um . . ." Athela's gaze shifted across the forest floor, from a stick, to a rock, to a stump—anywhere but looking directly at him. "Are you really mad at me?"

"YES, I'm fucking mad at you! Are you being serious?" Riven whirled on her, disbelief etched into his features.

She stuttered. "I—I'm sorry if I came across as disrespectful. I just—"

"You do it all the time." Riven cut her off with a frown, completely pissed about her jabs and jokes about that man he'd murdered in the dungeon. "I've been half tempted to just use the contract commands, but that'd feel like slavery to me. So I don't. Frankly, it's not even just about that guy. The jokes can be funny sometimes, but lean back on that shit—it gets really fucking irritating when there's this superiority complex you've got going on all the time. I thought we were friends, but you obviously don't want to respect me as a friend, because you trot all over the requests I give you like '*don't fucking tease me about the guy I killed and ate.*' It's pretty fucking simple, I'd think. Just give me some space, okay?"

She withdrew her fingers from his sleeve, nodded silently, and quickly blinked to get the water out of her eyes. "Sorry, Master."

Birds chirped overhead, the wind rustled the treetops nearby, and an awkward silence followed while Riven glared at Athela from a few feet away. That was when a high-pitched scream echoed from farther down the mountain, and more screams and shouts quickly followed it with other sounds akin to metal clashing on metal.

He turned his head. Was he hearing that right?

Riven shared a look with Athela, who clearly had heard it, too, but Azmoth was none the wiser as he trudged through the forest in a mindless, rambling way until he noticed the other two hadn't continued to follow. The larger demon's hearing just wasn't on par with the others', and he had no idea why they'd stopped.

The demon's armored head turned as well to look at them, despite having no eyes, and he curiously cocked his head to one side. "You not coming? Why?"

The sounds were faint, but Riven's boots began to shift in the mud as he turned right to adjust their trajectory. His amplified senses now allowed him to pick up sounds at a far greater distance. Athela had likely gained some sort of stat bonuses to Perception as well after her evolution, which was likely why only he and Athela heard the commotion while Azmoth had remained ignorant.

Riven motioned for the larger demon to follow before taking off. "Come."

The two nimbler members of their party melted through the underbrush like shadows on the wind of the early morning breeze, and despite Athela always having been much quicker than Riven previously, Riven found himself able to keep up with her rather easily, his body far more agile than he'd ever thought possible. He'd had little to no experience utilizing his body to its true extent, so he was far more surprised than he should have been. Foliage flew by as their enhanced bodies drove them ahead at speed and grace far beyond what they could have achieved in their past life in Negrada just a few days ago, and Riven felt himself beginning to wonder eagerly what it was he had the pleasure of taking out his pent-up anger on, while also wondering just how far he could go speedwise if he really pushed himself.

He didn't know what to expect. He didn't know who was fighting or why, but at the same time, he knew that he needed to find out. There was a good chance that they'd be able to help someone, or at the very least they'd be able to watch from a distance to glean some information about the locals.

Coming up the large hill and rounding a large outcropping of rock, they continued onward as the sounds of Azmoth barreling through the underbrush far behind them echoed out along with the crashing of trees. Meanwhile, the sounds of fighting ahead of them were growing louder, and the words that people were screaming were growing more tangible. Riven was able to hear swearing, threats, and begging—along with some garbled hissing, as none other than a medieval war horn sounded out just over the next ridge.

His breathing picked up and his heartbeat began to spike—simultaneously picking up the heartbeats of many of the combatants just over the hill. Making sure Athela was still with him after a single backward glance, he gripped his staff firmly and reached the next hilltop to discover a rather unusual sight far down at the bottom of the slope.

Dead bodies lay along a beaten dirt path through the oak trees of the forest. These bodies, however, were not human. Rather, they were the bodies of little green men with long snouts and ugly faces . . . likely goblins, if he had to guess. The bodies of elves, as designated by the sharp pointed ears, blond or silver hair, and fair features, were also present, and despite everything he'd seen so far, Riven was still surprised.

Both the goblins and the elves wore very little. The bald goblins had a mix and match of various shoddy spears, daggers, bucklers, and blow darts. They wore loincloths and sometimes thicker furs around their shoulders. The fair-skinned elves, on the other hand, usually had some form of designs drawn on their bodies with blue paint or paste, probably tribal markings, with a couple of them bearing blue handprints along their thighs, chests, or even foreheads. Many of the elves were barefoot, wearing furs or stretched blue-green material that looked like interwoven palm leaves, leaving little to the imagination for both men and women as they brandished long curved knives or bows and arrows.

Of the survivors, there were only a handful left for either side. The battle that'd been fought was drawing to a close. There were two men and two women, all elves, all of them obviously injured in some way or another with cuts and bruises evident. One of the men even had a long, deep gash across his front where a spear was still sticking out of his chest—though despite his screams of pain and horror, his allies were too busy fighting to help.

Meanwhile, there were still eight goblins left. They snarled and screeched, stepping over the bodies of the fallen as they tried to overwhelm the remaining elves with numbers as the woman on the left's last arrow sang through the air— clipping one of the goblins and leaving a deep gash along its skull.

But it kept coming, along with the rest of its green-skinned kin, quickly pushing the two women and the man who remained standing into an enraged, snarling ball of knife fighting. The ensuing bloody skirmish turned into desperate screaming and quickly became a one-sided battle.

CHAPTER 6

Senna had never been so scared in her life.

Her world had been flipped upside down, with the land the tribe had known for generations being mixed and matched with new landscapes and sceneries overnight. There were new creatures and dangerous monsters now appearing out of nowhere . . . appearing from ambient mana in what the Elysium system had called the world of **Panu.** These creatures had already killed many of her kin already, with numerous people mysteriously going missing. Her tribe was just one of many nomadic elf groups in the area, though, and they'd sent messengers to the other surrounding tribes to see who was still around . . . and who'd been taken to some other part of this new world.

In the meantime, she and her hunting party had been one of many to scout the surrounding area. It'd only been two days since the great migration, the apocalypse, and merging of her world with two others, and safety was their first priority. After discovering a human city within the nearby valley and seeing the chaos ongoing there, they'd retreated and tried to inform the elder council . . . only to be intercepted by goblins, of all things.

Goblins were native to her own home world, and they'd been a plague upon her people as long as she could remember. She'd grown up hating the little green devils. Often taking prisoners as slaves or meat, goblin raiding parties were not to be scoffed at. Though their individual strengths were weaker than an elf's, they made up for it in sheer numbers and could spawn infinitely, like rats.

A lesson that their hunt leader had learned the hard way, having fallen into what Senna had considered an obvious trap while bringing the rest of the party with him. They never should have chased . . . She'd tried to dissuade him from taking the bait, but she was low in the tribal hierarchy . . . and she was a woman. That alone made her opinion worth less to her peers in the eyes of the elder council.

Because of it, because of prejudice and arrogance, they were all going to die here.

"Ethel!" she screamed and began to sob, trying to stab at one of the goblins that was violently beating her with a small club just as another goblin latched onto her ankle, sinking in its sharp teeth and claws as she screamed. Blood stained her silver hair as it leaked from a head wound and matted it against her face, partially blinding her in one eye. "Ethel, help me! Please!"

CRACK

The young woman felt her clavicle snap as the goblin's club was brought back down with a jerk. She screamed again, horror filling her as pain radiated up her body. She kicked and flailed, desperation filling her as she began to hyperventilate, only for the goblins pinning her down to laugh at her misfortune with jeers and snarls. She felt the teeth of the goblin on her ankle sink deeper, through muscle and into bone, and she felt the goblin with the club slam it into her scrambling arms as she tried to get away. Bones shattered, and the pain was unlike anything she'd ever experienced.

"Please let me go!" Senna went rigid with a squeal of agony as her wrist snapped. "Please!!"

Her words trailed off, her chest heaved with every violent sob, and she recognized the bloodlust in the goblin's eyes under the forest canopy as it raised the club for a final time.

"Elf go die die!" it snickered—right before a crimson blur of motion abruptly slammed into the creature standing over her.

The goblin's chest rippled and exploded within the time of a single second, a torrent of red magic tearing through the small humanoid with a brief torrent of bloody wisps and a savagery that caught its peers by surprise. What remained of the goblin slowly went limp after that, dropping to the ground as its eyes went cold—the club going with it to thud into the dirt next to Senna's bloodied face.

She blinked twice, shock overriding her other emotions and senses as she tried to adjust to what had just happened. Had that really been blood magic just now? She'd seen it used once before when their tribe had expelled a man for meddling in the forbidden magics of the Unholy foundational pillar, but they'd been banished many years ago . . . No one in her village knew anything but nature magic from the Fae pillar.

So what had just happened?

By this point the elves had been completely overpowered. Ethel, Senna's best friend, was being tortured just as she was a few feet away and was missing a hand—pulsing blood from a lacerated wound with three goblins atop her. Bortris, who'd been speared earlier, now lay dead and unmoving in a patch of moss nearby. Then, lastly, there was Vorthem . . . the youngest son of a village blacksmith. Vorthem was beaten black and blue, barely breathing, and was being bludgeoned to death with his arms and legs at odd angles where the bones had snapped. However, all activity immediately ceased as the collective goblins realized what had happened . . . and, settling their gazes in the same general direction, all of them began brandishing their weapons to silently step back. Even the goblin latched onto her leg seemed to see something that made it go visibly tense, and it left her bare, bloodied leg a moment later to join its fellows as they grouped up.

Senna, still rigid with pain and crying silently as she clutched at her broken hand, was able to sit up with excruciating effort and a lot of pain radiating down from the shattered clavicle. Letting out a high-pitched grunt of pain and wincing, she came about to see what had put the goblins in such an obvious scare.

Two figures stared out under the morning shadow of trees. One of them was a demon, a spider-humanoid variant of some sort with bare, toned musculature, six bladelike appendages coming out of her back, and a wicked smile of teeth that were slowly beginning to sharpen. She had one of the goblins strung up between her outstretched fingers as either hand produced thin crimson strands of silk, and she was toying with him by making the terrified three-foot green man dance for her as if she was maneuvering a puppet.

The other figure was cloaked and carried a black wooden staff that radiated shadow energy at the gnarled tip. His features were hard to make out because of the runic mask he wore, but the pale skin and glowing crimson eyes . . .

She felt her blood run cold as she looked upon the newcomers. All hope faded, drastically and immediately, as she realized that it wasn't help that'd come . . . rather, it was another group of even more dangerous foes.

Apex predators.

Vampires were widely regarded as some of the worst opponents to go up against. Their senses, strength, speed, tracking abilities, and natural affinities for the Unholy pillar's magics meant that they were often incredibly dangerous. Add on that they could live for many millennia and weren't the mindless monsters that most creatures of the Unholy pillar represented: it meant that their collected knowledge, intelligence, and experience over their vast lifetimes was incredibly ominous for any who wished to fight them. On top of that, this vampire had a goddamned demonic summon with him. Demonic familiars were incredibly hard to acquire even for the most experienced of black magic practitioners; to have one with him made things all the more bleak in terms of outlook on her situation. Demonic familiars under contract could be banished, but they couldn't truly die unless the summoner died first. It made them expendable front-line fighters, ones that could and would without hesitation sacrifice themselves— temporarily—in order to save their masters from otherwise permanent deaths.

She'd heard the horror stories and had even seen a young vampire once, a long time ago in a trial that'd ended in its execution after it was caught feeding on one of her tribe . . . and this figure fit the bill perfectly. His eyes were a little bit more red than normal; the only other vampire she'd ever seen hadn't had eyes that glowed like that, but he was still no doubt the real deal. The goblins had certainly realized this as well, based on their reactions to the newcomers, which were a mix between anxiety, fear, and anger.

With a flick of her wrist, the demoness yanked on a couple of her crimson threads, and the yelping goblin she was using as a marionette abruptly exploded in gore. The otherwise beautiful demoness crowed with laughter, a malicious and heartless laugh as the little goblin's body rained down around her—and she sneered back at the other greenskins with bared teeth before extending one of her long arachnid limbs in an aggressive gesture.

There was a long silence after that as the six wide-eyed remaining goblins continued drawing back into the trees of the forest, away from the beaten path, while the vampire and his demonic familiar slowly progressed forward.

Senna felt a lump in her throat forming as she stared, dumbfounded, at what would probably be the last thing she'd ever see. She knew she couldn't run, not with her mangled leg . . . and her friends were all either dying or already dead.

This was the end . . . or so she thought, until she snapped out of her trance when she felt a gentle hand on her shoulder. She'd been staring off into space with sullen acceptance of her grim fate and, coming back around to reality—she saw that the vampire was now kneeling next to her.

"Are you able to move?" He gently asked in a low tone, removing his mask to reveal handsome features, his red eyes holding her gaze captive as he spoke.

Senna took in a deep breath, combating her fear and natural urge to scream, and all she could manage to do was shake her head no.

Why did he care? Was he just making sure she wouldn't get away whenever he finished doing whatever other business he had here?

The man frowned slightly and gave her a firm, reassuring squeeze—then withdrew his hand from her shoulder and stood back up. "You'll be okay. I promise, we'll get you out of here."

The elf just looked back, dumbfounded, and Riven seriously began to doubt that she understood him. He could have sworn he heard them speaking the same language that'd been incorporated into his mind ever since the transition, but maybe he'd been wrong . . .

A guttural barking voice called out to him from the line of goblins as they stood at the ready, warily taking an assessment of the newcomers for any weaknesses amid the cries of the elf they'd sawed a hand off—and the croaking, labored breathing of the broken man on the ground. "Why vampire here?"

The fact that Riven and Athela had killed two of their number already and the goblins remained almost frozen in fear and hadn't retaliated was an obvious giveaway to who held the cards in this standoff.

Riven snorted in disgust, snapping his fingers out in front of him to briefly spark with a crimson ribbon that quickly dissipated into thin air. His time in Negrada over the past month had jaded him. These goblins might be the same level as the ones he'd fought earlier, but the quality of their power was on a completely different scale. To see such relatively weak monsters in front of him, compared to the things he'd been killing back in the modified tutorial dungeon . . . it gave him no room for second guesses at what he was about to do.

"Bleed."

His hand shot into motion as a wave of crimson blades bloomed around him in the air, rapidly closing the distance between him and the little green men. Shredding the first and blowing at the leg off the second, Riven drew his staff up off the ground as it crackled with Black Lightning that ripped through another goblin, tearing him into paste.

BOOM

The trio of blasts sent the goblins shrieking and scattering, only to cry out when Athela blurred forward and ripped into another to cleave off the goblin's head with fingers-turned-claws—then she did it again, blurring forward and impaling a goblin's skull with one of her arachnoid legs, cackling loudly all the while. Her perfect set of white human teeth had abruptly turned into a lipless snarl of a piranha, with rows of razor-sharp fangs underneath her red eyes that'd each grown to twice their normal size. The beautiful features of the woman had truly turned into a monster, and her feminine muscles tensed while her six arachnid limbs turned rigid at their tips to produce spears of sharp black needlelike appendages.

"*SHRREEEEEEE!!!!*" Athela blurred forward with a screech of relish. Like a whirlwind of crazed rage, she ripped through another two goblins that'd been hiding in the bushes—ones Riven hadn't even seen or taken note of, as he'd been caught up in what was happening in front of him. It was something he'd have to work on, because he knew if he'd paid attention, he'd have noticed their heartbeats.

Limbs and heads flew skyward in sprays of blood, and the demoness hooted with laughter while simultaneously flipping head over heels in a cartwheel to rip through a small tree with her claws—along with yet another hidden goblin that'd been hunkering down behind it.

The rest of the goblins screamed and scattered.

Riven walked over with a malice to the sneer underneath his mask, whipping his staff around while grinning into a groaning goblin's eyes as it clutched at the bleeding stump of what remained of its leg. "Say goodbye."

The once-innocent man plunged the butt of his staff into the terrified goblin's chest, ramming it into the shrieking creature's body and sending an explosion of shadows down into the fallen creature. The blunt force impact of the on-hit shadow magic shattered the goblin's rib cage, jaw, and pelvis in one go—quickly sending the pathetically weak and broken creature into shock.

Licking his lips and letting his body slide down to the ground, Riven peeled his lips back to expose his fangs. His hunger gnawed at him, and he felt a need—nay, a compulsion—to drain the small body of all the lifeblood it had. His hand shot forward, quickly latching onto the dying goblin's neck . . . and he began to squeeze.

CHAPTER 7

Athela watched her master curiously . . . watched him sink his fangs into the dying goblin's arteries. Watched him give in to the hunger he'd been feeling over the past day. Then, letting out a long sigh of acceptance, she turned and bolted through the trees to kill the last of the little green creatures. Catching up to them over the next twenty seconds of sprinting, she nearly tripped over a tree root—but collected herself with an eye roll and drew back her head. When she stopped and suddenly lurched forward, Athela's long, slender tongue ripped through the air like a black viper—accurately striking the creature's cervical spine with a thud and dropping it to the ground after a brief gasp.

She could probably find them faster if she transitioned back into her normal spider form, but she was very opposed to doing that any time soon. She needed the experience in this new body, needed to hone her ability to manipulate it beyond the practice runs she'd done in the nether realms in a false body, and she was very much enjoying the new sensations she got from it.

In the distance, the sounds of other small green creatures quickly hustling through the trees met her ears, but she could tell that the monsters were running in the opposite direction, fleeing for their lives. There'd been a lot more than the ones battling here, though they may have been reinforcements, or they may have just been circling around to get the drop on the elves—who knew? She shrugged indifferently at the thought and yanked back her bloodied tongue—licking her lips to evaluate the taste of the short, green-skinned man and turning her more demonic features back into those of a young woman again. Her unhinged jaw clicked back into place, her elongated, sharpened teeth shrank down into normal-size human variants, and her abnormally hypertrophied muscles softened. Thinking about it and glancing over her shoulder to where the two elvish girls were, she paused and then withdrew her arachnid limbs back into her body as well—standing completely naked in the midday forest with blood dripping down her mixed white, gray, and mostly pitch-black skin. Her claws retracted next, and she brushed her long dark hair out as the droplets of goblin fluids seemed to roll off her silky, straight locks like rainwater off a windshield.

She giggled at the good fortune she'd had, bending over and crossing her legs to pick up the bag of Elysium coins that'd dropped in the form of a pouch on the goblin she'd just killed. A good master to serve, a newly integrating world, and boundless opportunities. "This is going to be so fun! I can't wait to tell Mother about what goblin tastes like . . . Auntie was right!"

Riven hadn't moved from his initial spot. He'd gorged himself on the lifeblood of the broken goblin, taking in deep breaths of air between bouts of slurping down the warm, red liquid. He continued to do this, ignoring Athela completely until she walked up next to him and jabbed her toe into his side.

Snarling reflexively and baring his fangs, Riven jerked back and got to his feet. Blood dripped down his face and he looked like a rabid dog until recognition sparked across his features. Slowly looking down at his recent mealtime plaything, and then back up to Athela, he furled his hands into fists in front of his chest . . . concern very evident.

"You do realize that they're bleeding out and dying, right?" Athela said with a casual snort.

She pointed to the blonde elf who'd had her hand cut off on the dirt trail to their right. She was quivering, shaking, and trying to stanch the blood from flowing freely with a makeshift tourniquet. She was failing miserably at shakily tying it, but nevertheless she was trying while giving the vampire and his minion anxiety-filled glances.

Riven shook his head to rid himself of the urges he'd fallen prey to and picked up his staff before placing his mask back on. "I need to get ahold of myself."

The man who'd been holding on to life by a thread, the one with the broken limbs who was battered to a swollen pulp, well . . . he had finally stopped breathing before Riven even approached. Faltering, then sinking down to his knees and feeling for a pulse along the man's neck, Riven frowned.

"Dead," Riven pronounced to the general area before hurrying over to the blonde woman and glancing over at the silver-haired elf briefly to make sure she was okay as well. The woman with silver hair had an obviously broken hand, a broken clavicle, and a shredded leg that was bleeding profusely, but she was in far better shape than her sole remaining comrade and was staring dumbfounded at him.

When Riven knelt down beside the woman with the stump, she shrieked and began begging while weakly trying to push herself away. Even aside from the loss of limb, she was in very bad shape. She'd been battered, beaten, and had numerous cuts all along her body—and even though she was utterly terrified at

Riven's approach, he couldn't help but stop and recognize how pretty she and her friend were. In fact, now that the battle was over and his adrenaline was down, he nearly did a double take before glancing over his shoulder to compare to the silver-haired woman.

Goddamn.

"Please d-don't eat me-ee . . ." the young woman sobbed, shaking even harder as blood continued gushing out of her left arm. "P-pleasee-eeee . . . I—I want to g-go home . . ."

Tears streamed down her face and her nostrils flared, her eyes squinting shut tight against the violence that was sure to come.

Riven gave Athela a look of bemusement, then snorted a sad laugh. "Calm down. I need to stop the bleeding before you die of blood loss. Here—"

He reached for her stump arm, and she screamed like it was the worst pain she'd ever felt before. It was mostly out of fear, as she flailed weakly on the ground, trying to push herself back along the dirt by her bare feet, but the elf was already in terrible shape and too weak to resist.

Was this his negative Charisma at work? He could only assume so.

"Use this." Athela held out a belt in one hand, and Riven's eyebrows shot up in surprise.

Taking the belt and examining it curiously, he looked back up to his demonic companion. "Where the hell did you get this? This is Earth-made."

The demoness hiked a thumb back into the woods and smiled sweetly. "One of the green midgets had it!"

Riven thought on that a moment, not thinking anything good could have been come from such news, then pushed it out of his mind.

Ignoring the elf's strained cries and thinking her actions a bit absurd, Riven grabbed her stump again and quickly wrapped the belt around the wound. When she wouldn't stop flailing, he pushed her back down and knelt on what was left of the bicep in order to keep her there while he made sure the belt remained tight. This only amplified her horrified screams, but it was for her own good . . . otherwise she'd likely bleed to death in the next few minutes.

He'd pulled it tight and snapped the belt into a secure position, cutting off the blood flow by over ninety percent, when he felt a rock slam into the back of his head. Dazed and immediately irritated, he clutched the back of his skull and hissed—fangs extending reflexively as he whirled.

There, barely able to stand and supporting herself against a tree, was the other living elf. She took in deep, ragged breaths and quivered fearfully with another rock in her hand—her knife having been thrown a good ways away by goblins so that she couldn't reach it. Regardless, she took in deep breaths despite the obvious pain she was in—snarling at him to try and hide her fear while her silver hair whipped about in a gust of wind. "Get off her!"

Athela was initially in shock that the silver-haired woman had attacked her master, but watching the elf throw that stone sent her into a rage. Her arachnoid legs ripped out of her back again, sharpened, and all six pointed menacingly toward the girl. "You little bitch!"

The elf who'd thrown the rock paled when she saw the demon getting ready to pounce, and her bravery faltered in the lines of her face just as Riven shot forward to grasp Athela's wrist.

He stood there, not saying anything, staring his demonic servant down with a firm and unwavering gaze until a stream of sunlight momentarily broke through the treetops and lit up his face. He winced, turning his face away from the uncomfortable morning light when it managed to penetrate underneath his hood, but he didn't let go of Athela's wrist until the arachnid legs withdrew into her back again.

"But . . . but she hurt you . . ." Athela whimpered, for the first time in a long time being anything but her usual ridiculous spider-demon self. She took in two deep breaths, looked over at the elf she'd nearly just killed, and then back to Riven. "She hurt you . . ."

Riven took in a deep breath, smiled at Athela's obvious care, and pulled her in for a hug that she hesitantly accepted and embraced. He relaxed his muscles and let the cool morning winds brush against his skin to calm his nerves with a light chuckle. "Keep your urges to kill in your pants, okay? Also, sorry for getting angry at you earlier. I was just on edge."

Athela stood there in shock for about five seconds, not knowing what to say, but then jabbed him playfully in his ribs. It caused him to yelp and let go as he fell over to the ground before laughing at the expression on Athela's face.

"If anyone gets to hurt you, Riven, it's me, damn it! Remember that! At least I do it lovingly, to build character! Humph!"

The demoness crossed her arms and straightened her posture while turning her back on him, but he didn't notice the moisture she wiped away from underneath her eyelids. Facing the terrified elf who'd thrown the rock, Athela bowed slightly and folded her hands in front of her with a widening and malicious smile. "Hey . . . I'm sorry. It's just that when you attacked my master, I got defensive, and I wasn't thinking . . . Maybe it's because I realized that since I hadn't been paying attention, you could have really hurt him. So . . . I'll forgive you. But do it again and I eviscerate you. Got it, slut?"

The silver-haired elf just sat there quivering, pale-faced, as razor-sharp teeth began to glisten one by one as they replaced Athela's more human set of pearly whites.

"And for the record . . ." Riven interrupted with folded arms as he came to stand ahead of Athela—glaring the scantily clad elf down, "I was putting a tourniquet on your friend to save her life. You're welcome."

Athela frowned over at the blonde, who was still clutching weakly at her arm below them. Then, stepping over a trio of dead goblins and another elf body, she made her way forward. Lightly touching the woman's stump arm where Riven's belt was wrapped tightly around, she shushed the abruptly protesting girl when the elf instinctively jerked back with a yelp. "Quit your whining!"

Gripping the stump arm with one hand and causing the blonde girl to scream, Athela rolled her red eyes and slapped the girl three times with quick successive strikes to silence her. "I DO NOT HAVE PATIENCE FOR THIS, MORTAL! BE STILL!"

Shocked, physically stunned, and not entirely all there due to blood loss, the second elf glared daggers up at Athela while the demoness used her free hand to spin out bloody threads from fingertips. Slowly the threads began to drift down onto the open wound of the stump arm she was holding, and the threads began to mend the flesh little by little.

The blonde girl's eyes widened in shock as the skin along her amputation site began scabbing over. It wasn't completely healed, but it was nevertheless *not* bleeding out after Athela had finished with it. Then Athela got up, snorted in disgust at the girl beneath her, and took a step back.

Riven was really impressed. He knew that abilities and skills could be utilized in ways the system hadn't described in the detailed notes concerning his own status page—an example of this was utilizing Wretched Snare as a net to slingshot the satyr warlord's club back at the demon in Negrada. However, he hadn't expected Athela to be able to partially heal someone utilizing her threads; it hadn't ever even occurred to him as a possibility.

Meanwhile, fear was still evident in the creases of the elf's face and the rapid, quite loud heartbeat Riven could hear. The stunned girl looked to her stump arm with a mixture of emotions, then gingerly sat up from where she lay bloodied on the ground. "Are you truly not going to eat us?"

Riven gave an awkward glance to the goblin's body, the one he'd fed on, and scratched the back of his head. "Um . . . no, we're not going to eat you. Sorry if I gave off that impression."

WHAM

CRASH

"WHERE THEY GOOO!!??"

Azmoth, obviously enraged, tore through the underbrush and collided with a large tree, toppling it completely and sending wood chips scattering. In one hand was the corpse of yet another goblin who'd been unfortunate enough to run into him while trying to get away from Riven and Athela. Azmoth promptly slammed the body into the soft earth before splattering its brains all along the dirt with a clawed foot. "Where they gooo!?!?!?"

The two elf women promptly let out terrified screams at the sight of Azmoth, the one standing falling over her own feet and scooting backward across the dirt.

Athela gave Riven a smirk and then rolled her eyes with a long, drawn-out sigh directed at the less intelligent of Riven's minions. "A little late to the party, idiot. While you were out and about playing Sasquatch, Riven and I already dealt with them. Try to put some points into Agility next time you level so you can begin to keep up."

CHAPTER 8

Jalel adjusted his dark, well-made, formfitting robes and smoothed out the sleeves where they meshed with fingerless gloves. The brunette slave girl attending him adjusted his collar, and he gave her an appreciating nod of respect, one she blushed furiously at before smiling widely and exiting the waiting area.

He smirked, finding it quite funny how little was required of him to make a slave's day like that. Despite being quite the ass in many circumstances, he at the very least could safely say he treated his slaves with a moderate amount of respect. The humans weren't all that far off from animals on the totem pole, but he treated them like pets and had even grown to like some of them very much.

Even if they were a lesser species.

The double doors began to open, and Jalel smoothed the flaring cloak-like tail of the garments he wore before taking confident steps forward into the room. It was a splendid attendance hall, with dozens of well-dressed nobles he'd grown up knowing—for better or worse—seated on either side in luxurious and elevated chairs. Slave attendants stood with notepads, platters of food and drink, or various substances to smoke that added flavor to the scented air wafting into Jalel's nostrils. Directly ahead and underneath an enormous banner of the crescent blood moon on a black backdrop sat the queen of their empire.

The queen herself looked not a day older than twenty years of age, though she was nearly a million years old now and had to restrain her aura in the presence of lesser creatures just so she wouldn't crush them under the sheer weight of looking at them. She wore a thin veil, bright-red eyes glowing from underneath it where strands of dark-brown hair flowed like silk over her shoulders down to a large ruby-colored amulet on her chest. Otherwise she wore a bright-white silk robe similar to his own, though hers had a more flowery look to it and spread out across the splendidly polished wooden throne she sat on that displayed carved depictions of lesser races holding up vampiric nobility. Her three sons and lone daughter stood on either side of her, Jalel's cousins, and all shared unimpressed looks with one another as he made his way down the red-carpeted aisle to kneel before the queen on her elevated platform.

The low muttering of the court quickly subsided under the dim light of lanterns overhead when the queen raised a hand, and all went silent.

"Raise your head, dear nephew, and tell me of what you found," Queen Nephridi commanded with a voice that whispered out across the room effortlessly, shaking Jalel to his very core under the sheer weight of the power contained in those words.

He shuddered involuntarily, then nodded and did as he was commanded to meet her own gaze from underneath the veil she wore. "It is indeed one of our own. The lost branch of our family has been found—at least in part."

Muttering and hushed whispers immediately tore through the room, echoing about the hall until the nobles got a harsh glare from the queen to immediately silence them. She turned back to her nephew and gave him an approving nod while her children all grimaced in turn. "Very good. You were able to locate them both, then?"

Jalel frowned, then shook his head and apologetically touched his head to the floor. "Forgive me, my queen. I was only able to find one, but I am certain that the other is of the same blood. The one I found was named Riven Thane, a rather unimpressive man but one able to use the gift of malignant prophecy. He spoke of his sister, Allie Thane, and I have no doubt that she, too, is the other beacon of prophecy you sensed. However, Elysium is unwilling to let me travel to their homeworld. It is still within a quarantined frontier sector, and I was only able to meet Riven due to special circumstances surrounding his tutorial upon initiation into the multiverse."

The queen's silent gaze quirked up in a small smile, and one of her pale fingers began tapping at the armrest of her throne. "Indeed. It appears that my granddaughter survived the tribulation after all . . . and no doubt had children of her own. How curious. Any signs of Sheline?"

"I'm afraid not."

"How unfortunate. I do hope she still lives; she was my favorite, after all . . ."

At this, all four of Queen Nephridi's children frowned even more deeply, and her eldest son even began to sneer.

"Nevertheless, it is a starting point for finding her again. And at the very least they will be useful assets to use in a century or two whenever the integration ends and the floodgates to their new world open for us." Nephridi leaned back in her chair and hummed thoughtfully, pushing her fingers up against her soft lips and rocking her head back and forth while smiling in deep thought. "Is there anything else you could tell me about this Riven character? Anything interesting?"

Jalel immediately thought back to when he'd discovered the shard of Gluttony Riven had acquired, but he actively avoided talking about it at all costs.

That shard would be his one day if he had anything to say about it, and no doubt telling the queen or any of the others here would immediately throw his plans asunder. "He was unimpressive in all regards."

One of Jalel's cousins snorted in amusement, getting a glare from his mother.

Nephridi frowned at the actions of her children and shook her head before sighing and crossing her arms. "Nothing at all?"

Jalel shook his head again. "No, Your Majesty. He was subpar in all standings. He lacks talent, lacks intelligence, lacks combat prowess, lacks good decision-making, and even spent a malignancy point for the life of a human girl he didn't even know or benefit from."

A snicker from the sidelines resulted in an abrupt scream, and then a man combusted into a flowering cloud of blood that rapidly condensed and flew through the air like crimson ribbons over to the queen's outstretched palm. She absorbed the noble, causing the hall to go deathly silent now that she was growing irritated with their disrespect toward her descendant, and she gave another meaningful glare over to her children on either side of her as they stood absolutely still under her angry gaze.

She shook her head, absorbing the last of the blood filtering through the air and crossed her legs. "Well, that is unacceptable."

"I thoroughly agree," Jalel stated in reply, hiding his savage smile underneath a mask of sorrow. If he could keep the queen disinterested, he'd be able to take Riven out in the future without much problem at all. "I suggest we abandon—"

"I will see to it that he gets proper education and training if he's lacking that much," Nephridi said thoughtfully, speaking over her nephew with indifference toward him. "Rhael?"

A large male slave attendant in shadowy robes stepped forward and bowed deeply. "Yes, my queen?"

"See to it that we figure out a way to access the quarantined frontier sector."

"Um . . . my queen?" Rhael replied with a confused look and raised eyebrow. "I am not sure that is possible. It is against Elysium's laws."

The queen nearly face-palmed, but she managed to struggle against the impulse and just let out a long sigh while massaging her forehead. "Dear God, I'm surrounded by idiots. No, you fool! I do not mean to travel there; I merely wish to—oh gods damn it, I'll do it myself!"

With a huff she stood up and walked out of the room and into a side hallway, leaving the entire gathering of nobility rather speechless and sharing glances with one another. The queen was certainly powerful, powerful enough to lead a bloodthirsty and violent empire for generations upon generations, but she often lacked what other leaders of other factions had in terms of patience or political maneuvering.

This time was no different, and Jalel's gut tensed in irritation. The way Her Majesty had reacted could be a potential problem, so he'd have to think of some countermeasures to offset this unfortunate state of events.

"Well, this throws a wrench in things," Athela stated absentmindedly while staring at the two wounded, blood-covered elves who lay half-exposed on a bed of furs and under blankets that'd been stripped from the supplies of the dead.

They'd settled into a darker recess of the forest half a mile away from the battleground, where the trees were larger and the brush was thicker, next to a large boulder the size of a truck that had a small stream passing by. Athela had set up traps and walls of red webbing all around the perimeter at a good distance away, and Riven was absolutely sure that if he crossed this kind of makeshift lair in the forest without knowing what had created it, he'd absolutely, 100 percent avoid it at all costs given how it looked. Despite this, it really was the perfect spot, considering they had all the shade Riven needed to avoid discomfort and water for cleaning the wounds of the two elves. Originally the wounds had been full of dirt and contaminants, and although the stream's water wasn't completely sterile, it was a hell of a lot cleaner after a washout than how they'd originally presented.

Not long after Riven had cleaned their wounds, both of the exhausted elves had fallen asleep. Quickly even, especially after their initial fears of being eaten had been somewhat put aside after an extended period of time with the strange trio watching over them. She'd set aside their bloody garments in order to better examine their bodies for further injuries, then covered them with blankets. Cleaner garments taken from the dead were used as bandages, and Athela had even gotten one of them to laugh at a stupid joke she'd made before the girl had passed out due to the battered state of her worn-out body.

"Yes . . . Yes, it does throw a wrench into things . . ." Riven stated slowly, tossing the guild-hall bauble up into the air and snatching it before it landed, repeating the action over and over again. He lay on his back, staring up into the canopy with one leg crossed over the other, and tried to keep his eyes off the two injured beauties not far off. "Elves, huh. Who would have thought . . ."

While they'd been waiting for the elves to at least somewhat recover, he'd been going over his options on how to proceed.

He still needed to find his sister, Allie, and his best friend, Jose. The quest log would tell him Allie's general direction every once in a while—it had happened little while ago, when it'd pinged her location for an entire minute that took the form of mental sensations confirming both person and place in the wreckage of the small city at the foot of the mountains. Last he knew, his sister had been about twelve miles from the gas station Riven had started at after leaving Negrada's hellscape.

He'd figure out if they'd been going in the right direction later with the next set of pings and would adjust as needed based on what happened. However, it was safe to say he was on the path to reuniting with them soon.

Then there were the two injured elves. Riven desperately wanted to question them . . . to find out what they knew and why they'd been fighting the goblins in the first place. To ask them if there were more goblins in the area, more elves, and why they'd reacted like that to seeing that he was a vampire. He was a monster now, and he knew he had a negative Charisma that would influence others to some kind of degree . . . but he was still more or less human in nature. Wasn't he? Surely Charisma wouldn't cause that kind of reaction from *everyone* he met, right? He still felt like the same person he'd been just days ago, only now he had vastly increased prowess—and a voracious appetite for blood. Didn't seem like too bad of a trade-off to him considering the change had saved his life. Hadn't they jumped to conclusions about him and his demons rather fast, considering that he and Athela had just saved the elves from a violent death?

Speaking of voracious appetites . . . he might end up going back to feed on some of those bodies. Just thinking about it made his stomach rumble, and the gnawing hunger in his gut grasped at him like a wild, rabid animal waiting to be unleashed.

He clenched his fists to quell the urge. Instead his thoughts traced back toward the city he'd seen farther down the mountain and into the plains. He had a feeling, based on how the elves were dressed—with hardly anything but furs and primitive wrappings—that whoever or whatever had built that distant city was not them. The other equipment that the elves had was also subpar at best, being nothing but long hunting knives, longbows, and steel arrows. Not a group he'd assume could make such large structures at such a distance. He couldn't make out the architecture very well from so far out, but it did look Earth-made from where he'd seen it on his vantage point up the mountain.

Athela walked over, poked Riven's shoulder with her bare foot, and smiled down at him. "Cheer up! You look miserable."

He raised an eyebrow her way as the arachnoid woman plopped cross-legged onto the ground beside him with narrowed red eyes and a wide, brilliant grin. "You good?!"

Dusting himself off, he shook his head and pointed a finger in her direction with raised eyebrows in mock aggression, pocketing the guild hall's bauble in a cloak pocket. "You'll be sorry for kicking me. I'm going to strike back in the near future, and you won't even see it coming when I do."

"Kicking you?! I just poked you with my toe!" She stuck her tongue out and pulled down an eyelid. "Bleh! But seriously, are you okay?"

He smirked, then nodded with a contented groan while adjusting his posture on the ground to rest his head on her thighs as a pillow. "Yeah, I'm okay. Just shut up and stay there—no funny business or messing with me while I'm resting. I'm going to sleep. Wake me up if something important happens."

Athela was about to give a snappy response and raised a finger to protest as her chest heaved to draw in air, but she thought better of it after she watched Riven close his eyes. Her finger dropped and a mischievous glint appeared in her eyes. Instead she merely muttered under her breath and to herself so that only she could hear, "Funny business?! I don't know what you even mean by that!"

CHAPTER 9

The mission was threefold—figure out what was going on with the city concerning the people he needed to find, find some more food, and find a location that would be suitable for Riven to stay in long term . . . if there even was one. There hadn't been any system notifications since leaving Dungeon Negrada, but Athela was utterly certain there'd be more to come.

"Each integrating planet has its own unique trials!" Athela said to him, trying and failing to contain a smirk right before he was to leave. "Sometimes many of them, sometimes less. Just depends, but they're coming!"

Riven frowned at her expression under the shade of the canopy, and that frown deepened whenever she started to snicker outright while covering her mouth with her hands. When Azmoth started to laugh, a deep, guttural barking sound, Riven could only cross his arms. "What's so funny?"

"You just look so handsome!" Athela said between giggles while Azmoth continued to cackle.

Riven didn't notice the large red mustache Athela had drawn on his face with her webbing until he put his mask on. When it stuck and he had a hard time prying the mask off, both demons began to howl with laughter even more loudly.

His eyes narrowed, but an amused grin spread across his lips. "Really?! While I slept?! Okay. So that's how we're going to play it, huh? I'll have you know I'm a master prankster! You don't want this kind of war, girl."

Keeping his hood down over his eyes, his body moved at superhuman speed—three times faster than his outright sprint prior to his ascension into vampirism while utilizing little effort to do it. The sun was beating down and he had to stick his hands in his cloak pockets occasionally in order to avoid a debuff, but overall avoiding the light touching his skin wasn't too much of a hassle. Meanwhile, the staff was attached to his back with a pair of straps he'd taken off one of the dead goblins that'd likely been meant for keeping prisoners or animals bound.

Trees began to disappear as he made his way into the plains, where fields of green grass, buzzing bumblebees, and beautiful wildflowers bloomed to life along either side of a long dirt road. The mountain behind him loomed with frosted peaks and jagged edges, making him feel small whenever he looked back.

The city in front of him was coming closer as the foothills completely gave way to flatter plains, and he began to make out buildings from a little ways off between a trio of lower-lying hills. Farther beyond the town and to the east, the plains led into a sprawling sea of grasslands and rivers before turning into patches of forests in the farthest reaches of his vision.

It wasn't but another hundred yards before he slowed his sprint, hardly having broken a sweat despite the long run, as his boots touched down onto a road made of familiar cement. There was a stark contrast between where the road and dirt path connected, and it looked like they'd almost been taken out of two completely different puzzles and placed alongside one another in cookie-cutter fashion. Even the grass, which had been a luscious green, was now slightly less vibrant in a noticeable straight line that struck out to his right and left—and beyond it even the trees were different. The change was subtle, but the leaves were certainly different when Riven looked closely. The oaks and evergreens that'd been present beyond the plains' edge and into the forest were now being replaced by small numbers of scattered maple trees, something that hadn't been present at all up until the city's border along that perfectly straight line.

How odd. Perhaps this is what the administrator had been talking about when it'd said his world was being meshed with two others? It was like two jigsaw puzzle pieces, albeit somewhat similar, had been slapped together.

The paved road led him around the small hill, presenting a main street that led into the heart of the city before disappearing with a curve about a mile out. Light poles, storefronts, houses, and familiar English lettering on street signs combined with a typical modern American–style architecture. It was definitely from Earth, and now that he was up close, he still couldn't decide whether or not it would be classified as a large town or a small city.

The odd part about seeing this was . . . the street was deserted.

There were broken-down cars scattered down the length of the road, two of which had been lit aflame and were smoking as they burned. A couple dogs barked in the distance, and he could even hear a gunshot in the far distance . . . though nobody immediately presented themselves out in the open. He briefly remembered how monsters had started spawning all around the world before civilization had turned upside down with the chaos it brought. Guess it made sense . . . seeing this place the way it was.

Surely there would be survivors, though . . .

That's when he saw the big blue road sign on the left-hand side. It read, **Welcome to Brightsville, Virginia! Home of the Fighting Prairie Dogs!** in large yellow letters.

He snickered at the thought of prairie dogs fighting. Must be a high school or college, but it wasn't any college he'd ever heard of. He'd been too poor to afford a college education anyway and hadn't really had an interest in further education because of that, and even though he'd been smart and gotten good grades in school, he'd dropped out early in order to help take care of his family.

His hand reached over his back to grab the staff strapped there with a tight grip, when he caught a brief glimpse of motion in a backyard to his left and pulled the staff out to hold in front of him. Turning to the fenced-off area, he squinted. Nothing presented itself again, though, and the heartbeat he'd heard began to fade into the distance. He shrugged it off and kept moving—wishing he still had a belt so that he didn't have to carry this damn staff everywhere, but he'd rather have it than not, even if it did make traveling at high speed a little less fluid.

With a grunt, he casually strolled down the main street, hoping he'd find some clue as to what was going on here and if there was anybody worth talking to still alive.

He came across a Walmart Supercenter, completely ransacked of all supplies with a couple of fresh bodies lying in the entrance area where a gunfight had obviously broken out. He visited a Best Buy, a McDonald's, and even a Home Depot. Only the Home Depot still had supplies, and even some of those were gone. In each of these places the electricity wasn't working, creating dark interiors in each. Running water wasn't working properly whenever he came across a drinking fountain or sink, and as Riven continued farther into the city's interior over the next couple hours at a slow walking pace, he began to see more signs of smoke and fire.

He turned down a side street into the suburbs, trying to stick to the shadows of the scattered maple trees along the sides of the roads. Still, there were no cars, no motorcycles, and no signs of any electricity being used. An hour into casually walking the streets, he was beginning to get discouraged about finding anyone—until he spotted a middle-aged man and woman jump a fence to his right and sprint across the road in front of him—stopping only momentarily in shock at seeing him before screaming at him to run.

"GET AWAY!" the brunette woman shrieked. Her clothes were ripped, bloodied, and she ran with a limp while holding her bleeding side. "SLAVERS ARE COMING THIS WAY! GO!"

Riven raised an eyebrow as the skinny man tugged at his companion, whispering frantically at her before they began running again toward the houses on the left. Slavers? Here in what was very recently a piece of Virginia?

The man and woman continued onward down the cement street a bit on Riven's left, panting at the exertion and fumbling with a pair of keys at a doorway as Riven took the hint and got behind a nearby minivan to hide. Glancing curiously over the windows and seeing out through the other side, he watched and heard as four bigger men clambered the fence after the duo. Two bald, muscular guys with tattoos wore gray tank tops and gold chains. The next guy had a mohawk and carried a machete, wearing a leather jacket, with another guy wielding a shotgun jumping the fence after them.

"Hurry it up!" the guy with the mohawk snarled at his comrades as he tore after the two fleeing people, who'd just entered a boarded-up two-story house and slammed the door behind them.

The house had a white-painted exterior up top with a brick first story. The glass of some of the windows had been shattered, but those on both floors were boarded up with numerous planks nailed into the interior side. The door itself was wooden with a circular glass window, but the brief glance inside before the two people had slammed it behind them showed Riven that they'd reinforced the door on the interior as well.

Gliding down the street after the four chasing men as they came up to the door, Riven curiously watched to see what would happen. He had to step quickly to the left, hiding behind a tree, when he caught the guy with the shotgun turning in his direction—but he successfully avoided detection. He didn't think his body would be able to withstand a shotgun blast at close range even with his newfound prowess, so he'd have to be careful here if he wanted to intervene in any way.

Riven peered back around the thick trunk of the maple tree, lips curling as the two men in tank tops took turns ramming the front door while the guy with the shotgun kicked open the fence to the backyard and circled the house to make sure their prey would not escape.

"WE'RE COMING IN, MY PRETTY!" cackled the machete-wielding, leather-clad man that Riven decided to call Mohawk.

Designating the two wife-beaters as Crony One and Crony Two, and the Black guy with the shotgun as Shotgun Guy, he quickly came to dislike all of them and realized that the woman who'd warned Riven had been absolutely right about their intentions.

"Oh, don't be shy!" Mohawk crowed while waving his machete at one of the windows, spitting and working himself into a frenzy. "A life of forced labor isn't that bad! Come on and let us in, and we may be a bit nicer to you before putting you both on sale!"

Yup. That's all Riven needed to hear.

A scream from the other side of the house, the sound of a quickly slamming door, and a follow-up blast from a shotgun made Riven scowl. Lunging across to his left and into the adjacent house's back fence, he vaulted over the wooden pickets and rushed toward the opposite side.

"Are you going to kill them?!" Athela asked excitedly, appearing out of nowhere to his left and almost causing him to scream in startled surprise. "How kinky!"

Athela was perched on the balls of her feet with a manic smile, setting herself promptly behind where Riven had been looking at just a moment before.

"Kinky?!" Riven whispered in a snarl before coming to a stop at the edge of the bordering fence between the house at his back right and the house that was being broken into in front of him. "How the fuck is that kinky? Where the fuck did you even come from and why can't I hear your heartbeat?! How'd you sneak up on me like that?"

"It's an ability I have. I can silence myself and do all kinds of sneaky things since my evolution! Though you did actually sense me earlier when you first entered the town . . . kinda disappointing, really. I'd been doing so good up until then."

"That was you behind the fence? And aren't you supposed to be watching the elves?"

"Nah. Azmoth has them covered. Now . . . How about we capture them for torturing and . . ." She abruptly paused like a deer in the headlights. Her excited grin melted away, and she looked down at the ground with mild amounts of shame. "Oh, wait. Sorry, I'd forgotten you asked me to stop that kind of teasing. Bad habits die hard." Athela gave him a sheepish smile. "I'll do better, I promise."

Riven's features softened slightly, and he gave her an appreciative nod. "Thanks. For the record, though, it isn't that I mind you getting excited about fighting. I know you enjoy it. I just don't want you to tease me about killing *innocent* people. Regardless, I appreciate the effort."

She beamed at the praise with a warm smile, clasping her hands in front of her and looking like she'd just gotten an A-plus on a test in school.

Their hushed whispers came to an end as Riven examined the scene again. Shotgun Guy had blown a small hole through the door halfway up and was kicking at it as screams of pain and fear echoed from the back.

"LEAVE US ALONE!" the woman's voice cried out as a pleading, wavering sob amid the ruckus. "PLEASE LEAVE!"

CHAPTER 10

Shotgun Guy just laughed, then he got tired of kicking and took aim and fired again. Another good-size chunk of wood blasted off the door, but the idiot had been too close when he'd fired and recoiled as chips of debris hit him in the face and eyes. "Fuck!"

He staggered back, rubbing at his face and cursing loudly until he managed to clear his line of sight . . . only to blink rapidly as he came face-to-face with Riven to his left and Athela to his right.

"Hello, chap," Riven said with a friendly smile underneath the black hood, leaning lazily against the side of the building. "Care to die for me?"

Athela's claws extended and flashed up, skewering the man's stomach and kidney before her arm protruded out the left side of his back. Shotgun Guy screamed in agony and horror, shock clear upon his features amid Athela's laughter right before Riven grasped the man's neck and brought it forward—headbutting the guy's face and breaking his nose in a gush of blood.

RIP

TEAR

SPLAT

"AAAHHHHHH!!!"

Riven found himself beating the man to death alongside his demonic minion. He felt no sympathy, no remorse, only a deep sense of satisfaction knowing he was—at least in his mind—doing the right thing. Meanwhile, the screams and gurgles intermixed with the occasional small explosion of shadow whenever his staff would make contact with the man's bloodied body.

Athela ripped the man's spleen out as the guy tried to fumble with the shotgun he held on to for dear life, but Riven easily knocked it aside as it fired again. Coming down hard on the falling man in a downward strike, one of Athela's sharpened arachnid legs whipped out of her back and severed the man's left hand, sending the appendage flying. Riven then brought his foot down onto the man's neck with an audible crunch when the windpipe collapsed.

Surprisingly, the guy didn't die right away. His eyes bulged, he coughed up blood, and he quivered there on the ground in disbelief. Riven cocked his head to the side in confusion at how he hadn't passed yet. Shrugging and walking over to the shotgun—he picked up the weapon and inspected it. Seeing that it had no bullets left in it, he walked back over and searched the dying man—finding only two cartridges.

"Good enough," Riven stated flatly, then stood up and gave his enemy a final swift kick to the face that sent his neck over at an odd angle with another crunch, and the man lay still.

Athela frowned his way. "Hey! That was my kill."

"Sorry, not sorry."

From the holes in the door, within the dark interior, he saw the man and woman who'd warned him watching with wide eyes. The man inside had been shot in the leg when they'd tried to make a break for it out the back door and was being bandaged by the woman on the kitchen floor. Both of them wore expressions of mixed hope and horror.

"Eyo!" Riven stated, smiling widely at the husband and wife with a thumbs-up while Athela did her best to give them an innocent look despite the spleen in her hand. "Just wait one moment and we'll get to talking!"

Shouting from the front echoed out and the pounding on the front door stopped, with the sounds of footsteps quickly coming around the side to the entrance to the backyard.

Riven quietly held up a finger, pocketing the shotgun shells and kicking the gun to the side as he turned to face the three men who'd come around the side of the boarded-up house. They were all in a line as they ran, giving Riven reason to grin before scowling when a ray of sunlight dashed across his vision when his hood had been drawn back a little too far. Regardless, it didn't stop him from beginning to summon the magic as he prepared a Blood Lance with his outstretched fingers.

Wisps of crimson began radiating off his skin, rippling down his forearm and into his hand as a thin, shimmering, bloodred spike a few feet across with sharp, lacerating edges materialized at his unspoken command. This time instead of the usual form of magic, he began to concentrate on making it more solid—forming a more permanent projectile instead of one that fizzled out after impact. He'd been thinking about practicing something like this, and although it probably wouldn't have much effect on the outcome, he thought he'd give it a try for the sake of science.

Mohawk, Crony One, and Crony Two all came to a sudden halt when they saw the display of power—confusion evident as they stumbled into one another when the spear of blood launched forward into the first of them.

The lance ripped through Mohawk's chest with ease, shredding his left lung and heart as the magic embedded itself into Crony Two's right shoulder. Mohawk gasped in shock, dropping the machete he carried to the grass, and fell to his knees while Crony Two shrieked and howled, stumbling back.

Riven cocked his head to the side curiously as he realized his attempt at keeping the lance in a more permanent state had worked—as it didn't disappear, but remained lodged in the second man like a flagpole.

"WHAT THE FUCK IS THIS?!" Crony Two roared, trying to rip the blood magic out of his shoulder before it vaporized right before his eyes when Riven snapped his fingers—leaving a seeping, bloody wound and exposing torn deltoid muscle. "WHAT THE ACTUAL FUCK?!"

Crony One was stunned, his eyes having grown wide at the sudden and unexpected death of his boss and the injury of his comrade. He scrambled for the machete, catching sight of Shotgun Guy, who was bloodied, missing a spleen, and dead with his neck at an odd angle behind Riven.

Cursing and adjusting his gold chain, Crony One screamed and rushed Riven to slash at him, only to have his eyes widen more in surprise as Riven easily avoided the predicted attack with a blurring sidestep—letting the machete slide through thin air while Riven rammed upward into the extended arm of the attacking man underneath the shoulder joint.

CRACK

Shadow magic erupted from the gnarled black staff and ripped completely through the shoulder joint. With Riven's enhanced speed and strength, the arm was completely severed with a single blow—but the shocked crony only had time to stumble forward before Riven's staff whipped back around and slammed into the base of the man's skull.

Riven didn't bother watching as Crony One's brains splattered across the dirt, and like a sack of potatoes his lifeless body hit the ground. Instead he kept eye contact with Crony Two, who was staring open-mouthed and clutching at his wounded shoulder in utter disbelief. That disbelief turned into horror as Riven gave his best impression of an evil laugh, extended his fangs, and pointed the staff Crony Two's way.

"Come here, child, I've brought cookies!"

It was a little ridiculous, Riven knew, but he didn't care. He was having fun, and as Crony Two let out a horror-filled scream and turned to run, Athela dropped from the rooftop above in a dive attack that skewered the man in six different places. Pinning him to the ground with her arachnoid legs, her hands and bladed tongue went into a flurry of motion as she tore his body into literal shreds that went flying as if she'd sent him through a woodchipper.

"KINKY!" Athela exclaimed with an excited shuddering, beginning to let out a giddy laugh of pure amusement.

Seeing the body parts drenching his minion, though, Riven had to take a step back and reevaluate whether or not she would be able to get all that gunk off, even with an hour-long bath.

He checked the dead men, not finding anything of value before proceeding over to the shotgun and picking it up. Casually loading the gun with the two remaining shells, he hiccuped and nodded in appreciation at his new loot.

[Shotgun]
[Shotgun Shell]

He sighed, again acknowledging that the identification information was still not nearly as good as it'd been back in the tutorial. He'd really have to find what the system had been referring to as an "Identifier," because being able to compare items, enemies, and ingredients for his totem crafting would be essential for the future.

Regardless, he assumed the gun had stats just like his staff did. He'd never thought of guns as having stats before, but now that everything else had stats . . . he could safely say it should be the same way. What DID surprise him was the abrupt sound of a strong heartbeat directly behind him that was inching closer . . . He whirled, and when he did finally see it . . . he froze.

There, not even five feet from him, was some kind of enormous cat creature. It was definitely not a native to Earth—it had six clawed feet and looked like a cross between a leopard and a tiger but had four fuzzy ears—the back set of ears being twice the length as the front set. Black spots intermingled with stripes along its otherwise yellow coat, and when it realized it'd been spotted, it lunged his way.

[Juvenile Wrath Cat]

Mana coursed through his veins and red sparks lit up across his skin amid Blessing of the Crow. Black Lightning exploded out of his staff a millisecond later, taking the cat head-on in midair. The magic had a recoil effect, which sent Riven slamming back into the side of the house. It also knocked Athela head over heels, sending her cartwheeling down the alley with a shriek. The cat had gotten the worst of it, though—its body erupted into smoldering fleshy bits amid a torrent of destruction. The fence behind it exploded and the ground underneath erupted to send dirt and debris skyward in a thirty-meter arc of desolation, and Riven's staff hummed in pleasure as he coughed and picked himself up off the ground.

[You have landed a critical hit. Max Damage x3.]

To any onlookers, it had appeared that he'd moved so fast that his body had defied time itself . . . and to Riven . . . Well, he was just happy to be alive.

Cursing jovially and getting up to evaluate the remains of the dead cat, he cackled gleefully at the dead monster and pushed himself up from the ground. "You thought you had me, didn't you—ya little bastard!"

Riven spat on the cat's corpse, picked up a coin purse that'd dropped out of thin air as a reward from the system, chuckled some more, and hoisted the shotgun and its remaining single shot onto his shoulder. His chest heaved with the thrill and excitement of the brief but stimulating fight, and he regained his normal respiratory rate seconds later. "Phew! That was a close one."

CHAPTER 11

"That's what's up, Riven!"

"Yes, I am the kinkiest." He referred to her earlier comment, glanced over his shoulder, and winked at Athela, who was licking her extremities with her elongated, ribbonlike black tongue—and he gave her a genuine smile. "Thanks for coming. Having you around has been a lot of fun."

Athela paused midlicking, and her red eyes focused on him for a moment before she blinked and turned around in embarrassment with her hands covering her face. "Oh, stop it! You're making me blush!"

Riven snorted in amusement and rolled his eyes. Turning heel and walking over to the back door, he nudged it open with his boot. After the locks and reinforcements had been blown off by the shotgun, the wooden door easily swung open at the small display of applied force.

The door creaked and came to a halt, and he stepped inside to close the door behind him—shutting out the light as well.

Given that Riven could now see in the dark, that was completely fine and even slightly more comfortable than being out in the sunlight.

A teapot was set along a stove to his right with a kitchen counter full of used, unwashed plates next to it. A turned-over table, some wooden chairs, and a hockey stick were also present before the kitchen led out into the front room.

Coming into the carpeted front room, which held a television and some bookshelves, Riven had the choice of going down a hall to the right, out the front door, which had been barricaded with a couch and boxes, into a laundry room just beyond that, or up a stairway.

Riven didn't need to ask which direction the people had gone, given the trail of blood leading up the stairs—and he could hear their frantic heartbeats directly above him on the second level when he concentrated hard enough. Wondering why he could pick up heartbeats with his sense of hearing yet couldn't hear what they were saying in hushed tones, he shrugged and began stomping up the stairs to make his approach apparent.

"Coming up! I killed the guys chasing—"

His voice cut off as he turned the corner and met a metal baseball bat square in the forehead.

"OW!" He nearly stumbled back and tripped down the stairs but managed to catch himself on the railing with a scowl. Rubbing his bruised forehead, he scowled back up the stairs where the woman and man both shrieked to run back down the hall out of sight.

But he could still hear their voices as they scrambled frantically into a room and slammed a door behind them.

"You goddamned idiot! That was the wrong guy! He just saved us, and you could have fucking killed him!" the man's voice said with a growl and a huff, saying some other words after that Riven couldn't make out. "Now he's DEFINITELY going to kill us!"

The woman's frantically sobbing voice came next. "I got scared! I wasn't sure if it was the slavers!"

"You knew goddamned well it was him when he yelled up the stairs! And what about that scary woman he had with him?!"

"It could have been anyone saying that! And what about the things he did out there? You saw how he moved! And that thing he summoned into the air and killed those men with, and the fangs?! He's one of them!"

"One of who?"

"The monsters that keep appearing! Look at the woman he was with! He came to kill us, too! That's why I swung, okay?! I thought I'd get him good!"

"Linda, for the love of God . . . You're such a damnable surly wench! Get it through your thick skull that you don't need to WHACK everybody we see!"

Surly wench? He actually really liked that insult and jotted it down in his memory. He needed to use that one himself sometime. Riven blinked and began to make his way up the stairs again with Athela still eating outside. Muttering to himself about how if he'd been any normal man he'd likely have died, he stepped into an open hallway cluttered with various children's toys and a couch halfway dragged out of a room on his right. A closed door led to a room at the far end of the hall on the left, where the man and woman continued to argue.

They were also completely engrossed in their arguing, to the point that they didn't even hear his footsteps outside.

Flinging the door open and easily throwing the man and woman behind it to the ground, Riven stepped inside to lay eyes on the dynamic duo of husband and wife. The slightly balding dark-haired man was bracing his left side with a crutch. He'd been shot in the leg, and he pushed himself up with a pained groan. He turned around, clambering to his feet again, limped over to his wife with a fearful glance Riven's way, and nearly stumbled when he saw Riven staring him down with glowing red eyes.

The man looked to be about forty years old. He was skinny and wore a gray checkered shirt and jeans that had holes where the shotgun had grazed him.

The woman with him looked to be about the same age, mildly overweight, with longer brown hair in a ponytail. She hid fearfully behind her husband with wide, teary eyes, carried a metal bat, and wore a dark-blue shirt depicting a guitar that was stained with blood along her hip where a cut had been bandaged up with gauze. The wound must have been shallow, though, because she paid it no mind and didn't limp like her husband did.

"Jerald!" the scared woman scolded her husband when he nearly fell before settling her gaze on Riven. She frowned and opened her mouth to speak but closed it immediately after with a shameful and avoiding glance to the floor.

"Didn't realize you would attack me for trying to help," Riven stated flatly, anger flaring to life again as he saw them. "Maybe I should have just let them do their thing."

The husband, whose name was apparently Jerald, tried to hold back a shaky frown and failed as he remembered what they'd just gone through. However, his emotions were only partially directed at Riven, and he limped over to sit on a desk with a groan—suspending his injured leg. "I'm sorry for what happened. My wife, Linda, was out of her goddamn mind when she swung at you."

The man's voice shook. His wife followed him over to hide behind him at the desk, both of their hearts beating frantically.

Riven raised an eyebrow and folded his arms in the doorway, watching Linda put a hand on Jerald's thigh. "Oh?"

The husband and wife exchanged looks, but neither of them caught Athela's lithe, black body leaning silently against the windowsill outside with a shit-eating grin as she snickered silently at Riven's bruised forehead. She was clinging to the side of the house with all six of her arachnoid limbs, and was utterly silent.

Riven just looked back at his demon, unamused, as she made silly faces at him while sticking out her tongue and pulling her eyelids up or puffing out her cheeks and wiggling her ears with her fingers.

They had no idea she'd been there the whole time. Athela really was one sneaky bitch, and she apparently thought this entire situation was hilarious.

"Well . . . we're sorry . . ." The man trailed off uncertainly, turning back to Riven a moment after glaring his wife down. "Now that she attacked you, I just wanted to let you know that we really meant you no harm. There are no hard feelings, right?"

"That hit would have killed a normal person," Riven stated sourly, turning his attention away from Athela and back to the couple. "Probably, anyways."

"Normal person?" Jerald repeated as Linda started to tug at his arm.

"See!" Linda stated, quickly becoming frantic as she jammed a finger repeatedly in Riven's direction. "He's not normal! Not human! He has RED EYES, Jerald! Humans can't do the things he did out there! Even LOOKING at him gives me the creeps! You feel it, too, Jerald, don't you?! He gives off terrible, scary vibes! You should just kill him now so he doesn't hurt us!"

Kill him now?

Was she daft? Riven glanced down to Jerald's bloody leg, the plastered image of fear of Riven and rage directed toward his wife frozen there after her words had come out without thought. The husband paled and slowly turned to the ranting woman, then aggressively pushed a quivering finger up to her lips to shut her up.

Ugh. Was this the negative Charisma at work again? He'd literally saved their lives, and this woman was telling her husband to kill Riven just because he was "different"? Or was she truly just that stupid? Perhaps it was a combination of both.

Riven gave her a flat look, then turned to Jerald. "And what if you're right, Linda? What exactly is it that either of you are going to do? Even if I'm not normal, I saved your lives. Didn't I? Do you really think your husband can take me in the state he's in?"

Linda hadn't been expecting the near admission of guilt after she'd accused him of not being a "normal" person. Her face puckered as she pointed a quivering finger in his direction when the words finally hit home, and her expression turned upside down. "Ah . . ."

She lowered her finger, nodding to herself as if a light bulb had gone off in that small brain of hers. "I suppose you're right. You did save our lives. Apologize to him, Jerald—what WERE you thinking?!"

She smacked her husband across the forehead with the back of her hand, and he recoiled, almost causing him to fall off the desk. "Idiot!"

"Idiot?! I'm not the one who hit him with a bat!"

"Keep talkin' to me that way, and you won't be gettin' sex for a week!"

"Are you serious?!"

Riven's flat look turned to one of confused amusement, and then one of sheer disbelief as he realized that they weren't joking—rather, they were actually stupid. Truly, truly stupid. The farther and farther down this rabbit hole they went, the more inbred they seemed, and he was seriously questioning just whom he'd saved when they finally came to a stalemate in the conversation about ten minutes later.

He'd only lost a couple brain cells. He'd be okay, but in the background Athela was clutching her stomach and reeling with silent laughter.

Sighing and coming around the back of the chair, Linda humphed and stepped forward with a sheepish bow. "Sorry 'bout that. My husband's a true moron at times; he had me convinced I had to smack ya, so I did."

Riven didn't really believe that for even a half second, but he was just happy he didn't have to kill them. Even though they were idiots, they seemed like nice enough people. Well, at least her husband did.

He closed his eyes, leaned against the wall, and shook his head. "So . . . how'd you two get caught up with those thugs?"

"Slavers, ya mean?"

". . . yeah. Let's start there. Why are there slavers here and who are they selling slaves to, exactly?"

The woman frowned and rubbed her chin thoughtfully, getting a better look at Riven in the dim light of their home. "You really ain't from here, are ya? Haven't you seen what happened with our town?"

Riven shook his head. "Obviously not."

"I'll answer your question if you answer mine first."

"Sure. Go ahead then."

"How'd you move like that? And what was that red spear thing you created in the air to shoot at those men? And the lightning? WHY does your staff occasionally ripple with black mist?!"

Riven looked down to his hand, then briefly summoned a Blood Lance through his arm and then up into the air to hover over the top of his palm like a sanguine blade. "It's magic. I also . . . changed, since the integration. I am from Earth, like you two, but I've gained a bunch of abilities that make me move faster. The Black Lightning was from my staff, which is actually semisentient, if I understand things right."

Jerald exchanged a look with his wife and snorted. "Told you. That administrator guy was the real deal—we didn't hallucinate him."

"That batch of weed brownies was laced with some sorta crack or shrooms!" Linda stated sourly, folding her arms in defiance of the husband. "Of course I'd have thought it was a hallucination! We had no reason not to!"

"We haven't had no weed brownies for at least a good week, you dumb wench!" Jerald growled while poking Linda with the butt of his crutch. "You have to think!!! THINK, woman, THINK!!!"

Oh, boy. Speaking of thinking, Riven really was beginning to think twice about these two. But he needed information, and because they were the first people he hadn't had to kill who could speak to him clearly and knew the situation from Earth—he might as well try despite their stupidity. Clearing his throat and sighing inwardly, he got their attention before they went off on another rant. "All right, so let's just cut to the chase. I'll give you a brief overview of myself and my story, and you can do the same for yourselves to cover the basics that you think I'd want to know about this city. All right?"

Both husband and wife nodded in agreement after glowering at one another.

"Good." Riven said, wiping a hand through his chestnut-colored hair. "All right . . . So, it's a long story. The short version is as follows: after the apocalypse, I was transferred to a trial to acquire a demonic companion, and then I was placed in a dungeon."

"Demons and a dungeon?" Jerald asked, interrupting only for Linda to shush him.

Riven nodded, modifying his story of what'd happened slightly to reduce the number of questions he'd get. "A dungeon that spawned monsters and things that tried to kill us. No interrupting, please. Anyways, we survived there for a couple weeks, and I drank some tainted blood in order to survive because there wasn't much food, and it also had healing properties . . . later on, I became a vampire."

CHAPTER 12

Riven took his runic mask off, pointed to a widening smile and extended his fangs for the two to see. The duo gasped in shock before he retracted both fangs with a shrug. "I became stronger, fought against a dungeon miniboss, and won a good number of Elysium coins. The dungeon was a sentient being and offered me a deal to get the coins back. I ended up teleporting out of the dungeon and into the mountains to the west. Fought some goblins, saw some elves, and now I'm here. End of story."

"Elves are real? I don't buy it," Jerald said stubbornly.

Linda, however, was overly eager to believe. She smacked her husband across the back of his head and scowled. "We've already been seein' monsters, and the goddamn world ended! The roads outside the town disappeared and the entire goddamned area was transported somewhere else! We've seen him use magic, Jerald! He even showed us his fangs! Why aren't we gonna believe him, you fuckin' idiot!"

She shook her head with an exasperated sigh and rubbed her temple. "All we know is the world ended and now everyone's gone mad. The city has devolved into chaos, people looting and stealing and killing one another. When the apocalypse started, it was bad, yeah, but since the administrator came down just a few weeks ago when the world changed . . . we ended up here—"

Riven held up a hand. "Wait . . . you said you just got here a few days ago?"

That's when he'd left the dungeon. He'd expected them to be here longer.

Linda nodded adamantly. "Yes. The apocalypse started a week ago, and the transition to this new world that the administrator person calls Panu happened two days ago."

Riven's frown grew. That didn't seem right . . . To him, the apocalypse had started well over a month ago. However, he'd also gotten here just two days past where he'd ended up at the gas station with his minions . . . had time run differently in Negrada than it did here?

"Are you absolutely sure that the apocalypse started a few weeks ago? How many weeks?"

Again she nodded, and Jerald confirmed this with a nod of his own.

"Maybe three weeks?"

"And did you ever go to a tutorial of your own?"

"I don't know what that is. A tutorial for what?"

Riven scratched his head and frowned in the dim light of the room. Huh. Well, this was something he'd have to think about, but not now. Another time, maybe. "All righty, then. You still haven't answered my question, though. How'd you get mixed up with slavers?"

Jerald grimaced, looking out the near window through a crack in the boards they'd nailed across the opening. He stayed that way for some time, examining the house's surroundings. "The city's gangs and thugs were the first to start leveling. People are growing stronger by killing things. That includes other people, not just the monsters that've been appearing, and criminals took advantage of that."

The man shook his head sadly while immersed in recent memories. "Some people were given quests; others were given abilities somehow, a lot like you. Ammo started running low, as did the food, all within a week. There aren't enough supplies in the city to go around anymore. I'm surprised at how fast it happened . . . but anyhow, the worst of it happened after the electricity stopped working. Even though the power plants were up, none of the lights would come on. I know because I used to work at the plant and the equipment is still in top shape—but nothin' comes out of it."

"Even the batteries in our flashlights and cars all died, and all at once . . ." Linda chimed in with a sad frown. "Anyways, we were at the hospital when it all happened. Our little girl has leukemia. This was her room before she started living in the children's quarters over at Mercy West."

"Mercy West being the hospital you were talking about?"

Linda nodded, her lips beginning to quiver. "Yes . . . They were doing a good job taking care of her. Sara is our daughter's name—she's only nine years old. Anyhow, she's still alive, and the hospital was running out of supplies. They didn't have enough of the medication she needed to continue treating her after it ran out yesterday, and we had some here . . . so we came looking for it even though we knew leaving the hospital was dangerous. Her life is worth more than ours, so we took a chance . . . and ended up here with you. As for the slavers—we heard about them before heading out, but then we saw them taking people a few streets over: tying them up and dragging them away to sell to other, bigger groups. They've been killing and eating people like cannibals because food is so low, or they use the slaves for their liking. That's what the word is, anyways. Hospital security warned us not to go . . . but that wasn't an option."

Linda pulled two large bottles of pills out of her left back pocket, rattling them for Riven to see. "We need to get back to the hospital so our little girl can continue living. The doctors there are taking care of her . . . but . . . we can't stay here."

Jerald and Linda stared at Riven hopefully, asking an unspoken question as it hung suspended in the stale air of their house.

[You have been offered a new quest: Admirable Escort. Escorting Jerald and Linda back to the Mercy West Hospital will result in a success for this quest. Completing this quest will result in an undisclosed system prize. If either Jerald or Linda dies, this quest results in failure.]

Riven blinked once, then twice, quickly walking to the window and peering out to where Athela was looking at him curiously with arms and legs crossed while her arachnoid appendages held her off the side wall. The sun had moved across the sky in the hours he'd been knocked out, but it was definitely still daytime. "How far is the hospital?"

"Just three miles . . . not far," Linda said hopefully, pocketing the medication and clasping her hands in front of her.

"And it isn't just a kids' hospital, is it?" Riven pressed with a plan formulating in his mind.

Linda shook her head with a confused frown, brushing her brown hair off to one side and setting her weight on one hip. "There are pediatricians there, but most of the doctors don't specialize in kids . . . Why?"

Riven let out a sigh of relief. "Because I have some people who need help, and a hospital is a perfect place to get it for them."

By the time they'd reached their destination, it was dark. Moonlight thankfully graced their passage with stars to aid it, and Riven had never known the cosmos could look so beautiful until now. Previous to this, city light pollution had made this kind of scenery an impossibility. But here . . . he had a real appreciation for what was out there in the universe.

The hospital was relatively small compared to most he'd seen before. It was a rectangular three-story building made of gray brick, and he'd been told it included a fourth level—the basement. It was a community hospital on the northwestern edge of the city, surprisingly close to where Riven had first entered along the main road, and it was surrounded by a circular hedge of tall bushes on the outer edge of a parking lot. Lanterns had been lit at the entrance and inside the building to give it a more illuminated appearance, with families in tents camped out in the parking lot between cars.

There was absolutely no sign of any electricity here or anywhere else under the night sky; the only other lights he saw were fires burning away various buildings in the interior of the postapocalyptic settlement.

Riven had insisted on going to get Azmoth and the others first before hitting the city, and introductions had been made before they helped carry the still-unconscious elf women back toward Brightsville. Both elves had drifted in and out of consciousness regularly, according to Azmoth, with one of them being able to utter the word *poison* before sinking into another feverish bout of unconsciousness. It didn't take long for Riven to realize that their wounds, wherever a goblin's teeth had sunk in, were now sprouting veins of black and green.

He'd come back not a moment too soon. They were dying and needed help fast.

The hospital's location on the outer edges of the city was likely a contributing factor to the lack of harassment on the return trip, as they avoided going deeper into the city, where most of the fighting between gangs over resources was concentrated. Instead they skirted along the edge of Brightsville until they saw the entrance with a sign saying Mercy West Hospital in big blue letters. Underneath the overhead sign and between the tall bushes encircling the hospital's parking lot were a pair of guards armed with pistols who shouted out to them from behind a makeshift barricade of overturned metal tables—commanding Riven's group to stop before getting any closer.

It was here that Riven's group made their case.

"It's me! Linda—and my daft husband, Jerald!" Linda called out from down the road as she pulled out her medicine bottles and rattled them at the two uniformed security officers. "We're here with the medicine for my daughter, Sara!"

The two guards quickly recognized the woman as she approached alone in the dim light of the lit lanterns, but they were still on edge. The older one, a man with a short, speckled beard, motioned for her to come forward. "I see you, Linda, but who are those others with you? I won't be letting them in if they don't give up that shotgun, even if they got injured people with 'em. We can't be having vigilantes running around the hospital causing trouble, and our security needs all the weapons and ammo we can get."

One of the other uniformed security guys nudged the first, nodding to Athela and Riven. "Man, I don't think those are humans . . . They both have red eyes, and I don't think I've ever seen a girl with that kind of skin color before."

"They give me bad vibes. Especially the hooded guy—just looking at him makes my hair stand on end," another of them chimed in while warily palming the pistol at his side.

The first officer and the one in charge gave them both a stern glare. He turned around, putting his back to Riven's party, and shook his head. "Of course they're not human. But honestly? We've seen a lot of *not human* ever since the fucking world ended, so as long as they don't cause problems and hand over that shotgun—which we sorely need—they're going to be let in. What are just two of them going to do anyways, eh? It's obvious those two girls they're carrying need help, and regardless of how that hooded man gives me the heebie-jeebies, I won't be pushing them out just because of a bad gut feeling. Got it?"

Linda and Jerald shared a glance, and both turned in unison to Riven, who was holding the shotgun he'd acquired over one shoulder and a scantily clad elf over the other. Meanwhile, his black staff was strapped to his back.

The young vampire frowned, realizing he should have probably kept the gun underneath his cloak to look like less of a threat, but also knew that he didn't necessarily need the gun, either. It'd be nice to have, but it wasn't necessary.

"I'd rather keep it!" Riven shouted back over the stretch of distance. "Given the state of things, can you blame me?!"

The older guard adamantly turned around and shook his head at a distance as more security personnel began to walk their way. "No. If you want in, give us the gun and ammo. We'll put in a good word with the docs so you can get your friends healed if you do—that's the trade. A win-win for us all, and we promise we won't be using that gun on you if you choose to give it up. We have enough fuckers runnin' around these parts already to worry about some pale pretty boy."

Pretty boy?! Riven was about to retort when he caught Athela chuckling. From within the nether realms and through their connection, Riven could feel Azmoth laughing as well. He hadn't summoned the enormous demon because of the reactions he'd doubtless get, and even Athela was pushing it. "Shut the hell up, the both of you."

"That goes for you, too, naked lady!" the other guard called out as he pointed at Athela. "What's your story? Walkin' around like that without any clothes! There's no way you're human! Linda, Jerald, can this one be trusted?!"

Jerald attempted to hold up both his hands as Athela took in a deep, exaggerated gasp of offense. However his leg was still badly hurt after the slavers had attacked earlier that day and he nearly fell over but caught himself on his wife instead. "Ugh. Yes, they're trustworthy. Come on, she's basically the same as us! Just 'cause she has additional legs coming out of her back don't mean nothin'!"

"Additional legs?" The guards all frowned at that, not seeing any spider legs on display because Athela had withdrawn them into her back to make her look more like normal people. They all exchanged glances with one another, and eventually the older guard and lead man of the troop shrugged. "Jerald's been doing drugs again . . . But it can't be too dangerous—she doesn't have any weapons. And it wouldn't be the weirdest thing we've seen over these past couple weeks. Just hand over the shotgun and you can all enter. Come on, man, make this easy on me."

Starlight twinkled overhead in a cosmos-filled sky, and in the distance an explosion across the city echoed while a distant downtown condo erupted with fire. It was enough to draw all their attention for a minute, but only a minute due to how far away it was. No doubt there were other groups fighting it out over God knows what over there.

Riven pooched his lips, placed his mask back on, and let out a grunt in response. Then he grudgingly held up the weapon. To say Athela wasn't dangerous only meant that these people either didn't know how to identify or were getting even less information when they tried to identify her than he'd been getting recently. Jerald and Linda hadn't had tutorials, either, so it was safe to say they really didn't know how to use the identify feature. Yet people like Hakim and Riven had that ability? Either way, he wouldn't complain.

A minute later, Linda had been sent over with the shotgun, informing the two security guards how there'd only been two shells left. Despite this, the guards were happy with the exchange and informed her that they had more ammo for it back in their cars. They did, however, give Riven curious or even outright hostile stares as he walked by, and they eagerly gawked at Athela's lithe figure. The pointed ears of the two elves gave them pause last, and one of them actually held up a hand to stop them from continuing farther when he saw it.

"Are those elves? Like the people from fantasy books with pointy ears?" a younger, uniformed, clean-shaven man with bright-blue eyes and a muscular frame asked. He cocked his head to the side while walking out of a small crowd of tents and refugees on a nearby patch of grass between parking lots and scratched his head curiously while examining the unconscious silver-haired woman Riven had slung over his shoulder. Then he turned to the blonde girl who was being carried by Athela.

Riven nodded, relieved he could speak so openly without a hood covering his face after the sun had set. "I believe so, yes."

"Huh. I'd heard there were sightings—guess it's true. Well, have Jerald and Linda lead you to Dr. Brass. He's the head of medicine. We're not a big trauma center, but he'll be able to set you up with one of the two orthopedic surgeons we have on staff and should be able to get them some proper bandaging and antibiotics. Should be on the first floor, left wing. By the way, cool mask. Goes with the creepy vibe you give off."

Riven smiled awkwardly underneath that same mask, not sure what to make of that statement, and gave him a nod of appreciation. But that smile turned into a grimace when he caught sight of the elf girl's leg wounds. The bandaging he'd used earlier had fallen off after collecting green and black drainage. She was breathing heavily now, and the lines of poison streaking up her leg had made it all the way to her knee. "I'll go get him now."

Then he heard a jingling of coins as a sack was added to the backpack he wore.

[You have completed the quest: Admirable Escort. Escorting Jerald and Linda back to the Mercy West Hospital has resulted in success, and you have acquired sixty Elysium coins.]

Not an amazing reward, considering he still hadn't found an altar to utilize the coins he possessed, but he'd take it without complaint for now.

The hospital had become something of a refugee camp. The people out in the parking lot or along the grass surrounding it numbered a couple dozen, supplied with sleeping bags and camping equipment, but inside was even more packed. They slept on the floors, chairs, couches, and were cramped beyond belief as the security forces—which numbered only ten, according to Linda—tried to maintain order. Small rations from what the hospital had left were being passed out, such as saltine crackers and orange juice, but Riven absolutely knew that the food would run out soon with this many people here.

Nurses in green and blue scrubs were also coming in and out of rooms, using any space they had left open for the injured and sick. They were exhausted, outnumbered, and almost in a frenzied state as they barked orders at one another. One room had a couple doing chest compressions and running IVs, another had a man screaming and being held down as a doctor used a medical instrument to pull a bullet from his arm without any anesthesia, and yet another had an old woman who'd been stabbed and stitched up—left to recover with her family.

CHAPTER 13

The scene was chaotic. The only things still holding people together were the occasional armed guards patrolling the halls and the hope offered by the medical staff as they treated hurt or sick loved ones.

"This is absolutely crazy . . ." Riven mumbled, taking the brunt of the elf's weight on one leg when he pivoted around a kid running past.

Jerald motioned them to follow him farther through the hospital hallway, limping heavily to relieve pressure on his wounded side and using the crutch as support. "Come on, Dr. Brass is a good man, and he'll see you as long as he isn't busy."

Normally in a hospital setting Jerald's bloodied leg and Linda's cut would draw immediate attention. As would the two injured elves Riven and Athela were carrying in. But here, in this madhouse, it was just a free-for-all. It also probably didn't help that the medical staff kept a wary distance from Riven and Athela, as if they could smell danger on their very being.

They went down a less crowded hall to the left and then took another turn around a corner. Wood paneling along the walls with pictures of the hospital's founders decorated the interior, and the lights that'd once illuminated the hospital had all been replaced with gas lamps.

"How many lamps do they have?" Riven asked curiously, a little impressed with just how many were present.

Linda laughed, lightly clutching her injured side. "This hospital is really, really old, and they kept a lot of supplies from the colonial days in the basement, believe it or not."

Riven couldn't help but think about how ridiculous that sounded, but it'd certainly come in handy. "Wow."

The couple led them to a glass door. On the other side, two old men with gray hair and wearing white coats were talking at a desk. They both looked tired, haggard, and were pouring each other cups of whiskey while speaking in low, hushed tones.

Linda knocked on the door, and the man with glasses facing them from behind the desk motioned for them to come in. The door swung open, and the other old man—who was beginning to bald in the back—gave her a smile of recognition. "Oh, Linda! Good to see you! Did you get the medication for Sara?"

Linda smiled widely and pulled out the two bottles of pills. "Dr. Telsky, I did! Hello to you, too, Dr. Brass!"

The man with glasses chuckled, downed his mug of alcohol with one go, and slowly exhaled. "I'm glad you found it. You should start your daughter back on her regular regimen immediately—her leukemia treatment was almost done, but she's still immunocompromised. Go ahead upstairs to see her and give her the starting dose tonight. Two pills. And . . . you both look terrible. Jerald, were you shot?"

Dr. Brass, the one with glasses, got up from his desk and came around to look at the leg wound—but startled himself half to death when he saw the state of the two elves slung over Riven's and Athela's shoulders in the hallway. Completely forgetting about Jerald and eyes going wide at the state of the bite wounds and obvious infection rapidly spreading, his jaw dropped. "By sweet baby Jesus, these poor girls . . . what the hell happened to them?!"

He didn't seem to notice or care about their ears at all, nor did he mention the state of the less-than-human features Athela and Riven had, and quickly gestured for them to follow him. "Come with me. Are you two able to carry them down a flight of stairs? We only have room left in the basement now."

Riven and Athela both confirmed that they could, waving goodbye to Jerald and Linda as they continued to talk with the other doctor before following him to wherever their daughter was located.

"By God, I did not sign up for this kind of shit . . . the world's gone mad." Dr. Brass muttered, shaking his head as they passed the crowds and through another hallway toward a stairwell behind a door. Opening the door and ushering them down, Dr. Brass closed it behind them. "It's just down one level and to the left. There'll be a sign that says, Operating Room Waiting Area. We're going past that and into operating room five. Watch your step! It's dark in here."

The light the candle-lit lanterns threw didn't penetrate the stairway almost at all. Dr. Brass had to use the handles along the side of the stairs to make sure they didn't fall, but Riven and Athela navigated them in the front without any issues.

Coming to a door and pushing it open with his free hand, Riven found himself in the waiting area. Only a couple people were lounging in chairs, some of them asleep and others whispering to one another in the dim candlelight. They all looked over as Riven walked in, but many of them paid him no attention after that. All of them were too scared, worried, or hungry to care about more newcomers.

"Is that an additional limb coming out of your back?!" Dr. Brass asked incredulously, pointing to Athela's arachnid appendage that'd come out to casually scratch her neck. "Actually, you know what? I don't care. I really don't, not after all the other baffling stuff I've seen. Follow me; operating room five is straight ahead."

They pushed through a set of double doors and continued on, hearing the screams of someone on their right as they were held down to a table for surgery.

Dr. Brass sighed and adjusted his glasses. "We ran out of propofol, other anesthetic agents, and most pain meds two days ago when the world split apart and was rearranged. Anyone needing surgery has to be bound, and it's causing complications . . . God, what I would give to have a coffee right now."

He pushed open the operating room door that had a big number five hanging above it. Pointing to a rolling bed, he coughed once and turned to the others. "Put both of them on the bed. We don't have enough to go around for individuals, but you can stay here for now after I'm done. I'll hook up some IV antibiotics and do an I&D on them each myself. It'll probably take an hour."

"I&D?" Riven asked curiously.

Dr. Brass adjusted his glasses again. "Incision and drainage. They're going to need surgical debridement to clean out their wounds, some Lactated Ringer's for fluids so they don't go into shock after their already obvious blood loss, and then we'll just hope the antibiotics will be enough. I have no idea what the hell kind of infection they have, and our micro and pathology labs are down, so I'm just going to hit them with the big guns and give them broad-spectrum antibiotics. Probably vancomycin and Zosyn . . ."

The old man muttered medical lingo to himself and dismissed Riven with a wave and headed over to a drawer where he began fishing for supplies, so Riven walked ahead to the rolling bed, making sure the wheels were locked in place before gingerly setting the unconscious girl down.

She groaned, sweating from her illness and was still obviously feverish as he pressed a hand to her forehead. The blue tribal elf paint was beginning to come off due to the perspiration, and her breathing was labored.

"What about their fractures? This woman's clavicle is broken, and—"

"I'll do what I can to reset them properly," Dr. Brass interrupted with another dismissive backward wave. "I'm no orthopedic surgeon, though. All I can do is my best since the others are busy with more urgent emergencies."

The room was square, with pristine white walls and overhead lights that could be rotated to get a better view of things while operating—but there was no electricity to power them, so Dr. Brass had to use a lantern. He had Athela hold it up for him to see while occasionally adjusting his or her position for a better look. Using a scalpel, he cut away small pieces of necrosed tissue, drained a couple abscesses that'd quickly formed over the last day, and then washed out the wounds with a good amount of saline before starting an IV.

During that time, Riven absentmindedly looked around. There were supplies stacked in one corner, some of which were obviously not native to an operating room under normal circumstances. There were a couple boxes of crackers, juice boxes, water bottles, and granola bars. There were stacks of scrubs in different sizes, masks, gloves, syringes, and various medications.

It was all pretty barren aside from that, with only a long metal table on the right side next to a shelf with a dead computer. But it was comfortably warm, and by the time Dr. Brass had packed the girls' wounds and bandaged them up, washed his hands, and dried them off, Riven was comfortably dozing off in the corner with his head slumped to one side.

"Now all we can do is wait," Dr. Brass stated with a grunt. "I'm surprised neither of them woke up. They squirmed a little, but nothing that I couldn't handle. You'll likely know over the next couple of days whether or not they'll make it. That's if any of us make it . . . with all the gangs and monsters roaming around since the apocalypse set in."

The old man solemnly shook his head a final time, wiping away the last remnants of blood and washing his hands for a second time with a bag of saline and some hand sanitizer. He'd used gloves, but his forearms had still gotten a little bit of the wounds' fluids on them while he'd operated. "What's your name? Your friend Athela has already introduced herself, but I left you alone because you were half-asleep."

Riven blinked twice, yawned, and stood up as the words struck home. He noticed how the two elves were tucked under blankets on the wheeled hospital beds, and he extended a hand. "Riven. Nice to meet you, Dr. Brass, and thank you for all you've done."

"Don't mention it," Dr. Brass replied, smiling back under tired eyes and taking Riven's hand to shake. "I'm not even going to ask about your situation and what's going on, because I have too much to worry about, but eventually if things all calm down . . . Well, I'll have questions for you then. Good luck to you, and feel free to help yourself to some of the supplies—but please ration them. This stockpile is for the entire hospital, and we don't have anywhere else to hide it at the moment."

Riven's eyebrows raised as he glanced over the stacked boxes. "This is all you have left?"

Dr. Brass shrugged. "Not all, but still . . ."

The old man waved as he exited through the door, leaving Riven and Athela to themselves.

Athela smirked, picking up a couple water bottles and flinging them across the room into Riven's waiting hands. "Well, this is certainly a situation . . . You should eat and drink some normal human sustenance, too. Blood alone isn't going to do it."

"Indeed," Riven acknowledged with a lightly growling stomach, still blinking to wake himself up with another yawn. He was about to say something else when there was a sudden boom from up above—and the hospital shook. Screams, abrupt gunfire, and the sounds of mayhem followed immediately after that—with yet another shudder as the very foundation of the building rocked.

Riven's eyes widened, and his teeth clenched. "What the hell . . ."

Athela's smirk faded, to be replaced by worried furrows. "Well, that doesn't sound good."

Without another word, Riven and his demonic servant exited the room. Immediately the screams grew louder as they opened the door of OR five, and the sounds of more gunshots rapidly echoed across the building's upper floors.

"Fuck me . . ." Riven muttered as people downstairs began to scream and scramble back. A handful of terrified nurses sprinted down the stairwell and found places to hide as Dr. Brass tried to calm them.

The old man threw up his arms and rushed to place himself in front of the last nurse—a skinny young man in his early twenties—as the others blatantly ignored the doctor in their mad rush to find cover. "What the HELL is going on, Jim?"

The nurse was pale, breathing heavily, and he pointed shakily back up the stairwell as others in the area watched with wide eyes. "We're being attacked!"

"By who?!" Dr. Brass roared, beginning to surge past the nurse to reach for the door handle.

"DON'T!" Jim yelled, grabbing Dr. Brass by the shoulder and whirling the old man around forcefully. "It isn't who, it's WHAT! I . . . I can't describe it completely . . . It's enormous. It looks almost like a person, but it's rotten . . . has gray flesh and is unbelievably strong! At first it was just a weird-looking guy with a sick smile in a bloody clown suit, and then his body erupted and he became something else! It was like he shape-shifted and blew up to three times his size! He began eating people and ripping them apart with claws and a multitude of mouths! The officers were shooting it with bullets but they had no effect—they just kept shooting and people kept dying—body parts were everywhere and—"

Another boom rocked the basement as the screaming upstairs continued—but the gunshots had stopped. The nurse looked frantic as everyone listening paled, and Dr. Brass was certainly one of them.

The old doctor took off his glasses, wiped them on his white coat, and slowly placed them back on his face. "You're saying that this is another one of those monsters?"

The nurse frantically nodded, his chest heaving fast due to his obvious horror at what he'd just seen. "I . . . I wouldn't go up there. They're all goners if they don't run, and there's nothing we can do except hide and hope it doesn't come down."

CHAPTER 14

Riven had heard enough and was about to start walking toward the two men when he heard Athela whisper, "Don't."

Riven shot the demoness a look of anger. "What do you mean, don't?"

"That's what I mean," Athela stated flatly. "Whatever that creature is upstairs, I can sense its aura from here . . . and there are more of them coming. It feels like . . . like a hive-mind creature of some sort. We can expect a swarm soon."

Yet again the building rocked, and there was a crashing sound as another shudder caused dust to filter down from the ceiling.

"I can summon Azmoth."

"Sure. Summon him, but it may not be enough. You are not a coward, Riven. I know that, but please trust me on this. Swarm creatures are very dangerous and can be composed of multiple bodies with one entity controlling all of them."

Riven stared blankly back at the demoness, desire to go up and save those people battling with how certain Athela was of their failure. He couldn't sense the heartbeat of the creature, which was disturbing in itself since he'd gained his newfound abilities—but he could certainly hear and sense everyone else upstairs as their own heartbeats were rapidly snuffed out one by one. He also couldn't sense any aura that Athela was talking about. He'd certainly need to talk to her about her new demonic capabilities since the evolution.

Riven snarled, clutching his fist as he thought about Jerald, Linda, and their little girl, Sara. "What about all the people upstairs?"

"They're dead," Athela stated confidently as her arachnoid limbs began ripping out of her back, all six producing bladed tips that gleamed ebony in the candlelight—to the gasps or further screams of the already terrified people nearby. "Or they will be. If you go up there, whatever those creatures are will likely kill you. It has the ability to seek out living auras, a lot like I do, a form of magic that can track down creatures based on their life force. It's probably some kind of high-tier undead variant, and I'm absolutely certain that it has already identified our presence and will likely make its way down here even if we continue to hide. We need to seal off the stairway. You may be a vampire, even a pure-blooded vampire, but you are still not anywhere close to the top of the food chain. You have a long, long way to go, and now is not the time to play hero."

A ball in his gut started to form. He wanted to go up there and save all those people. All those families, the children, all those people who had the last remnants of hope being stripped from them now in this new world that Elysium had created.

It was so fucked up, and Riven felt his face flushing as he realized what he needed to do—yet still didn't want to do.

Then he realized that everyone in the room was looking at him.

"Goddamn it, AZMOTH! Get out here!"

Riven pulled down his shirt and touched the pentagram sigil on his chest, lighting it up as a swirling portal of hellfire erupted in the middle of the room, sending many of the others scrambling. The armored, muscular tank of a demon stepped out of the netherscape portal, which winked out a moment later to reveal the colossus, his newly acquired spiked tail whipping back and forth in anticipation of the fight to come and all four of his clawed hands visibly itching to start the violence. "You called, Master?"

Athela scowled but responded to Riven's choice as well, her six bladed arachnoid legs whipping out of her body on full display and claws extending from her fingers in the blink of an eye.

In total, there were probably three dozen people down here—the nurses who'd run down from upstairs, Dr. Brass, a couple people operating on some guy in one of the rooms they'd passed earlier, who now were sticking their heads out to see what was going on, and three families with children. All of them had heard what Athela had said, and all of them were staring wide-eyed at the two demons with mixed emotions.

Dr. Brass flinched as another scream echoed farther up the stairs, and he hesitantly approached Riven to look up at where Azmoth had burst into flames a few feet away. "I'm not sure what that is, boy, or how you've made friends with these creatures, but if you have a way to save us, then please do it."

The man completely ignored the fact that Riven had been called a vampire or how Athela had called herself a demon, something that Riven appreciated. Maybe the reality of their situation had set in on the old doctor, but regardless, Dr. Brass had put his public support for Riven on display.

They all shifted their gazes to the stairs as another individual pushed through the door, sobbing and clutching at her throat. It was another nurse, her usually pretty features contorted with fear as she tried to stanch a gushing wound the size of Riven's fist, to no avail. Blood sprayed all over the door, the floor, and she gurgled something to the rest of them before passing out and dropping to the floor.

"GET HER INTO A ROOM NOW!" Dr. Brass screeched as her coworkers rushed to the downed woman, lifting her up in a mad scramble as the families tried to calm their screaming, terrified children.

Without another word, the warlock grasped his black staff and headed for the stairs.

In the stairwell, the steps leading up were already slick with blood, and a recently deceased body was sprawled unceremoniously along their path. Screams got louder as Riven vaulted upward, quickly coming to the door of the first floor and pushing it open to reveal a madhouse of death and carnage.

Bodies were everywhere, and the floor was thick with rubble and blood as people tried to scramble while slipping or tripping over one another as five large, faceless humanoid monsters killed indiscriminately in the dim glow of lanterns and starlight seeping in through a large hole in the wall one of them had made.

Though they were humanoid in shape, these five monsters looked like fleshy, gray-skinned gorillas devoid of any hair or genitalia. They stood six to seven feet tall and were two times thicker than an average man with muscular, clawed limbs. They had no eyes, no facial structures, but did have circular maws where thick tongues whipped out to pierce people—dragging them alive into their mouths. Their mouths could extend to massive proportions, enabling them to feed on people whole before they dragged their prey into some kind of abyssal core that seemed to suck the terrified, dying men and women into an internal black hole after being shredded to smaller pieces with long razor teeth.

And even more horrible was that right outside the hospital was even worse. There were dozens of these monsters, all of them slaughtering with wild abandon amid the refugee camp that'd been set up outside. A bloody gun in a hand missing a body to Riven's right on the ground spelled out what'd happened to the security forces.

The nearest monster was just about to slam a clawed hand down on a screaming, crying little boy's head when Riven blurred across the room and slammed his black staff into the gray creature. Black shadow magic pulsed and exploded from the magical weapon, rocketing the large brute across the room and over bodies to slam into one of the other monstrosities as yet another, sixth creature ran in through the outside.

"Die."

Riven stepped in front of the child and launched a flurry of Bloody Razors, pushing his new body and heights of power to the limits to create even more of them. His Blood subpillar quivered and his body pulsed with red light. The fluids of the numerous dead began to rise up off the ground and from the walls amid swarming people—the environmental resources heeding his call. A dozen razors became two dozen in an instant, and the spray of blades left red ribbons in a crimson tide after their passing.

ZIP-ZIP-ZIP-ZIP-ZIP
CRASH

The room turned into a blur of red for just an instant—blasting into the gray-skinned creatures and tearing off limbs and heads and eviscerating the beasts in a multipronged attack that left them looking like a Gatling gun had just mowed them down. Some people stared in wide-eyed shock, while others just continued to run for their lives or hide while doing their best to collect loved ones.

The light left Riven's body, and he felt the environmental pool of available blood around him diminish as the magic dissipated. Ignoring the notifications about XP and the small system-made bags of money, he turned to the entrance where screeches and howls of anger roared in unison. His eyebrows rose when he realized that not one, not two, but every single one of the odd, grotesque creatures was now glaring his way with those eyeless faces and gaping round maws.

And then they charged, their large gray bodies pounding over pavement, grass, and flesh in a simultaneous howl of anger that echoed across the city blocks.

"Come on, you cocksuckers, let's see what you've got!" Black Lightning ripped out of Riven's weapon while he simultaneously threw out a wave of red ice that covered the floor through the large hole in the wall. Bodies melted into sizzling piles of ash, and their comrades slipped over the debris or on the ice itself while piling up over one another.

Riven quickly charged two Blood Lances and shot them directly into the choke point where dozens of creatures were pouring in to attack.

The lances of solid crimson mana split open eight of the creatures in a single devastating strike, leaving their bodies as corpses for more of the swarm to stumble over.

And just as the mass of bodies finally made it to the entrance, Azmoth's roar bellowed out and a giant, flaming demon shot forward into the wave of beasts—tearing them apart one by one in a tidal wave of violence.

Blessing of the Crow activated, and lightning crackled along Riven's skin. His eyes glowed red, and his staff flickered with shadow. Many of the heartbeats of nearby civilians had disappeared; either the people had run off through other entrances or had been snuffed out by death. However, there were still many of them left, watching from their hiding places in rooms nearby or remaining as hidden as possible while the sounds of battle raged in the entrance hall of the health-care center.

Athela blurred left, tearing open another of the monsters Riven hadn't seen coming due to a lack of heartbeat—and he gave her an appreciative nod before she disappeared noiselessly behind a pillar and clambered up to the ceiling to view the action from thirty feet above. He didn't have to ask what she was doing; he knew she was prioritizing his own life over the immediate battle because she was worried. The expression she wore was that of obvious anxiety, and she quickly darted her eyes around to different avenues of entry.

"AAAZZMOOTTHHH CRUUUSSSSSHHHHHH!!!!" The brutalisk roared and picked up two of the slightly smaller and significantly weaker human-oid beasts in front of him, burning them alive and smashing their skulls together while whipping his spiked tail around and around to slash and maim.

Athela provided a hail of red needles in the form of solidified webbing from up above, showering the choke point in carnage while continuing to glance around anxiously.

Riven lowered his hand, smiling underneath his runic mask with a content hum. He hadn't been the only one to become stronger since his evolution. That, and compared to the denizens of hell, these monsters were significantly weaker. There was very little chance that their level difference was that far off from the Negrada undead or demons, considering Negrada's surface level had contained even creatures as low as level 2, but the quality of race and base stats was just miles apart. It had to be, considering Azmoth was beating these things senseless like a violent child with squishy pinatas.

[Nightmare Fledgling, Hive Mind Dream Creature]
[Nightmare Fledgling, Hive Mind Dream Creature]
[Nightmare Fledgling, Hive Mind Dream Creature]

Feeling a bit more secure and wondering just why Athela had been so alarmed by these relatively weak creatures, Riven turned around and knelt in front of the quivering little boy covered in dirt and someone else's body fluids. The child's lower lip trembled, and tears streamed down his face. He had to be only five or six years old, and seeing the boy shake even more violently when Riven reached out to him only made the vampire's heart drop.

"You'll be okay," Riven said, withdrawing his hand and motioning to a room's doorway where other people were staring wide-eyed at the battle in a hushed cluster of bodies. "Go over to them; they'll keep you safe."

The boy was frozen in shock, looking up at him, but a young mother already holding a young child of her own raced forward and grabbed the boy by his hand, yanking him back and sparing Riven a wary glance before running back to the relative safety of the other room.

CRUNCH

Athela smashed into the floor behind Riven a dozen feet away, impaling one of the dream creatures in six different spots before using lightning-fast strikes to rip open its head. She glanced his way, muscles tensed. "Riven, I can feel more coming!"

The vampire rolled his eyes.

"Well, there are lots of them out there!" Riven said with a nonchalant wave of his hands toward the piles of monster bodies gathering in the choke point—the swarm of beasts still having failed to bring Azmoth down or even slow the cackling, flaming demon.

"No! I mean the aura is drastically increasing! I think—"

Athela's voice was cut off as a deafening howl reverberated all around the hospital. Dozens, then hundreds of voices rose as feral screeches toward the night sky that shook the building to its foundations—and Riven's glowing eyes went wide.

Glass windows shattered and doors were thrown off hinges all around the hospital's first floor when hundreds of the beasts came surging in from hallways to his left, right, back, and front.

It looked like things had just gotten a whole lot more interesting.

CHAPTER 15

Doors from nearby rooms slammed shut, and people started barricading themselves inside immediately upon hearing the rushing wave of oncoming monsters, and soon Riven stood alone with his demons as enemies flooded into the main entrance hall from four different directions. Rippling muscles and rounded abyssal maws full of teeth and writhing tongues bore down on him with clawed limbs, racing ahead like hairless great apes.

But he remained calm. He'd survived far worse enemies than this. To his surprise, the sacrificial dagger he'd acquired from Negrada seemed to agree and began to quiver with primal rage—reminding Riven that it was still there and wanted to be used. It'd been a while since he'd even attempted to use the item, or at least it felt that way. In reality he'd only just gotten it back after trading with Negrada.

He took a brief moment to glance down at the exquisite weapon. The intricate patterns on the blade resonated with his soul, and the flesh bond between his weapon and his body began to connect again with wisps of muscle that crept across his lower leg.

Athela, to his left, began to shriek in rage and yelled at him to run before vaulting ahead into the oncoming swarm of enemies at his right—claws outstretched, black hair whirling out behind her, and six scythe-like arachnid legs flashing forward. Azmoth was already busy mowing them down by the dozens in his own little choke point and couldn't be concerned with the other three pathways leading to the main hall where Riven stood.

Yet despite the oncoming swarm of roaring monsters that made the hospital shake with their simultaneous charge, Riven was not concerned. He found himself oddly at peace, a content sigh of resignation parting his lips to escape the runic mask in a small cloud of bloody mist.

As he smiled at the dagger and felt it continually resonating with his body, the totem weapon crept up his free arm and placed itself through stretching fleshy connections into his palm opposite the staff he carried.

It wanted to be used.

And you know what? Riven wouldn't deny its request.

In a flash of inspiration, Riven slammed the hilt of the Sanguis Foedus down into the top of the shadow-imbued staff. The flesh of the dagger roiled and writhed, rapidly encircling and intertwining with the black wood of redemption, and their screens simultaneously displayed.

[Sanguis Foedus (Totem, Sacrificial Dagger): 12 average damage on strike, high chance to apply Amplified Bleeding debuff on biological enemies when struck. Requires a 20% or higher Blood pillar affinity to wield. This item has an abnormally high endurance and is hard to destroy.

- Totem Soul: Low-Grade Primal, Incomplete Fragment, 6 Willpower requirement
- Flesh Bond: This totem binds to the wielder in a unique way, allowing you to manipulate it at a limited distance through a flesh bond. If the flesh bond is severed, it must be restored before undertaking further distal manipulation.
- Sacrifice: Use this dagger to sacrifice an enemy and mentally activate this ritual ability to create a portal back to Negrada at any distance. Creating a portal will take up to twenty-four hours.]

[Black Redemption (Tier 1 Awakened Staff): 74 average shadow damage on strike, with each hit drawing a small amount of mana from you to apply a knock-back effect with a minor explosion of shadow magic. All cost of Shadow spells is decreased by 7%; mana regeneration is increased by 68%. Shadow magics all have damage modifiers applied by +27% while channeling through this staff.

- Black Lightning: This staff can passively build up charges of Black Lightning. Power of Black Lightning depends on the amount of charge emitted.]

His thoughts raced while Riven instinctively internally drew on a fragment of his soul, chiseling off a tiny part of it and incorporating it into the blood magic now running down his fingers and across the shaft of his black wooden staff. Crimson Ice ripped through the weapon from where his hand held it midshaft, intermixing with black shadows that radiated out from Black Redemption and fusing with the strings of flesh that were rapidly digging into the wood from the top end. The staff hissed and the dagger screeched, but their sounds were not of agony—rather, they were of bliss. To them, this was the truest form of trust. To this awakened weapon that had no soul at all, yet lived in physical form, and to the fragmented totem soul that was incomplete, Riven was making them whole. He was generously re-forming them into something new, something unique, by giving them a piece of his very being through pure will and inspiration.

And his inspiration was not off the mark.

The flesh of the dagger, the shadow-imbued wood of the staff, and the crimson blood with Riven's soul fragment all collided with one another and intermingled to form an explosion of power that was directed straight upward—ripping a large hole through three ceilings and sending a shock wave outward from Riven's position. Enemies were blown back and even his two demons were knocked down, while the barricaded rooms around him all shuddered and jolted furiously until the aftermath of power died down.

And there, standing under the light of the stars after all the lanterns had been blown out or utterly destroyed by the blast of power, was Riven. He held an entirely new weapon now, one created from the concepts of Shadow and Blood.

It looked very similar to the previous weapons he'd put together. They weren't necessarily changed in terms of looks when one studied their individual pieces that'd been fused in both spirit and the material world, but rather, they were changed by identity. The system now considered it one single item, with the other pieces having been absorbed into the weapon.

The gnarled staff now had fleshy strings of muscle weaving around the black wood that continued to ripple and flare with shadow. A smooth stream of actively flowing crimson blood washed along the staff's insides and on top of the wood in various pathways. It had once been Riven's soul-infused blood magic, but now it laced in interweaving patterns beside the fleshy strings. Beyond that, spikes of crystallized crimson ice now decorated the top of the gnarled staff, reaching up and out. The spikes grew more numerous in all encircling directions until reaching the top. There, at the very top of the staff, the dagger that'd once been a sacrificial totem was now planted like a spear's tip—the hilt having fused entirely into the black wood with red crystals further reinforcing the connection at the base of the blade. Even more enticing was the fact that Riven could literally feel the weapon. He could feel its thoughts, its wants, its inherent abilities, and he could control its functions by sheer Willpower.

[You have created a unique soul-fused sorcerer's staff. Congratulations!]

[Vampire's Escort (Vampiric) (Unique Soul-Fused Weapon, Sorcerer's Staff): 104 average damage on strike with each physical strike dealing minor shadow-explosion knock back. Mana regeneration is increased by 102%. All Shadow and Blood spells cost 9% less mana while dealing 22% additional damage. This item has an abnormally high endurance and is hard to destroy. Requires vampiric heritage to wield.

- Sacrificial Kill: Killing strong opponents has a chance to imbue this weapon with additional attributes, stats, or bonuses.
- Scorpion's Sting: The blade at the tip of this staff can extend through flesh molding to cut down enemies. Enemies hit with the blade portion of this weapon do not experience shadow-explosion knock back like the rest of this staff, rather, the blade portion of this weapon will imbue stacking bleeding damage to all biological enemies.
- Black Lightning: This staff can passively build up charges of Black Lightning. Power of Black Lightning depends on the amount of charge emitted.
- Portal Master: This weapon can sync to any stabilized portal you have permission to use by the portal maker and master. Current locations available for access: Dungeon Negrada.]

Riven had never read anything about soul-fused weapons before, and it certainly piqued his curiosity. However, he was brought back to reality when a shrill and simultaneous scream broke the silence from hundreds of throats around him.

His crimson eyes lifted from the marvelous weapons in his hands, and he slowly began to grin.

Moving the carnage out from the hospital interior and into the parking lot had definitely been a wise decision, as it kept accidental civilian deaths to a minimum while Riven fought like a man possessed over a growing mountain of corpses— monster and human alike. It also brought the dream creatures an obvious target, drawing the vast majority of them out of the hospital and onto a waiting open battlefield.

Bladed fleshy tongues lashed out at him, and claws ripped through the air, trying to pin Riven down, but torpedoing Blood Lances and waves of spinning bloody blades tore through the masses in a blitz while he dodged and swerved to avoid close combat.

He might be a vampire with enhanced health, speed, and strength now— but there was still no way he'd have ever been able to take on this many enemies in melee. He was, however, able to deal with them at a reasonable pace while kiting them at range.

"EEEEEEEEHHHHHHHH!!!" A monstrous and faceless dream creature rocketed over a smashed pickup truck, jumping at Riven only to receive a spike of Crimson Ice directly into its face.

SQUELCH

The large monster fell limp and slid lifelessly down the solidified blood magic it was impaled on, its position quickly being overtaken by more of the zealous creatures that chased the vampire in droves around the medical campus grounds.

Black Lightning crackled along the fleshy black wood of his staff before ripping through the forest of gray monsters with a resounding ***BOOM*** and an explosion of body parts. Riven wasted no time and opened a rift in space behind him, quickly vanishing through the shadow portal and closing it to appear on top of a storage shed on the opposite end of the campus. His portals, he was quickly learning, actually left an afterimage of his traveling route. It was something he hadn't realized in the short time he'd been experimenting with Riftwalk, but was thankful to know it now. Each time he entered the rift, a very brief flash of black wisps flickered along the path he took in a direct line—leading the hive-mind monsters to catch on and quickly redirect their course with every attempt to outpace them.

[Riftwalk (Shadow): Channel mana into your Shadow subpillar and focus on the place you wish to travel to. Then rip open a portal in space and pass through it, allowing you and other people or objects nearby to pass through until you close the rift. Mana cost is dependent upon length of space traveled and time maintaining rift.]

Thankfully, though, Azmoth and Athela were making their own waves in the horde.

"RRRHHAAAAAA!!!!" The titanic flaming demon stampeded through the apelike dream creatures with wild abandon, seemingly untouchable despite their numbers piling on top of him. They were just slightly smaller than he was, but the strength difference was massive, and those that did manage to tie him down with numbers soon found themselves simply being burned into ash over time before he was freed again.

Meanwhile, Athela was zipping in and out of their forces—following Riven like a silent shadow on the wind that he only saw in brief glimpses when a spray of viscera or flying, decapitated head was noticed. She was doing quite a good job at keeping the pressure off him, too, as there'd been more than one incidence where he'd been hard-pressed to maintain his barrage, only for her to take the brunt of the frightening and allowing his mana to recharge.

And now, standing on the storage shed, he used her intervention to yet again prepare a devastating attack. Arcs of red ribbons raced along his staff and the bladed tip of Vampire's Escort launched skyward. The arcs of red followed it, Crimson Ice flowing down the fleshy string that attached the blade to the rest of his weapon, before expanding in full bloom when he swung the weapon horizontally.

The skyward blade came down and around like a whip, lashing out with blurring speed that left a trail of mana-infused ice and red ribbons in its strike path and over two dozen through-and-through lacerated bodies that toppled over like dominoes.

"YOU ALMOST HIT ME!" Athela screeched over the torrent of roars and charging bodies while ducking and glaring back at him from the ground.

"Don't give me that much credit!" Riven laughed, reeling in the blade of his newly created toy and summoning the environmental blood of the most recently fallen enemies to do his bidding.

Blood ripped out of the corpses of the two dozen he'd just killed, filling the air with fluid before it condensed into spinning blades that rocketed toward the oncoming mass of enemies in a storm of carnage.

He turned to glance at his minion, who stood shaking her head in bewilderment at the absolute destruction he was wreaking. Then he looked back to the massive number of enemies who now lay dead or dying on hospital grounds. He smiled to himself, his heart pounding with excitement, and he felt truly alive. How ironic, seeing that he was actually undead now, but regardless, he was having a lot more fun than he should be.

Not only that, but Riven was quickly beginning to realize the true extent of his powers. When environmental resource pools like hundreds of dead bodies and the now-available blood in them presented themselves for a blood mage like him to use, Riven could quite quickly become a fully-blown harbinger of destruction.

CHAPTER 16

Allie sat meditating in her bone garden under a starry night sky, atop what had once been one of the downtown skyscrapers. Well, she supposed it was still a skyscraper—but it'd been converted into her home base of operations and had a rather spooky feel to it after the makeover. The building itself had an aura to it, with ripples of teal and black mana occasionally shimmering across the structure while it was being pseudo-terraformed into a death-oriented zone through ritual magic Mara had introduced her to. The bone garden on the roof, forty-two stories up, where she now sat, was also littered with bodies and intricate bone structures—each having their own unique function in producing sentient undead.

Opening her eyes as another soul passed through the veil, Allie smiled underneath her skull mask when another of the bodies began to twitch. Slowly the ghoul began to move, examining her environment as Allie's accomplices, Nin and Vin, the skeletal skresh brothers, got up to greet the newcomer. Their forces were growing . . . and now it wasn't only the mindless minions that aided them. Oh, no, they now had fully thinking, sentient beings working on their side as they brought new life into the bodies of the enemies Allie's forces had killed—born anew. And this new bone garden had thus finally brought about a turn of tides in the war that Allie had been hoping for.

It was rather peaceful tonight, and she took in a deep breath of crisp air before pushing herself to her feet and walking over to where her friend Mara was standing. The ghoul necromancer's dead, milky eyes panned over the city beneath them, where rogue groups of survivors still battled one another for supremacy over their little pockets of remnant civilization. Battled over what little food and medicine they had left, or to subjugate and enslave. It was all the same in the end—people killing other people instead of working together.

And it made Allie sick with disgust.

"You look angry," Mara said, glancing over at Allie with a small smile. "Still thinking about Jose?"

Allie slowly nodded, her piercing crimson eyes glaring down at the shouts and small fires in suburbs not far off. "Humans."

Mara chuckled and clapped a hand onto Allie's shoulder. "We used to be humans, too, you know."

Allie's frown only deepened, and her eyes did not move from where she heard and saw the gunfire many stories down. "Unfortunately, you're right. Even when I was human, though, I always felt like the human species was . . . gross. Evil, even. People in general were always out for themselves, always greedy, always eager to undercut others to get ahead. It's why Jose died, too—those fucking bastards from Prophet's domain thought they could just waltz right in and declare everyone subjects."

Mara raised an eyebrow and folded her arms, turning her head to watch the firefight below and a couple blocks away alongside the woman who was quickly becoming a very close ally and friend. "And look what it cost them. Thousands of their holy order have died, they've been pushed back into the northern section of the city, and they've resorted to allying with the other, larger groups there to fight us off."

"They call us monsters," Allie sneered, kicking a small rock off the side of the building and watching it tumble through the air to the street far below. "Yet they were the ones who brought this on themselves. They started this. I will merely finish it."

There was a long pause, and the silence stretched on with only the echoes of the firefight and the sound of the breeze flowing through their cloaks to be heard. Yet, despite all the anger she felt inside, Allie couldn't help but look around at their surroundings and feel a sense of awe at the majesty. Beyond the city, snow-capped mountains loomed in the distance to reflect moonlight and starlight. The cosmos above glittered in a way that no city back on Earth could have done due to light pollution, and rivers leading out to an ocean in the far-off distance shimmered and sparkled.

It made Allie want to explore after this little war was over. After she set the foundations for a new undead community in the wreckage of what had once been Brightsville. It was abundantly clear to her now that humans would never have a place for her; she'd been shunned many times already, and she didn't want to be one of them anymore, anyway. So she'd just make a place for herself instead—through brutality and force.

Her thoughts were interrupted when an explosion of massive proportions bloomed on the western edge of the city. Her eyebrows lifted in surprise when crimson mana exploded upward into the air—illuminating the buildings over that way for just a brief moment before it disappeared just as quickly as it'd come.

"What was that?!" Mara asked, mouth slightly ajar and in awe of what she'd just felt. "Was that a magical attack?! Did you FEEL that mana pulse?! That must've been an *enormous* sum of energy if we could feel it at this distance!"

"Yes . . . That was blood magic," Allie stated curiously, turning her body and tilting her head to the side as if to study the aftermath of mana fluctuations that she could still barely feel before they faded away entirely. "How very interesting . . ."

Vin and Nin both raced over next, abandoning their talk with the newcomer to one of their undead assistants with curious clicking noises that their teeth made when on edge.

"Was that a mana signature I just felt?" Nin asked—only to get slapped across the back of the head by Vin.

"Of course that was a mana signature, idiot. Don't ask stupid questions. The REAL question is, who could produce that kind of power output?" Vin turned his head and motioned to Allie. "That kind of raw magic is on your level, Allie, if I read the signature correctly. To think there'd be two monsters of your caliber here! Who'd have thought?"

"Another person to be wary of," Mara interjected with a long sigh. "Hopefully not someone who'll join that system quest of Purge the Undead that so many have already signed up for. Whoever that was, I don't want him or her on the wrong end of a conflict with us."

Mara, Vin, and Nin all began chatting about what they'd felt, with Mara describing what she and Allie had seen. Meanwhile, Allie continued to study the western edge of the city with a curious glare, tapping her slender fingers on her bone bracers while humming slightly to herself and swaying side to side.

Perhaps she needed to go investigate. As the others had said, that kind of power was on her level—and she couldn't let another person that strong remain in the city if they were going to be a threat. She had to find out just who and what that was, and she would then deal with it if necessary.

Normally he'd never have been able to make this kind of attack by himself, but with the army of the dead around him, he'd actually done it. The drawback was that he'd nearly killed himself and damaged his soul during the attempt. This would very likely not be something he tried to do again.

CRACK

Riven screamed in agony as his left forearm exploded. The battlefield around him rippled and surged skyward—pillars of Crimson Ice spearing hundreds of the apelike gray dream creatures in one massive attack. All the environmental blood was utilized, his internal mana reserves were completely drained, and he'd very obviously overexerted himself due to the backlash that'd nearly ripped his entire body apart before he'd managed to quarantine the fallout into just one limb.

But in turn, that push had granted him the gift of further insight. Visions he didn't entirely understand started flashing before his eyes, and he began to slowly enter a mental state caught between reality and inspiration from the Blood subpillar. Pathways to power opened up before him as images and meaning, insights and secrets, the stairway to the heavens brought him brief glimpses of true meaning. Of true control of the abilities he used. Of the Dao of Blood.

He gasped, dropping his new staff to the ground and shuddering uncontrollably while his vampiric regeneration began to rebuild his mangled arm. And above him, the pillars of red exploded in an ocean of shrapnel that blew through enemy ranks like a high-powered cannonball through Wonder Bread.

Despite his agony and rapidly decaying control on the violent mana surge he'd set into motion, he did manage to angle the explosions enough to avoid himself, the hospital, and his minions. Notifications pinged him over and over again, but he didn't have time to acknowledge them at all.

WOOOM

The air current of the shock wave blew Riven over anyway and caused him to skip across the ground a few meters, only to be caught by Athela and cradled in her arms while the parking lot around them essentially blew up. Fragments of concrete were ripped out of the ground and intermixed with the ocean of blood overhead, and the roar of the mana around them was entirely deafening. It also caused his ears to ring for almost a half minute after the initial blast.

Riven blinked and looked around, trying to regain his focus and shake off the dizziness. He felt very weak, shaky even, as Athela fetched his staff with a thread of webbing. His left arm was still growing back tendons and flesh, or even bone in some parts, but his vampiric body was definitely resilient in the dark. All around him, a shimmering mist of glowing red mana specks floated down from high above and landed in the devastated outer area of the medical campus grounds. The monsters were utterly gone, the last of them decimated by the all-out attack that had been in large part enabled by so many of them dying in the first place to fuel Riven's power surge.

Azmoth's flaming figure lumbered out from the red mist, grinning wickedly and cackling with deep demonic laughs—though Riven's ringing ears could only make it out partially.

"I feel sick . . ." Riven muttered amid swirling visions that continued to berate his consciousness. He fell farther into the madness of insights and desperately tried to grasp at their true nature, letting himself go now that he was safe and slumping down in Athela's arms. The demoness could tell that something wrong was happening and picked him up bodily to carry him over the debris toward the still-standing hospital.

He started to tremble, internally screaming at himself to capitalize on these visions before they left him forever. His body felt sluggish and weighed down, but his mind was on fire as image after image presented itself—only giving him glimpses of the possible pathways to greatness should he attain even a fraction of the true meaning he now saw.

"I do not feel okay."

Athela chuckled and softly said something with a gentle smile directed his way, but he had no idea what it was she'd said through the ringing in his ears. Funnily enough, staring up at her while she carried him, it reminded Riven of the times when he was a child and his mother used to hold him like that to make him feel better.

The memory made him smile.

And then he heard a roar from beyond the ruined parking lot, one that even Riven in his weakened state with ringing ears could hear. He and his two minions turned to see a large, hulking figure moving toward them at a rapid pace a hundred yards away—but Riven didn't get a good look at it because Athela began to sprint.

With Azmoth directly behind them, they rushed into the hospital, and Athela headed directly for the stairs to the basement below, still carrying Riven's rapidly weakening form in her arms.

Riven's body was going into overdrive trying to repair his mana channels, and he'd started convulsing due to the visions—but she knew he'd be okay as long as they were able to hunker down and didn't move him around too much—moving him around a lot while he underwent these kinds of repairs could potentially be very bad, and the safest bet they had to keep him in a stable position was to seal the basement off.

Athela waved Dr. Brass down with a yell, literally threw one of the male nurses off a nearby couch with two of her arachnoid limbs, and dropped her unconscious master onto it instead. "Hey! Are there any other entrances down here?!"

The panicking staff and fugitives now huddled here in the basement were some of the only ones remaining in the hospital after the surge of hive-mind creatures. Athela hadn't had the heart or time to let Riven know, but many of those who'd been holed up upstairs had been devoured during the fight after he'd try to lure the oncoming horde his way. It'd been a valiant effort on Riven's part, but in the end he'd only partially succeeded.

"Only the elevator, and it doesn't work!" Dr. Brass called back upon seeing who it was before rushing into another operating room to try and save someone else dying from blood loss.

Athela gave a quick nod, and crimson webbing began spilling out of her fingers as well as the four arachnoid limbs. "Azmoth! If that thing tries to come down before I'm done, you need to tank and buy me time! Got it?!"

The previously flaming, four-armed demon lumbered forward toward the couch.

He made sure Riven was okay, and then gave a grunt of acknowledgment before backtracking to the stairwell. His armored body still simmered with embers, and his large claws extended in anticipation should the pursuing monstrosity actually attempt to force its way down. A crowd of onlookers either cried, yelled out questions about what was coming, or fearfully stood back all the while. If these demons were running away, just what on Earth was coming for them?

Weaving the strings of ribbon in the air, Athela's nets began lacing back and forth across one another and into the passage leading up to the first floor. They crisscrossed and overlapped innumerable times, faster and faster as she poured out webbing in condensed layers while Riven reinforced the plug at the stairway with nets of his own. Threads continued attaching from wall to wall against the heavily reinforced cement layers that were easily a couple feet thick down here in the basement area. They wove over and over again until Athela began to feel a real drain on her stamina reserves, and she eventually backed up all the way to the end of the stairwell where Azmoth was still standing ready for a fight. By the end of it, the entire stairway had an eight-foot-thick layer of sturdy webbing to stop whatever creature was up there from coming down here.

She just hoped it'd be enough.

She heard a distant roar and then felt the ground shudder. It shuddered again and again, and she even saw slight ripples in the plug she'd made . . . but the resilient layers of webbing held firm. Then she heard a pounding up the stairs again, and screams from up above echoed distantly through the ceiling.

The monster must have found other survivors that hadn't been snatched up yet.

From her left, she felt a light tap on her shoulder and turned to see a teenage boy. The boy shot his parents a look over his shoulder for encouragement and gulped, pushing trembling hands through wavy blond locks. "Uh . . ."

Athela blinked twice. "What is it, twerp?"

The teenager gave a half-hearted and nervous laugh while fidgeting with the hem of his shirt, and looking at the floor, he nodded. "I have a mapper's class. I like to draw maps, and it was given to me by the system in the tutorial along with a few minor abilities. One of them is that I can envision a three-dimensional map around wherever I am . . . so if it'd help, I can show you what's upstairs. We've actually been watching parts of the fight down here with my power . . . But I can't maintain it for long and have to take breaks. So . . ."

Athela's eyebrows raised from underneath a couple locks of black hair, and she glanced over at her still-unconscious master, passed out on the couch nearby. "Well, that'd certainly be helpful, if not at the very least quench my curiosity. Go ahead and do it."

The boy nodded, held up his hand, and a spark of light illuminated the surroundings. In an instant, Athela's worldview changed.

It was an out-of-body experience. Completely and utterly. She was looking at herself as a phantasmal projection and was able to shift around the room at will. Her top right-hand side vision displayed a miniaturized, three-dimensional map of her surroundings, too—displaying everything within a small sphere of influence. She could see deep into the earth, all around the parking lot, and each and every floor in vivid detail—or vague detail, depending on if she wanted to use her direct sight or watch the minimap.

Athela soon got a hold of her ability to zoom around. Quickly adjusting and orienting herself to how the map worked, she enlarged the minimap and identified the happenings upstairs. Then she zoomed in for an up-close glance.

Simply put—it was carnage.

A pocket of three dozen or so survivors had come down from the second level in an attempt to run after thinking the coast was clear, and it'd been a mistake. Fresh bodies by the dozens littered the first floor, and the entire right outer wall had collapsed—leading to that side of the small hospital collapsing with it—all three floors of the right eastern wing. Dust and rubble filled the halls and floors that remained, and the remaining people that weren't buried, dead, or unconscious were running for their lives like rabbits from a hawk.

Chasing them was a creature that Athela didn't really know what to make of. It was similar to the other hive-mind monsters that they'd already fought, but this one was a much more evolved version. And a creepy one at that, even to her.

It was large, very wide, easily a couple tons, standing over ten feet tall, and was essentially a giant rotting humanoid with writhing tendrils ending in leechlike mouths—containing hundreds of teeth apiece. It had stark yellow eyes and, oddly enough—the face of a clown . . . red nose and all. It had huge, clawed hands, small, webbed feet, and a thorax that looked like it'd been stitched together with sewing materials and fleshy strings alike.

"Identify."

[Nightmare, Dream Creature]

Well, it wasn't undead, then, but it certainly looked that way. More so than the other dream creatures, anyways. Maggots ate at its exposed, necrotic muscles, and as it tore a man in two, pieces and bodily fluids of its meal sprayed out of its throat while it swallowed.

It dashed from person to person, rending and tearing people apart or picking the screaming people up to slam them into one another like bloody piñatas. The tendrils in the meantime continued to eat anything and everything around it, living or dead, as they ripped off pieces of flesh if anything got close. Men, women, and, disgustingly enough, even children fell in violent deaths to the creature as the horror scene unfolded.

CHAPTER 17

Visions of towering monoliths flooded Riven's mind as his mana channels surged and re-formed themselves. Riven wasn't out cold or out of action like the humans around him thought him to be; rather, he was attempting to craft an evolution that was rapidly taking shape even as he lay convulsing on the couch. After he'd thought the fight was done when he'd basically blown up the entire parking lot, he'd had to make a choice due to a surge of inspiration that came with his massive attack: grasp the moment when it'd come to him and immerse himself in the visions—or ignore them.

He was guiding that evolution, molding it to his body, and simultaneously he was experiencing scenes that were not of this world.

He couldn't quite interpret them yet, but he felt like he was on the precipice. Oceans of blood, tidal waves of death, and the birth of new life. Blood was the key to mammal physiology, the life bringer, and when it was taken away, it stripped that life with it. Even certain plants and elementals had blood in their bodies, though it came in different forms and shapes. Different colors flashed in front of his eyes while he occasionally glimpsed the real world around him in flashes of heat and light, but he struggled to continue the visions—one after another—while doing his best to interpret their meaning.

Each vision held immense amounts of meaning. Meaning that he could only glimpse snippets of but that held the truths of the universe in quantities far surpassing his own knowledge. His mind was expanding, his soul structure reaffirming the rightful place as the master of the sanguine, while his pillar began to churn and change.

He almost had it . . . and yet he grew frustrated as the minutes rolled by in what seemed like eternities to him. He was so close, yet he could not reach the summit of that knowledge. He was only able to grasp part of it.

Not yet. Riven wasn't able to unlock the entirety of the greater truths and insights of his pillar despite how hard he tried. Just not yet . . .

His eyes blinked rapidly, and he came out of his pseudo-coma with a frustrated scream that shook the room around him when his soul pulsed, giving off an aura of rage that wasn't necessarily directed at anything in particular other than himself. Yet the people around him, the humans, all scrambled backward with terror in their eyes while Azmoth continued to brace himself against Athela's makeshift plug in the stairway.

The creature on the opposite side was now done massacring everyone upstairs and beating on the plug's opposite side, tearing away little by little with its immense strength while Athela fidgeted nervously and children around the room began to cry. But upon his scream, she whirled around, wide eyes not understanding how he was even awake after burning through his mana channels so thoroughly. Then she gawked as an aura unlike anything she'd ever felt out of the nether realms before began to simmer around Riven's body—and it was the same power that'd been carried on his voice when he'd yelled out in anger.

Crimson eyes flared, and the vampire slowly sat up. When he stood, the floor underneath him shuddered and quaked, and the couch underneath him shattered as his aura exploded. A vibrant red cloud of power engulfed his body, and everything within miles of their current position came to a standstill as he took a single step forward.

Even the beast on the other side took pause and stopped its hammering to let out a low whine.

With lightning speed, far faster than he'd ever moved before, a Blood Lance charged and rippled up his arms with wisps of energy before ripping out of his outstretched hand to collide with the plug Athela had made.

It passed right in between Azmoth's armored left arms, and a feral scream of rage was heard on the other side of the plug as it shredded and began to fall apart. Riven's staff shuddered with an influx of mana, and his demons both hastily stepped out of the way when the blade blasted out from the top of the shaft and crashed through the decaying plug, whipping backward and dragging a gargantuan beast back through with it. It was large, a grotesque clown's head snarling with long, carnivorous yellow teeth while it squealed and tried to latch onto anything and everything it passed by. Eel-like appendages with bulging muscles and maggot-ridden flesh whipped around and sought Riven's death right before impact. But right before the monster reached Riven, a torrent of red ice torpedoed through the conduit of fleshy, whiplike rope attaching the impaled blade to the rest of the vampire's staff.

BOOM

The room shook, and Riven's aura faded slightly when a torrent of power collided with the creature in the underground basement, eviscerating and mutilating the creature with thousands of spikes, needles, and blades all created from the blood magic he'd just unleashed.

With a crash, the dead nightmare monster smashed into the cement walls of the stairway and then was buried in rubble when the stairway collapsed. Dust and debris were sent scattering amid shards of solidified crimson magic, and when it settled, the mangled remnants of the beast could partially be seen scattered through the glass-like portion of the underground passage.

Riven glared at the dead foe, continuing to seethe and radiate power that rippled the very air around him. Slowly, though, as Athela's hand gently touched his shoulder, he calmed down and closed his eyes. The route up was sealed off, and the monsters in the immediate vicinity were all dead.

At least they were still alive.

A final bloodcurdling scream and a bestial roar of excitement was heard from up above while Riven and the few dozen others present silently watched the ceiling above them. More of the dream creatures, the hive mind, had come looking after their initial battle was ended—and they were truly pissed off. But it appeared they either didn't know where Riven or his forces were, for some reason, perhaps being another of the same species but a different hive mind, or they simply couldn't find a way down into the basement after Riven's magic and the collapsed stairwell had led to an impassable blockage.

Dr. Brass had come out of the room shaking his head in dismay after the loss of the last woman he'd tried to save. He was in bad shape, and his hollow eyes accepted the strangeness of his situation despite not knowing how it was being done. "There were hundreds of people up there that we left to die."

Riven frowned in consideration but felt a tight squeeze of reassurance from Athela to his left. "We did what we could. Would you rather have died as well with them?"

"*You* did what you could. I just hid down here like a coward," Dr. Brass scoffed, taking off his glasses and slowly walking over to the desk at the front of the surgical waiting area, plopping down into a cushioned rolling chair. "Obviously I would rather not have died, too. It's just incredibly sad, frustrating, and somewhat unbelievable. How has it come to this?"

The old man threw up his hands to either side as the staff, families, patients, and one other doctor present all listened to the exchange in silence. "What the hell is even happening here? What IS Elysium, and why did it do this to us? We all saw the messages about that bullshit apocalypse—half of us even went to some forsaken tutorial event—but am I really supposed to believe that our world merged with two others and is now connected to some sort of intergalactic labyrinth of planets?"

The old man then pointed to Riven accusingly. "And you! You come in here with two demonic pets and have the ability to do shit like cast APOCALYPTIC

MAGIC?! We watched your fight through the kid's mapping ability! You took on hundreds of those beasts by yourself! And WHY do you have elves with you, of all goddamn things?!"

Dr. Brass slammed his fists down onto the desk in frustration, biting back tears and flaring his nostrils. He then pointed to where the door had once been, now completely sealed shut by stone to form a thick wall. "How?! Why?! What the fuck is going on here?! I demand answers! My friends just DIED up there, goddamn it!"

People around the room began to murmur, with only an occasional groan from the guy who'd recently had surgery to remove a piece of metal from his arm in the next operating room over. Riven didn't know how to approach the situation. He knew the doctor was hurting. This entire situation was fucked up.

Athela, fortunately, was there to explain things for him when Riven found he lacked the words. "I believe I may be of some assistance in explaining our situation, now that the tutorial is over and I'm at liberty to divulge slightly more information."

Lightly nudging Riven's side with a finger, she turned around and hummed happily. "My name is Athela! I am a rather young demon, which is an immortal entity that generally isn't allowed into the mortal realms unless certain requirements are met. This is my master, Riven, who contracted me so that I could safely get out of the nether realms and then saved me from being cannibalized by another group of demons in the realms of hell. The big guy who occasionally lights himself on fire is Azmoth; he's another of Riven's demons, and he's basically a dumb ape. It is very nice to meet all of you!"

Nothing but awkward staring and silence ensued, other than an irritated and guttural growl from Azmoth behind her.

"Well, then!" Athela stated sourly, her sharp feminine features become visibly irritated at the lack of reply. "Tough crowd! Anyways, I'll start with some of the already posed questions and statements. Yes, your planet Earth has been incorporated into Elysium's multiverse. The multiverse is a vast and sprawling universe of planets that you can travel between at different portal zones. However, because this planet, Panu, is newly formed from Earth and two others, Panu will have a cleansing of sorts in the form of trials."

Athela waited for questions again, but there were none. So she continued with an eye roll. "I don't know what those trials will be, but they will either be surpassed or billions will die for every one of them that isn't passed. I'm not at liberty to say what those trials will be, and a lot of the time they even differ. I could even be wrong with my own guesses, but you'll all find out soon enough. Moving on—now that you are all part of the multiverse, you are part of a magic-dense existence. Ambient mana can be controlled and wielded in various useful tools, such as ascensions, but many forms it takes materialize as monsters, such as the creature that killed most of the people upstairs. You will also soon find yourself able to cultivate and grow various Dao pillars, which are insights and pathways to power that stack on top of your normal stats, levels, and magical abilities. Unfortunately for most of you, the death rate for newly integrated worlds is very high and you likely won't ever get to begin leveling—and you'll likely get nowhere near cultivating. But fear not! If you take a pledge of allegiance to my master and allow him to feed on you regularly, we will keep you safe."

The demoness turned gracefully to focus on Riven, ignoring the shocked looks of horror from the mortals around her. "Was that a Dao vision you were experiencing earlier? You're able to produce an aura now. Oh, and I highly suggest that you keep these people as subjects. Finding cattle to feed on regularly will mean you don't have to hunt, and it can make finding a good thrall or two a lot easier."

He ignored her first question and narrowed his eyes. Riven didn't even know what a thrall was, but he was more concerned about how she was openly talking about turning these humans into cattle, scaring the living daylights out of them after they'd just been trapped in a basement with him and his demons. He gave her an angry glare, and her smile turned sheepish when she realized she'd fucked up and mouthed the word *sorry* with a pout. She truly looked sad about it, too. Habits were tough to break, but at least she was trying.

Even the teenage kid who'd come up and shared his mapping ability with them looked visibly shocked at Athela's words, and people began silently looking for another way out soon after.

A small child with a pink bow in her blond hair, about six years old with a teddy bear held to her chest, slowly inched out from behind her mother near the cushioned chairs on Riven's left. "Are you a vampire, Mister? I heard that lady talking, and she said you were."

"A friendly vampire!" Riven said awkwardly, taking off his mask and smiling gently down at the little girl. "I promise."

A burly man nearby with a basketball logo on his shirt scoffed and folded his arms. "Vampire? Really? You're going to ask us to buy that? You just look like a creep in a cosplay outfit to me."

Riven's smile turned to the man, and he extended his fangs for everyone to see. A couple people gasped sharply, and even more backed away, but Riven's smile returned to normal seconds later. "Is it really that hard to believe after everything that's happened? I cast magic, have demonic summons with me, and you're questioning . . . that? Are you a fucking idiot?"

He shook his head with a snort. "Unlike all of you, I was flung into a hellscape. I was changed because of it. If you don't want to stay due to that, I'll let you all leave after this is over . . . but you're all going to have to wait for those monsters to leave first."

Murmurs flooded the room as they looked to the area where the door had been and then to Riven. Some of them continued to inch back with fearful looks cast his way, while others were just simply curious.

"So you were human at one point, then? How does that work, exactly?" the doctor who'd been performing surgery not even five minutes ago asked with a curious glare. She was tall, thin, middle-aged, and had blood spots along her blue scrubs, which bore a name tag that read Dr. Beth Waters, Physician, across the front. She stepped forward, brushing her brunette hair to the side and peering at Riven's face. "Open up again."

Athela sneered at the absolute lack of awareness of personal space on the doctor's part. Or at least that's what Riven assumed she was sneering at.

"Sure . . ." Riven stated hesitantly, opening up and extending his fangs for the doc to take a look at.

Ten seconds later, Dr. Waters nodded absentmindedly and shut his mouth for him by lightly pushing up on his jaw. "Fascinating. We should talk later, but I have to make sure my patient in the other room remains stable. Keep me posted if anything happens."

The woman walked back into the operating room with a nurse in tow, obviously a no-nonsense kind of person and seemingly not bothered at all by everything that was going on around them.

"I'll not have my kids around monsters like you three," a Latina mother snarled from across the room, holding a little boy in her lap as her heavily tattooed husband next to her sat tensed and ready to spring. He was with another mean-looking bald man who wore no shirt and carried a baseball bat on his left. "You'll keep your word and let us out when those creatures leave?"

Riven snorted, partially in amusement and partially in disgust at the way she was talking to him. "You'll be more than free to leave. I could give less than a flying fuck about where you go, lady. For now, I'm going into OR five. Don't come in without knocking first, and try not to bother us unless something interesting happens. Athela, Azmoth—let's go."

CHAPTER 18

Riven turned heel and walked out of the room, cloak flowing behind him, leaving the other people to talk among themselves about what had happened. Tensions were high, and he could still hear the creatures above occasionally roar through the ceiling despite how thick it was.

Riven gazed upward. "They probably just found new prey."

"Actually . . ." The teenage boy interrupted his thoughts with a nervous laugh, having followed them inside OR five without permission but not seeming to care. "Those creatures are trying to find a way down here and are expressing their rage. I've been watching on my map. They tried the stairs but couldn't dig through the rubble."

"Oh, really?"

"Yeah. Those layers of stuff you packed in there after that awesome attack held them back . . ." The teenage kid gave an awkward thumbs-up. "So thanks for that! My name is Jake, by the way."

"Nice to meet you, Jake. My name is Riven."

He shook hands with the smaller, blond young man and gave an appreciative nod. "Thanks for the help. Do me a favor and continue to watch out for it, all right?"

"Will do!" Jake gave a quick salute, a more firm smile than his previous ones, and turned around to march out the door toward his parents on the sofas.

The visions had returned.

Riven found himself surrounded by an ocean devoid of life. Only the warm, rolling waves gently tossing his body back and forth were causing any noise, and his body relaxed amid the never-ending massage of the waters around him.

Slowly he opened his eyes, and as he did, his body began to rise up out of the ocean and into the air. Demonic wings sprouted from his calves, his lower back, and his upper back, one after the other, as flesh tore and gave way to greater substance . . . but this rebirth did not hurt. If anything, as his red eyes finally opened fully to meet the visage of a brilliant crimson moon ahead of him—he felt the grip of a god on his soul pulling him home.

The moon was so close . . . barely hovering above the horizon of the otherwise dark and starlit sky. Yet it encompassed well over a third of the sky above him—with pockets of craters and mountains visible even from here.

He felt it getting closer now, felt the pull of his ancestors calling to him—and in a flash, the sea around him began to roil and churn. Water turned to blood, sending cyclones of spinning red torrents cascading about him. The calm sea turned into a hurricane, and the bodies of those he'd slain rose up from beneath him as a mountain of corpses, all of them reaching out to him with dead eyes as they worshipped the one they now called master from the afterlife.

But beyond all else, and within the eye of the storm about him, a sword forged from the blood of his enemies was created before his very eyes. The legions of dead men and women he stood upon screamed in anguish while they withered away and fell into the ocean of red beneath. One, two, and then three of his thralls appeared in explosions of shadow in the air around him, all bowing their heads toward his divine form while he rose up into the sky and took the gleaming red weapon from where a tornado of rage swirled about them. Then he lifted his hand, shimmering crimson light encompassing it as a rocket of power launched itself into the heavens with a blast of power that tore through the heavens and exploded overhead—creating a nova blooming above them to finally signify his return. The world trembled under his power, the oceans roiled, and the air about him simmered. All would see it, and all would know it was him.

The king was coming home. Though his enemies and usurpers might try, they would not be able to stop him now.

Yes . . . He was finally coming home.

[Quest Update: Finding Your Family—As promised by the administrator, your completion of Chalgathi's Trials and the Tutorial Trials have brought you together in close proximity with your family and friends. Once per day, you will receive a ping on Allie's general location to let you know which way to go. Locating the position of your sister, Allie, now.]

Riven's notification woke him from the dream, and he rubbed his eyes with a yawn. He hadn't slept well, his mind repeating the strange images of the man in the ocean, the blood moon, and the sword created from a mountain of the dead.

Was it supposed to mean something?

Why had it repeated over and over like it had? Though he'd been asleep, he could distinctly remember having it numerous times over . . .

But then he saw the hologram notification and his heartbeat began to spike. Through the cement walls and dirt, through the city and not that far away, was a gleaming figure. He couldn't make out the true identity just yet, as she was only represented by blips of light, but he could tell exactly how far away and which direction she was in.

Finally. Fucking FINALLY! A huge smile tugged at his lips, and he clenched his fists with an inward scream of triumph. She was alive and not far off! But just why hadn't he already had a notification appear before now? Had it appeared when he'd been undergoing transitional pains during that first night in the broken-down gas station? Or had it happened during one of his fights and he'd accidentally dismissed it?

He was half tempted to rip through the ceiling and just charge through the waves of enemies to get to her, but he knew doing so would result in the deaths of dozens of people that hid here with him. Inwardly cringing that he was stuck down here in this hospital basement, he could only hope that next time he'd be ready to move and out in the open.

Athela's voice spoke from behind where she sat against the wall, playing patty-cake or something akin to it with Azmoth. "Looks like your friends aren't that far off. I'm excited to finally meet your sister."

She'd gotten the notification, too, then.

He nodded, yawning one more time and reviewing the vivid dream he'd had again. Secretly feeling rather jealous of the two recovering elves on their relatively comfy hospital beds, Riven rubbed his forehead and yawned again before coming over to sit next to Athela. "Can't sleep?"

"Don't feel like it. You're supposed to be nocturnal now, ya know. As a vampire. You'll hunt better that way, and you won't have to worry about debuffs."

Hmm. That was probably true, but Riven also liked being able to walk around in the day. Was needing to wear extra clothing to block the sun's rays really too much of a hassle? He didn't think so.

"Yes, yes," Azmoth stated profoundly, giving Riven a knowing look as he gave up on the patty-cake game and swatted at Athela instead—easily missing her as she dodged backward. "You want hunt at night."

Riven smiled slightly, chuckled, and leaned his head on Athela's shoulder to relax a bit when she settled down next to him. "It may take some adjusting, too, but you're right. Moving around in the daylight is a little . . . uncomfortable."

There was a knock on the door, and the familiar voice of Dr. Brass echoed through a moment later. "May I come in?"

"Come in."

The doorknob turned, and the door opened wide to reveal the old man's haggard appearance. He looked like he'd aged a decade in the short time they'd known him; his gray hair was frazzled beyond belief, and it looked like he'd just woken up. His white coat was dirty and spotted with blood. Dark bags were under his eyes, and he rubbed his temple with a tired expression as he shut the door behind him. "May I sit?"

He motioned to the floor in front of Athela and Riven.

Riven silently gestured for Dr. Brass to do as he pleased, and the old man came over to plop right in front of the others. "Most of the others are still asleep, so I thought this may be the best time to get away from them and have a word. I . . ."

His words faded away. Dr. Brass sat silently, inspecting Athela, then Azmoth, and then Riven. Putting his hands over his face and sputtering something under his breath, he rubbed his tired eyes and removed his glasses. "Riven, right? That's your name?"

Riven nodded once, taking a pack of saltine crackers from the floor nearby and opening them. He was beginning to feel hungry again. Specifically, he wanted blood . . . but he was curious as to just how long he could stave off the hunger and was self-experimenting by eating other food in the meantime. He obviously wouldn't go too far, as he didn't want to have another insanity attack, but he could feel how far the tipping point was, and he hadn't even come close yet. This gave him some measure of relief, meaning he wouldn't need to actively gorge himself all the time—but rather could probably put days in between each feeding if he really needed to.

Dr. Brass grunted, pulling his knees up to his chest and slowly rocking back. "So . . . how did you come across your magic, if I may ask? Surely you didn't learn it on Earth. You can shoot piercing bolts of blood at creatures to kill them. And you can obviously summon demons. Is this some kind of sick joke? I want to believe this is all just a bad dream, but over and over again, I am disproven. I know what I saw, but I can't seem to grasp the reality of it. Can you please show me one more time? A spell?"

Riven frowned the doctor's way with a raised eyebrow, realizing by the way the old man's voice shook that he was nearly at a mental breaking point, and he pointed at the far wall. Crimson ribbons flickered along his forearm, licking his skin and engulfing his hands until they reached the fingers a half second later—and a thin shard of blood magic materialized out in front. "It's true."

The three-foot shard of sharp, pointed magic rocketed forward into the wall, piercing the stone without much effort and sending chipped pieces of concrete skipping onto the floor. Dr. Brass gawked, shook his head, and sprang to his feet to inspect the projectile. He gingerly touched it, withdrawing as a warm sensation began to spread along his hands when he did—and watched the solidified blood magic slowly fizzle away into nothingness a couple seconds later.

"So I'm not dreaming. That's . . . that's real magic . . ." Dr. Brass gasped, putting a finger into the hole in the stone wall where the magic had almost cut cleanly through. "This isn't a dream. This isn't a dream. This really isn't a bad dream. How is this possible?"

Riven was truly confused. Had Dr. Brass actually been trying to convince himself that this was all fake? And if so, why would a simple act of magic like what he'd just done be enough to convince him when everything else the old man had seen was just as convincing? This doctor was about to mentally shatter.

"You're really going to ask that after all you've seen?" Riven asked sincerely, cocking his head to the side and looking down as he felt Athela's covered head land in his lap when she scooted across the floor.

Dr. Brass was still dumbfounded. He whirled on Riven and stomped over, pointing back to the wall. "Do it again!"

Riven slowly shook his head. "I need to conserve mana in case that thing breaks through our barrier."

"What are your other abilities? I know you can teleport, because I saw you rip open space and travel through it in the visions conjured by that boy in the front room. What else are you hiding?"

Dr. Brass was breathing heavily. There was a long pause, and Riven raised an eyebrow.

"I'd rather not talk about them right now. I don't know you that well, and giving away all my secrets doesn't seem like a wise decision, considering the postapocalyptic scenario we find ourselves in."

". . . Are you really a vampire then? Like, really?"

Riven chuckled. "Just recently became one. Yes . . . you saw the fangs, didn't you?"

"I thought that was some kind of weird trick to try and intimidate people."

"It wasn't a trick. I'm also a hell of a lot faster and stronger than most people now, too."

Dr. Brass narrowed his eyes suspiciously. "You're not a threat to us, are you? When I first met you, I did get a rather bad feeling about you . . . but I always like to take people for who they are rather than go at face value. I hope I didn't make a bad choice."

Riven rolled his eyes. "No, I'm not a threat. Not unless you cause trouble for me first."

"Good. You seem like good people . . . I'm deciding to trust you. Please don't make me regret that decision."

The old man sat back down, trying to collect his thoughts. "I'm sorry to bother. I'm just trying to wrap my head around all this and what's happening. You seem to know more than anyone else that I've met. It's a goddamned mess out there! Everyone in the next room looks up to me, and I have no answers. I'm just a man doing his best, but my best is not nearly enough."

Riven smiled, genuinely, as he recognized the sincerity in Dr. Brass's words. "That's all we can ask of ourselves. As for what I know—it's very limited. I'm counting on Athela here, mostly."

"Even I don't really know that much!" Athela stated bluntly with a chipper smile from where her eyes were covered up by the blanket she'd thrown over her face. "I'm rather young for a demon. I was only in the nether realms for two hundred years until Riven freed me!"

"Two hundred years?" Dr. Brass repeated disbelievingly.

"Mmm-hmm!!!"

"That's an absurd amount of time. Are you certain it was that long?"

Athela wiggled her fingers at him like a witch casting a spell, pulling the blanket halfway down and cackling. "Mmm-hmm!!! Really, it was 197 years, if you want a specific amount of time. I know what you're thinking, though! Demons can live for indefinite amounts of time through the ages if they acquire enough power."

Dr. Brass scowled back at Athela and adjusted his glasses again—a habit that was quickly becoming overly repetitive and, to Riven's eye, seemed like it was something Dr. Brass did whenever he got flustered.

The old man coughed into his closed fist, addressing the demoness again. "What is Negrada? I heard you and Azmoth talking about it earlier."

"The dungeon that was going to eat me!"

"Dungeons eat demons?"

"Not all the time, but sometimes. Their minions can absorb our essence, and sometimes they even bind other demons to do their dirty work."

"That's barbaric."

"It's the circle of life! I'm just happy I got out. I didn't want to die, and I really want to make Riven proud after he picked me as his first companion. I think you made quite the lucky steal by binding me, Riven!"

"I did?" Riven asked with mock curiosity. "Didn't realize you were old enough to be my great-great-great-grandma, by the way. You old fart."

Athela growled and narrowed her eyes dangerously. "Yes, you did get a steal, idiot! AND I'M NOT OLD!"

"Not just old, but really old."

"Shut it, twerp!" Athela tried to sucker punch his kidney, but Riven quickly deflected and aggressively smacked her forehead, eliciting a feminine *UMPH* when she fell backward. This got an amused laugh from Azmoth to their right.

"Riven . . ." Dr. Brass began in a low tone, staring at the floor between his legs. "Where did you grow up before all this started?"

Riven's red eyes found their way to the old man, and he blinked, wondering why the doctor would care. "Well . . . that's a long story. The short version is Dallas, Texas. Let's just say I didn't have the greatest of childhoods . . ."

Athela woke to the sound of a pained moan. The clock on the wall said it was four a.m.—meaning she'd slept four of her usual eight hours, but she still felt completely refreshed. She blinked, yawned, and clucked her lips a couple of times. She could hear children playing out in the waiting room down the hall. The sounds of happy, carrying voices were enough to make Athela's heart swell in a way it almost never did. It'd been a while since she'd been so relaxed, as odd as that was given their situation.

Riven was peacefully asleep next to her, and Azmoth was in a rather uncomfortable position next to the metal surgical table. The large demon did give Athela a nod of affirmation, though, clarifying that he wasn't asleep but merely bored out of his mind as he went back to staring at the ceiling.

Another low moan of pain echoed out from one of the two elves, and Athela saw the one with silver hair adjust her posture underneath the blankets, blinking rapidly and coughing as she sat up with a startled yelp.

"Why, hello there!" Athela said, reaching out a hand and patting Riven's hair while he slept.

The elf blinked in surprise. "We're not dead . . ."

Athela gave the other girl a confused frown and then stood to grab a small box of orange juice. Walking over to the bedside, she noted how tired the elf looked. The IV was still in her arm, and the poor girl barely had enough strength to sit up properly—her head sagged and there were bags under her eyes, yet she was still very pretty. The blue paint across the elf's face was partially gone or smudged, and given how the injured woman grimaced when she moved it, her clavicle was still obviously broken even after the doctor had set it into its proper anatomic location.

The woman groaned again, wincing and eyeing Athela suspiciously before lying back in the bed under the warm covers. She looked to the IV in her arm a little worriedly and then underneath the blanket to see that her clothes were missing.

Lastly, the elf looked to her leg, which Dr. Brass had bandaged properly. "What are you doing to me?"

"Healing you," Athela said with a wink, using a straw on the back of the juice box to puncture its seal and then handing it to the other young woman. "Take this and drink. What's your name again? I forgot. Or did I ever know?"

The elf took the box gingerly, trying not to move much and looking the object over without understanding how to work it.

Athela snickered, pointing to the straw. "Suck out of that. It's fruit juice . . . Oh, don't give me that look! I could have killed you anytime. Just shut up and take our hospitality whether you like it or not!"

The elf frowned again, eyed the IV again, and hesitantly put her lips against the straw to suck. She was too weak to argue or protest anything, but her brilliant blue eyes shot open wide when the juice hit her tongue. She began sucking it down hungrily, quickly draining the box while Athela laughed and handed her another.

Athela gave her crackers, a couple granola bars, and then a water bottle after that. All of it was quickly downed as if the poor girl had been starving for weeks, and after she was done, Athela capped the water bottle for her and set it on the steel surgical table next to Azmoth.

"So what's your name?" Athela pressed again—a little more forcefully this time.

The girl parted her hair with her left hand—the side that didn't have the clavicular injury—and smiled lightly. "My name is Senna. Thank you for helping us . . . but I must ask, why did you do it?"

Senna's gaze shifted to Riven sleeping on the floor, and then to the faintly glowing cinders flaring to life at random along Azmoth's body. Her eyes shot wide-open, and she gasped in disbelief. "Is that a Hellscape Brutalisk?!"

". . . Yes. A baby one. How'd you know?"

"I've seen pictures in my uncle's archive!" The disbelief was written along with momentary shock on the elf's face, but she quickly regained control of her emotions and let go of the breath she'd been holding in. "Wow . . . I never thought I'd see one in my lifetime. Much less one that was casually trying to sleep."

"I don't sleep." Azmoth's deep voice came from where he continued to lie on his back and stare upward.

Senna looked back in surprise, and an eyebrow raised. "Really . . . All right, then. How do you all speak my language?"

"Your language?" Athela repeated. "Are you sure it's your language?"

Senna was about to answer when she stopped and thought about it. Her jaw dropped in surprise. "No . . . no, this isn't my language. What's happening? Is it your language?"

Athela shook her head with a pleasant smile as Azmoth giggled uncharacteristically. "Nope! Our languages likely merged or converted to the universal language upon entering the multiverse."

Senna nodded slowly, then turned to look at her friend—the blonde elf who was missing her entire forearm and part of her bicep. "Ethel . . . is she going to be okay?"

Athela shrugged hesitantly. "This old-looking baby stomper, Dr. Brass, said he thinks so . . . but I didn't press the matter. Honestly, we weren't sure either of you would live after what happened. Apparently, those goblins spread some pretty nasty infections through their bites . . ."

"Poison," Senna spat with venom in her words, anger flaring to life across her pretty features. "Those wretched goblins . . ."

Athela shook her head slowly. "No . . . Dr. Brass said it was definitely an infection. That's why he put you on medication." Athela pointed to the IV. "He's directing medicine these humans call antibiotics into your blood vessels for faster access. Be sure not to take those out; they have limited supplies here after the hospital was attacked."

Senna coughed again, this time a little more violently, hacking up some phlegm and spitting it out onto her covers between closed hands and looking to Athela apologetically. "I'm sorry . . . Did you say hospital?"

Athela frowned and folded her arms over her abdomen. "Well, it was a hospital from Earth. Then that monster attacked, and most of the people here died . . . Riven and I sealed off the entrance down here for now."

Senna's face slowly fell, and she sighed. "Earth, you say? Where is that?"

"My master's home planet," Athela replied promptly. "Part of Panu now. Your world was incorporated into Panu as well."

CHAPTER 19

Senna nodded yet again. "My people called the planet I come from Zazir, though neither of our worlds exist as they once did, if what the administrator said is to be believed. I cannot grasp the meaning of all this . . . I . . . I need to get back to my family. How long have I been asleep?"

Athela thought back to the battle in the forest. "Almost two days now."

"Two days?!" Senna repeated, dumbstruck. "Were there any other survivors other than Ethel and myself?"

"Not from your group. We almost got there in time to save one of the men with you, but he died shortly after we killed the goblins."

Water began to tear up along Senna's lower eyelids, and her lip trembled slightly, but she got a hold of her emotions soon after that and swallowed hard to bring herself in check. "Um . . . okay. May I ask again, though, why did you help us?"

Athela shifted her position, leaning against the bed with her arms folded—and her smile went cold. "Because my master has a bleeding heart. Personally? I would have let you die. It isn't that I want you to die or have any ill will toward you, it's just that I don't care if you live or die. You are as unimportant to me as the grains of dirt underneath my feet, but he'd have been unhappy if we didn't help you out. And believe it or not, I've taken a keen liking to my master and don't want to see him upset."

There was an awkward pause. Senna's eyes went wide at the admission, but they softened as they fell on Riven's sleeping figure nearby. "Well, you are a demon. I should have expected as much. Still, I'm surprised that he would have wanted to help. He is a vampire, after all."

Athela snorted, suppressing a laugh, and then beat her chest twice to expel a belch. "Nice! That was a good one. Anyways, Riven wasn't a vampire up until recently. Or maybe he was and just didn't know it? He drank some sinner's blood from the hellscape and unlocked a dormant bloodline. Not sure how that works out, but that's what happened."

"And . . . he was human before?" Senna asked uncertainly, shifting to a more comfortable position on the bed.

Athela nodded. "Human. He's been a vampire for a grand total of a few days."

"He certainly took to feeding on that goblin without much of a problem for someone who's only been a vampire for a minimal amount of time."

Athela's stare turned cold, and her unusual features were set into hard lines that made Senna visibly shiver. "I'm trying to be nice for my master's sake. If you want me to leave you alone, I can certainly do that. I'd appreciate it if you weren't so judgmental with the people who saved your lives, though."

Senna opened her mouth to speak, then shut it again. She shook her head, eyes downcast, and sighed. "I am sorry. I apologize . . . I am just not accustomed to the idea that . . . Well, usually his kind views my kind as cattle. If you say he was just turned, though, I will believe you. There is no reason not to since I am still in the land of the living . . . You are very pretty, by the way."

Athela immediately beamed. "Thanks! You're very pretty yourself! For a mortal, anyways."

Senna blushed and half smiled, glancing over at Riven again. "As is your master."

The room's mood immediately soured, and Athela's face darkened. "Don't even think about it."

The way Athela got so protective over Riven in that single instant was somewhat funny to Senna, and the elf suppressed a laugh of her own when Azmoth also began to laugh.

"Not funny!" Athela snapped at the brutalisk, only for Azmoth to wag his tail even faster with amusement. "I'm serious, Azmoth! It isn't funny!"

"I am promised to another," Senna stated with a sly smile. "Though he is good-looking, I must admit. What is your master's name?"

"Don't press your luck! You aren't worthy!" Athela replied, half joking and half threatening with a finger pointed the elf's way. "His name is Riven."

Senna raised an eyebrow. "Do you intend to vet all the women who chase him, then?"

Athela raised an eyebrow daringly. "That or I intend to kill them. Unless of course they meet my standards . . . I'd allow it if they were up to par."

Senna's face paled, but she began laughing again when Athela's composure broke and she couldn't keep a straight face.

"I'm already beginning to like you, Athela," Senna said with another sigh, closing her eyes and letting her head sink into the pillow behind her. "This is such an odd situation I find myself in . . . when I tell my father of this, I'm sure he'll not believe it until he meets you."

"Until he meets me?" Athela repeated with an eye roll, using a finger and wagging it in front of Senna's face. "Don't think that's a good idea. Just look at how you reacted. At how the goblins reacted. Let me ask you a question: If you had a larger group of people with you and encountered us—would you have tried to kill us?"

Senna opened her eyes and met Athela's gaze, then winced in pain when her clavicle moved when she breathed. "Certainly. However, I will be able to convince him and the council. Your master has proved himself a good person. I am in his debt, and my tribe needs to know of this place. The more allies we have, the more protection we can bring to one another against the monsters that roam these lands."

Athela wasn't buying it one bit. "I am incredibly skeptical that any elf tribe would want to ally themselves with a vampire and his demonic servants. You may broach the subject with him when he wakes, but I will advise him against meeting your father or any of the rest of your kind. Do not think that because *he* is newly turned and unaware of your people's histories that *I* do not know them. Just as I studied his realm before the integration, I studied yours, too."

Azmoth got up from the side of the surgical table, standing to his full height and peering down at the elf with a scrutinizing gaze unbecoming of anything friendly. "They will not know of the master unless he wants it."

The elf was not to be persuaded otherwise, though.

"But people can change, and we must change if we are to survive. Why not try?" Senna asked hesitantly, looking a little sad and lightly clasping her hands. "I understand that you don't want to let my tribe know about Riven, for good reason, but can we not at least find a common meeting place to leave each other messages or set aside times to talk? I'm in his debt and wish to know more about all of you after I leave here."

Athela's sly smile quickly spread across her lips while she examined the visibly nervous elf. "No . . . you're just fishing for information." Athela took a step forward and jabbed a finger into Senna's sternum. "You're just afraid he's going to select you to become his thrall. Azmoth, should I tell Riven about how to make thralls now that he's got such a fine specimen here that seems so easy for the picking?"

The elf's face quickly paled, and a look of horror overcame her, and Athela followed up with a shrill, cruel laugh. "Do not play games with me, mortal. But be comforted, as he would be appalled by such an idea anyways. However, if you truly are interested in meeting us again after we let you go . . . you may speak to Riven about it when he wakes."

Senna's horror vanished, and she let out a deep and shaky sigh before she smiled brightly. "Good! I am excited to let my family know that I have made friends with a vampire! It's actually quite exciting . . ."

A quiet knock at the door drew the attention of the elf and the two demons, and the voice of Jake, the teenager from earlier, called out to ask if he could come in.

Athela quietly exited the room, not making even the slightest of sounds as her bare feet traveled over the tiled operating room floor. It was uncanny. Even the swing of the door made no noise, her body's passive abilities dampening the sound just because she was in contact with it—as she didn't want to wake Riven for no good reason.

He needed his sleep.

Exiting the room and staring down at the teenager, who gawked at her breasts with wide eyes, she slapped the boy with an open palm to get his attention and startle him back into reality. "The hell do you want, runt?"

The blond, curly-haired teen stammered a reply and hastily tried to reconstruct his composure while blushing immensely. "I, uh, just wanted to update all of you. I've found something important with my maps."

"Oh? Are the monsters gone?"

The boy slowly shook his head. "No . . . they're still sniffing around upstairs. It actually looks like they're making a nest, or trying to find a way down here, or both. They're not having much luck on the second."

"Then what is it?"

The kid pointed back toward an old closet and motioned for her to follow. Taking one of the lanterns from a nearby table and using the dim light to lead the way, he opened the closet and pointed at a thin metal sheet on the floor that was clipped down to another metal ring via padlock. "If we can break this, it actually leads into a sewer system. We can get out of here without ever needing to fight the creatures up above, even if they're nesting."

The next two hours passed with little to do for Athela, but eventually Riven yawned and woke up with a stretch.

"HOLY shit!" Riven exclaimed and reared back his head, whacking it against the near wall when he opened his eyes to see Athela staring daggers at him from only half an inch away.

He grimaced and rubbed at the bruise with a frown. "OW!"

The demoness snickered, and Riven smacked her upside the forehead before pushing her away and sitting up. "You think you're funny, huh?"

She gave him a brilliant smile. "I know I'm funny! Anyways, Jake, that teenage brat, has some information from scouting out the surrounding city. We also found a passage out of here, so get your ass moving and let's go talk to him!"

Riven smiled at her chipper attitude and massaged the back of his head some more, then took her hand to pull himself up when she offered it. A minute later he approached Jake, who was nestled in between his parents on a couch, and a few minutes after that he was in the three-dimensional mapping system alongside Jake, who was pointing out various details about the surrounding environment. It was a very useful ability and class, if Riven had any say, even if it wasn't combat-oriented. The main sphere of his map was updated live, in real time. The issue was that his 3-D mapping sphere only extended within a certain radius of his current spot, which was maybe a couple hundred yards, and Jake couldn't be paying attention to all the details at once. But he was able to use summoned dragonflies to go beyond this sphere, looking through their eyes as they zipped about to scout for him and map out other parts of the area that were stagnant based on the last thing Jake saw. The teenager apparently could create up to five of these mana-based scouting dragonflies at one time, too.

First thing the kid had scouted were the monsters upstairs. They really were beginning to nest there, dragging piles of corpses over to feed on and integrating body parts little by little of what they didn't need to eat.

Jake had also combed through the western edge of the city with his dragonflies after he'd investigated the surrounding area in thorough detail. This had been done over the past couple days, actually even before the monster attack, and the kid had even adopted a pattern of developing intelligence on surrounding groups only for his own curiosity—which he was happy to share with Riven.

The city was a lot bigger than Riven had initially thought, situated mostly in between two mountains in a large valley but also extending out into the plains beyond. Of the scouting Jake had done thus far, three areas were most noticeable.

First was an old prison on the other side of a large neighborhood where looters were frequenting various houses. Watching and listening through the eyes of the dragonflies, Riven had come to realize that this prison was now one of the city's hubs. Inmates, once prisoners there, had overthrown the guards and taken control of it. The prison was basically a fortress, with heavy-duty barbed-wire fences in multiple layers and easily guarded points of entry. Being two stories tall, it also had a lot of room to keep people. They'd killed all the original guards, and the inmates had replaced them with slaves while forming a hierarchy around one man named James. These people raided the surrounding city wherever they were able to find supplies or other humans, killing anyone that got in their way, taking their things, and raping whoever they chose to take for their own pleasures. They had a stockpile of guns, with a few of them even having earned classes, levels, and abilities by killing monsters or finishing their own tutorials—the most noteworthy of these being James himself.

James was a big, bald white man with a bushy brown beard who always remained shirtless, having long, X-shaped scars on his chest and back. Heavily tattooed sleeves inked his muscular arms up to the shoulders, and he was quick to anger, killing people who even thought of challenging his authority with some kind of earth magic that enveloped his skin in rock with strength and defense bonuses. Given the way they conducted themselves, Riven had already marked him as an obstacle they'd have to take care of sooner or later if he wished to stay in Brightsville.

The second noticeable area was a very large church next to a sizable lake located on the northern edge of the city, where hundreds of people, mostly rednecks and adamantly religious types, had congregated. A priest named Benjamin had acquired a form of holy magic and some divine book of miracles he'd likely found in a tutorial dungeon and had called upon his fellow followers of God to pray with him and take up arms. In typical redneck fashion, they'd brought their guns and Bibles and created something of a religious cult—referencing Benjamin as their lord and savior reincarnated and a direct messenger of God, who would lead them from the apocalypse to greater destinations. Benjamin's followers called him Prophet, and according to Jake they'd been very aggressive in their recruitment tactics—often forcing other people to join via threat of violence. Rumors were going around that Benjamin's men had actually murdered the previous city mayor and had killed the remnants of the police force as well.

The third noticeable group was a bit more . . . scary. At least according to the teenager. Other survivors who'd witnessed the fights or even those who'd just happened to be in the wrong place at the wrong time swore up and down about a new undead faction in the downtown area. There was a lot of debate about whether or not they were actually people who'd just obtained necromancy magics after the integration or whether they were monsters feeding on people to grow their own numbers. Whatever the case, Jake had scouted it out as well—and he'd found hundreds of various undead species holed up within the tallest tower of the downtown skyline. The tower was very tall, and in the snapshots Jake had taken, it was pulsing with teal and black magics that slowly warped the building from steel into . . . something else. The process was still underway, but it was very obvious from the patches of ivory and black along its surface that the base structure of the tower was actually being converted into new materials. Unfortunately Jake's creatures had been spotted rather fast when exploring this particular area, so he hadn't been able to glean much information on it yet.

The neighborhoods to the northwest of the city were also a madhouse. Entire blocks had been lit aflame and burned down street by street as gang wars erupted between a multitude of different smaller factions fighting over resources—food, ammunition, toilet paper, medical supplies, and, sadly enough, women. From what Riven could tell, most of these smaller groups were spread out amid the anarchy without any major leader unifying them just yet . . . but many of the gangs actually bartered and traded with one another within these five categories of goods. Apparently Elysium coins hadn't become a really big hit yet with the local populace, and Riven couldn't blame them. He had yet to see any Elysium altars since getting here, so how was he supposed to spend these damn coins?

Quite frankly, Riven was quite surprised to see that society had fallen so far and so fast as to resort to slavery within weeks of becoming a postapocalyptic wasteland, but Athela wasn't as surprised as he was.

CHAPTER 20

"No, Riven, this is typical of your species," Athela had stated flatly with an uncaring yawn as she watched unspeakable things done to various victims across the city through Jake's vision. "You people call us demons bad, but really there are a lot of humans out there who are easily comparable to the worst of demonkind given the opportunity to obtain power."

Marketplaces had all been looted by this point, and as the dragonflies scouted farther into the city, they found more and more anarchy following suit. The police were gone, either disbanded completely or having hunkered up somewhere farther east, but more than a few cop cars had been flipped over and set ablaze. There were still a couple patches of city blocks where families holed up and tried to wait it out, but more often than not, this was no longer the case. People were becoming frantic, desperate to scramble and fight over the last resources of the old world instead of trying to make something from the new.

They also learned that the monsters in this area, though certainly appearing in small packs or at random, were usually rather weak. There were a few stronger ones, such as the hive-mind dream creatures that'd made their new nest in the recesses of the hospital, but even they were individually weak for the most part. And the scouting revealed only a handful of these stronger creatures. Some of the monsters were also somewhere in between, like that six-legged tiger cat that'd tried pouncing on Riven—but even those weren't very common. They'd seen more wargs, a couple large birds with blade-tipped wings, some semitranslucent mana-wisps that were more passive than other creatures and only attacked if provoked, a large, ugly-looking troll, and even some more war parties of goblins that raided along the outskirts of the city.

Despite all this searching, though, they didn't see any sign of Jose or Allie. Riven was anxious to get out and up aboveground so he could better evaluate where the glowing lights indicated they were—rather than be stuck down here in the basement when the next brief interlude of the system's quest happened again.

Riven spent another three hours exploring the surrounding area using one of Jake's dragonflies. Meanwhile, Ethel—the blonde elf who'd lost part of one arm—had come around. She'd woken up in a state of panic and had taken a lot of time talking to Senna in order to calm down. By the end of their talks, however, both elves were on uneasy speaking terms with Athela, whom they'd taken a hesitant liking to.

The feeling was not entirely mutual, but Athela did her best to put on a face, keep them company, and answer any questions since Riven had gone out of his way to save them. Even if they *were* disgusting elves.

Food distribution was also going very poorly, very fast. Rations were already scarce because most of the food in the hospital had been left upstairs before being sealed off—and the lack of sun made the place feel rather gloomy despite the candlelight. Groups had already started to form in the basement: the handful of nurses with Dr. Brass and Dr. Waters, the few families who'd been here with relatives undergoing surgery around the time of the attack on the hospital, and a number of people who had just been down here to seek refuge and find an out-of-the-way place because the rest of the hospital had been too packed. This didn't include Riven, his demons, or the two elves, of course. These groups generally kept to themselves, except when Dr. Brass came to talk to Riven or Athela about various magic things or to take some of the food rations out to the others, but there was a definite sense of fear whenever other people looked Riven's way. It was the same fear that both elves had expressed when they'd first set eyes on them before Riven and his demons had saved their lives.

"I wouldn't take it personally," Senna bravely stated at the end of the day through a forced smile, speaking to Riven directly for the first time since she'd woken up, as the tattooed husband of the woman who'd called Riven a monster walked by with a stout glare Riven's way. "You're just a threat to them, and your Charisma . . . it's a bit jarring to look at you. Even now. But Charisma is always worst with first impressions, and the longer you know someone, the less their Charisma stat affects you . . ."

Well, that was good to know. Nevertheless Riven was standing, leaning against a wall with a dull look in his eyes. He didn't like the way people were looking at him. They were scared, almost all of them, and other than Dr. Brass and Dr. Waters, none of them wanted anything to do with him.

It probably hadn't helped that they'd taken the corpse of the nurse who'd died to feed on . . . but Riven had been seriously hungry. He wouldn't have lasted much longer that day—given the severe stomach cramps and bloodthirsty way he looked at the people around him until he gave in and sank his fangs into the dead woman's neck. They'd tried to keep it on the down-low, but word had spread like wildfire anyways—and Riven had determined that his silent experiment into how long he could go without feeding on blood had concluded that the time was rather short indeed.

At least, it was short in terms of serious hunger cravings. He didn't know how long he'd last in terms of insanity kicking in.

Even the elves had been scared to death when they'd first laid eyes on him, terrified of when he was going to eat them. So when Senna finally managed to muster the courage to talk that day, both his eyebrows shot sky-high and he did a double take to his right. "Are you talking to me?"

Senna's confident features faltered as his gaze shifted to her, but with an encouraging touch from Athela, who sat on a metal chair next to the bed the elves were still recovering on, she hardened her resolve. "Yes. I also wanted to personally apologize for my rudeness. Our rudeness—"

Senna corrected herself by motioning to her friend Ethel on her right, and her friend quickly nodded with wide green eyes. "We both wanted to apologize. You and your demons have been nothing but kind to us. We are sorry for ignoring you, it's just . . ."

"You're intimidating," Ethel stated bluntly, then she flushed a deep red and tried to cover her face with her hands—only to whimper sadly when she realized she was still missing one of them. She dropped her head, long blond hair falling over her face in a look of utter defeat.

Riven gave them both a warm smile and slowly came over to stand beside the bed, looking down on them. "Thank you both. It means more to me than you realize. I've never been great at making friends. I was worried that becoming what I am now would seriously damper my efforts."

He glanced down at the stump of an arm that Ethel was tearfully staring at, sighing lightly as the beautiful elf never took her eyes off it. The wound was bandaged up nicely, but the bandages had to be changed every day to keep the wound clean. Underneath there was exposed bone, muscle, and granular tissue starting to fill in, even after Athela's original efforts to seal it up with her webbing.

"Are you two doing okay?"

Ethel sniffed, wiped her eyes and nose on the blankets, and adjusted the scant fur top she'd put on the day before. "I'll be okay eventually. Probably not soon, but I know I can overcome this."

Senna gave her friend a sad smile. "You'll be okay, Ethel. Thank you for asking, Riven. As for me, my leg is recovering . . . The infection is under control, from what your Dr. Brass has told me. He said it might take a couple weeks to heal completely, though . . ."

She frowned, wringing her fingers and suddenly seeming lost in her thoughts.

"Worried about your family again?" Athela asked curiously. "That's the look you get whenever you talk about them."

Senna immediately gave a dry chuckle and nodded. "Yes. They likely think we're both dead. If they've found the other bodies by now, then they think the goblins took us to eat."

"Or worse . . ." Ethel mumbled blandly.

Senna nodded and wiped at some of the dirt on her face. "Or worse. My kind has been at war with goblins for as long as I can remember . . . They are the mortal enemies of woodland elves. They breed at rates far beyond my own people, so although one elf warrior may take down many before he or she dies, they just keep coming. They are stupid, greedy, ugly, evil little creatures that kill and eat everything they can. The world would be a better place without them."

She grumbled, swinging her legs over the bed and gingerly putting weight on her good leg—only to cringe and shrink back when she moved her upper body in a way that put pressure on her broken clavicle. "By the gods, I am going to kill those little green men by the scores when I leave this place."

"As am I," Ethel muttered under her breath.

The obvious hate for goblins was only emphasized by the anger visibly showing on both elves' features. They truly meant it when they said they were going to go kill the little green men, Riven had no doubt about that.

He raised a hand to get their attention and posed a question. "Do you have any means of regrowing that arm?"

Both elves looked at him blankly, then Ethel burst into melodic laughter as Senna sputtered.

"Magic to regrow limbs?" Senna repeated as if to make sure she'd heard him right. "Not in our village."

"Didn't your people have magic before the apocalypse?" Riven pressed curiously.

Ethel held up her remaining right hand, calming herself and wiping a tear away. Still smiling and genuinely amused despite the partial loss of her left arm, she waved her stump at him. "The shamans have some basic nature magic in the village, but nothing like what you're talking about. That was funny, though. I needed the laugh. Thanks for that. You know, for a vampire . . . you're quite nice. Athela is great, too, even if she tries to come off as uncaring!"

She beamed up at him, a little shyly at first but growing more confident. "I'll get used to not having my hand, I'm sure. I'm just happy that I'm alive. It's more than we can say for our friends, and I know our families will be happy beyond belief when they realize that Senna and I are still with them."

Riven felt himself flush at her beaming expression and cleared his throat when he caught himself staring—averting his gaze to Athela, who remained narrow-eyed and scowling his way. "Right. I'm glad I made enough of a fool of myself to be amusing, then!"

Azmoth was sipping on a juice box with a poorly hidden smirk through his obsidian-dagger teeth, which frankly looked ridiculous. But as Riven walked by to exit the room, he nudged the vampiric man and whispered so Athela couldn't hear, "Quite the lady-killer."

Riven just flushed even harder, and Azmoth laughed as they both exited.

"I'm not going to give you the satisfaction of replying to that, Azmoth, but I've gotta admit your speech is coming along nicely."

"Thank you, Riven. I've . . . learning fast after listening to all you interact. It's almost entirely what . . . been focusing recently. I still make mistakes, but Athela always quick to correct me. She's good teacher."

Coming down the hall and then to the closet that Athela and Jake had showed him earlier, Riven opened the door and nodded approvingly at the latch in the center of the floor. It was made of steel; the padlock had already been ripped off, and it was big enough for him to easily fit through.

It was time to go exploring.

"This is entrance to sewer systems?" Azmoth asked curiously.

Riven nodded. "Indeed. Funny that a building like this would have it, but I don't think this was always a hospital."

He bent down, gripping the latch and flinging it up to reveal a dark path into the ground. The tunnel was a straight shot down, measuring around six feet in diameter. Rungs had been added on two sides, allowing two different people to go up and down at one time.

Athela had followed along right behind the others, and with a nudge she prodded Riven down the hole. "It's now or never, just like we talked about! Let's go find your sister!"

Azmoth waved down at them, his armored limb slowly moving back and forth in the light of the cinders across his body. He was to stay behind and keep the others safe long enough for them to escape down into the sewers themselves if those dream creatures somehow found a way inside the hospital basement—and if Riven really needed him, the vampire could always portal him to Riven's given location. "Be safe."

Riven gave the demon a friendly grin and a thumbs-up. "Will do, man! Make sure you look after Ethel and Senna; they'll need you to fetch their juice boxes like a good little peasant!"

"I am a B-class demon, you runt! Not a peasant!" Azmoth said with a laugh.

"Yeah, well, I'm still not sure what a B-class is, really—does that stand for 'sissy'?!"

Athela laughed loudly at Azmoth's expression and hiked a thumb Riven's way, pausing her descent. "If he gets us killed down here, just know that I died valiantly trying to save his useless ass as *he* screamed like a sissy!"

Riven scowled back at her over his shoulder, and Azmoth laughed even harder.

"You shut your dirty whore mouth, Athela!" Riven shot back.

"I am a VIRGIN! I've never had the opportunity to be a whore!"

CHAPTER 21

"Oh, shoot, hold that thought! I forgot I needed to check my status page after that fight with the dream creatures. I got some notifications but was busy experiencing that Dao vision . . ." Riven's words trailed off while he was halfway down the ladder into the sewers, and his eyebrows rose in shock.

He'd killed goblins, men, and hundreds of dream creatures over the past two days. He'd been thoroughly caught up in events—so much so that he'd simply failed to check his notifications concerning said level-ups. He hadn't known what to expect since the last time he checked his page, but this . . . this was not it. He'd grown by . . . a lot and had jumped from level 18 to level 27. He had a whopping number of free stat points to use, and preapplied improvements had already been placed.

[Riven Thane's Status Page:
- **Level 27**
- **Pillar Orientations: Unholy Foundation, Blood Specialty, Infernal, Shadow**
- **Core of Original Sin—Gluttony: (Under Construction) (???)**
- **Traits: Race: Pure-blooded Vampire (Extreme Darkness Regeneration) (Sunlight Decay) (Extreme weakness to silver weapons, Sun pillar, and Light pillar attacks), Class: Warlock Adept, Adrenaline Junkie (Blood) (+15% to Agility)**
- **Abilities: Blessing of the Crow (Unholy), Wretched Snare (Unholy), Bloody Razors (Blood), Crimson Ice (Blood), Blood Lance (Blood) (Tier 2), Hell's Armor (Infernal)**
- **Stats: 59 Strength, 116 Sturdiness, 224 Intelligence, 134 Agility, 1 Luck, -335 Charisma, 164 Vampiric Perception, 91 Willpower, 9 Faith**
- **Free Stat Points: 63**

- Minions: Athela, Level 23 Arshakai [36 Willpower Requirement]. Azmoth, Level 24 Hellscape Brutalisk [27 Willpower Requirement].
- Equipped Items: Crude Cultist's Robes (1 def), Vampire's Escort (104 dmg, 102% mana regen, Shadow and Blood dmg +22%, Black Lightning, Scorpion's Sting), Chalgathi Cultist Amulet (???), Leather Boots (1 def), Backpack of Supplies (Guild Hall: Stone Manor), Witch's Ring of Grand Casting (+26 Intelligence), Cloak of the Tundra (22 def, +56 bonus def vs frost), Breath of Valgeshia (48 def, +13 dmg & +9% mana output dmg for blood dmg, 6% mana regen)]

"You're just now looking?" Athela teased with a grin while hanging on the opposite ladder and waggling a finger his way. "You need to be better about that after battles—you killed lots and lots of enemies. Azmoth actually gained a fire breath ability from his level-ups, courtesy of the system. I didn't get any new abilities, but the power boosts were definitely nice."

Riven blinked. "Why do I not feel any different after all these stats were applied?"

"You underwent a Dao vision, didn't you?" Athela stated with a polite smile. "Often Dao visions and inspiration will mask changes to your body. Or, better said, they sometimes come as a result of many gains and help your body and soul integrate the new stats. That isn't always the case, but it certainly was here."

"I see." Riven slammed all sixty-three stat points into Intelligence again, shuddering when he immediately got a killer headache—but he could literally feel his mana channels expanding and a new flux of power flood through his body as he went from 224 Intelligence to 287 Intelligence in an instant.

He shuddered slightly and squeezed the bridge of his nose. It wasn't anything unbearable, but it definitely hurt, and Athela laughed before continuing down the ladder when he shook it off.

They dropped to the bottom soon after, landing on the sewer's main pipeline floor with a set of squeaks from some nearby sewer rats. "Man, that stat boost was a little rough. Athela, were you able to memorize the layout of this place from Jake's maps?"

"Somewhat. I think we'll be fine, and I'll mark our path with webbing to keep us on the right path when we come back."

Riven's feet hit on the stone floor, and he turned, his eyes easily adjusting to the dark without any problem, as what would have appeared black to normal people now appeared in various shades of gray. The tunnel split at a crossroads farther ahead, and the tunnel behind curved around to the left. It was a good thing he and Athela could see in dark places, because otherwise this would have been a real nightmare trip.

Riven watched as rats ran ahead through the waste and trash. Whichever way Riven and Athela looked—there wasn't anything of real interest to them.

It also smelled rather terrible down in the tunnel, and Riven got a really good whiff of it when he walked ahead to a rail posted along the walkway he stood on. In the middle of the sewer was a small river of vile, stagnant liquid, rotting garbage and human feces apparent in the mix of swirling gunk. It likely had once been a moving, flowing river that carried the trash out before the sewer systems had been detached whenever the land had been rearranged with the three worlds merging—but Riven couldn't be sure. He just couldn't see why anyone would let it all stay down here like that—it could cause a serious disease problem if they did.

Or so he assumed.

Athela's bare feet glided over the floor in silent grace, but she grimaced in disgust as the stench hit her nostrils full force. "By the hells, that's disgusting!"

Riven nodded in agreement. "Yes, it certainly is. Now, let's find a way out of here so we can start exploring the city ourselves without having to face any more of those dream beasts. I'm all for leveling up, but who knows how many of those things are out there?"

"And so we can get the naysayers out of our lair!" Athela chimed in, extending one finger to produce a claw and tapping Riven on the head with it.

"Our lair? No way. We're finding somewhere to set up that guild hall I got from Negrada."

Wanting to make the most of their time, they went toward the crossroads. Moving straight ahead instead of following the first rat as it took the path to the right, they continued in silence amid the gloom of the dark underground.

And then, without warning, a new set of prompts appeared for both Athela and Riven to see.

[You have been made a target by a regional quest: Crusade Against the Undead. Benjamin, known as Prophet to many of his followers, has declared a holy war for the control of the city of Brightsville. Enacting a holy ritual and with his request being backed by a minor god, all humans within Brightsville will receive additional Elysium coins, XP toward leveling, and other undisclosed prizes based on performance when culling the undead in this area.]

[You have been offered a guiding system quest from the administrator: Covens—Either find a coven to join or grow your own coven to a minimum number of five vampires including yourself. To create new vampires, you must inject vampiric essence into your target via your fangs. Be wary of doing this too fast, as if you do not recharge your vampiric essence in between attempts to turn others, you will become sick and, in a worst-case scenario, die. Rewards: one portal ticket for an attempt to acquire another piece of Valgeshia's Item Set.]

[You have been offered a guiding system quest from the administrator: Acquire Cattle and Create a Thrall—As a newly born vampire, you will need to acquire cattle, or, in other terms, people to feed on regularly. It does not matter if you do this through persuasion or force. Then after this, select one of these cattle to create a thrall. Thralls are mortals bent to a vampire's will and are essentially more subservient and powerful cattle, as many vampires like to say. Though they do retain their Intelligence, personality, and to some extent their own free will, their desires are instinctively and heavily oriented to align with your own. This places them in the minion category of your status page when acquired successfully. Thralls also acquire some vampiric strengths, although they are able to retain their own pillars and abilities outside the vampiric influence. However: retained pillars and abilities will be corrupted—sometimes modifying them slightly for better or worse. Lastly, thralls are able to provide greater amounts of nourishing blood than normal mortal cattle do, and their bloodlines may be modified over time to evolve to your liking. To create a thrall, you must feed on them regularly for an extended period of time, and they must in turn feed on your blood numerous times throughout their initial evolutionary cycle. Reward upon acquiring thrall: one combat level, a stable food source, and a new avenue to acquire minions.]

[You have been offered a guiding system quest from the administrator: Kill the Dream Creatures—Kill the dream creatures building a nest over the hospital's basement before they grow in power and become a larger threat to the surrounding area. As the hivemind dream creatures feed on souls, they will continue to grow in strength and numbers over time. Time limit: thirty days. Rewards: one Elysium altar.]

"Huh?" Riven muttered, cocking his head to the side with his hands on his hips. Not a moment later, he felt Athela repeatedly jab him in the side excitedly.

"Ooooh! OOOHHHH, OOOOOOHHHHH! Look at these!" Athela crowed, continuing to jab excitedly at her master's rib cage until he swatted her along the back of her head. Scowling up at him, she flipped him off. "Jerk."

"Is it normal to get system quests like this?"

"Early into integrations it is. After that, when the world has been settled down and trials have been completed for failure or success, they're harder to come by."

"So other people across the planet are also getting quests like these?"

"To greater or lesser extents, yes. It's usually all individualized."

A bubble rose up out of the sewage, causing both of them to look over to their right with tensed muscles—but they relaxed when they saw it was just another rat making its way out of the disgusting mess down here.

Athela waved a dismissive hand in front of them as they started to walk again. "Meh. Let's get a move on and worry about the quests later. We need to find your sister, and being underground when the system pings her location again won't be any help to us."

Riven had to agree. "Yeah, that's true. However I'm not exactly overly enthusiastic about these other quests, either. Creating a coven is one thing, but creating a thrall sounds rather awful. Semi-evil, even."

Athela let out a snickering laugh. "Oh, you're so soft. Look, it's either create a thrall or two or go around and hunt people. Even if you let them go after feeding, do you really think their families and friends or the communities you're preying on won't come for you?" She gave him a wry smile. "Let's be realistic here. Thralls are an evolution and adaptation that vampires perfected over countless millennia in order to keep and maintain willing participants that they feed on. There is always the other option of actually enslaving people, which is another common method many of the vampiric societies throughout the multiverse work with, but I don't see you being that kind of person."

"There's a thin line between slavery and making thralls, or at least that's how it appears to me."

"True, but many people will willingly give themselves up to a vampire in order to acquire power. Being a thrall isn't all bad as long as you have a good vampiric master. Think of it like a demonic contract, only that the strict set of rules has been replaced with urges to further the agenda of whatever vampire created them."

Riven blinked. "Will thralls require Willpower stat points as well?"

"Yes. It even said that doing so is another avenue to creating minions, right?"

"Well, you can add needing more Willpower to the list of reasons why I won't do it. I'm already going to be investing in all my demonic contracts, and each demon will need more and more Willpower with every evolution. Too many minions will mean I'll stifle my own growth."

"Oh, just think about it. Class upgrades will also increase the amount of Willpower you get if you choose the right ones. Your thrall's bloodline evolutions will also upgrade with your personal Willpower, a lot like how my evolution required additional Willpower. However, when a thrall dies, they're *dead* dead.

Not banished-to-the-nether-realms dead. That's the big difference between us demons and a thrall when using them to fight. Got it?"

"I get it, but I still don't like it. I'll think about it, though, and if there is a unique situation where someone actively wants to become my thrall, I guess it wouldn't be too bad. But there won't be any slavery or forcing them to do it against their will. I refuse to do that. What I don't get is the other quest concerning creating new vampires—it says I have to inject my vampiric essence into my target and not to do it too fast or I'll die."

"That one I can't help you with, sorry. I have no idea how to inject vampiric essence into anything."

Riven pulled up his status sheet and then reviewed the quest log again. "I guess it'll have to wait then. I'll figure it out. The problem is finding people we trust enough to create vampires out of . . . and honestly, I'm not even sure being a vampire is all that great. It's definitely a power boost, but at what cost? Each additional vampire will also mean finding ways to feed them, too, and we would all need to be sustained on the blood of mortals."

Having a rather surreal feeling about being contacted by the administrator about this, Riven shook his head and continued ahead while motioning for Athela to follow. He wondered how many other people had been contacted about such outrageous things. How many billions of people were struggling to survive right now? How many other unique scenarios or quests had been given out, like the Chalgathi trials? What were the other people who'd escaped Chalgathi's starter event doing now? Why had they been chosen to participate? He still had so many questions and so few answers it made his head hurt.

They continued on another fifteen minutes and took another right, coming to an immediate stop as both of them saw a blur of movement at the far end of the next passage. Dim moonlight illuminated the far end of the tunnel through an open manhole—easily discernible to both Riven and Athela.

Athela nudged him with narrowed eyes, and all six of her arachnoid legs came out to stand poised for a strike. She was still working on regaining her arachnid form via shape-shifting and likely would have transitioned here due to the tight space in the tunnels around them, but she'd been struggling with shape-shifting beyond what'd been expected and could only stay in her demonic humanoid form.

"Did you see that?"

Riven silently stared into the dark from underneath his hood, crimson irises scanning the area intensely as he gripped his black staff more firmly. For the second time since they'd come down into the sewers, the filthy waters of trash and sewage in the middle of the tunnel weren't stagnant. Ripples in the dark waters originating from farther up passed them by.

"Yes, I did see that . . ."

He looked over the railing, not noting anything else or anything that was an obvious threat. He pushed ahead a little bit more, again seeing nothing new, and Athela began crawling up the tunnel's wall and onto the ceiling in absolute silence to scout out the area. He scratched the back of his neck, blood vapor blowing out of the holes in his runic mask, and was about to take another step forward when he began to hear the faint sounds of a heartbeat only a few feet from him.

Then the tunnel exploded into motion.

CHAPTER 22

A lithe, snakelike figure measuring at the very least a couple dozen feet tore up through the trash and scummy water at insane speed, its roar an earth-trembling screech. The creature was covered in armored, spiked chitin, with a round mouth full of rows of teeth. It had no eyes and two large pincers in the front of its maw but no legs.

[Infantile Spiked Wyrm, Great Beast]

Riven didn't have time to take in the rest of the creature—not entirely sure just how big it was considering part of its body was still submerged—as he screamed at a pitch unbecoming of a fully grown man and instantly activated Riftwalk.

A black fissure in space erupted directly behind him and swallowed him whole, ripping him into it and sending him teleporting backward out the other end of the fissure as he barely managed to avoid a stone-crunching body slam.

CRASH

Riven instantaneously exited the spatial fissure in a burst of shadows ten yards down the tunnel, grinning with excitement at the utter shock of almost dying. The pincers tore through the stone floor where the opposite end of the portal had been just a moment ago, making Riven's heart beat fast as he realized how close to death they'd just come, and his staff lit up with crackling power with the mana he began to channel into it.

"MOTHERFUCKER!" Riven's excitement and simultaneous rage boiled over, and with an outstretched hand he unleashed a piercing Blood Lance. The red projectile rocketed toward the armored creature, which squealed and screeched, the magic ripping into the long body while it struggled to dislodge its pincers from the stone floor.

If only he had more bodies and blood to utilize. Unlike the last battlefield, he didn't have the luxury of free resources—so he'd have to make do with his own innate mana.

Snarling with bloodlust and focused on the thing that would dare attack them, Riven reengaged with a burst of Black Lightning from his staff that shredded and cooked one side of the creature. His outstretched weapon radiated an aura of malice and tore thick plates of chitin completely off, entering the creature's head just above where the right pincer was. Immediately after that, six red ribbons of hardened webbing flew through the air and slammed into the creature's side—sending bits of the snakelike insectoid's body airborne while it screeched even louder.

WHAM

Athela catapulted off the ceiling, her bare shin colliding hard against the beast, cracking more chitin plates while her bladed spider legs pierced deep into the squealing creature to hold her down as her claws blurred. Each strike applied necrotic venom, and her deeply entrenched spider legs pumped it in continuously. Digging into the beast ferociously, her tongue ripped out of her abnormally widened mouth and began digging into the creature's side—sucking it dry while it was still alive in a horrific display of carnage.

But the creature was an absolute tank, and with a screech it ripped out of the floor and yanked its head back so fast that it nearly crushed Athela up against the tunnel's ceiling. Athela barely managed to yank herself out of the beast and flip off its back, but she was caught in midair by a sideswipe of one of the pincers. She was sent sprawling head over heels down the sewer, splashing into the muck amid a writhing, forty-foot-long body that sought out its prey with avid conviction.

A rapid series of strikes tried to catch Riven off guard, each one of them tearing stone out of the sewer's walkway with bites that'd easily cleave him in half. He jumped, dodged, and rolled while desperately batting away the few strikes he couldn't avoid with his staff. Each time his staff made contact, a burst of shadows and a knock-back effect would counter the monster's massive strength, but it'd also send Riven reeling backward because he didn't have the Sturdiness to take these hits without being thrown off his feet.

"SHIT!"

BOOM

Stone shrapnel scattered in all directions, and a deep gash quickly opened up on Riven's stomach where he'd almost been eviscerated.

He snarled and clashed with the monster again, using his staff like a baseball bat and smacking the creature in the side of the face with all his Strength and a little bit of mana infusion for an extra effect of Black Lightning. The combination of the knock-back effect with the shadow explosion and the black lightning being channeled into it was doubly effective and would have taken out any normal human like a bug under a boot.

WHAM-CRACK-ZAP

The Black Lightning channeled from his body into the staff sent the creature into a brief spasm and it flailed about, causing the walls to shake in a violent temper tantrum before it let out a hiss of anger. Zeroing in on him again, the wyrm made a choking sound—opened its throat—and shot out an enormous glob of acidic mucus.

Riven Riftwalked again, this time teleporting behind the creature with steady footing to avoid the attack altogether. Where he'd been just a moment before was now being eaten away, smoke rising from the point of impact where the acid had landed on the walkway.

The tunnel shook.

SMASH-THUD

He felt himself gasp as the air left his body just as the creature's tail whipped out of the muck and slapped him hard across the side—launching him right into the tunnel wall like a bruised pancake. If he hadn't been turned into a vampire with the Sturdiness he currently had, he'd have definitely been dead.

"RRRAAAAAAAHHHHHHHH!!!!" Athela's scream of rage was quickly followed up by a blur of black, red, and white. She blurred forward, easily outpacing any movement Riven had ever seen her perform before when she made a mad dash to get to him before the pincers of the monster did.

Athela's claws clashed with the huge pincers right before they closed around his body, and the demoness snarled something at the monster in a language Riven didn't understand before her long, slender, pitch-black tongue snaked out of her mouth again and slashed into the insides of the monster's gaping throat.

The creature reeled backward and twisted, but Athela followed.

Snorting and trying to clear his head, he reoriented his surroundings and watched Athela grip a chitin spike while riding the wyrm.

She spun around the creature's body lightning fast, using her webs to launch herself to and from the ceiling or sides of the tunnel with in-and-out dash attacks that left him almost speechless while inflicting incredible amounts of necrotic venom buildup. Even now, black patches were forming across the exposed fleshy bits where the chitin had been ripped off or damaged.

Unfortunately for Athela, she got a little too carried away and failed to check a blind spot despite Riven's shout of warning.

SNAP

Athela screamed in pain, and one of her arachnid legs went flying through the air, completely torn off when the creature had properly identified her path of attack and countered.

It head-bashed Athela into the murky ground after that, following up her stunned state with repeated head bashes as she screamed and cried out.

Though she might be able to come back with a blood price, hearing her whimpering cries made Riven absolutely furious. A hot rage unlike anything he'd experienced before began to seethe in the very depths of his soul, and a violent, silent roar echoed within his mind.

He was on the precipice of a breakthrough, and he'd been in a constant state of enlightenment since his last vision. Here, in this moment, spurred on by his rage, the insights began to re-form. Riven's thoughts flashed with a vision of his recent dream. A blood moon, the storm, a mountain of corpses rising up out of a red ocean, the three thralls that surrounded him as they called a self-proclaimed king back home, and the nova explosion to announce the king's return. His hands blurred instinctively, without thought, rhyme, reason, or practice. It was as if he'd always known how to do it, and his body just reacted. Immaculate hand gestures were intertwined with the proper intent, meaning, visualization, and a perfect understanding of what was about to happen without knowing why he knew. He tossed his staff to his left, letting it hover there next to him of its own accord. His fingers twisted and incorporated complex two hand patterns, unlocking the seals that would allow him back-door access to the spell he wanted to perform.

And then he had it. It was just a whisper, a voice of some long-lost ancestor gently pushing thoughts into his mind, but it was certain. With all the other parts performed, he uttered the chant that would seal this monster's fate. "NEFAJIA CRECUS BLOOD NOVA!"

[Tier 3 Blood Spell: Blood Nova, has been discovered and added to your status page.]

[Blood Nova's mandatory eight-hour cooldown has been triggered.]

The creature lunged for him, huge pincers each the size of one of his legs open wide with rows of spiny teeth right behind them.

But it was not fast enough.

A sphere of bright crimson blood quickly began forming between Riven's cupped hands, quicky rotating and picking up speed as a bright-red glow illuminated the passageway. The sphere grew in equal stride with the rate of spinning and the brightness of the red glow until it reached the size of a bowling ball. Thrusting his hands forward to release the energy was like trying to push back a freight train, but he managed to do it—and in that instant, space shattered.

First the area immediately around him was ripped apart, sending a shock wave of crimson energy in an area-of-effect explosion centered right on top of his head. Stone melted away and the incoming monster was blown back, shattering its skull and pincers in an instant. Then the glowing, spherical crimson torpedo tore through the tunnel with an aftershock as it grew to nearly the size of the entire tunnel and then broke the sound barrier. Ripples of power scattered the ambient mana in the air and left a vacuum in the passage behind it as it expanded and burst like a missile from hell.

CRASH

The entire tunnel shook, and Riven was thrown backward by the secondary part of the spell as the creature's huge body just burst open like a shaken can of soda pop that'd had a couple dozen Mentos dropped into it. The huge monster just simply ceased to exist, and its remains were scattered to all sides of the tunnel—top, bottom, left, and right for dozens of yards. At the end of the tunnel there was a large, gaping hole in the side of the wall where exposed earth was trickling in, and a cloud of dust quickly filled the air, causing Riven to cough.

His ears rang from the sound of the impact and his body felt incredibly weak, as if he'd just sprinted five miles without a break. He had a headache that felt like a jackhammer had been tapping against his skull for the past week. But he remained in control, and his red eyes simmered with remnants of the power he'd just unleashed—accompanied by a confident grin underneath his runic mask.

[You have gained one combat level. Please visit your status page to assign stat points.]

A sack of coins dropped somewhere within the canal, splashing in the muck that hadn't been sent flying by his spell while he continued to vomit. His world began to spin slightly, but he rested with one hand on the wall to stabilize himself for a few seconds until the dizzy spell passed.

Unfortunately the fight wasn't over yet.

Three much smaller versions of the creature he'd just killed surfaced from the murky, disgusting sewage waste like bullets out of a gun and lunged for him. One skewered his right shoulder, causing him to scream in anger and roll left to grapple with it as the other two overshot their mark due to the premature attack of the first.

Feeling the pincers of the three-foot-long monster sink deep into his ligaments and muscle, he snarled and grabbed it by the base of its neck. He channeled his rage, feeling mana flood his Infernal subpillar inside the depths of his soul as he activated Hell's Armor. Power ripped through his mana channels with brilliant flames, exploding across the tunnel in all directions to roast the little bastards with incinerating heat.

The creatures abruptly died, withering under a torrent of hellfire that roasted them alive, but his attention was quickly diverted again at another noise just as he deactivated Hell's Armor and the inferno died down.

CHAPTER 23

CRASH

The tunnel echoed as yet another one of the larger creatures made itself known. A good thirty feet in length and coming down from a side passage, it ripped around the corner at breakneck speed with pincers gnashing and chitin plates scraping loudly along the stone walls. Gunk and sewage splashed like it was in the middle of a tsunami, and a horde of the smaller wyrms followed in its path—some of them crushed under the mad rush of the bigger one.

But that supplied Riven with the environmental resources he needed to excel.

Riven's hand shot out, and the crushed corpses of the smaller wyrms went up in a light show, bathing the entire underground tunnel system in an ominous red glow as Crimson Ice ripped from their bodies and rocked the huge creature with dozens of spikes right before Athela's figure blurred forward. Leaving huge lacerations along the underbelly of the monster, Athela swung around the beast with one of her webs and vaulted back down. With an audible crunch, all of her remaining arachnoid legs buried deep in the beast's skull like spears. It twitched a couple times, splashing in the muck, but eventually it settled down in death while Athela dodged gobbets of acidic bile being spat at her from farther down the tunnel.

Dozens of coin pouches dropped into the water just seconds later, each of them marking the site of the death of a beast they'd killed, yet the fight was still not yet won.

Earlier Riven hadn't been able to pick up the heartbeats of these creatures until they were very close by—perhaps they had much smaller hearts than most creatures—but something behind him from beyond the battle was quickly picking up tempo and approaching him with its heartbeat ticking up in speed as it closed the distance.

This was something new.

Riven turned to see what was rushing him, temporarily leaving Athela to deal with the wyrms, and cursed when he saw a gigantic ratlike ogre barreling down on him with the speed of a freight train.

The brown-furred creature was semihumanoid, with large yellow eyes, a scar running down its face, and large, sharpened front teeth. It wore spiked metal knuckles almost akin to gauntlets and a leather armor chest piece with a belt and pack strapped at its side. Its huge, muscular arms reminded him of a gorilla's, and the beast roared in excitement about twenty yards out.

To Riven's confusion, though, its large ears perked up upon seeing him, and it actually hopped to the other side of the tunnel to avoid running him over. It clearly gave him a quizzical look, stopping in its tracks, and started participating in a short staring contest, then rushed farther in to begin helping Athela kill the swarms of wyrms that she was battling not far off.

Riven blinked. This was a friendly monster? He quickly tried to identify it and raised his eyebrows in surprise.

[Rat Man]

Huh. How interesting.

Getting up onto his feet, he flung another spiraling arc of Black Lightning that blasted through a number of the swarming wyrms. Then, summoning a batch of Bloody Razors that bloomed in the air about him, he sent over a dozen of the blades spinning through the air—utilizing their minor lock-on features to twist around Athela and their new ally before ripping through the still-incoming swarm.

The rat man and Athela were going ballistic, tearing through one after another of the endless tide of these creatures while Riven supported them with a barrage of magic. Athela was quick and nimble, easily dodging most of the acidic gobbets the smaller creatures aimed at her and using her claws, blades, and sharp, elongating tongue to rip wyrms apart. Meanwhile, the rat man smashed everything in sight and just took the acidic barrage head-on without any real effect.

Riven was curious just what the rat man was made of, if that acid that'd eaten through stone didn't put any damage on him, but he was just glad it wasn't another enemy to contend with.

It had become an all-out battle zone.

Spike wyrmlings died by the dozens as they clashed with Athela and the rat man. Even more died as wave after wave of Bloody Razors flew through the tunnel over the heads of Riven's allies to crash into the oncoming hordes of enemies—though Riven occasionally had to wait in between casting times to let his mana recharge with the help of his staff, and he found himself occasionally smashing his weapon into some of the wyrms that had made it past the two front-line fighters with explosions of on-hit shadow magic. More of the larger spiked wyrmlings joined the fight, and Riven quickly found himself yearning for his new Tier 3 Blood Nova spell—but the mandatory eight-hour cooldown was kind of a bummer. Just one of those spells would have torn through the entire tunnel and wiped out the swarm in a single go. Occasionally he was able to use environmental blood for a cascade of ice spikes and take out another large section of enemies, but corpses and their fluids could only be drained once before the blood magic started to dissipate into something less energy-dense.

However, he couldn't really blame himself for using Blood Nova prematurely. He hadn't even known he could use the spell until now and had no real explanation for how he'd learned it. Had that dream been a Dao vision? Or had it been some kind of vampiric lineage thing where he'd come up with the memories of an ancestor? He had no idea.

Regardless, he was just happy this unknown rat man had arrived—as he was quite the fighter and was keeping up with Athela in kills. The rat man's arms or gauntleted fists would occasionally light up in a dull green, empowering his physical strikes, and his skin was often coated in a similarly colored light to deflect attacks or repair wounds. Riven briefly thought about summoning Azmoth down here but thought better of it when he was more certain they had a handle on things.

[You have gained one combat level. Please visit your status page to assign stat points.]

[You have gained one combat level. Please visit your status page to assign stat points.]

Twenty minutes later, the tunnel was littered with corpses. The huge rat man was covered in small wounds, huffing in pain and pulling himself to sit up against a wall. Meanwhile, Athela was sprawled atop a pile of the small corpses.

Riven and Athela likely would have been able to handle the battle themselves, but he was still appreciative that this creature had come to his aid. He gave the unknown rat man a thumbs-up and a head nod of thanks from a wary distance. "Appreciate the help."

The muscular rat man just nodded in silence, still panting against a wall.

The next few minutes were spent collecting the pouches of coins that'd dropped into the muck of the sewer—or what he could find, anyways. The pouches always disappeared shortly after he'd obtained the coins, leaving him with mostly clean Elysium coins of bronze, silver, and gold to add to his backpack's collection. Reviewing his status sheet, he also saw that he had collected over three thousand coins just from this one fight alone, and on top of that he'd also grown three levels. It was likely the best single haul for a fight other than the prize he'd gotten from Dungeon Negrada's bet with Chalgathi.

Riven applied his remaining stat points and focused more than he'd normally do into Willpower upon reviewing his status page, as he'd been ignoring that stat compared to Intelligence. Azmoth and Athela needed those points for future evolutions, and he would likely be obtaining a third minion soon. That, and he applied a couple points to Luck. He wasn't sure what Luck did, exactly, other than brief explanations from the system or Athela on how it was able to sway events in marginally small degrees, but one Luck was the bare minimum. It certainly wouldn't hurt to occasionally dump a point into it here or there considering it was his second-lowest stat.

[Riven Thane's Status Page:
- **Level 30**
- **Pillar Orientations: Unholy Foundation, Blood Specialty, Infernal, Shadow**
- **Core of Original Sin—Gluttony: (Under Construction) (???)**
- **Traits: Race: Pure-blooded Vampire (Extreme Darkness Regeneration) (Sunlight Decay) (Extreme weakness to silver weapons, Sun pillar, and Light pillar attacks), Class: Warlock Adept, Adrenaline Junkie (Blood) (+15% to Agility)**
- **Abilities: Blessing of the Crow (Unholy), Wretched Snare (Unholy), Bloody Razors (Blood), Crimson Ice (Blood), Blood Lance (Blood) (Tier 2), Blood Nova (Blood) (Tier 3), Hell's Armor (Infernal)**
- **Stats: 61 Strength, 120 Sturdiness, 295 Intelligence, 142 Agility, 5 Luck, -341 Charisma, 166 Vampiric Perception, 105 Willpower, 9 Faith**
- **Minions: Athela, Level 25 Arshakai [36 Willpower Requirement]. Azmoth, Level 24 Hellscape Brutalisk [27 Willpower Requirement].**
- **Equipped Items: Crude Cultist's Robes (1 def), Vampire's Escort (104 dmg, 102% mana regen, Shadow and Blood dmg +22%, Black Lightning, Scorpion's Sting), Chalgathi Cultist Amulet (???), Leather Boots (1 def), Backpack of Supplies (Guild Hall: Stone Manor), Witch's Ring of Grand Casting (+26 Intelligence), Cloak of the Tundra (22 def, +56 bonus def vs frost), Breath of Valgeshia (48 def, +13 dmg & +9% mana output dmg for blood dmg, 6% mana regen)]**

Other than needing the Willpower for Athela and Azmoth, he wasn't entirely throwing out the idea of acquiring a thrall, either. Honestly, he hated the idea of slavery, but if he could find someone who'd do it of their own free will, then he'd be all for the idea. Athela said some people did it for the power boost they got by being a thrall, so he was holding out hope. He was already working on ways of selling the idea to potential mortals that he could use as a frequent food source, as he was deathly afraid of going berserk and killing someone else like he'd done to that poor sod in Dungeon Negrada when he first turned. His vampiric body back then had been completely devoid of mortal blood, and it'd gotten someone killed without Riven even realizing what he was doing until after the fact.

Coming out of this thoughtful trance, Riven couldn't help but give a strained laugh upon seeing how filthy both he and Athela were. His body ached everywhere after pushing so much magic through it, but his new Intelligence stat points had enabled him to pour out power far beyond what he'd have normally been able to do. He also had numerous small wounds and two large ones on his torso, but they were healing rather fast—even to the naked eye. He looked down to evaluate his mending body, seeing his flesh heal so rapidly that he could witness the skin growing over just a minute later after having taken a pincer entirely through that shoulder.

So this was what vampiric regeneration was like. Given he was in a dark tunnel and wasn't so sure it'd work like this out in broad daylight—given the key phrase *extreme darkness regeneration* listed on his status page.

Athela, on the other hand, was in worse shape. She was panting, grimacing, and there was a large wound along her thigh, along with the spots on her back where her spider legs had been ripped off. That first monster they'd fought had been the biggest of the bunch, though, even compared to the other large wyrms, so thankfully she hadn't lost any more limbs after that. She gave him a weak smile and limped over to him to meet him halfway as he waded through the muck toward her, ankle-deep in sewage. Putting her head on his chest and wrapping her arms around him, she gave him a weak hug. "You made me worried there, Riven. Glad you're okay."

Riven grinned, hugging her back and examining her for any other serious wounds. "Just glad you're okay, too. Are you needing to go back to the nether realms for a bit? You look rough."

She nodded solemnly, then let go and gave a backward glance at the rat man. "I'll go recover, but if you need me, I'll be ready to hop right back here. Or you can take Azmoth with you. Talk to you later."

A portal appeared in the tunnel to swallow Athela whole, leaving Riven and the rat man staring at each other in silence for almost an entire minute before Riven made a move to get closer to the large creature. It was still breathing heavily from the exertion of fighting so much, occasionally glancing over at the mountain of corpses. However, as Riven got back up onto the walkway along the tunnel's side, he definitely recognized intelligence in the rat man's eyes, and the creature's ears perked up when Riven sat down a couple feet away.

"Again, thanks for the help," Riven stated, removing his mask to reveal his face and placing it on the blood-covered stone next to him. His staff leaned up against the wall while he crossed his legs. "Can you understand me?"

The rat man blinked twice, then coughed and spat out something like a hairball. Its scarred features quickly turned back to Riven, however, and its hairless tail flitted back and forth while it removed its bloodied, spiked gauntlets. "I can-can."

CHAPTER 24

The rat man's voice was definitely a little on the rough side of raspy, and it was only moderately deep. Not nearly as deep as Riven had expected. It also sounded like he'd been hacking fur balls all day. "Why do you come-walk here in upper-top of the dark-black of the tunnel-ground?"

Well. This rat man certainly had an odd way of speaking, but Riven could deal with it. "I was trapped and had to get out using this sewer system."

"Trapped-stuck? Have you been-visited here much-a lot in your time since the integration-fall?"

"No, this is actually my first time. Are there more of you?"

"Of me-me?"

"Yeah, more of you rat people."

"Oh. You humans-apes not know-see us down here. We try not to visit-see your people-humans if we can avoid-hide. But yes, many-lots of us-we are down in the tunnels-ground. The underdark has lots-many species, with us-we being just one. Many caves-pits down here, a new world-planet in the dark-black that is not for human-apes to see. But you are vampire-bat; you are not normal human-ape. Not drow-elf, either, but still home to dark-black. As a member-rat of my nest-brood, I welcome you to our part-home of the underdark."

The rat man gave his best version of a smile, which was a little bit freaky, truth be told—but Riven smiled back, subconsciously flexing his fangs and quickly retracting them a second after. The words the rat man had used . . . *drow-elf*, *dark-black*, and *underdark* all pointed to one thing he'd previously read about in fantasy novels.

"The underdark? A second world in the dark-black? You're saying there are lots of different species down here in cave systems?"

The rat man seemed confused by the question. "Yes-yes, lots-many."

"Interesting. So what's your name?" Riven held out his hand to shake. "Mine is Riven. Nice to meet you."

The rat man curiously looked down at the extended hand, then back out at Riven. "What is this-this? Do you want-need something from me-I?"

Riven chuckled. "No, we shake hands to greet one another where I'm from."

The rat man looked back down, then his huge, gnarled fingers reached out to grip Riven's own. They shook, the rat man being intentionally gentle so as to not crush Riven's fingers, which Riven appreciated immensely.

"My name-sign is Snagger. Me-me is warrior-killer."

"Snagger? Good name. Are all rat men as big as you?"

The rat looked startled for a moment, then gave out a squeaky laugh that was actually kinda cute. "I was born-made for fighting-killing with claws-teeth and strength-body. I am a fighter-killer for my nest. Most rat-kin are small-short when compared to me-me."

"Gotcha. Well, have you been around humans or vampires before? You looked rather surprised to see me down here."

Snagger and Riven talked for a few hours as the rat man recovered. Riven, on one hand, wanted to leave to find his sister, but on the other hand, he didn't want to leave Snagger alone after the rat man had helped him fight off the wyrms. He didn't know how many other wyrms were down here, and he wouldn't just let Snagger fend for himself when he'd so selflessly defended Riven and Athela.

And because of that, Riven got to know a lot more about Snagger's people as well as the so-called underdark while he waited for the rat man to recover. It was absolutely fascinating, and some of it pertained directly to Riven.

The underdark was a vast, complex network of cave systems that'd been native to the planet Zazir prior to integration and merging of the three worlds. In the truest sense of the words, it was another world. If Snagger wasn't exaggerating, there were thousands of kingdoms, countries, and nests of creatures down here—and Snagger, as a forward scout, said these tunnels led directly to where his nest was located on the fringe of the underdark.

Most of the species living down here were able to see in the dark, obviously. They included certain types of dwarves, rat-kin, gnomes, dark elves or drow, trolls, certain types of goblins, and a much larger variety of not-so-intelligent species. What was most interesting to Riven, though, was that there were actually certain types of demons that lived down in the underdark, too, and beyond that, Snagger claimed there were actually vampire communes as well. Snagger hadn't been overly surprised to see Riven when he'd identified him as a vampire because of that, though he had been surprised about the eyes.

"Most eyes don't glow-shine like you-yours," Snagger said confidently while stretching an injured arm out. "I not-no talk to vampire-bat people often-much; they think they better-good than we-we. But I never see-watch them have bright-glow eyes like you-you."

"The glowing red eyes aren't normal for vampires?"

"No-no. They are red-dull, not red-bright. I not know why-how, but you are different."

Well, that was curious. Riven thoughtfully scratched his chin and nodded slowly. "I wouldn't know—I just recently changed. Anyways, I have to go find my sister, and my demon companion is likely healed by now. Would it be all right if we met up sometime? I'm very interested in seeing what your people are like and maybe visiting the nest, if you will allow it."

Snagger gave Riven the most joyful, teeth-filled smile he'd seen in a very long time. "Yes-yes! Clan mother will be happy-joy to have vampire-bat friends! We are looking for ally-friends in new world-dark, since we have been stranded-lost down here. The underdark twisted-shifted, and other colonies-nests no longer present-here."

So the underdark had been rearranged, too, then.

Riven gave Snagger another handshake, noting that he was good to go again and not as exhausted as he'd initially been postfight. "Good. The same can be said for me. I'm very much looking forward to meeting you all—do you want to set up a spot for some time in maybe a week or two?"

"Yes! Follow me-me, I will show you to spot-area where we meet-arrive!"

Athela was summoned back after that, and her wounds had completely healed. Something about being in the nether realms for periods of time let the demons he'd contracted with heal up quite quickly, though not as fast as his extreme regeneration. Thankfully they also didn't bump into any more monsters and safely found a way out of the sewers not long after Riven had resummoned his minion.

The manhole from the sewers led them into a fenced-off area meant for city maintenance people back on Earth. The cover had been thrown to the side, and there was a man's stripped corpse not far off that was beginning to attract flies in the dead of night. There was also an open shed that had probably once contained tools but now only held a desk, a broken chair, and empty racks. Beyond the chain-link fence and through an open gate where a broken padlock hung was an apartment complex—and then the rest of the small city was sprawled out beyond it.

They were still on the city's western edge, though a little farther to the northeast than the hospital had been. Moonlight dimly illuminated the landscape along with a myriad of stars, and without the light pollution Riven had been so used to, he was able to make out extraordinary sights amid the cosmos. Beautiful nebulas, a comet shooting overhead, and what was probably a distant planet due to the size and orange color were obvious in the clear sky above—though he knew it probably wasn't the Milky Way anymore. In the distance across the city, fires still burned, and the occasional gunshot was heard. Once, while pondering the sights, they even heard a far-off scream, and he hoped that his friend and sister weren't some of the victims of whatever violence was happening right then.

Riven shook off his cloak, half tempted to leave the disgusting thing beside the manhole. Hopefully the stench would somewhat alleviate itself after it had time to dry, but stat bonuses were stat bonuses. So he kept it on.

Not that he had anything else to wear aside from the clothes currently on his back anyways.

"That motherfucking . . ." Riven trailed off, angrily mumbling to himself about the monster swarm attack and wringing out his other smelly clothes before strapping his bag to his back again.

Athela suppressed a laugh.

"Maybe we can stop by a clothing store?" Athela suggested a minute later, covering her nose when he stood up and groaned. "You still smell terrible."

He glared her way. "That's probably a good idea. If we see any, then we will, but by now they're probably all looted."

"For clothes? Really?"

Riven shrugged. "Wouldn't put it past people. The last pandemic on Earth had everyone scrounging for *toilet paper*. People are fucking animals, ANIMALS, I say! Clothes definitely wouldn't be off the list, and they'll get even more valuable as time goes on."

She smirked, her red eyes narrowing, then she shrugged and leaned against the chain-link fence while looking over at the apartment complex. "All right. So now that we've found an exit, what's the plan?" She waved across the landscape around them. "Mass murder everyone until we find Jose and your sister, Allie?"

Riven snorted with amusement. "No mass murder. Sorry."

Athela put on a pouty face and crossed her arms as crickets started chirping nearby. "Well, what do we do?"

"We explore a bit, and in the meantime we wait for the quest pings to light up their locations. We weren't able to see what area of the city they were in because we were underground in a basement, but now that we're outside, we'll be able to get a good idea."

"Ugghh!!! Nooo!!! Let's go kill stuff!!! That last fight was fun!" Athela stamped her foot angrily in the dirt and was about to retort when a gunshot rang out from the apartment complex at their backs. They turned as one, and a flurry of gunfire followed the initial shot with resounding screams and flashes of light on the third floor.

Then the apartment building's top blew off in a flash of white light, which was quickly followed up with subsequent blasts of teal and black fire that took out a nearby wall. One of the buildings began to collapse, and people started running from where they'd apparently been packed inside like rats.

Somewhat startled by the not-so-far-off eruption of fighting, cursing, and screams, Riven and Athela quickly focused their attention on the nearby complex, where dozens of humans wearing varieties of makeshift armor flared up with gold and white fires, forming a line and yelling at one another before a wave of undead scrambled out from the other side of the collapsing building and through an alley. Skeletons wielding hatchets, swords, shields, or just their claws came barreling ahead in a wave that crashed into the terrified defenders.

Meanwhile, crying women and children were trying to flee the scene where their husbands and brothers held the line against the oncoming horde of Unholy creatures—running right on past the spot where Riven and Athela stood gawking at the scene.

The holy caster threw up a large barrier between their group and the oncoming tide of death, only for it to shatter when a powerful surge of death magic slammed into it—sending some of those at the front line smoking and dead onto the cement and causing the screaming caster to reel with backlash damage from his failed spell.

"SHE'S COMING!" one of the soldiers screamed, fear causing his voice to shake. Sweat beaded down his forehead, and his shoddy club flared with purifying light. "IT'S HER! THIS IS NOT A FIGHT WE CAN WIN!"

Yet the rest of the line held, and with stoic expressions they met what they knew to be their end at the claws and weapons of the skeletal horde with screams of rage—all in order to buy their loved ones time to escape. No one bothered replying to the man, for in their hearts they knew he was right.

CRUNCH-SNAP-WRENCH

The warriors entered the melee and were quickly overtaken due to sheer numbers. The lone caster in the back line regained his senses and sent holy fires blasting into the oncoming enemies, but a palpable aura that made the air quiver with cold and relentless rage caused him to abruptly stop in his tracks.

For a brief moment, all eyes turned to the outline of a shrouded woman wearing a skull mask who stood along the edge of a nearby rooftop. She looked down at the humans with a disgusted snort, and her body flared with neon-teal light while she raised a black wand that screamed a high-pitched wail—condensing a magical attack meant to end them.

But to everyone's surprise, a flare of red pulsed and bloomed skyward just as the woman released the attack, and two slender but highly condensed lances of blurring crimson magic intercepted the strike.

BOOM

The shock wave sent both skeletons and humans sprawling from the clash directly overhead, knocking many of them completely head over heels as a whip of flesh skyrocketed and swerved in midair from one of two figures farther back, maybe forty yards away. Crimson Ice began spiraling up the red leash, and the tipped blade whipped forward, aiming directly for the woman on the roof.

The woman's eyes narrowed from underneath her skull mask, and she blurred in turn, dashing across to the opposite rooftop right before the one she'd been on was splintered apart from third to first floor in a single strike.

Black Lightning followed up in an audible clap of destruction, obliterating dozens of the skeletons from the side as they tried to recover and sending bone splinters in all directions.

The humans all gawked, many of them scrambling to their feet to chase after loved ones or helping injured comrades up from where the residual blast had thrown them. Even more just lay there, stunned at the power displayed by this new participant in the battle.

Riven stepped forward, easily smashing one of the skeletons that had managed to break away to lunge at him with a downward swing of his staff. He stepped over the remnants of the undead with a crunch underfoot, then his eyes went wide when three flaming skulls bloomed around the woman and roared toward him. The attacks split the sound barrier and let off a sonic boom.

In a split second, his body lit up with hellfire as an explosion of flames radiated out from his very soul—blasting the surrounding area and eradicating the oncoming projectiles while simultaneously being blown back. He skidded across the ground, shrapnel from the concrete spraying as his heels, which were gluing him to the ground with crystallized blood magic, tore through the earth. He slid to a stop in a cloud of debris, glaring up at the woman, who stared down at him in equal measure.

The crowd of skeletons, remaining humans, and the two mages stood very still and quiet while they evaluated the situation. The wide-eyed humans glanced from the woman on the roof to the man on the ground, and then to the demoness that stepped forward with bladelike arachnoid legs shimmering in the dim starlight.

"Athela." Riven slowly pointed up at the woman above them, clicking his tongue in annoyance. "Deal with her."

Athela let out a terrifying, unearthly scream of malicious glee. Her claws extended, her razor-sharp black tongue whipped out of her mouth, and she blurred ahead as a torrent of death mana began to surge around the caster above in a whirling storm.

CHAPTER 25

Allie's eyes went wide when the demoness lunged for her, and she quickly erupted with power, encompassing the area around her and demolishing the rooftop she stood on to blast the creature backward. However, the demon was far faster than Allie had anticipated, and she used strings of red webbing to adjust her trajectory and avoid the blast entirely before catapulting underneath the roaring death mana to clip Allie's right leg with one of her elongated arachnoid blades.

Crimson liquid flew through the air, and a searing pain ached through Allie's calf, but the bone armor that covered her shins had blocked the majority of the blow. Only a small area of unarmored flesh was truly hit, but her body quivered in recognition as venom began seeping into her body from the wound.

She'd been poisoned? By such a glancing blow?

Though the poison quickly disappeared due to her vampiric blood, which nullified most toxins almost immediately.

Half of Allie's bone minions rushed ahead, spreading out to avoid spinning discs of crimson blades, while the other half exploded and flew skyward. Allie whirled and slammed a foot into the demoness, who spun backward under the blow—surprised herself at Allie's own speed before redirecting her attack using numerous shards of red webbing.

But Allie jumped off the devastated building to avoid the flurry of small needles, cursing under her breath while her heartbeat escalated to levels of simultaneous anxiety and excitement that she hadn't felt in quite some time now. Bones flew through the air from the minions she'd sacrificed and collided with her body fifty feet off the floors crumbling below her, forming a monument of bone armor around her with protective ivory layers and spikes.

First came the legs, then the torso, then the arms and helmet—almost doubling her normal size and making her look like a linebacker. She was somewhat slower in this form, but her defenses skyrocketed when green runes began glowing along the newly constructed bone armor. Layered barriers of death mana also radiated out from her construct, rebuffing the slashing and projectile attacks of the infuriated demon, who screamed her rage Allie's way.

"You little bitch!" the demoness screeched, her black tongue whipping forward like a lightning strike and bouncing off the flaring black-and-teal bubble surrounding Allie. But the bubble did shimmer, and Allie had to pour more mana into it in order to keep it intact against another crazed flurry of strikes.

Allie then summoned her obelisk—a towering, ghostly visage that bloomed over the battlefield and began empowering her while simultaneously weakening . . .

She stopped dead when she realized that although the humans she'd originally been tracking were quickly weakening under the aura effect of her obelisk, the Unholy caster's attacks were seemingly empowered. The flurry of red discs continued to come, cutting down her horde of skeletons with more and more power behind the attacks. And when she identified him, she was both startled and confused by the result.

[Vampire]

That's all she got. Well, no wonder the obelisk wasn't weakening him; it was very likely they were both being empowered by the obelisk—not just her.

But why would a vampire be protecting humans?

She had so many questions. She was somewhat excited to meet another of her kind. He probably knew the secrets of her race that she'd been so clueless about since unearthing her old heritage, but she was also midbattle with him, and he obviously had a motive to defend the people below. Again, that posed the question—why? These people were hunting her and all the other undead down in this area; they'd even spawned a system quest in this city to slay all the local undead through that damnable holy book Prophet had found.

She didn't have time to dwell on it for too long, though, and kicked off the building to launch herself toward the street while avoiding two more blurring Blood Lances that shredded her barrier and nearly ripped her left arm off. She could feel the power behind those strikes, and they'd left her barriers absolutely decimated.

She quickly dismissed the bone armor after realizing speed would be more valuable than defense in this fight. The armor shredded itself and flew forward in a hail of shrapnel that took the enemy caster by surprise.

A wall of Crimson Ice flew up in front of him in an instant, catching the bone fragments to completely block the blow while Allie flipped up into the air to avoid another slash at her back from the demon.

What an irritatingly fast minion to deal with. Allie was used to being the fastest one in any given fight, but this creature was even faster than she was—if only barely.

Cursing and turning her wand on the arachnid-humanoid hybrid, Allie launched a blast of black power from her weapon. The wand screeched and howled during its strike, briefly paralyzing the demon midlunge and giving Allie's attack just enough time to connect.

BOOM

Athela's right breast and arm were ripped off entirely, but Allie's mind raced with panic when she realized the grinning demon had just shrugged off the momentum of the blow by turning her body sideways. Instead she used that momentum to spin and kept coming forward in a tornado of blades and claws.

Allie screamed when a flurry of attacks hit her all at once—most of them glancing off the soul-woven bone armor she still wore but many of them landing on weak spots her armor didn't cover. She had to act quickly, and in turn she mentally grasped at a nearby skeleton to fling it at the demon.

The skeleton cracked and re-formed, rapidly morphing into a spear of ivory and impaling the demon through the left thigh. The demon screeched when the spear ripped through her leg and she was launched across the parking lot.

One of Allie's minions crashed into her, knocking her out of the way of a blast of Black Lightning that scorched the ground and ripped up cement where she'd been only a moment before. She sneered, her wounds quickly healing under the dark night sky and her red eyes glistening behind her bone mask.

In front of her, about twenty yards away, dozens of spinning red blades appeared amid a swirling vortex of red ice. An aura of malice, almost physical in nature, radiated out from the enemy vampire and caused her to stagger under its weight—his brilliant crimson eyes glowing with power while his staff of flesh and wood crackled with Black Lightning.

How did he have such a palpable aura this early after the system set in? Did he have background knowledge on the inner system workings before the worlds merged?

She needed to either finish him or subdue him before the others got back into the fight. She could see the humans were positioning themselves to attack at her back, and the demon was yanking out the bone spear she'd impaled it with while cursing loudly in an infernal language Allie didn't recognize. Most of her skeletons were out for the count, though she still had about two dozen of them left.

She sent her remaining skeletons after the humans to buy her time and decided on the demon first. To the other vampire's surprise, she vaulted left and ignored the caster—going straight for the demon to finish her off instead. Three flaming skulls came into being, encircling Allie before she fired them off with another sonic boom.

The target hit true, and the demon's shocked expression was locked onto her face right before she was sent crashing into the parking lot again, creating a crater that left her body mangled and twitching.

But the decision to focus on the downed minion also cost Allie. To her right, the other vampire's power built and exploded. Crimson Ice immediately blasted across the cement, covering the parking lot, and hundreds of red spikes climbed up from the frozen ground to shoot Allie's way. Black Lightning burst from the staff imbued with shadow energy. Dozens of homing blades sliced through the air and matched her trajectory despite her attempt to dodge, and over half of them made impact.

The blinding pain Allie felt after that was . . . immense.

Her bones broke and shattered, the black cloth armor she wore was absolutely shredded, and without her vampiric healing and endurance or the soul-woven equipment she wore—well, she'd be dead.

Allie's body crashed through a burning apartment wall and out the other side. Her body skipped across the ground like a stone on a lake, crunching and breaking with each impact until she came to an abrupt stop against a car. The car's metal bent under the impact, and it skidded across the ground for a dozen yards with Allie wedged into it.

Nevertheless, she got up, pulling herself out of the twisted metal with a groan and cracking her neck as she felt her bones and muscles reconfiguring themselves.

She grimaced. "Fuck, that hurt . . . Looks like I'm going to have to get serious."

Riven cast a worried glance Athela's way and rushed over after sending the enemy necromancer blasting through the apartment complex. He didn't get any XP notification, so he was sure she wasn't dead, and when he reached Athela, he could only grimace. His minion was still alive, but her body was absolutely wrecked. Her jaw hung off by threads of flesh, and she looked like she was in severe pain.

He bent down to one knee, putting a hand on Athela's cheek, and pushed the bloodied, matted hair out of her eyes. "You did well. Go home. I'll call you back after it's done. And don't worry, I'll summon Azmoth if things get bad enough."

Without another word, he banished her back to the nether realms before she bled out. Hopefully that'd be enough to heal her wounds, and he was pretty certain it would be. But he was without help now, facing down an opponent who was far beyond anything else he'd faced so far. She even surpassed the satyr warlord he'd slain in Dungeon Negrada, but at the same time, he'd also gained significantly in terms of power since then.

He was not the same man he had been back in the hellscape.

CRACK

The sky overhead broke apart, almost literally, as another realm presented itself before Riven's very eyes. It was only for a brief moment that the enemy caster held this spell intact, but that was more than enough to cause Riven's jaw to drop.

Out from rifts in the void, an enormous black-and-teal eyeball wreathed in death mana focused on his position. The rift wasn't entirely complete, nor was it able to last more than a second, but that gaze from some other world bore down on him with all the weight of a malicious god.

His body shattered and the ground cracked and splintered—erupting all around him in a split second. His clothes were left in tatters. He felt his skull, ribs, arms, and legs all break at the same moment, and internal organs ripped apart in sprays of viscera that left him reeling in pain while he screamed.

Out of the burning wreckage between two collapsing buildings, a figure walked through the smoke. She limped slightly, her red eyes glaring at the man who'd managed to push her this far, and she breathed heavily after exerting so much force.

On her way forward she stumbled twice but picked herself up and became more sure-footed as her regeneration continued to heal her broken figure. She stopped twenty yards away from the other vampire, heaving and taking a hesitant step back when Riven pulled himself from the wreckage of the shattered cement.

She saw an arm snap back into place, the torn flesh rapidly mending itself while muscle regenerated at astonishing levels. His lacerated right foot quickly grew back bones, pale new skin covering his body just as quickly as her own did. He, too, was obviously injured, though, and they stared one another down.

It was only when Riven coughed up blood and removed his mask to let the fluids drain that Allie's eyes opened wide in astonishment—and in that second, all the fight left her body instantaneously. Her right hand dropped the wand she'd been holding, and she took an involuntary step forward while Riven eyed her and began to conjure new blades.

". . . Riven?" Her voice quivered when she spoke, and her body visibly began to shake while her arms wrapped around her shoulders in an attempt to contain her roiling emotions.

Riven abruptly stopped the formation of his spells, recognizing that voice just as fast as she'd recognized his features. His sneer of defiance became a shocked look of panic, then dismay, and then confusion. Then he looked horrified after realizing what they'd almost done.

"Allie? Fuck, Allie, is that you?"

CHAPTER 26

The girl removed her mask, allowing Riven to confirm that it truly was her.

It was Allie.

His little sister broke down into violent sobs and rushed toward him, and he met her in the middle, sweeping her up off her feet and crying along with her as he hugged her to his chest in a death grip.

They just stood like that, neither one of them saying anything as they shook and held one another for well over a minute. Riven's breathing was ragged, and he was experiencing a flood of mixed emotions that included relief, horror, confusion, and worry. Eventually he let go of her, looking down and wiping tears out of his eyes while smiling at the sister he'd grown up with.

"I'm glad you're alive," Riven said shakily, laughing when Allie grunted something intangible and refused to peel off him—keeping her arms wrapped around his chest with her face buried there. "I . . . um, I'm glad we didn't kill each other."

There was a pause, and then the two of them erupted into laughter intermixed with Allie's continued sobs. She eventually snorted, pushed off him, wiped her own eyes, and glared up at him. "I was kicking your ass."

"Was not!"

"Was, too!"

Riven let out a sigh and grinned, ruffling her hair when his smile began to fade. "Allie . . . why were you killing those people?"

CRASH

White light exploded from behind Riven's back, but it was met by an Unholy barrier that crackled to life when Allie's body sheathed itself in bone over the course of an instant. The bone armor she'd previously dismissed was now back in full force, and the runes lit up again to produce layers of these shields while battle cries and shouts from beyond the magical clash went skyward.

"They've killed my remaining minions; it's just us," Allie stated curtly, ignoring Riven's question for the time being and glaring out beyond the explosion when the magic began to fade.

Riven's expression soured, but he slowly nodded while evaluating her—then turned around. All the men he'd saved were now barreling toward them with glowing white weapons—they must be under some kind of buff—while the lone caster behind them prepared another magical attack. Some of the charging melee fighters drew guns and started blasting, others blurred right or left to flank the vampires using movement abilities, and the bigger, tankier guys just went charging full speed ahead. They carried a variety of weapons and wore makeshift armor and looked more like a street gang than anything else.

A cold sensation crept over Riven's body. Perhaps they were attacking after seeing him embracing the girl who'd been chasing them. Perhaps they'd seen he was a vampire and thought Riven would turn on them, too. But they'd had the chance to run and a chance to try and broker peace. Instead they'd not given Riven the benefit of the doubt, immediately turning on him in a sneak attack and attempted assassination.

He couldn't help but feel like this had to do with his negative Charisma, and his mood darkened even further. Was this truly what his life was going to become? First the elves and their reaction to him. Then the comments from the people at the hospital about how he felt creepy. Now this.

A wall of Crimson Ice shot up to block incoming bullets after a couple pierced Riven's shoulder and gut, though he didn't think much of it as his vampiric body started pushing the small-caliber bullets out over the course of seconds here in the dark. Looking over at the women and children who were watching their brothers and fathers rush the two vampires, Riven couldn't help but feel disgusted at what he was about to do.

He turned to Allie, nodded once, and began to summon crimson power along his arms.

Riven's gut twisted into knots after paving the ruined ground with the bodies of the charging men. They hadn't stood a chance, but some kind of strange conviction had led them all to fight to the very last—even though it was futile. "I don't understand."

Allie snorted in disgust and finished raising another corpse—the flesh melting off its bones while the skeleton stood erect with pale, glowing eyes. "Don't understand what? Why these fuckers attacked us?"

Riven blinked, a little bit disturbed at how brutal his little sister had become. He turned his gaze to her, seeing no remorse whatsoever for the way they'd slaughtered these people or for the sobbing, fleeing families of those they'd killed. Then he noted how the system identified her armor as "soul-woven."

Realization struck him then. All Unholy bloodlines had been present in Chalgathi's trials, which would include his sister, since they were related—and he obviously had been there. So she would have been, too. Not only that, but she'd chosen to sacrifice her tutorial group for legendary-tier items?

Just what the fuck had happened to the timid, happy girl he'd known before? It'd only been a month or two, but the system had already shown its hand in terms of time warping, so perhaps it'd been longer for her. Regardless, it bothered him. He'd need to address these things, but not now. Not after he'd just found her.

". . . Yes. Why would they attack us when they knew they'd lose? They saw what we did fighting one another. There was no way people this weak could take us individually, let alone both of us."

"They're religious fanatics, that's why. They think they're fighting for some higher purpose. That, and they thought we were weakened after beating the shit out of each other." Allie spat at a dead man she hadn't raised yet, then planted a bone-covered boot on his face while grinding it into the ground in an act of overt disrespect. Suddenly, though, her features fell into a hard grimace and then an expression of sadness. She clasped her hands together, the bone gauntlets partially covering her hands grating against one another. "Um . . . Riven, there's something you have to know before anything else."

The seriousness of her tone caught him by surprise, considering she'd treated the killing of all these people as a trivial act. And when she looked up to hold his gaze, his heart suddenly clenched. Unspoken words were traded in those moments, and Riven felt his blood run cold. He looked around, not seeing Jose anywhere, and a lump started to form in his throat.

She merely nodded, and tears began to collect under his eyes.

Beginning to tremble, Riven silently stared at the ground where a pool of blood had collected from a recent victim. Allie didn't move.

"How did it happen?" Riven eventually asked in nothing more than a whisper. "Did you bury him?"

Allie nodded slowly. "I buried him. It was the same group of people we just fought. They're led by a man called Prophet, who found some sort of holy book—a relic delivered to this world by the system. They think he's the second coming or something like that . . . and his followers are real nutjobs. When Jose and I first came out of the tutorial, they demanded he join their group. When I appeared and they realized what I was and who he was with, and after he'd told them that he wasn't going to join some religious cult, they called him a race traitor and . . . they killed him before I could do anything."

Riven's eyes didn't leave the ground, and Allie eventually continued.

"One bullet to the skull was all it took. They tried to kill me, too, after that, calling me a monster." Allie's voice began to tremble slightly, but her composure remained solid after a few deep breaths. Her long brown hair whipped about in the night breeze, and a clap of thunder in the distance echoed across the ruined city. "I . . . I am responsible for his death. Because he wouldn't have—"

"You were not responsible. Don't ever think that," Riven said in a low whisper, feeling hollow inside and clenching his fists. He looked up again, walked over to her, and lifted her chin to meet his eyes. "He wouldn't want you to ever think that, Allie. He was essentially a brother to us, we grew up with him, and he would never blame you for what happened. Do you understand?"

They were the words that Allie had been needing to hear, and with trembling lips she mumbled a half-hearted, "Yes," before her brother wrapped her in another hug.

"Is that why you were hunting them?" Riven eventually asked after a few minutes of standing there in the decimated parking lot.

"Yes."

He nodded once and brushed his fingers through her hair before kissing the top of her head. "I see, and I think I understand."

[Quest Update: Finding Your Family—You have successfully found Allie. Congratulations! This quest is complete. Pings will now be deactivated.]

Riven nearly scoffed in disgust at the pop-up notification. Yeah, some help the system had been with that one.

"You *think* you understand?" Allie pushed herself off him and sniffled, a confused glare holding him almost contemptuously.

He didn't waver but shoved his hands into the pockets of his ruined cloak. "This Prophet person . . . he's going to die for this. The followers of his who actually did the deed should die, too, but I assume you already killed them. However, slaughtering his followers like this tonight . . . Especially when they're so much weaker than you? They were terrified of you. They had families and friends dying in front of them. You made them experience what you went through a dozen times over just tonight, let alone any other times you may have acted similarly. Allie, that isn't who you are. Just how many people have you killed because of this?"

Anger flared across her features, and she quickly bit her lip to hold back a cutting reply, then swallowed and closed her eyes. "Lots of them. Hundreds. Maybe a thousand. Maybe two thousand, I don't know."

Riven frowned. "How many of them do you truly think deserved it?"

Allie's mouth opened to reply, but then it quickly shut. As she seriously thought the question over for a time, that tight-lipped smile turned into a full-on grin of pride. Confidently, she straightened her posture and took a step toward him with fangs exposed in a blindingly white smile. "All of them."

Riven had a lot to think about concerning the changes his sister had undergone, the loss of his best friend, and this new Prophet character. Regardless, Allie was family—and although he didn't necessarily agree with her choices, he did understand them. In some ways, he felt like they were even justified—but not to the extent she'd taken it after the stories she'd told him. He'd seen the looks of shock, anger, denial, and extreme grief of the families who'd fled after he and his sister had cut down Prophet's men tonight. There had been emotional agony written all over those people, and he couldn't help feeling guilty despite his own emotions over his oldest friend.

But he also felt angry. Angry that this vampiric curse of theirs had in some ways been responsible for Jose's death. Angry that it was now responsible for a pseudo-war between this apparent undead faction Allie was creating in downtown Brightsville, and the groups of humans banding together on the northern outskirts of the city to purge the undead.

She'd told him all about it. About her friends Nin, Vin, and Mara. About the bone garden at the top of a skyscraper she was now using as a home base and terraforming with death mana to better suit the undead. She'd told him about their battles, won and lost, and how she'd experienced far worse than he had when trying to contact other groups of humans in earlier days.

She'd apparently even begged others to take her and her three undead friends in after Jose's murder. It'd been another, separate group from the new-age holy crusaders gathering in the north, but even they'd looked at her with both fear and hatred. They, too, had called her a monster, and they'd also tried to kill her without any real reason. They'd just seen she was a vampire, and they'd attacked.

No doubt this was likely due to them thinking she was another system-spawned monster, a vampire trying to trick them into trusting her. Or perhaps it'd been the negative Charisma at play again; perhaps it was both. But it was hard to tell whether those people had just been skittish or if this vampiric curse had really been the cause of their choice to strike out.

Regardless, those people were all dead now, too, fuel for the bone garden Allie had built where new undead—mostly a humanoid variant of ghoul—were being created as independent and sentient creatures. They were being reborn from the void, from the fragments of souls that'd once been the people whose bodies they inhabited. But they were not the same.

It was all very concerning . . . especially given that Riven had two elves and a bunch of refugees holed up with Azmoth underneath a hospital right now. Were they all going to turn on him, too?

His vision snapped up, and he focused when a light touch of Allie's fingertips brought him back to this world. He'd been internally pondering all these things without really looking where he was going, too deep in thought to care, but her soft touch and warm smile reminded him that this was still his sister—regardless of how much she'd changed or the choices she'd made.

"We're almost to the perimeter," Allie stated, gripping her older brother's hand and pulling him along. Their footsteps echoed through a dark alley, and they came out the other side between buildings to gaze upon the remnants of downtown.

Riven's eyes widened slightly, and he took in the area that'd obviously been a war zone for quite some time now.

Blocks of buildings had been demolished. Scattered piles of debris burned, ruins smoked, and crumpled vehicles lay smashed and destroyed. Light poles had been knocked down, bloodstains were occasionally seen in patches, but there were no bodies left to speak of.

Beyond all this desolation was downtown. A couple skyscrapers still stood relatively intact, with scattered office buildings in between. But one stood out above them all—towering overhead and radiating power. Teal and black flickers occasionally trickled along the sides of this large structure, the tower showing spots of ivory bone where metal beams had once been, and even from here Riven could see undead patrols hidden in ambush along various nooks or crannies.

From the shadows of one of these crevices between rocky debris, a woman stepped out—only to be followed by four heavily armored skeletal warriors carrying large shields and swords.

The cloaked woman clasped her hands in front of her and bowed her head slightly, her raven hair drifting out from the hood she wore and her pale white eyes giving her a very gothic appearance. She was beautiful, but her body was stitched together in patches that she'd likely carved off other bodies in the past—and an aura of calm, submissive power radiated out from her when she addressed the two vampires.

"My lady," the ghoul said with a sweet smile directed at Allie. Then her dead eyes flickered and she evaluated Riven with a curious cock of her head. Her gaze shifted to the way these two were holding hands, and her eyebrows raised instantly. "Allie, who is this?"

Allie's hand clenched more firmly around Riven's fingers, and she gave her friend an eye roll. "It's not what you think."

Another clap of thunder echoed out from the storm rapidly closing in on their location, and raindrops began to pitter-patter across the stone.

Allie stepped forward, letting go of Riven and putting a hand on the ghoul woman's shoulder. Turning back, she softly smiled in the dim light of the stars and embers around them. "This is my brother, Riven. Riven, this is my new best friend, Mara. Get to know one another as we walk—I want to show Riven all we've built while he's been gone."

CHAPTER 27

Riven couldn't help but be impressed with what Allie had built here.

Hundreds of sentient undead walked, talked, bartered, built, and laughed with one another as Allie and Mara took him on a grand tour of the tower. The skyscraper's walls had been knocked down in some areas, terraformed in others, and in some places they had been kept up. A mix and mash of steel, bone, death mana, and even sometimes sinewy muscle created various parts of the structure, with a huge spiral staircase that'd obviously not been there to begin with leading up and down. Shops selling various wares were set up, living quarters had been spaced out, and training areas or food courts were available. It was all quite homey, with a friendly feel to the environment.

Most of the undead were ghouls, more humanoid and put together than the mutated ones Riven had seen in hell. Then again, there were also more bone-type or skeletal undead, too, like the skresh friends Vin and Nin, whom Allie had described earlier. There was even one enormous and sentient flesh golem, lacking any skin but with huge, rippling muscles, applying metal armor directly into his body. They mostly bowed or waved or even had a word of praise thrown Allie's way whenever she and Mara passed them by with the escort of four heavily armored death knights following. Occasionally the tower's occupants would give Riven a curious look, but no one said much about him otherwise.

"You created all this? It's like an undead city!" Riven said with awe while staring around, smiling slightly when he saw a ghoul man flirtatiously bragging about exploits he obviously hadn't achieved with a ghoul woman in a dark corner while they drank some kind of . . . slime?

"Mara, Nin, and Vin all helped. I couldn't have ever done it without them." Allie beamed back, a wide smile on her face as she clasped her hands together behind her back. She motioned over to the enormous spiral staircase made of bone and made a gesture to proceed up to the next level, letting a group of five robed skresh talking about magical theory bypass her on their way down to the first floor. "And, to be fair, the bone garden does a lot of the work for us. Once we set it up—which was a hard feat, mind you—all we have to do is supply it with the proper materials and it'll create new undead."

"Yeah, you've mentioned the bone garden before, but how exactly does it work?"

Allie opened her mouth to reply but thought better of it and nudged Mara, who came to stand next to her. "You're the real mastermind behind that one. Go ahead and tell him."

The stitched-together beauty grinned, and if she could have blushed, Riven thought she would have just by the way her posture shifted to an uncomfortable pride or bashfulness. "Well, it took a lot of time—but my master in my old life told me how to make them before I . . ."

There was a pause, and Riven's right eyebrow raised in confusion. "Is something the matter?"

Mara seemed to stumble over her words while she muttered, and then she shook her head—pushing her raven hair to the side while her pale eyes shifted back to him. "I just can't remember exactly how it happened. One day I was with my old master, a necromancer on another world, and then something . . . A long time ago, something happened to him. To me. Then I remember waking up in Chalgathi's trials and Allie was pulling me out of a crypt."

Riven's features turned grim. Allie and he had spoken a little about their experiences of Chalgathi's rites and the tutorials afterward. It hadn't taken much of a genius to figure that one out after he'd seen the soul-stitched items she had, but they still hadn't gone into details with so much already buzzing about their heads due to their reunion. Either way, it had initially come as a real surprise that both of them had been in the same starter trials and not even known.

Quickly he wiped the grim look off his face and proceeded with a polite smile, pushing thoughts of Chalgathi out of his head. "Well, I don't mean to dig into your past if that makes you uncomfortable. You can skip that part."

Mara nodded slowly, seeming troubled, but she blinked rapidly and returned to the issue of the bone garden. "Well, I learned how to create one from my old master a long time ago. I didn't have the proper amount of mana to do it by myself, but Allie is quite the font of power, so we were able to use her as a conduit to create the structure. Bone gardens can systematically raise up new undead by drawing in souls from the void, or the shadow realms, or really any of the outer realms that have free-floating souls that want a body. Or they can use fragments of an old soul to create new ones if the soul shards are incomplete. Souls instinctively look for bodies, so the bone garden acts like a beacon and is able to fuse the soul with the material if there is enough compatibility. Most people here are ghouls, because the bone garden was able to identify those forms as the most compatible with the settings I laid out—"

"You can create 'settings' with a bone garden?" Riven cut in curiously, folding his arms.

Mara brightened, obviously eager about the subject, and her excitement on the "science" behind it began to show through. "Oh, yes! For example, I could set the bone garden to spawn less sentient undead—like the types we use for minions. We can draw in more powerful souls or souls with different affinities, souls that have . . . Ah, that can get a bit boring. But the short version is, yes, you can essentially tell the bone garden what to look for and what types of bodies to create. As long as you have the proper materials, proper know-how, and proper soul affinity, you can create all sorts of undead."

"Why not just create really strong minion types and be done with this war, then?"

"Well, in theory you could, under the right conditions. But there are a couple problems with that. First, stronger undead require stronger, rarer souls with higher affinities for that body. Second, those kinds of souls take longer to find, and in the meantime the bone garden isn't harvesting any other souls. Third, you still have to subjugate the created creature. If you set the bone garden to create a monstrosity you can't control, it may destroy the bone garden and simply eat you, because most of the nonsentient undead are ravenous by instinct. Fourth, we would still need materials, and materials are in high demand. There's even a market upstairs that focuses on selling or buying body modifications, like the flesh golem you saw earlier was doing, but most body modifications aren't metal. Instead, they're usually body parts stripped off other creatures or even other undead."

"Or plants," Allie cut in.

Mara rolled her pale, dead eyes. "That has only happened once, and I have no idea how he did it. There's an entire list of reasons why that isn't really possible right now for practical purposes. Those were only four reasons, but there are many more. The bone garden can definitely supply us with sentient undead, or feral ones using soul shards we can use as minions, but everything comes at a cost, and we can't just snap our fingers to say, 'Hey, create a giant bone dragon that I get to use as a pet' or something to that effect. It just doesn't work that way. Our queen also asked me about this the first time I offered to create the bone garden."

"Queen?"

Mara shot Allie a look, and Riven's little sister DID go bright red with a flush. Apparently vampires still had that ability, whereas ghouls—or Mara, at least—probably did not.

Riven's grin was slightly mocking as he stared at the silently brooding girl in front of him. "Queen?"

"Oh, shut up!" Allie said with a humph, stomping up the stairs while Mara began to laugh. "I was NOT the one to come up with that title! That's just what everyone is calling me, okay?!"

"I see." Riven gave an amused chuckle and followed Allie up the stairs with Mara beside him. He shot the ghoul a sideways glance. "So . . . all these undead really are newborns then? Does that come with any problems, like orienting them to their new lives or dealing with repressed memories of their past lives? Or are they like little kids?"

"Not all of them have past lives." Mara corrected with a hum and a raised pointer finger while they walked. "Those are . . . the most problematic. Yes, they are essentially children, and yes, it's a burden on the rest of us in the immediate timeline—but they'll be of use when they grow older. We actually have a kind of day care for them—it's on floor five—and we basically have to treat them like toddlers while teachers we've assigned educate them. Most, however, are either brought in from the void or are created from fragments of old and splintered souls. These ones do have glimpses of their past life from time to time—but aren't nearly as incompetent. They still feel like they're new people, but many describe it like occasionally experiencing a dream or fragments of a dream. They usually don't feel connected to these old memories or emotions, rather like they're watching a theater performance."

"There are also a couple others who the system allows to traverse worlds, but only in select circumstances." Allie butted in again, glancing over her shoulder and slowing down to keep pace with the two behind her. "Very specific criteria have to be met."

At this, Riven blinked and gazed up through the hole in the middle of the tower that the skyscraper's main staircase was centered around. Far, far above them was the roof, and it'd take a while to get there no doubt. "Two questions. First—how tall is this tower? And second, what the hell do you mean, undead are traveling here from other worlds?"

"I can't remember how tall the tower originally was, but it's rapidly grown in both height and width. We've added a couple floors, and it's still adding new ones. I think we have forty-two now?" Mara murmured with a scrunched nose.

"Forty-three as of yesterday," Allie stated proudly. "It's not a living building, but it has the potential to be one eventually. Right now the bone garden is continuing to terraform, and that's why there's such a transition."

Mara nodded. "Yes, well, anyways—what Allie is talking about concerning other worlds is that undead under a combat level of four without any advanced skill sets or ties to what Elysium considers 'major factions' across the multiverse can come here through a one-way pilgrimage. Did you see that system notification concerning a holy crusade against the undead? It should have been citywide."

Riven slowly nodded. "Yeah, I saw it. I was a target."

"As we all were." Mara motioned at the dozens of undead, who were playing cards on the floor they were passing now. "The crusade was enabled because of two things. The first was our bone garden, and the second was the holy book

Prophet found. It gives the system a scenario to work with, and oh, does the system love its scenarios . . ."

"I don't understand. Why would these things cause a system quest to target us?"

Mara raised an eyebrow. "Because the system drives conflict in order to fuel growth. The system is designed to create stronger, more talented individuals by fueling them with the deaths of weaker individuals. Some think this is a system with the goal to create gods or godlike immortals, while others believe it is for the system's own amusement. Other theories from my old world state there is no real rhyme or reason and it just exists as a fundamental law, like gravity. Regardless, there are certain scenarios that the system often focuses on and uses to further its agenda of conflict—and sometimes, though certainly not always, these scenarios are focused around the Charisma stat."

Now Mara had Riven's attention, but she didn't seem to notice when he perked up. He'd been wondering how he'd go about life with slowly building negative Charisma, and it appeared she was about to give him some much-needed insight on the matter.

She held up her hands and motioned about her. "All of us are oriented toward negative Charisma. About half of the undead races, as a general rule of thumb, acquire negative Charisma for each level gained. Some races don't gain negative Charisma as a default but feel more attracted toward those with negative Charisma and repulsed by those with positive Charisma. Most demons, blood elves, drow, vampires, certain species of orc, and a couple other races are oriented toward negative Charisma, so the more negative Charisma you have, the more these types of races will like you. Meanwhile the humans, high elves, dwarves, gnomes, fairy folk, angels, and others are focused on positive Charisma. These races will be able to go into the negative Charisma, but doing so will cause others of their kind to instinctively dislike them—especially upon first impressions. So why would they?

"And some naturally acquire positive Charisma per level gain—namely angels. Negative and positive Charismas reject one another when races meet; those with negative Charisma feel uneasy, afraid, or disgusted around those with positive Charisma, and vice versa. This leads to distrust, and eventually it leads to natural conflict between races with negative and positive Charisma orientations on a far greater scale than what is normal otherwise. That is why demons and undead are often hated by humans and angels, almost as a universal rule across the cosmos, even though realistically there are friendships between angels and demons in some corners of the multiverse. That's just very rare, and in order for this to happen it takes unique situations where those individuals make an effort to throw aside their differences and work very hard to overcome the stigma their Charismas set."

Mara let out a huff, taking a breather from the explanation while continuing to pump her legs. "Long story short, as soon as we started building an undead faction here in close proximity to a holy-oriented human faction, it meant an easy opportunity for conflict. Prophet was likely given the choice of whether to pursue this quest for war and extermination when we started building our forces, with the system giving bonuses to the crusaders for our deaths. When he accepted the quest, we in turn got our own leveraging. We got the unique function Pilgrimage added to our bone garden, allowing our small bone garden to allow weaker, unaffiliated otherworld undead travelers to join us for a new start at life using one-way tickets to this world of Panu. It is unlikely Prophet knew this would happen, though, otherwise I'm not sure he'd have taken the offer. Regardless, the holy crusaders outnumber us by a lot and are absorbing dozens of other human groups in the northern end of the city despite our victories. They're likely going to make a push to reclaim territory soon."

"We also got a quest to 'survive' for the next six months, which doesn't seem promising," Allie grumbled in irritation. "It's like the system is expecting us to lose even though we're currently winning this war."

"I never received those notifications. I only got the quest saying I was a target," Riven stated flatly.

"Likely because you hadn't joined our faction yet," Allie shot back with a shrug. "No idea, honestly, but that's the only thing that makes sense. Everyone else here got it."

CHAPTER 28

The storm had died down to a low drizzle, but lightning was still flashing over-head when Riven stepped outside.

The bone garden was open to the air on the wide tower rooftop and heavily guarded. A door from the large staircase with an arch made of bone led into it, where over a dozen armed warriors and an equal number of robed mages stood watch. There was even one bone giant, standing three times Riven's height, who wielded an absolutely gargantuan bow with arrows the size of Riven's thighs, and another ghoul man with a sniper rifle, of all things, peering out a scope onto the city below.

The garden itself was . . . beautiful, for lack of a better word. It wasn't the type of beauty one would expect out of a normal garden, but Riven could see why they called it that. Intricate ornamental bone structures hovered and floated about the air in a palpable wave of death mana and little orbs of light that slowly churned around a central spire. The spire itself was very tall, very thick, and made mostly from cords of interwoven spines or vertebrae, as well as various skulls and sinewy strings of flesh.

The palpable cloud of black-and-teal death mana was cool to the touch and felt a little bit like a swimming pool when Riven followed his sister into the dense mist, and the droplets of rainwater falling from the heavens slowed down to a crawl whenever they entered the sphere of power. The tiny lights in the area bounced, laughed, or even sang while they danced about in the air—and many of them brushed by Riven's skin or even went through his body to give him sensations or flashes of memories or emotions that were never his. The general feel he got from these glowing lights was that they were actually spirits, and they seemed . . . happy. Happy to be here, from what he could tell from the thoughts they transferred on contact.

"Beautiful, isn't it?" Mara said while smiling at a pair of souls chasing one another around her legs. She giggled when they brushed by her, imparting another set of emotions, and she rolled her eyes at what was certainly a thought that'd been shared with her.

The dozens of rotating bone structures softly orbiting the pillar came in all sorts of shapes and sizes. Riven could feel the connections of mana between them, though, and upon focusing further, he could almost see the intricate webbing where each floating piece of carved bone held meaning and purpose in this setup. Some of them were star-shaped, others were rectangular and could fit into the palm of your hand, and others were odd shapes that didn't really fit the norm—yet they each had tiny runic sigils that glowed a soft teal.

"It is beautiful . . ." Riven said quietly, almost a whisper while he reached out and touched another passing soul—getting a brief sense of happiness before it joined its brothers and sisters in the slowly churning vortex of power around them.

Allie absentmindedly pushed one of the larger bone structures, watching it float away into the dense mana and through hundreds of slowed raindrops with a small smile. Then she turned to stare at her brother with crimson eyes. She let out a sigh and came over to hug him again. "I'm glad you're okay. So . . . what do you think about all this?"

Riven blinked as she let go to the sound of rumbling thunder and gave an approving nod. "I think I'm very impressed."

He didn't mention his misgivings about how she was handling some of the humans in the city, because honestly, after his talks with Mara and Allie, he wasn't sure if conflict was avoidable at this point. And who knew—if he'd seen Jose get killed like that, maybe he'd have been thrown into a rage, too. In fact, he certainly would have.

His features fell, and he let out a sigh. "Where's he buried?"

Allie's smile faded, and her eyes hit the ground. She then gestured over to the edge of the rooftop, where the wet, glistening bone giant stood watch, then pointed to the horizon along the southern edge of the city. "Under an oak tree on the outskirts of the city. It seemed appropriate at the time—there wasn't really anywhere else . . ."

"I see. Do you mind taking me there sometime?"

"Of course I can."

Riven nodded in appreciation and set the butt of his staff down on the rooftop to better support himself, and his shoulders silently slumped.

Allie, however, had been giving his staff curious glances every now and then, and it was here that she decided to address it, likely to take Riven's mind off their dead friend. "I know you said you went to hell and came back. Is that where you got that staff? It's very neat. Crystallized blood spikes with flesh and flowing blood, set into black wood. Even the name, Vampire's Escort, is suitable, considering what we are."

[Vampire's Escort (Vampiric) (Unique Soul-Fused Weapon, Sorcerer's Staff): 104 average damage on strike with each physical strike dealing minor shadow-explosion knock back. Mana regeneration is increased by 102%. All Shadow and Blood spells cost 9% less mana while dealing 22% additional damage. This item has an abnormally high endurance and is hard to destroy. Requires vampiric heritage to wield.

- Sacrificial Kill: Killing strong opponents has a chance to imbue this weapon with additional attributes, stats, or bonuses.
- Scorpion's Sting: The blade at the tip of this staff can extend through flesh molding to cut down enemies. Enemies hit with the blade portion of this weapon do not experience shadow-explosion knock back like the rest of this staff, rather, the blade portion of this weapon will imbue stacking bleeding damage to all biological enemies.
- Black Lightning: This staff can passively build up charges of Black Lightning. Power of Black Lightning depends on the amount of charge emitted.
- Portal Master: This weapon can sync to any stabilized portal you have permission to use by the maker and master. Current locations available for access: Dungeon Negrada.]

"I got the pieces in hell, then put them together here on Panu." Riven stood stock-still and shifted the status information he'd already acquired to Allie so she could take a look. Then he went back to taking in the view of the city from such a high vantage point. It was pretty from so high up, and somewhat breathtaking. This was the highest point in the city and the surrounding area until reaching the mountain range to the west.

"You created this, then?" Allie said with surprise. "How is that possible?"

Riven nodded, still staring out across the landscape while rainwater dripped off his hood. "A surge of inspiration. The Blood subpillar . . . it almost speaks to me sometimes. It's even my specialty pillar now, after I had an epiphany of some kind with the Dao."

Allie nodded, then dismissed the information screen he'd pushed to her. "Ah. I've had some insights, but only two, and they've both been related to the Death subpillar. Question . . . do you think Mom and Dad knew?"

"Knew about what?"

"Knew that we were vampires? Do you think they were vampires like us?"

This was the first time many of the guards had ever seen Riven, but upon her words, some of them outright stared. They hadn't known who Riven was, but to see that their leader's brother was now among them made some of them all the more curious.

Riven shrugged. "I have no idea. But if we both have it, there's a good chance they did, too. I wish they were here."

There was a long pause.

"Yeah, me, too." Allie fidgeted uncomfortably, then cleared her throat and asked the question she'd been wanting to ask since she'd brought him here. "So what now? Do I get to meet your demons without them killing me? Athela and Azmoth both seem very nice, from the stories you've told me, and that Athela is very fast, by the way! I was impressed with her fighting capabilities. When are you going to move in? I have a spare room next to mine down below, and I can get you furniture! Oh, I could even decorate for you! The girls here will be all over you, by the way—be careful who you pick to date. There are some very pretty ghouls here. Hey, Mara is single!"

Mara slapped a hand over her face in embarrassment and outwardly cringed.

Riven's red eyes met Allie's own, and a chuckle escaped his lips. "Yes, you'll meet my minions soon enough. However, I have a problem I need to take care of before I move in."

"Problem?" Allie repeated with narrowed eyes. "What kind of problem?"

Riven gestured over to the hospital on the western edge of Brightsville, only barely visible due to the rain. "Remember how I told you about the elves and those people in the basement?"

Allie frowned and reached out to touch Riven's arm. "They'll just try to kill you in the end. Just leave them. Stay here—with me."

Riven shook his head, tapping a finger on the wand at her waist and then the soul-woven bone armor she wore. "I'll come back, but unlike you, I still seem to have some of my humanity remaining."

He gave her a sour grin; the comment obviously stung. She looked at her soul-woven pieces of equipment and grimaced, knowing he was commenting on what he deemed to be unethical decision-making, but she didn't give a snappy reply. He hadn't been there to see what she'd been through, and she knew that he knew this as well.

So instead she merely accepted his decision while ignoring the jab. "I have to stay to run things. Though, honestly, after fighting you, I don't feel as worried about your odds of survival as I once did. We're probably some of the most powerful people in this city. When you get back . . . are you going to help us with the war?"

The question was hesitant, and Riven's response even more so. But he gave a slow, solemn nod. "Yeah. I'll help, but I don't want to mindlessly slaughter everyone. I hope you haven't done that already, Allie. If you have, I forgive you, but it's not something I'll just stand by and tolerate."

Allie pursed her lips, looking back down at the city beneath them. "Okay."

Riven noticed she hadn't denied or confirmed anything, and he grimaced inwardly. Honestly, though, she could have murdered a whole damned continent and he'd still love her—because he knew who she was on the inside. She might have changed somewhat due to recent circumstances, but she was still the kind person she'd always been. It might take a bit for her to get back to where she'd been after the trials and loss she'd experienced since the system took hold, but she wasn't evil.

She was still Allie.

"How long do you think you'll be?" Allie asked, gesturing over to Mara, who came over to stand beside them.

"Hopefully just long enough to deal with the remaining dream creatures, and I need to figure out what to do with the survivors . . ." Riven rubbed his forehead and could feel a headache coming on. "Goddamn it, and I need to escort those elves home, too. They're sick and injured, and I can't have them just lying around by themselves. Azmoth is there now, but I need them out of my hands."

"I'm surprised you're helping them at all," Mara stated flatly. "Most elves back in my old world would kill you for being a vampire. They're high elves, right? That's the most common type."

"How do you tell?"

"What color is their skin?"

"White."

"Well, they're either blood elves or high elves, then. What about their eyes and hair?"

"Blond hair and green eyes, silver hair and blue eyes."

Mara nodded in confirmation and began to dig around in a bag at her waist. "They're high elves. They were terrified of you when they first saw you, weren't they? You're going to be attacked by their kin if they see you hauling two unconscious or sick elves around."

Riven outwardly groaned and began to rub his forehead more furiously. "Grreeaaaattttt."

Mara and Allie both chuckled, and Mara pulled out a bauble made of obsidian. "Here, take this. It'll allow us to communicate while you're gone. Allie and I both have one, as do Nin and Vin . . . Where are they, by the way?"

Allie shrugged as Riven took the bauble. "Probably downstairs working on their mad scientist projects."

The women both laughed, obviously having some kind of inside joke about the two skresh.

Meanwhile, Riven examined the bauble in his hands and pulled up a status screen.

[Communication Orb: This orb is part of a fifteen-orb set and has an effective communication radius of 203 miles. After that range, you will be able to sense location but not actively communicate with other holders of these linked orbs.]

"Interesting." Riven pocketed the bauble and gave a nod of thanks. "That makes things a lot easier."

"You could always turn the elves into thralls instead," Mara stated with a shrug. "It'd make things easier, for you and them. It'd heal them and would give you two sources of sustained feeding."

Riven's lip curled in disgust, but then he thought about it. Perhaps that wasn't a bad idea, in terms of obtaining a thrall, but he wouldn't do it to someone unwilling. "I only intend to create thralls from people who want that done to them."

Allie snorted. "Good luck."

"Do you have any thralls?" Riven asked curiously, turning his gaze on her amid the drizzle.

"Um . . ." Allie's face flushed slightly, and she shrugged.

Riven's eyebrows rose. "Really?"

"That's a complicated story . . ." Mara eventually said in the awkward silence, receiving an appreciative glance from Allie, who fidgeted with her wand. "One that will likely take time to explain. Either way, thralls are an easy solution to what is otherwise a life of hunting down victims to eat. Right?"

Riven gave them both skeptical looks but eventually shook his head. "All right, this is a conversation for another time. I'm off for now. Allie, I love you. Be safe. Mara, it was nice meeting you."

He extended a hand to Mara, who declined it and instead bowed to him while taking a knee. Riven was a bit surprised by the act of submission but didn't comment on it and withdrew his hand before Allie came over and gave him a kiss on the cheek.

"Be careful. I love you, too," Allie replied with a wide smile. "And don't get into any serious fights while you're away. Just run if you need to. I feel safer knowing you have the same bloodline I do, and we might be superhuman in some ways, but still . . . we're not immortal. I've almost died more than once, even with my regeneration."

"Yeah, me, too." He roughed up her hair and got a scowl, to which he laughed and waved. "All right, 'bye now."

Allie gave him a confused stare when he stepped toward the edge. "What are you doing?"

Coming up to the precipice, he took one last look back at his sister and the ghoul Mara, who was now getting to her feet. He grinned, then let himself begin to fall. "Taking the shortcut!"

WHOOSH

Seeing the shocked faces of the two women become smaller while he fell, he waved to them amid the flapping of his tattered cloak and laughed. Whirling around in the air to face downward, he cast two Wretched Snares from either hand, reinforced them, and then gripped each one before slinging them at the side of the tower three-fourths of the way down. Then he yanked. Angling his body to use momentum properly, he swung himself around and launched himself at another office building two streets away. Hurling through the drizzle and crashing through a glass window like a comet, he rolled across the floor, through a wooden door, and into an adjacent hallway with a cackle. Brushing himself off and standing up, he wondered just what Mara thought of that stunt.

Then he started walking. It couldn't be all fun and games, and he had responsibilities to attend to.

Night turned into day.

Their first stop was a department store wedged between a heavily looted shopping center and a four-way intersection. It was called Annabelle's, and Athela had seen it while exploring the city on the first day after the merging of worlds. It was a redbrick building with a white and yellow sign overhead, and the glass windows that'd been set up to display wares had been shattered. The sliding doors in front had largely been ignored in favor of the broken windows, as there was no electricity anymore, and a couple of looters were going in and out even now.

As Riven and Athela approached, many gave them wary glances, and a woman pushing a stroller screamed and rushed away with her baby when she saw one of Athela's arachnoid legs loop around to scratch an itch.

"Why didn't you let me meet her?!" Athela asked for the tenth time that morning. "I had so much I wanted to say! So much I wanted to ask! Like . . . what kind of BLACKMAIL she has on you! All the nitty-gritty secrets she knows—oh, I can't wait!"

Riven rolled his eyes and ignored the screaming woman, stepping over the ledge and shattered glass to make his way inside. "I told you, I wanted you to heal up completely before calling you back. You're important, and I want you to be healthy while you're here. You'll have all the time in the world to talk to Allie about the dark secrets of my mysterious past!"

He let out a snort of amusement when Athela playfully shoved him with a grin.

One man wearing a scarf around his face and a leather jacket looked up from where he was trying to hush his two little boys. His eyes went wide upon seeing Riven's system description, and he slowly backed away against the wall while holding the children's hands. "I don't want any trouble."

Riven glanced over and smiled, gesturing to his own tattered garments. "Don't worry about us. We're just here for some new clothes."

There were a couple other people inside the rather large store—almost a warehouse, with thousands of racks and about half of them still loaded with clothes. Piles of discarded garments that people had been riffling through also littered the floors, and skylights illuminated the building at intervals.

They went through the aisles of turned-over shelves and racks, picking out various articles of clothing each of them wanted. Surprisingly enough, Athela was even open to the idea of wearing clothes from time to time now, though she made it very clear that she'd only do so in special circumstances. What she meant by *special circumstances* was still up for debate, though.

As they shopped, Riven and Athela avoided other people just as much as those other people avoided them. Within minutes, the other small groups of friends and families continued their looting with minimal fear, seeing that the newcomers weren't hostile despite the oddity of their appearances and system descriptions. By now everyone had seen varieties of monsters and how their city had been meshed into a new landscape. They'd seen the messages the administrator had sent to the entire populace of the three merged worlds, so this particular group of people just chalked it up to another oddity and kept hands on their weapons if they had any.

Riven bent down, picked up a black trench coat, and grinned Athela's way, throwing it into a cart he'd scavenged before taking his demon's growing pile of clothes and putting it in the cart as well. "This must be like a dream come true for you—being able to finally shop to your heart's content. Be sure to pick some stuff for formal wear, too, and not just . . . whatever this is."

Riven held up some pink lingerie with a quizzical side-eye.

"Don't you question my choices!" Athela humphed, folding her arms with a glare and posing defiantly with her pitch-black legs planted firmly apart. "You said you wanted me to wear clothes, so I'm wearing clothes. Deal with the choices I make, plebian!"

"I'm just sayin'—"

"Nope! Enough!" She smacked him upside the back of his head and abruptly turned into a spider in a whoosh of motion.

Riven startled and stepped back, then laughed when he saw it was her original form. "You've mastered the shape-shifting now?! Very cool."

Athela's black-and-red spider body turned abruptly, and she pointed a quivering spider foot up at his face, eyes narrowed. "Any more of that backtalk and I stay in this body forever! Got it?!"

Riven's grin only widened. "That's your choice, Athela. I like you just the way you are, no matter what body you take."

"Shut it! I don't need your sarcasm!" Athela dramatically rolled over onto her back, covered up her mandibles and arachnid face with a couple of legs, and got another chuckle from her master.

Another scream from a little girl nearby caused Athela to quickly shift back into her humanoid form, though, and she gave the kid a scathing glare. "Oh, come on! I'm not THAT scary!"

"You're pretty damn scary-looking, Athela."

"Shut it, twerp! Unless you want more mustaches drawn on your face when you sleep!"

That's when Athela's bright-red eyes lit up in excitement as she picked up a long white dress and spun around—keeping it close to her body to mimic what it'd look like. "What do you think about the dress?!"

Riven's eyes softened, and he put his hands on his hips. "You'd look beautiful in it."

There was a pause in the conversation, and the quirky expression faded from her face along with her grin as her eyes slowly fell to the ground, avoiding his gaze. Athela blushed, rolled up the dress, then slowly walked up to him and gave him a firm hug. "Thanks, Riven. You know, you're not a bad master."

She gut punched him and peeled off with a smile while avoiding a retaliatory kick, then stuck her black tongue out with a wink and continued surfing the wares.

Riven stood there thoughtfully under the skylights of the dim, spacious room for a long, long time, waiting for her to be done. All this was fascinating to Athela, who'd never been outside the nether realms until she'd met him, and the demonic entity was a whole lot less demonic in scenarios like this one. She was smiling a lot, spunky, full of energy and enthusiasm, and was basically having the time of her life on this new adventure. It'd only been a few months, but he'd grown a very strong bond with her in that short amount of time. He was very glad that when given the choice in Chalgathi's trials, he'd chosen her.

He wished he'd been able to introduce her to Jose, too, but that was something that would now never come to pass. His heart sank at the thought—they'd have liked each other. And he knew she'd get along with Allie.

His thoughts came to an abrupt halt when the voice of that teenage kid Jake rang clear in his mind.

"Riven, can you hear me? This is Jake, from the hospital. I'm using a telepathy skill I have—it's complicated and came from my tutorial. Can you hear me? Okay, good. Anyways . . . you may want to come back to the hospital. We've had some problems in your absence."

CHAPTER 29

Riven stormed through the sewers to the rungs leading up the tunnel. He grabbed onto them, and Athela followed closely behind. The clothes they'd gathered were strung up in large, sturdy bags they'd procured from a back room in the clothing store, and they were dragged up along the tunnel's side, too.

The hatch unlocked and swung open to let in the light of the lanterns. Riven continued up and out of the tunnel—not bothering to wait for the others, eager to see what Jake had told him about.

There in the hallway was one of the male nurses, a young African American man who'd been severely injured with a clearly broken leg that Dr. Brass was wrapping up with the help of another female nurse and Dr. Waters. Senna and Ethel, the elves, were crying on the floor outside room seven—obviously still injured themselves, but with a few new bruises that hadn't been there before. A shirtless bald man on the floor was obviously dead—a huge set of claw marks had been gouged into his chest—and there was a screaming family in the far corner of the waiting room throwing profanities at everyone else. They were being backed into that corner by Azmoth, who was obviously not having any of their shit and bored out of his mind as he stood there with folded arms waiting for Riven to arrive.

The dead man on the floor was none other than the guy who'd been with the Latina woman's family—the same woman who'd called Riven a monster when he'd first arrived and had wanted to get out as soon as they could. The guy hadn't been wearing shirt then, but he'd had a baseball bat and had looked rather thuggish. Now his lack of a shirt did very little to hide his innards from the rest of the room. The screaming woman's husband, a heavily tattooed man whose friend was dead on the floor, was waving that same baseball bat around, trying to intimidate the large, simmering, armored demon ahead of him. "You FUCKER! You killed my brother!"

The man's son, probably about six, screamed and cried at the top of his lungs while clinging to his mother, who was throwing whatever she could get her hands on at the demon. Each item bounced harmlessly off the bored creature. The other small families, nurses, and people present just watched in silence or muttered among themselves—though none of them seemed at all afraid of Azmoth. Rather they cast judgmental looks at the small family of three instead.

Riven glowered at them a moment, then knelt next to the male nurse and clapped him on the shoulder. "You okay, man? Looks like you've got a bum leg now."

Dr. Brass snorted and adjusted his glasses. "He'll live."

The nurse scowled at the old man, causing the middle-aged brunette woman, Dr. Waters, to chuckle. "No! I'm dying, goddamn it! DYING! I'm not meant for this kind of abuse!"

"He's certainly not dying," Dr. Waters said with a grin Riven's way, gripping onto the young man's leg to hold it down. "Tyson is just . . . overexaggerating. He loves drama."

"I DO NOT!"

"We'll put a splint on it soon; we just did an evacuation of the hematoma. He'll walk with a limp for a while but should recover normally as long as the break heals properly."

"DYING!" the young man named Tyson insisted, running hand across his dreadlocks and groaning in pain, leaning back on the floor and closing his eyes when Dr. Brass was a little too rough with his leg.

Riven nodded once, upon further inspection noting a huge, swelling bruise right under Tyson's hairline, then let out a sigh over the yelling and ruckus of the family. "I heard you were rather heroic. According to Jake over there, you stopped that guy from assaulting the elves."

Riven hiked a thumb in the direction of the blond teenager, who gave them all a wave from where he sat next to his equally blond mom and dad on the couch again.

"And his brother!" Jake called out over the yelling. "The man with the bat was trying to strip them down before Tyson intervened. Your demon Azmoth only left him alive because he backed off, and they've tried to escape a couple times now."

Riven nodded to Azmoth in approval. He got up, passing the nurse with the broken leg while he glared daggers at the dead man on the floor and then over at the still enraged and screaming family in the corner.

He came to a stop next to the elf Ethel, kneeling next to her as she remained slumped against a wall, crying—trying to hide her face from him with her bandaged, damaged arm. She had bruise marks around her neck, a black eye, and scratches along her torso.

Meanwhile the other elf, Senna, had numerous bruises along her rib cage and left cheek and a swollen lip. She, too, was tearing up, and some of her clothes were ripped, though unlike Ethel she was able to look him in the eye and brushed her silver hair out of her face to get a better look at him. "We want to go home."

Riven took a look at their still-festering wounds, frowned, but then nodded his agreement. "All right. Where is your home?"

Senna's lips trembled as she glanced over at the bloodied, torn corpse of the man who'd tried to assault her. "Maybe forty miles south of here, farther into the forest at the base of the mountains."

He nodded again, inwardly raging about the situation but keeping his outward composure. "All right. We'll escort you back home tomorrow."

Senna sniffled and wiped away a tear. "Thank you."

She went back to comforting Ethel, and Riven stood up. Inhaling deeply, he whirled and quietly walked toward the muscular, tattooed man with the baseball bat.

"YOU FUCKERS!" the man screamed as he swung again at the demon, the bat easily bouncing off Azmoth's armored torso. His eyes narrowed upon Riven's approach, and with a roar he stepped up to swing at Riven—focusing all his rage at losing his kin into that strike.

The wooden bat landed right on target—or it would have, but Riven's hand shot left and caught the weapon as it struck.

The man's eyes widened at the speed and strength Riven possessed, and he stumbled back when the wood splintered and shattered in Riven's grasp.

The vampire sneered and, drawing one hand up to his right, he formed a single, large disc of blood magic over an open palm.

Riven's fingers snapped, and the projectile blurred forward, cutting cleanly through the entirety of the man's right arm. The man screamed and panicked, stumbling back just as Riven's foot nailed the side of the man's left knee.

The man's screams of anger immediately turned to horror and pain. And as Riven stood over him, anger and bloodlust flushed through his mind. He raised his free left hand, red magic rippling across his skin to condense ahead of his outstretched hand as a slender, crimson spike. "Say goodbye."

He abruptly grimaced in surprise when he felt a sharp pain in his side, and slowly turning his gaze downward, he saw that the man's wife had stabbed him with a small blade. It was a minor wound considering his enhanced body, and he'd taken far worse over his time in Negrada, but it was still painful. She was screaming at him in Spanish, and he had no idea what she was saying, but the look of revulsion and terror on her face was unmistakable. Her child was sobbing on the floor in the background, hiding his face as he rocked back and forth, and despite the things this man had done . . . Riven suddenly couldn't bring himself to kill the would-be rapist.

His mind briefly went blank with incomprehension. Why was it that without law and order, people who had once been civil became absolute animals?

Why was this such a common theme ever since the system ended? This was not the first time he'd seen this scenario play out. He'd also seen slavers and looters, his best friend had been murdered, the entire city had gone up in flames with infighting despite monsters roaming the streets . . . it was all so infuriating.

Gritting his teeth and sneering, Riven knocked the woman backward. She tripped over her own feet and fell to the ground as he drew the knife out of his side and casually tossed it away, and he went back to staring down the man on the ground.

Taking in a deep sigh, he clenched and unclenched his free hand repeatedly while trying to calm his nerves while the basement's occupants watched him. "You're banished from this side of the city. Go north to the holy crusaders—you'll fit right in. Or perhaps the city prison—that group of slavers seems to think a lot like you, and you should get along. I'll have one of the docs save your pathetic life because you have a family, but if I ever see you around here again, I'll assume you're trying to take revenge and kill you on the spot. Remember that."

Without warning or waiting for a reply, Riven slammed his foot into the man's face—breaking his nose with a crunch and knocking him out cold. "Dumb son of a bitch."

Everyone in the room was silent now, save Athela—who was chuckling loudly in the background. "Riven, you ruthless bastard!"

Riven ignored the looks he was getting from the small crowd and walked back over to Dr. Brass. "Sorry to inconvenience you, but do you mind patching that guy's arm up with a basic bandage? We're kicking him out as soon as he wakes up."

Dr. Brass huffed in irritation, brushed off his white coat, and stood up. "Goddamn it, I really didn't sign up for this. Fine, but you owe me."

The vampire smiled slightly.

"I already do," Riven replied, giving the old man a pat on the back and heading back toward the elves. "Come on, ladies, let's get you back in bed. I'll dim the lights so you can get some rest before the return home tomorrow."

Riven finished updating his sister through the communication bauble about his decision to escort the elves home and that he'd be leaving the city in the morning. Allie hadn't liked it, but she'd expected something like this and just told him to keep her updated as he progressed. The crusaders were continuing to gather their forces, cannibalizing other human groups while using a carrot-and-stick method. They were giving holy powers to their new followers through the relic and banding together against the common enemy of the undead. People were terrified that the undead were real, and the slowly morphing tower in the center of the city was very ominous. This in turn meant Allie's forces were fortifying their home base, setting up traps or ambushes, and attempting to assassinate higher-ranking enemies to wreak havoc, but they didn't expect a full-blown attack for at least another month or two due to sheer lack of organization on Prophet's part. The current plan was to let the enemies come to them so that the undead could fight on their own terms and in their own territory.

Riven closed the communication channel and let out a frustrated sigh, leaning back against the stone wall and mulling over the many things swirling about his mind. This war between the humans and undead was a really sad outcome, in his opinion.

He took a look at the corpse of the man Azmoth had killed, now drained of blood to satiate his appetite. That was another thing that needed to be addressed—he needed a more permanent source of blood. He couldn't keep finding or creating corpses to feed on . . . well, he could, but that wasn't how he wanted to go about it. He needed something reliable.

Then there were the elves he needed to escort home when morning came. And he needed to figure out what to do with all these people who—although they feared him—looked to him for protection. They'd stayed here this entire time, in the basement of the hospital, waiting for his return because they were more afraid of the monsters outside than they were of him. Jake had kept them all updated on the activities of the dream creatures above that had set up a goddamned nest in the building while feeding on local wildlife, other monsters, or people.

And that was yet ANOTHER problem; he couldn't just let a swarm of hive-mind dream creatures in the middle of Brightsville continue to devour everyone on this side of the city. He needed to annihilate those fuckers to the last one.

After all that, there was the rat man Snagger, whom he'd met in the cellars. He had a scheduled appointment with him so he could venture into the underdark and explore. There was the guild hall he needed to find a place for, too, and figuring out who Chalgathi was and what his goddamned amulet did—the list just kept going.

"You look stressed," Azmoth muttered in a deep grunt, slamming down onto the floor beside him, his weight shaking the room slightly. His tail flipped back and forth, drawing Riven's eyes while the vampire leaned his head back against the stone wall.

"He's had a rough couple days," Athela said, coming to sit on the opposite side of Riven and leaning into him, resting her head on his shoulder. Then she peeled the plastic wrapping off a straw, inserted it into a juice box, and sucked the sugary liquid out with loud—definitely intentional—slurping sounds.

Riven glanced her way, then chuckled at the obnoxious demoness while running his hands through his hair. "It's just a lot. I wish things were simpler."

"Yeah . . . me, too," Senna stated softly from her hospital bed across the room from them. She lowered her eyes when she noticed Riven had heard but then shrugged and began to examine her injuries in more thorough detail. "I miss my old world."

The other elf, Ethel, nodded in silent agreement.

SLUUURRRRPPP

Riven's crimson eyes slowly shifted over to Athela, who was making an overly dramatic attempt to garner his attention, and he swatted the empty juice box out from her grasp with an amused smile. "You don't need those—save them for the humans."

"Hey!" Athela protested, shifting back into her spider form and jabbing his thigh with one foot. "Don't be a jerk!"

"Your mother is a jerk."

"DON'T YOU TALK ABOUT MY MAMA, YOU PLEBIAN DOG!"

"I do what I want; you can't tell me how to live my life."

Athela's eyes narrowed dangerously. "I am a PRINCESS! You will do what I say, OR YOU SHALL SUFFER THE CONSEQUENCES!!!"

She lunged, screeching and barreling into Riven to knock him over onto Azmoth while rapidly swatting at him with all twelve of her legs. Laughing and wrestling the spider to the ground with rapid swats of his own to the top of her head (which only egged her on even more), Riven and the spider battled on the floor for supremacy.

"TAKE THAT! AND THAT!"

"You little shit! Hey—HEY! DON'T YOU—"

"AND THAT!"

"DON'T SPRAY THE FACE—THAT'S CHEATING!"

"CALL ME KUNG-FU SPIDER BITCH!"

SMACK-SWAT-SLAP

"Ow!"

The two elves stared at the battling duo for a solid ten seconds before bursting into laughter, and Athela's screeching drew the attention of Dr. Brass and a few other curious onlookers. Seeing that Riven was cackling while he duked it out with his minion, the humans quickly lost interest and returned to discussing their options with one another. They knew of Riven's departure in the morning, and he'd asked them to brainstorm among themselves while he did the same. They couldn't just stay here—they had to leave—but what options did they have?

WHAM

Riven pinned Athela to the floor, using his vampiric strength and superior body weight to weigh her down while she flopped like a fish underneath him. "Well, well, well . . . Looks like I have to put you in spider time-out!"

"THERE'S NO SUCH THING! SPIDER TIME-OUT IS A MYTH!"

"Spider-princess time-out?!"

"EVEN LESS OF A THING!"

Riven's chuckle and their banter caused the wary elves to smile, and they outright laughed again when Riven's blood magic quickly condensed and formed a half block of Crimson Ice around the majority of Athela's body. Her twelve legs stuck out straight where they'd been frozen in place, and only her head was left out of the block when Riven sat the ridiculous, snarling spider down in her new time-out container with a thud.

"LET ME GO, PLEBIAN!"

Riven smacked his hands together as if to dust them off and nodded to himself while smiling wickedly at his demonic spider minion as Azmoth laughed. "No, no—this is spider-princess time-out. Just like I said."

Athela's red eyes bulged, and she raised her mandibles into the air with a rather dramatic ear-piercing wail. "AAAAAAHHHHHHHHHH!!!!"

"Oh, shut your tantrum down and be a good girl. You WERE the one to start this, after all. Tut-tut." Riven patted the screaming spider's head like he would a dog's. "Good girl."

"AAAAAAAAAAAAAAAAAAAHHHHHH!!!"

Azmoth was finding this absolutely hilarious, and his laughter was rising in pitch to join the elves'. He then pointed to the iced spider with one of his four arms. "Obnoxious spider girl looks like brick."

"She does look like a brick. Doesn't she? A rectangular red brick of spider ice."

"CURSED, FOUL-SMELLING PEASANTS! UNLEEEEEASH ME SO I MAY UNVEIL MY TRUE FORM AND WRATH!" Athela tried wriggling her legs, but they were frozen absolutely still, and it only made her arachnid features tense in concentration, like she was trying to figure out a hard math problem.

Riven blinked, then turned to the elves, who were the only other occupants in the room. "Sorry for how ridiculous she can be. But may I ask, why are you two still up? Aren't you supposed to be getting sleep for tomorrow's journey? You're both still rather sick and injured."

Ethel let on a slight chuckle, then gestured to the wailing spider in the middle of the room. "I doubt we'd be able to sleep with that dramatic creature causing such a ruckus. That aside, we tried . . . or at least I tried. I can feel the exhaustion beginning to overtake me, but it'll probably be some time before I find the Willpower to rest again. What happened earlier today . . . it was traumatizing."

Riven solemnly acknowledged her words. "Understandable."

"AAAAAAAAHHHHHHH!!!!"

Riven rolled his eyes and snapped his fingers, unleashing his arachnid partner and shattering the Crimson Ice, which shimmered and disappeared.

Athela shook herself off, glaring up at the vampire with a dramatic humph, then strutted out of the dimly lit operating room with her head held high. She only stopped briefly to give him the stink eye before departing, and called back over her shoulder, "I'm off to get another juice box, as my previous one was so rudely thrown away."

"Ridiculous. Truly, that spider has a knack for melodrama," Riven stated, unable to wipe the amused smile from his face. Then he went back to his original position next to Azmoth but kicked his legs out and lay down instead of sitting. "All right, well, I'm off to sleep. Good night, ladies. Good night, Azmoth. And tell Athela not to fuck with me this time—if I have wake up with mustaches on my face, I'm going to throw a hissy fit."

"That will encourage Athela more," Azmoth stated blandly.

"Then smack her if she tries. You don't sleep, right? Guard me."

"What I get?"

"What do you MEAN, what do you get?! You're my minion, damn it! Do what I say!"

The demon looked skeptical but managed to mutter a response. "Fine."

CRASH

Riven jolted from his slumber, bolting upright when the basement shook. "The fuck was that?!"

Catching his reflection in a piece of metal, he saw a big red mustache had been drawn on his face.

Screams echoed from beyond the operating room, and both injured elves were wide-eyed in alarm when Dr. Brass burst through the door. The doctor was a disheveled mess, and he shakily pointed back out of the room toward the waiting area. "There's a crack in the ceiling over the waiting area! Something's trying to break in!"

People were rushing through the hallway, trying to get into the empty operating rooms that were farther away from the crack in the ceiling. Jake quickly pulled up his 3-D map, and it showed that an absolutely enormous dream creature was furiously clawing out chunks of pipe now, right over the waiting room, where it'd been pinned down in a net of red webbing. Other dream creatures waited behind it by the dozens, hundreds, even, and Riven had to rub the sleepiness from his eyes with clenched fists.

Ugh.

"All right, I guess we're going all out. Athela, Azmoth, get ready."

Both demons were already up and waiting for orders. Athela had taken her humanoid form, with all six of her bladelike arachnid limbs at the ready, and Azmoth was beginning to burn hot with embers as a large, obsidian smile devoured his face in anticipation.

"We'll take care of it, and if we don't—you can all take the tunnel out," Riven said to Dr. Brass, pushing him aside as he, Athela, and Azmoth walked out to the front.

Riven stretched and yawned. The unconscious man whose arm Riven had cut off had been bandaged, a tourniquet applied, and he was being dragged by his sobbing wife off to the side. Everyone else had already run from the waiting room to hide elsewhere.

Riven felt a little guilty in that moment, seeing how distraught she was, but then he thought about how Ethel and Senna had been assaulted. The pity for the man immediately disappeared.

He felt a nudge at his shoulder, paused, and turned to see Dr. Brass.

"Hey . . ." the old man muttered under his breath while screams and the crying of children became louder with every successive crunch from the ceiling above. He looked down at the pistol in his left hand. "I've never fought a monster before. But can I help?"

Riven eyed the man and his gun, setting the butt of his staff on the tiled floor. "Just blast through your bullets as fast as you can. Maybe you'll even get some levels for helping kill these things. Have you killed a monster since the system arrived?"

Slowly, Dr. Brass shook his head no.

"Well, here's your first chance. Grow some levels—it's going to be a good opportunity for experience."

The old man nodded hesitantly, adjusting his glasses and shaking only slightly. "Yeah . . . will do."

He didn't look too confident, but he held his ground anyway and stood with Riven in the waiting area along with the two demons. He was the only one to do so—everyone else was clustered together in the hall or the operating rooms farther back.

The ceiling shook, rattling with every strike as the tiles overhead cracked farther down the center. Already there was a large fissure in the ceiling about five yards across and half a foot wide, though dust, tile, and pieces of metal pipe were raining down, though they couldn't see the monster just yet.

Riven yawned again, covering his mouth and grumbling to himself. "And just when I was getting some good sleep . . ."

Out of all of them, Azmoth was the only one who was excited. Flames began to flicker and rise off the monstrous creature, and he began to utter a deep growl in anticipation of the fight to come with claws flexed on all four of his arms.

Athela, meanwhile, scrambled up the wall, onto the ceiling, and paused overhead—watching the fissure widen with every earthshaking strike from above. "Let's give it hell, ladies!"

THUD

THUD

THUD

The continued battering of the ceiling gave Riven a building headache, and he briefly asked himself whether the people behind him should just make a run for it through the sewers. But there was no way so many people would get out in time with a single exit, and it was probably safer to barricade themselves in the rooms while Riven used the hall as a choke point. Because knowing what creatures lived down there in the sewers, these people would likely die without an escort. He'd already told them this; some had even watched his first battle through Jake's mapping skill. They were all very aware that they were caught between a rock and a hard place right now.

"I'll engage first. Azmoth, Athela, wait for my initial barrage before you head in. Azmoth tanks; Athela, you're on crowd control, making sure they don't get near me or past me. We hold the choke point here," Riven said groggily, listening to the beating continue overhead. "Dr. Brass, once you're out of bullets, you need to go back with the others. That magazine should gain you at least a few levels after I take out the big bastard we saw in Jake's video feed."

His instructions came to an abrupt end when an unearthly screech echoed from above. It was harsh, guttural, and filled with rage, and a final blow against the ceiling from above sent a creature falling through on a wave of dust and debris. Slamming hard into the floor below among a flow of old electrical wires, metal pipes, and rock, the creature was momentarily stunned. That didn't take away from its ominous aura, though, and fear began to flow through the braver onlookers behind Riven who hadn't hidden the moment this creature hit the ground.

It was about fifteen feet tall, if Riven had to guess. The clown face wore a wide-set grin filled with rows of crooked, sharp teeth that literally split the head from ear to ear. Swaths of writhing appendages extended from its back, ending in mouths that screeched and grasped at the air with gnashing teeth. Large, bloodshot eyes flicked back and forth in different directions, not in conjunction with one another—but as if they had minds of their own. Maggots riddled its muscular, stitched-together body from the head down to its large, clawed feet. Its gray skin flexed and rippled with each movement it made while it tried to push itself up out of the rubble, but the gaze swerved right and locked onto Dr. Brass immediately.

Cold, humid air escaped its mouth as it opened its jaws to gasp in excitement. The words it spoke next were predatory, hungry, and wet with saliva as it started to drool. "Precious little meatling! I am glad you stayed to play!!!"

CHAPTER 30

Frankly, none of them had expected the creature to talk—but as surprised as they were, it was equally surprised when it saw Azmoth.

"Demon? What is a demon doing here?"

The Hellscape Brutalisk roared in challenge, slapping his spiked tail against the ground and blooming into flames. Azmoth took one step forward, heaved back, and then let loose a cannon of fire from his throat.

Had Azmoth always been able to do that? Riven didn't think so.

The creature screamed as it was bathed in the fires of hell, the smaller dream creatures above shrieked in unison, and the battle was instantaneously on the move.

Waves of spinning razors launched themselves into a horde of gray-skinned monsters that poured through the hole in the ceiling and into the basement, and a blast of Black Lightning erupted into a crowd while Azmoth fought with the big guy who'd begun to charge Riven.

The two titanic creatures smashed into each other while dozens of muscular, gray-skinned humanoids continued to launch themselves Riven's way—dying like flies in sprays of viscera and blood. Combined with Azmoth's flames, Athela's needles, and the larger dream creature's writhing appendages that regrew with each one torn off, it was like a violent fireworks show.

A clawed gray hand whipped toward Riven's head when one of the monsters got underneath the barrage but was sent flying—along with the monster's head—as Athela intercepted the beast. The ovoid mouth full of teeth screeched in rage at having been so close to striking the mage, but Riven paid it no mind. He had confidence in Athela to keep him safe while he dished out damage from the back line. Athela whisked back and forth like a bullet, catching one here, two there, launching herself between the floor and ceiling to get better vantage points while on protect-Riven duty.

The two brutes in front of him were an even match. Azmoth's flaming claws would collide and rip at the fleshy, maggot-ridden clown while the larger beast would try to throw Azmoth aside to get at Riven. Eel-like appendages with toothy maws tried to bite down on Azmoth's armored body, only to be burned away in the hellfire coating the demon before they regrew moments later. Their clashes and the brute force of their strikes caused the room to vibrate, body parts spraying along the ground with each new dream creature that entered the meat grinder.

But the numbers of the incoming swarm were too great, and though Riven was using a choke point and environmental blood from the bodies of those slain to launch more razors, one of the enemies got through.

CRUNCH

Rows of sharp teeth tore into Riven's arm. He grimaced as he was tackled to the ground, but he rolled and slammed his afflicted forearm into the nearby wall. Repeatedly slamming the creature that'd latched onto him into hard stone, he felt its body give with a loud crack—and the monster fell to the ground, limp.

But that was all the time these monsters needed to overrun his current position.

ZIP

A rift in space tore open, and Riven jumped through, yanking an absolutely stunned doctor with him and teleporting farther down the long hallway before spinning. Throwing Dr. Brass to the ground and grimacing at the lost ground, Riven watched the screaming horde barrel past where Azmoth and the clown were battling toward him and the barricaded civilians.

Shrouds of Unholy mana bloomed in front of his position, black snares attaching themselves to either side of the hallway in a blockade that was further reinforced with a wall of Crimson Ice. The horde slammed into the barricade, and the ice cracked, even as more of the crimson magic surged from nearby bodies, flowing overhead along the ceiling and walls. The power rapidly condensed, layers of jagged spikes the size of his leg coating the path in front of him while he heard his demons continuing to battle on the other side of the barrier.

"THEY'RE BREAKING THROUGH!" Dr. Brass screamed in horror, still not having fired a single shot and shaking terribly. His skin had a thin film of sweat on it, and his hand gripping the pistol had gone pale white due to how hard he held the object.

Riven ignored the man, finishing his long passage of spikes while rapidly making curving motions with his hands. Blood magic began surging up his arms, charging Blood Lances one after the other before depositing them to the side where they floated, radiating in the air. Four. Six. Eight.

He got to ten before the reinforced barrier broke down. Athela had been cutting down many of the monsters at the front line, but this hive mind was intelligent. They knew taking Riven out was the key to victory and would rid them of the demons, too, so they for the most part ignored his demons and shattered the wall to keep on coming.

Like a tidal wave of elongated tongues, toothy maws, and sharp claws, the monsters poured through, clambering over one another in a mad rush for Riven.

Riven calmly held back and gave Athela a signal to make way for friendly fire, waiting for the monsters to get halfway to him while they impaled themselves on the spikes for their brethren to clamber over. More snares appeared around him, pulling tight and elongating while he attached each to one of the ten Blood Lances.

Almost there.

Riven let loose and used the snares to give his Blood Lances an extra boost. Blood Lance was already a high-velocity and long-range spell, able to pierce through most things like an absolute missile. It was by far his fastest projectile when compared to the snares, spinning blades, or even his new Tier 3 spell, Blood Nova. But when he was able to line up his targets like this in a narrow hallway and use ten lances at once while boosting their speed with slingshots created from Wretched Snares—the effect was devastating.

Ten red-and-black torpedoes blasted forward in a straight line, decimating the enemy ranks in an instant and clearing the hallway all the way down to the waiting room where Azmoth, Athela, and the clown were still battling. Nearly a hundred of the monsters had been wiped off the face of the planet in an attack so fast that a sonic boom rocked the basement. Glass windows of the operating rooms shattered, and people behind him screamed as their eardrums took a hit, with Dr. Brass reeling on the floor in pain while clutching his head.

The attack had been much better than Riven could have hoped for, and he made a mental note to use this combination again in the future, given that he had time to prepare.

"Line 'em up," Riven said through gritted teeth, and he suddenly felt his decreasing mana stores weighing down on him. He'd used a lot of mana in a very short amount of time, his Blood subpillar was beginning to become rigid from overuse, and he could even feel cooldowns starting to accumulate should he continue at this pace.

And that was even if his mana stores held out long enough.

Still, the blood from his fallen enemies was great material to fuel his magical reserves. With a raised hand, his Blood subpillar reacted—with blood all around the hallway ripping from bodies and flowing toward Riven's position to circulate around him like the eye of a small storm.

A primal wave of hunger hit him then. He could feel the razor's edge of intent flooding through him, permeating his already-thick aura with an even greater bloodlust as the shard of Gluttony inside his soul resonated with his will to kill.

Crimson eyes grew brighter, and a wide smile lit up his face to replace the calm. The shard urged him to kill more, to eat more . . . He began to salivate, the swirling storm of blood energy whirling around him and crashing against the stone walls—causing Dr. Brass to run back to avoid being ripped apart by the sheer force of the fluctuating power.

"THERE ARE MORE COMING! WE'LL KEEP THE BIG GUY HERE!" Athela screamed over the ruckus, vanishing a second later and slamming six of her arachnid blades into the back of the shrieking clown while it tussled with Azmoth and barreled out of sight into the surgery waiting area. It was still trying to get at Riven, and unlike the other, weaker members of its hive mind, that one was certainly able to take a hit.

On cue, shrill screams pierced the air and another wave of fleshy, muscular gray bodies barreled down the hall—this time with even greater fervor. Piles of bodies were climbed over and stomped on in their quest for Riven's head, uncaring of all that they'd lost and completely lost in rage.

Gluttony simmered and snarled, rejoicing in the violence to come, and his body began to drink in the surrounding blood at a rapid pace. The storm poured into his body, flooding his mana channels and flesh before it was transformed into a more viable source of power. His Blood subpillar screamed at him, nearly at its breaking point, but Riven continued to maneuver the energy with the shard of Gluttony spurring him onward.

Intricate hand gestures began racing across his fingertips, combining both hands as he let go of the staff to conjure his newest spell. Magical seals to the power he craved unlocked with every hand motion, and the Blood subpillar in his soul began to vibrate. Though his body radiated and his aura pulsed a sinister, tangible breath of malice, the words he spoke were soft. "Nefajia crecus Blood Nova."

KABOOM

A shock wave radiated out from his body in all directions, though he was able to focus most of it forward to avoid seriously hurting anyone behind him. Immediately after that, an orb of crimson rapidly expanded to the size of the entire hallway. Everything it touched evaporated, and another sonic boom tore through the hallway and through dozens more of the creatures, leaving nothing but red mist and debris in its wake.

CRASH

The entire building shook. An explosion of red light blinded Riven for a moment after that, and a round tunnel smoldering with crimson cracks was left in the wake of his attack. What had once been a hallway was now gone; the ceiling, walls, and floor had been completely ripped out and eaten by the mana he'd unleashed for well over a hundred yards in a straight line.

[Blood Nova's mandatory eight-hour cooldown has been triggered.]
[Your Blood subpillar has become completely rigid. All blood spells have a mandatory cooldown for the next twenty-four hours.]

His soul clenched, and Riven winced in pain. He'd never had a pillar go completely rigid before, but pushing himself to the absolute limit had finally done it. His connection to the blood mana around him was gone, and attempting to draw on it at all resulted in an even greater spike of pain that pierced his skull like a migraine. "Fuck, that hurts."

Leaning against the wall next to him right before a drop-off in the floor where he'd created the simmering tunnel, he looked forward and saw that most of the dream creatures were now dead. Farther ahead and to the left where the waiting room was still partially intact, Riven could see swaths of flame and red needles launching across his line of sight and smaller versions of the dream monsters being flung this way or that way.

Fortunately, though, he still had access to his spells that weren't blood related. Wretched Snare still worked, his staff had acquired another charge of Black Lightning, Riftwalk was available, Hell's Armor hadn't even been used yet, and Blessing of the Crow was on standby.

Despite the killer headache and lack of sleep, Riven hopped on down into the trench he'd created and started moving toward the remaining battle. The edge of Gluttony had receded, his mind was clearer, and he wasn't even close to being out of the game just yet.

He had a clown to kill.

CHAPTER 31

He turned the corner just as Athela was thrown across the room—face-planting against the wall but recovering quickly to turn on the giant, grotesque clown. His demons were winning this fight, but the monster had incredible regeneration and was battling back fiercely. Maggots wriggled, and sightless, eel-like appendages with sharp teeth grappled the other titanic combatant while Azmoth's fire-imbued armor slammed into the beast.

Riven drew up his staff and pointed it at the creature's face, pouring his mana into the weapon, and put on his mask to feel the item's effects empower him in the same instant. "Mind if I help out?!"

Black Lightning blew a hole the size of a dinner plate through the writhing, squealing creature's rotting flesh.

[You have landed a critical hit. Max damage x4.]

The dream creature shrieked in surprise and fury, having already been pressed to its limits by Athela and Azmoth. It stumbled back, still screaming, not even knowing what had happened to it after being blinded by the torrent of flames from Azmoth's mouth. That scream then turned into a roar when a wave of rapidly fired bullets slammed into its head, with none other than Dr. Brass having followed Riven in order to finally help.

Riven glanced back at the doc, gave a head nod while the old man fumbled for a reload, then snapped his attention back to the main fight. The bullets wouldn't do much to a monster like this, but it'd certainly help the old man get some levels after Riven and crew finished it off. Hopefully, anyways.

Azmoth's fire breath soon began to fade while Athela repositioned herself along the ceiling, and it was apparent that the Hellscape Brutalisk could only keep up the fire breathing for so long. Still, it numbed the effect of the monster's regeneration, and pieces of its body were beginning to fall off.

"YOUR RESISTANCE IS FUTILE, LITTLE MEATLINGS!"

They heard the monster's defiant challenge through the gunfire and small explosions, its voice echoing in hatred as it surged out of the rubble and fire—rushing straight at Riven now that the warlock had finally exposed himself.

Though it didn't get far before Athela slammed her six arachnid blades into its side, causing the creature to topple over. Claws began rapid-firing strikes into the smoldering monster, trying to dig into the chest to find its heart.

Azmoth's tail whipped around and landed a devastating strike to the monster's knee when it stumbled under the Arshakai demon's attack, and Athela immediately capitalized. She made for its exposed weak spots—skewering it entirely through the neck with a shrill squeal of delight as her hands morphed into claws and, yanking on the creature's spine, she began ripping savagely away to try and dig out its bones.

Azmoth did not remain idle, either, charging like a linebacker to connect head-on with a roar. His huge obsidian claws and teeth tore into the enormous monster and nearly knocked it off its feet while it let out a surprised shriek of anger.

The nightmare creature was absolutely dominated, rolling on the ground and fighting off the two demons to the point that Riven almost felt bad for it. Blows that would have crippled normal men, such as slamming Azmoth's armored head into the floor with the power of a pickup truck, had little effect on Riven's armored demon. Meanwhile, Athela was simply too fast for the nightmare creature to land a hit. Despite this, it wasn't what the nightmare had been expecting, and its many jawed appendages began flailing about trying to catch Athela since it couldn't make it to Riven. Though the beast certainly tried, every time it attempted to rush Riven's position on the sideline, it was met with devastating attacks.

"Your demons are . . . very good at what they do," Dr. Brass stated numbly, pistol held limply at his side. "My ears are still ringing."

Riven grinned. "Sorry about that."

The flaming brutalisk was putting in serious damage, playing tug-of-war with the mawed appendages to rip them off whenever they got too close. The nightmare creature had to resort to its larger front limbs instead of the myriad of lithe jaws protruding from its back—and it sneered through its creepy clown-like face while trying to bite back at Azmoth with everything it had. This resulted in Athela playing on hit-and-run tactics to induce necrotic venom with her tongue strikes.

"Wow. That thing's regeneration is amazing; it's even better than mine," Riven muttered under his breath, charging up another Black Lightning bolt and waiting for an opportune moment to blast the clown with another brutal shock.

He scored a perfect hit to the head. It hadn't been where Riven had intended to shoot, but the creature had jerked in an odd angle to cover the pelvis. Riven's eyes went wide as his attack completely obliterated the monster's skull, only to have it re-form seconds later in a smattering of gray flesh.

The nightmare creature laughed, glaring in his direction with that bloodied, sickening clown face snarling amid the chuckles. "YOU WILL MAKE A FINE MEAL!"

But the clown's laughing snarl was quickly reduced to a bruised mess of flesh before having to regenerate again.

WHAM
THUD
RIP
CRUNCH
CRASH

"RRAAAAAAHHHHHHH!!!!!"

It barely had time to respond due to the constant barrage of attacks.

Minutes later, the fight was over.

"That is one ugly motherfucker," Riven stated calmly while looking down at the husk of the creature that slowly tried to drag itself toward a nearby wall. It glared back at him, its regeneration finally having come to a grim end. It only had a single arm left, half of its face, and a hole in its chest.

The beast screamed in a furious denial of its situation, spit flying out of its mouth while pieces of it dropped off over the ticking seconds. "YOU WILL DIE, LITTLE MEATLING!"

Riven blinked, folded his arms, then nodded to Azmoth, who stood over the monster like a flaming executioner come to collect souls for the lords of hell. "Do it."

Azmoth's clawed hand crashed down.

There was a moment of silence as the nightmare's tormented screeching came to an abrupt stop. Its body twitched three times and then lay forever still. Then, to everyone's surprise, something odd happened. Slowly illuminating the room, a long, rectangular red box began to form over the corpse—hovering over the body, only to be joined by yet another container, this one a wooden chest that slowly drifted down to settle on the nightmare's body.

[**You have completed the guiding system quest from the administrator: Kill the Dream Creatures—You have successfully killed the dream creatures building a nest over the hospital's basement before they grew in power and became a larger threat to the surrounding area. Congratulations! Rewards: one Elysium altar. An additional reward has been given due to overcoming heavy odds stacked against you. An additional number of gifted stat points has been randomly distributed to you due to your performance in this quest.**]

Huh. Riven had completely forgotten about this particular quest. He'd been more caught up in other events, but it was nice to see that he was going to get a reward . . .

And a good one at that. An Elysium altar would finally allow him to spend all the money he'd earned by killing—

As if on cue, bags of money immediately dropped over the corpses of all the creatures he'd slaughtered. The sound of many thousands of coins clinking against one another when they hit the ground marked where he'd vanquished his foes. In turn, two boxes appeared in blips of white light, hovering in the air in front of him. One was long, thin, and red, while the other was a smaller brown chest.

[You have gained six levels. Congratulations! Be sure to visit your status page to apply points.]
[Your minions have both acquired new skills from the system after leveling up multiple times. Congratulations!]
[You have reached combat level 36. Congratulations! Your class allows you to create one additional demonic contract at level 35. When ready, please select the option at the minions tab to interview potential partners.]

Alongside levels he'd gained from killing Allie's skeletons and then the new-age crusaders, he'd recently gained nine levels in total. He shot a look to his demons, and his grin grew wider. "Good job, Athela, Azmoth. Couldn't have done it without you."

It wasn't until twenty seconds of heavy breathing had passed that Riven turned and saw Dr. Brass, Senna, and Ethel all watching wide-eyed and silently from the large tunnel behind them.

[Riven Thane's Status Page:
- **Level 36**
- **Pillar Orientations: Unholy Foundation, Blood Specialty, Infernal, Shadow**
- **Core of Original Sin—Gluttony: (Under Construction) (???)**
- **Traits: Race: Pure-blooded Vampire (Extreme Darkness Regeneration) (Sunlight Decay) (Extreme weakness to silver weapons, Sun pillar, and Light pillar attacks), Class: Warlock Adept, Adrenaline Junkie (Blood) (+15% to Agility)**
- **Abilities: Blessing of the Crow (Unholy), Wretched Snare (Unholy), Bloody Razors (Blood), Crimson Ice (Blood), Blood Lance (Blood) (Tier 2), Blood Nova (Blood) (Tier 3), Hell's Armor (Infernal), Riftwalk (Shadow)**

- **Stats:** 68 Strength, 147 Sturdiness, 366 Intelligence, 170 Agility, 10 Luck, -362 Charisma, 182 Vampiric Perception, 112 Willpower, 9 Faith
- **Free Stat Points:** 0
- **Minions:** Athela, Level 29 Arshakai [36 Willpower Requirement]. Azmoth, Level 30 Hellscape Brutalisk [27 Willpower Requirement].
- **Equipped Items:** Crude Cultist's Robes (1 def), Black Redemption (74 shadow dmg, 68% mana regen, shadow dmg +27%, Black Lightning), Chalgathi Cultist Amulet (???), Leather Boots (1 def), Backpack of Supplies (Guild Hall: Stone Manor), Witch's Ring of Grand Casting (+26 Intelligence), Cloak of the Tundra (22 def, +56 bonus def vs frost), Breath of Valgeshia (48 def, +13 dmg & +9% mana output dmg for blood dmg, 6% mana regen)]

Everyone else had left in a mad rush to escape the fight. Jake and his parents had gone; Tyson the nurse had left. All the families with kids had left. Even the man Riven had maimed had woken up and followed his wife groggily down into the sewers, according to Dr. Brass. Many of them had carried away lanterns and food supplies from room seven when Riven and his minions were preoccupied.

That, however, would hardly damper his good mood over the next few minutes as the team explored their spoils of battle. Money, levels, stat boosts, minion abilities, a new demonic partner, an Elysium altar, and some other unknown prize were all more than enough to keep him in good spirits.

He gave both his demons a hug and a huge number of compliments before offering to send them back to the nether realms for healing, but both demons declined, as they were curious about what additional reward he'd gotten. It was also obvious they were excited about their own power gains, having pulled up their own status screens to go over the new abilities they'd been granted. It was the first time Riven had seen a straight-up ability gained purely by leveling, even though Athela had mentioned it could happen.

So after Riven plopped down next to Dr. Brass with a groan, Athela distributed the limited crackers, granola bars, and juice they had left as a celebratory gesture.

He held the long, rectangular red box in his lap. The coins had all been collected, though there were thousands of them and the bags they'd come in all disappeared after ten minutes—so they lay in a pile off to one side. Azmoth had also carried in the second box, a small brown chest, and he put it on the floor with a grunt. Riven hadn't wanted to stay in that main room due to the mess and smell, so they'd gone back to operating room seven along with everyone that'd stayed.

"I can't believe you won . . ." Dr. Brass stated giddily at Riven's side—smiling widely and showing Riven that he, too, had gained quite a few levels just from firing bullets at the slain clown. It was apparent that whatever level that clown had been, it'd been quite high. So for someone like Dr. Brass, who'd started at level 0, to help kill such a beast meant that the gains were far higher for much less effort.

Riven let out another groan of relief and rested his head against the cold stone wall. "Wanna see what's in these boxes?"

"Definitely!" Athela chimed in happily, nudging Azmoth's almost-shattered arm and causing him to yelp. "Oh, don't be such a wuss, Azmoth! You're a big boy now—you gotta act tough!"

Azmoth just growled back, coddling his injured limb with a sideways glare.

The others remained quiet, watching wordlessly while Riven opened the long red box. It looked like something one would see in a jeweler's store—only far larger than any jewelry box Riven had ever seen. The lid popped off rather easily, and Riven gently laid it to the side as his eyes gleamed with excitement.

CHAPTER 32

Captain Vros Kinal stood on a large hovering platform that loomed above his marching legions. Their heavy armor gleamed in the bright rays of sunshine illuminating their glorious planet. The soldiers chanted, slamming their spears into the ground in unison time after time—an act that caused the very city around them to quake.

Meanwhile, the crowds in the stadiums on either side of the military parade were going wild. They screamed, cheered, and roared their approval for the assault to come, for they—the glorious Empire of Dying Suns—had been granted an invasion token by the system.

Kinal's gaze shifted under his helm to his right, where the emperor and three generals that oversaw different areas of their intergalactic territories stood side to side, chatting idly while they watched the oncoming soldiers march happily to their deaths. Those deaths would be worth the blood they paid, though, as long as they were successful in overthrowing the other invaders and securing planet Panu for the glory of Dying Suns. Panu was on the other side of this sector and would give their empire a much-needed foothold for expansion on the rim that wasn't so boxed in by competitors.

"Captain Kinal," one of the generals stated absentmindedly, turning from his talks with the emperor and putting the spotlight on the one who would be leading the invasion on Panu. "Are you excited for your first expedition into the outlands?"

Kinal did not hesitate, and his blue cape shifted with the winds as he gave a quick salute. "Sir, I am honored to be chosen to lead this expedition. I will do the empire justice and bring this planet under our control without fail."

The general smiled, and even the emperor seemed pleased with his response. Kinal was only level 80, which was the cutoff for any invading armies that set their sights on the integration trials. Every newly integrating planet had underwent between one and ten worldwide integration trials, and this planet—Panu—had dice rolled Invasion as one of theirs. Invasion was a classic of the multiverse for integrating planets, but it didn't always show up. When it did, the system offered bidding wars to various nearby factions in the sector and sometimes even more distant ones, depending on circumstances. Invaders, this time numbering just five, could bring in a certain number of soldiers with a max level of 80. Kinal was considered the empire's most competent leader that fit this description, and thus he'd been chosen as the one to lead their invasion.

This could only be done after the designated tutorials were over and an orientation period was complete, but the time for the invasion of Panu was nearing. Captain Kinal didn't know what other integration trials the Empire of Dying Suns would encounter there, or what the locals were like, but he did know of the other four invading groups. All of these would be hostile factors he would have to crush, but he did have faith that their legions would prevail.

"I remember when I led my first expedition," the emperor stated, gazing fondly into distant memories with a wide smile on his face as he stroked his long gray beard. "Had to slaughter entire cities by the dozens until the locals finally gave up. That was back when my father was still emperor, rest his soul. How I do wish for the youth of my younger days . . . But I am sure you'll be fine, Captain Kinal. I have faith in your abilities, and your superior officers all have nothing but praise for your past performances."

"Thank you, my liege." Kinal bowed low. "Your words humble this poor servant. I will perform to the best of my abilities."

The emperor nodded and placed a hand on Kinal's metal pauldron. "I pray you are right. This is a big opportunity for our empire, and your name will go down in the history books once you succeed. Hopefully Elysium opens up the gates sooner rather than later, for I can tell that the bloodlust of our soldiers is growing. Heroes will be born here, Kinal, so make sure that you are one of them."

In the abyss, the vision of these future enemies flickered and began to fade.

From beyond their plane of existence and in an entirely other dimension, Chalgathi remained caged by Elysium's administrator. Yet he still saw the preparations of the Empire of Dying Suns, and he heard the words this ambitious emperor spoke.

Thus Chalgathi cackled wickedly in the abyssal black of his temporary prison. *"We will see, humans, just how many of your* heroes *are left when I am done."*

Closing the scrying image entirely and refocusing on another, Chalgathi set his gaze upon his chosen few. In particular, there were three that interested him most. The two vampires, Riven and Allie Thane, and another man who was rapidly gaining power beyond even Chalgathi's expectations.

Chalgathi's grin grew wider. *"We will see just how many of your soldiers remain on Panu when I am finally set free, invaders from beyond. For this new fledgling world is not yours to conquer. It is already spoken for. It is already claimed. It is mine."*

Riven, in the basement of the hospital, opened the long rectangular box without much effort, and there in the bottom of the box was a single item. It was a rod, beautifully crafted with golden trimmings along a porcelain shaft. A mesmerizing white jewel was fitted into the top.

[Elysium Altar Planting Rod: Plant this rod into the ground to begin creating an Elysium altar. An altar requires at least three square miles of space in all dimensions in order to place it.]

Huh. That was neat. It appeared the altar was actually not fully formed yet, rather that this rod would create it when planted. But three square miles? Just how big was this thing supposed to be?

He took the rod out and examined it in detail, feeling the warmth of the item underneath his fingertips.

[Please select the planting area and insert the rod.]

He ignored the prompt and put it back in the box, closing the lid and passing it over to Azmoth for the moment. "Looks like we get to choose where we plant this thing. It'll be nice to finally have access to Elysium's system stores."

"And others!" Athela chimed in happily.

Riven and the others all looked her way with confused expressions. "What do you mean, others?"

"Other factions across the multiverse."

"They have stores accessible via Elysium altars?"

Athela vigorously nodded her head. "Oh, yes! Though you have to unlock them first. That usually includes a sum of money, a trade, or an alliance of some sort. There'll be some smaller and weaker factions that allow anyone to use their system-registered stores, but they're usually desperate and don't have much to trade with. The Elysium administrator's basic store is more expensive than other ones most of the time, and it also doesn't have any exotic stuff, so it's in your best interest to acquire access to other stores, too."

"What's the point of not allowing other people access to your store if you want to sell anything?"

"To prevent monopolies and make sure you have materials for friendly factions, mostly. There've been circumstances where larger factions will completely buy out everything and prices skyrocket across the board, making it harder for all the smaller factions in a galaxy or sector."

"I see."

Athela cleared her throat and rattled the medium-size wooden chest in her lap. "So . . . if that was the original quest prize, what's this?"

Riven nodded her way. "Why don't you open it and find out?"

She grunted, then tried to open the latch. "This is my third attempt. It isn't budging."

Frowning, Riven took the chest from her and inspected it. It seemed like an ordinary, rather heavy treasure chest from the medieval ages. Clinking glass or metal could be heard inside, making him wonder what exactly was contained. He gripped the handles on either side of the lid and pulled, but just like Athela he had no success.

"You can probably bash the lock open," Athela muttered after frowning awhile. "It's likely just a monster drop."

Monster drop? Riven only ever seen monsters drop sacks of coins. Those were probably considered monster drops, too, and the system probably gave more due to the way this monster had been particularly hard to kill. Shrugging and peering at the front lock, he didn't see anything that looked out of the ordinary.

"I'll just pick the lock. I don't want to damage whatever is inside." Riven made a helicopter motion around the room. "Anyone have anything I can use as a lockpick?"

Luckily, they found a small piece of metal that did the trick. A minute later the lock swung open, revealing hundreds of Elysium coins. They were each about the size of a quarter and were a mixture of platinum, gold, and silver.

"Oh . . . even more money." Riven picked up one of the platinum coins, examining it thoroughly.

[One platinum Elysium coin (equivalent to one thousand bronze coins)]

He picked through the small chest, suddenly realizing just how much money he really had now. There were hundreds of coins in here; about half of them were platinum and the rest gold. One platinum equaled ten gold, one hundred silver, or one thousand bronze. After killing hundreds of dream creatures that dropped smaller bags of money, he'd probably had just earned somewhere in the realm of a couple hundred thousand Elysium coins in flat bronze value. The excitement at seeing so much was somewhat amplified by the fact that he would soon have access to goods via the altar.

But he stopped short as he rummaged around and noticed yet another item. It was a card of some sort, colored black, green, and yellow with various scribbles that he could describe only as the equivalent of a child's unruly drawing. The edges were hard and firm, though, and it glowed when he held it up in the light. Turning it around, he squinted and then read the description aloud.

[Ascension Card: The Carnivorous Maw, Trait—acquire the Curse of the Carnivorous Maw. Grow appendages that can extend and retract (even completely), and whatever they eat rejuvenates your health—healing you from any wounds at accelerated rates.]

Oh. This brought up an entirely new area of exploration. He'd never heard of Ascension Cards before, and he'd had no idea that one could use a thing like this in order to evolve a trait, of all things. Thus far his traits had been his vampiric race, his vampiric bloodline, and his class. So realizing now that he could actually get more of them was a bit of a shock.

"The carnivorous maw . . ." Riven chuckled slightly, imagining those things growing out of the nightmare's back on his own body—then he shuddered. "Well, do either of you want this thing?" he asked his minions.

Athela shook her head. "It wouldn't work for me—it counts as a back modification and would likely replace the blades I have. Azmoth might want it, though."

Riven's head swiveled to where Azmoth was curiously looking the card up and down. The large demon gestured for it, and Riven handed it over without a word.

Scrutinizing it some more, Azmoth slowly nodded and looked back up with his sightless, armored head. "It will cost more Willpower."

"How much?"

Azmoth looked back down. "Seventeen more points."

Riven did a quick check concerning his Willpower cap and the minions' stat demands.

- **Minions: Athela, Level 29 Arshakai [36 Willpower Requirement]. Azmoth, Level 30 Hellscape Brutalisk [27 Willpower Requirement].**

It was a little more than Riven had thought, but it was still very doable after growing so many levels. He currently had 112 Willpower, and if he let Azmoth take this upgrade, it would boost the demon's Willpower requirement to forty-four. Combined, that would mean he needed eighty Willpower for the contracts of Azmoth and Athela, leaving thirty-two Willpower left over for his final contract. If need be, he could even go and grind some more levels to put more points into the stat—but it was still enough for at least some contracts based on their original costs before evolutions.

"That's not bad at all. If you want it, go ahead and use it! Having maws that can eat enemies during battle to regenerate your health will only better your tanking abilities."

Azmoth grunted his acknowledgment with a smile and abruptly snapped the card in half—and the card vanished into dust. Immediately he began to absorb the particles, and seconds later the armored demon began to shudder. He leaned forward and looked like he was going to vomit, letting out a gasp as he clutched his sides with thick obsidian claws.

"You all right?" Riven asked, concerned.

Azmoth didn't reply—but instead puked and then gasped again. Bubbling masses of flesh began to flex and pulse along Azmoth's back with disgusting popping noises, and everyone slowly backed up when it began to look like it was going to explode like two grotesque pimples.

Then the demon's back did explode—revealing two long, eyeless, snakelike appendages with toothy maws a lot like the nightmare creature had sported. Again, it was only two—unlike the numerous ones that the nightmare had borne—and these were made of dense red muscle instead of the sickly gray the clown had. They were also slightly larger than the multitude of smaller ones present on the dream creature.

Azmoth took a minute to adjust to the new appendages, looking them over curiously as they looped around to the front. He opened them, closed them, felt how sharp the razor-like teeth were, and opened up the throats to examine the inner tubing. "I like these."

"A man of few words," Athela stated with an eye roll while tapping her foot against the ground. "Azmoth, what new ability did you get?"

The titanic creature shifted his attention from the new appendages when they resorbed into his back. "Shock Wave."

"Shock Wave?"

Azmoth nodded. "Remember goat man we fought in hell? I take his ability, new martial art. I learn Shock Wave when stomping!"

Riven's eyes widened. That was actually a really damn good ability to have! It'd torn up his Crimson Ice in the mini-boss fight and sent both him and Athela flying with each detonation. "Wow, congratulations, man! Happy for you! Is it normal for the system to hand out abilities that you've already come across, or is it just coincidence?"

Athela paused, then nodded hesitantly. "It isn't necessarily about things we've come across, rather than what you've accomplished. Azmoth probably got the option for that upgrade because he was able to help kill the satyr, and the system deemed it an appropriate prize because of this. Just like how we got the Ascension Card from this dream creature."

"Hmm." Riven steepled his fingers thoughtfully and leaned over his legs, elbows on his knees. Meanwhile, the elves and Dr. Brass just silently watched the warlock and his two minions discuss their winnings. "I see. What'd you get, then?"

"You're not going to guess?" Athela replied with a wink.

Riven thought about it a moment. They'd fought a necromancer in the Chalgathi trials, his zombie wolf, a bunch of undead and demons in the Negrada hellscape dungeon, wargs, goblins, slavers, Allie and her skeletons, the crusaders . . .

No, wait. Athela had been sent back to the nether realm when he'd killed the new-world crusaders.

He shrugged. "We've killed a lot of creatures, but I can't think of anything that stands out in terms of abilities. Unless you're going to be shooting blue fireballs or black orbs of destruction like the Jabob Demons and their lurker demon master. But I doubt the system would give you those as options, because you use stamina and martial arts instead of magic and mana. Right?"

"You'd be correct." Athela nodded with an amused smile. "I'm proud of you for coming to that conclusion all on your own—you're taking my lessons seriously. I ended up getting an ability called Flurry."

Flurry. He'd heard that somewhere before . . .

"That was an ability offered to me with the Reaper class, which I turned down in favor of being a Warlock Adept," Riven eventually stated after seconds of thinking. "Is that right?"

"Oh." Athela shrugged. "No idea—I don't remember. But yes, my new ability is Flurry. It's a pretty common one, but it's very useful; it gives me a burst of damage and speed—empowering my attacks and negating damage to my limbs when I strike during the attack. I can use it to block attacks that'd otherwise be far too strong, or I can use it offensively to barrage a single target. The problem with it is I don't actually control my limbs when I use Flurry—I have to preprogram the ability to attack a certain way. I can change up the preprogrammed motions, but the motions are otherwise always the same."

Riven pooched his lips with another nod. "That's actually pretty interesting. Do I get to see it in motion?"

"Haven't programmed it yet. I'll let you know when I do, but I have to think of a combination attack that will hit all angles and give me the best chance for a successful hit."

That made sense to him.

Meanwhile, Azmoth was extending his carnivorous maws again—reaching up above to about twelve yards beyond his back, maxing them out and stretching them before retracting them completely into his skin as if they'd never been there to begin with.

Decent range, definitely not bad. They'd almost function like scorpion stingers.

Riven put all the Elysium coins from the chest on their pile of money, then pondered a bit on what they were going to do in terms of carrying all that cash. They couldn't just leave it here, but they didn't have any real containers.

"I think it's time to take a look at the potential new partners we have available . . ." Riven eventually said, motioning for Athela to come sit next to him before the demoness plopped down beside her master. "Any advice on what to expect?"

"You're contracting your third demon right now? Azmoth, get over here!" Athela chuckled with a hand motion toward the Hellscape Brutalisk. She rubbed her hands together and gave Riven a seriously sinister smile. "Oooohhh, boy, I can't wait to see that list. As for advice, certainly. The big points are these: number one, don't sign any contracts until Azmoth and I read them over. Number two is don't sign any contracts until Azmoth and I look them over. Number three is definitely DO NOT SIGN any contracts until we look them over. I encourage you to go to these interviews on your own at first, as a courtesy to them, but we can look at the contracts and talk to them afterward, and you do NOT have to say yes or sign anything in a timely manner regardless of what those stupid bastards tell you. This is your first time signing a contract the normal way, so be careful. My kind are ruthless suckers; they'll try to steal your soul away without you even knowing it using complex verbiage or loopholes, and you're not going to be manipulated by some dumb twat if I have anything to say about it. Go on, pull up the list, and we can start looking it over together!"

CHAPTER 33

[These four demons have been following your progress and are interested in obtaining you as a partner. Click on each for further details concerning the potential minion and their contracts.
- Beholder, Unholy, Level 27—predominantly a buffer- and siege-type demon with long-range high-cooldown attacks and shielding abilities. This particular Beholder is very good at identifying enemies or objects. [25 Willpower required]
- Blood Fiend, Blood, Level 3—a close-range brawler with passive regeneration, this demon often uses its teeth, claws, and stinger to inflict stacking Bloodbite afflictions that do damage over time. [11 Willpower required]
- Succubus, Unholy/Depravity, Level 21—caster demon, good crowd control and debuffs, moderate damage. This particular Succubus specializes in curses. [29 Willpower required]
- Abyssal Wyrm, Chaos, Level 12—a massive tanking-type demon, very stupid, prone to experiencing uncontrollable rampages. Feels little to no pain or fear. [30 Willpower required]]

"Is four demons a good number?" Riven asked as he shared the screen with his two demonic familiars. Athela climbed up Azmoth's back to sit on his shoulder again.

"I not sure," Azmoth stated.

But Athela was more happy about it. "Definitely! You did GREAT! The variety is rather good as well—most contract applications only come in ones or twos at a time. Let's take a little bit to go through the list. Something to keep in mind is that the levels matter, but they don't matter nearly as much as the traits they give you and the contracts they try to throw at you. We can always power level them by killing random monsters in the wild. Some demons will try to trick you into giving them various benefits or loopholes without you noticing, such as time off to do whatever they want or an easy out of the contract if you say a certain word. Doesn't happen often, but you should watch for it."

Riven raised an eyebrow, folding his arms thoughtfully. "So . . . why does this Succubus have Unholy and Depravity pillars listed? When I saw the Succubus offered as an option previously—back when I ended up choosing you in Chalgathi's trials—it was only listed as Unholy. The description here is also a bit different than the first . . . Does this mean this Succubus is special, somehow?"

"No. It just means that this Succubus has acquired both those pillars and is probably transitioning to create her own specialty pillar with Depravity. Depravity is pretty common with succubi—an easy-to-acquire subpillar for them, for obvious reasons. As for why there's a unique description, that's because they've acquired levels and the system is evaluating them at a more in-depth level than the level-1 demons who've never been in combat." Athela clicked the first item on the list and started reading, and Riven began to do the same.

Beholder, Unholy, Level 27—predominantly a buffer- and siege-type demon with long-range high-cooldown attacks and shielding abilities. This particular Beholder is very good at identifying enemies or objects. [25 Willpower required]

The level-27 Beholder was a giant, floating, central eye above a large maw of sharp teeth. It had purple skin and multiple other eyes at the ends of long, tendril-like appendages. The details were described in further detail with a click of the option. The trait it gave was called Observer, which allowed itself and the bonded warlock to see stealthed opponents far quicker and at a much longer range. It also came with a description concerning identifying enemies or objects, which Riven desperately needed, in his opinion—this creature would fill a massive hole in his party. Not being able to see enemy identification information was a serious problem, and he remembered how nice it was to get that information back in Negrada when he was still under system tutorial parameters.

Blood Fiend, Blood, Level 3—a close-range brawler with passive regeneration, this demon often uses its teeth, claws, and stinger to inflict stacking Bloodbite afflictions that do damage over time. [11 Willpower Required]

Next was the level-3 Blood Fiend. This creature's body was unsurprisingly created from bright-red flesh. It had two thin, abnormally long arms with similar but shorter legs across a spiked white torso—and all its extremities were clawed and covered in sharp, jagged spikes. A long tail twice the length of its body had a stinger attached to the end. Its face was of a crocodilian nature, and it had two pale white eyes on either side of its face before a long snout full of teeth. The trait it gave was called Marine, and it would have allowed Riven to swim at high speed and breath underwater at a very, very small cost of mana over time. Other than also calling the creature a "newborn" in expanded details when the option was clicked, there wasn't much said about it.

Succubus, Unholy/Depravity, Level 21—caster demon, good crowd control and debuffs, moderate damage. This particular Succubus specializes in curses. [29 Willpower required]

Then there was the level-21 Succubus. The description of these demons was the same as it'd been before, when he'd first entered Chalgathi's pretutorial starting quest, describing them as "caster demons, good crowd control and debuffs, moderate damage"—but this time it had a little bit more detail concerning the "specializes in curses" part. When clicking the option, it gave even more details and talked about the demon's ability to fly. The system even talked about how they were often used as nothing more than sexual playthings for their masters and had a historical habit of being abused or pimped out to wealthy men over the centuries due to their natural beauty.

Riven felt a little bit bad about reading that, thinking it was something of a shame that they'd been treated so poorly . . . and he determined that IF he was going to choose the Succubus, he was going to make an extra effort not to let her feel like an object, but rather like a person. Unsurprisingly, she was also incredibly pretty. Her skin was a light-blue complexion. She had bat-like black wings attached to her back, a long, slender black tail, white hair that came down to her back, black eyes, and short black horns sticking out of her forehead. The trait the Succubus came with was called Silvertongue, a very high-mana-cost trait that was able to increase her persuasion abilities drastically. This trait only worked on people with significantly less Willpower than the user, would transfer to Riven as an Unholy spell similar to what had happened with Azmoth, and it only worked for a short period of time depending on the amount of mana spent. Considering he had negative Charisma, this could be utilized well when interacting with humans.

Abyssal Wyrm, Chaos, Level 12—a massive tanking-type demon, very stupid, prone to experiencing uncontrollable rampages. Feels little to no pain or fear. [30 Willpower required]

Lastly there was the level-12 Abyssal Wyrm. This chaos-type demon was essentially an armored, titanic tank that looked very similar to the wyrms he was familiar with in fantasy lore back on Earth. As a low-leveled youngster, this one was only the size of a small school bus—but Athela promised they could get much bigger. It was black, red, and gray, and covered in jagged plate armor all around its body before the circular, toothy maw at the front end. The in-depth description talked about how it could burrow into the ground or break through walls with minimal effort, and they had often been used for siege breaking in many of the histories across the multiverse. The system talked about how these creatures were basically mindless killing machines and were rather hard to control even under contract, but if one did manage to control it well enough, it'd be a great asset as a front-line disaster to enemy forces. The trait was pretty good considering it stacked onto his defense, as it was called Sturdy—and applied a flat +40 to the Sturdiness stat, along with an additional passive effect that would negate two percent of all damage taken.

Frankly, each of the traits was pretty damn good. The only problem was that none of them were based in healing . . . though the Beholder and Succubus were technically more support type demons than the other two front liners. It was a little disappointing not having an option for a healer, as that'd been what he was really looking for when building up his team. He could still definitely work with these options, though, and given that he had massive amounts of passive regeneration in the dark, it wasn't something he needed to worry about immediately. More than anything, he was concerned about the day he ran up against enemies with silver-imbued weapons or sun and light affinities. Those . . . would be a real pain in the ass to deal with. A potentially deadly pain in the ass for a vampire like him.

[Would you like to interview your contract applicants? Yes? No?]

Riven looked around the room at his two minions, Dr. Brass, and the elves. They didn't say much but merely watched him in silence, and he selected yes. Time seemed to slow before he abruptly found himself standing in an ethereal room made of purple mists. Azmoth and Athela were standing to his right and left, and in front of him were the four demons that'd applied to receive his level-35 contract. All of them were in the same ethereal, semitranslucent state as he was.

"Ah . . ." Athela said as she turned around to look at the vast expanse of purple mists. "Back to the nether realms, I see."

Azmoth gave a nod but kept his gaze fixed on the four demons in front of them.

The pictures had been rather skewed in terms of the size of Riven's applicants. The Succubus was the size of a regular woman—but taller than average, probably about five ten, but shorter than Riven. The Beholder was a little bit smaller than her, maybe three feet in diameter for its main body with numerous eyeball appendages making it seem a little larger than it actually was. The Blood Fiend, however, was significantly larger than its picture—about twice the size of the Succubus—and the Abyssal Wyrm was about the size of a small bus at this point in its life cycle.

Still, each of the demons, though they were moving about restlessly, did not appear to see him.

[Touch each of the demons individually for your designated interview time. Your own perceived notion of time has been sped up drastically while you complete your transaction. The hells and nether realms send their regards and hope that you find your new partner up to satisfaction.]

Riven scratched his head as Azmoth and Athela waited patiently, and he approached the large wyrm first. Moving closer was the equivalent to shifting his body's position at a thought when he blipped ahead, disorienting himself momentarily while he adjusted to this realm's odd set of rules, and he reached out a translucent hand to touch the Abyssal Wyrm.

Immediately all the other demons disappeared, including Athela and Azmoth, and he stood alone underneath the creature's towering figure on a vast landscape of ice and snow. A blizzard encircled them, crashing down onto Riven's head . . . but he did not feel cold as the snowflakes pelted his skin. He subconsciously knew, somehow, that this was a visage given to him by the wyrm itself . . . and that this was its ideal habitat that it conjured while remaining here in the nether realms.

In person the monster was even more intimidating than he'd originally anticipated. It coiled up around itself like a snake, deep rumbling sounds vibrating the ground underneath his feet, and it sparked with crimson lightning similar to how Riven's own Blessing of the Crow worked.

Riven backed up to get a better look at the monster as the wyrm uncoiled, and it silently watched him move.

Neither spoke.

Frowning slightly, Riven raised a hand. "Nice to meet you . . . do you talk?"

CHAPTER 34

The wyrm continued to stare blankly back at him, raising its neck and rearing back like a cobra.

Riven's eyebrows raised, and he cleared his throat. "Do you understand anything I'm saying?"

The wyrm's mouth slowly began to open, and it displayed rows upon rows upon rows of jagged black teeth all around its circular maw. Dark light that was a pale purple-gray color intermixed with sparks of red accumulated inside the beast, and the power began to form a large sphere of almost palpable energy. In the next instant it roared, striking at him with the ball of furious mana that dissolved his apparitional body as the vision faded and the wyrm disappeared.

[Tundra Wyrm has declined the contract.]

Riven blinked with a confused scratch of his head. He was now back with his already contracted familiars, puzzled and not sure what he'd done wrong as he watched the wyrm's huge body begin to fade away until there was nothing left of it. "Well . . . that wasn't expected. Definitely a little discouraging."

Athela sighed, holding up her hands to either side with a bemused expression. "We saw the whole thing. They're truly stupid creatures, and it likely just couldn't understand what was going on. Tragic, but there are better options here anyways."

"I'll be your primary tank—no need for stupid worm," Azmoth said with a grin and a low, demonic laugh. "When I get bigger, older, I stomp that parasite into the ground. Do not fret."

Riven smirked back at them and nodded in appreciation at their words of encouragement before moving on to the Beholder demon next. Upon touching the large floating-eye demon, he was instantly transported to the nether realm's plane of existence—this time showing a vast expanse of bright, swirling balls of light that scattered in various directions upon his arrival amid innumerable floating islands of various sizes in the depth of space.

"Hello . . ." came a sophisticated and confident male voice from the demon in front of Riven, almost with a British accent, and the eyeballs surrounding the central body and maw began to pulse with various lights similar to the ones floating about them. "It is good to meet you, Riven Thane. I was hoping for an introduction and am pleased to see that you made the effort to contact me."

Riven blinked, smiled, and nodded in affirmation while crossing his arms. "I'm happy that you applied. What's your name?"

"Jarmosh," the Beholder said without missing a beat as his floating body circled Riven—examining him with all his eyeballs. "Shall we begin? Feel free to ask me anything you'd like."

Riven nodded, taking in his surroundings again with a slow nod. "Yes, of course. I'm currently on a newly integrated planet in the early stages and am just now getting used to this new system. Are you aware of the other demons I already have under contract?"

"I am," Jarmosh stated with a bob of his floating eyeball-head, smiling widely through a toothy maw as his other numerous eyeballs connected to stalks hovered about him. "I am very excited for the potential to become part of that team."

"Then tell me what you can offer, and why you'd even want to join in the first place."

The Beholder paused, giving him a curious look. If he could have scratched its head, he likely would have. "Are you not aware of the benefits we receive by taking on a summoning contract?"

"Go ahead and enlighten me as if I didn't know."

Jarmosh nodded. "Very well. We gain a form of immortality outside the boundary of the nether realms by taking on a contract and can move straight from the nether realms into the mortal realms of Elysium, instead of endangering ourselves by moving into and through hell to get there. Many demons of hell prey on one another to level up and grow stronger, devouring the souls of their brethren. I have remained here in the nether realms for some time now and do not intend to put my life at risk by entering hell just yet . . . I believe it would be wise to find a quality partner to bring me to Elysium instead. You have not only shown yourself to be competent but have the ability to formulate prophecies of unique origin. Beyond that, you also have shown yourself to be quite capable and unlikely to die when compared to your peers. As with your other demons, I, too, wish to develop by serving someone competent enough to keep me there a long time . . . New contracts always take a toll on us demons, and we are not always able to re-form them with new partners immediately after a summoner's death. So having a contract with one like you that will last would benefit me. Otherwise bonding to a self-serving partner who is uninterested in my personal growth would also be folly, and you do not seem to be that type of person—which is unusual, considering your class choice. That is why I wish to join you."

Riven shifted his weight, looking the floating creature up and down thoughtfully. "You haven't answered my question about what you can bring to the team. And I mean long term . . . What will you be able to do in the future if I develop you? What kind of contract would you want?"

Jarmosh narrowed his large central eye and gave another sickly smile. "It is good that you ask such questions. I have been watching you . . . that time that you were nearly killed by the satyr in hell? That wouldn't have happened if I'd been there. The creature snuck up on you without you having noticed their presence until it was almost too late . . . so my trait would benefit you greatly there. Stealthed opponents count as those nearby who you are simply not aware of but are still hostile, not just those who are using stealth abilities."

"Fair point." Riven waved a hand. "Go on."

"Other than that, my kind specializes in buffs and long-range attacks, as the system decreed—but it failed to mention my ability to be used as a scout. My kind has a natural ability to see into and through close objects or barriers, we can scry and visualize things at a great distance if I become developed enough, and our identification abilities are far above normal. My kind usually generate new abilities every eighteen or so levels during the early stages, but it is random, like all the other kinds of demons you may get. My current buff is a shielding ability, a basic barrier that encompasses a target. My ranged attacks are twofold. The first is a high-powered mana beam, and though it is a very high-range attack, it lessens in damage output the farther away the target is. The second attack I currently possess is a pulse detonation surrounding the area around me; it silences all but myself and the one I am bound to and prevents nearby enemies from using abilities for a short time if they don't resist the effect."

[**Black Barrier (Unholy)—Create an Unholy barrier of energy to counter enemy attacks. Your own attacks cannot pass through this barrier either unless broken through and can form many different shapes depending on your vision of this spell. Short cooldown.**]

[**Sin's Cannon (Unholy) (Tier 2)—Create a very long-ranged beam of Unholy energy with high speed and piercing potential. Very high damage. High cooldown.**]

[**Fool's Silencing Act (Unholy)—Detonate the area around you, with damaging effects ignoring you and bound allies. This detonation has a high chance to silence enemy abilities for a moderate amount of time. Very high cooldown.**]

Riven proceeded with numerous other questions after that. Some personal questions about the life here in the nether realms, what combat experience the Beholder had, and various other small talk. The contract Jarmosh wanted wasn't a simple one, and it was very long. It stated overall that Riven would give him opportunities in equal measure to the ones he'd given Azmoth or Athela and would not regularly keep Jarmosh from seeking out his own opportunities for growth, lest the contract become null and void. There was a clause in there talking about how Jarmosh also wanted to set aside time for "experiments concerning the anatomy of mortals" as well, though the way it was worded made it sound like the demon would be dissecting creatures alive—and if Riven took this contract, he'd be sure to scratch that out before accepting.

"It was good to meet you, Jarmosh. I'll get back to you soon," Riven said with a smile as he accepted a handshake from one of the fleshy tendrils snaking out from the main eye. "I think you'd be a great asset to have."

The Beholder grinned evilly back at him, though Riven was rather certain that's just how the smiling Beholder looked every time he grinned. "The pleasure is mine."

He vanished out of the Beholder's personal realm with a thoughtful downward gaze. Jarmosh hadn't been all that bad—an identifier would be nice, and the abilities were all right. He gave a thumbs-up to Athela when she gave him a questioning stare, then silently approached the Succubus next.

She was likely about his age, maybe a couple years younger . . . though this might just be how all succubi looked. He couldn't be sure and would have to ask Athela about it later. The girl was a unique blend of three colors. There were the black eyes, black horns, black tail, black wings, and the long white hair and light-blue skin. She was easily one of the most attractive women he'd ever seen, but he had to remind himself that this species—according to the system—had a very sad history concerning their treatment. They'd historically been used and abused, and he was hesitant about how to approach this contract because of it. He didn't intend anything of the sort and instead was focused on her potential for the team he was building, but the implications of even considering a Succubus were certainly there.

He touched her shoulder, and in a whirling of colors he found himself sitting in a beautiful garden on a lawn of brilliant green grass. They were sitting underneath a large oak tree's canopy, and rays of sunshine filtered through the leaves above to shine onto the Succubus's bare body in patches as she stared back at him with a hesitant yet excited smile.

His eyebrows raised as he looked around, and then he met her gaze with a smile to match her own. "Hey."

The Succubus gave him an even nod and a soft smile, then stood up and dusted off her thighs before cupping her hands in front of her. "Hi, Riven. How's your day going?"

He paused as he thought it over.

"Honestly? Not terribly. Could be better. I was just swarmed by a hive-mind creature, and that got in the way of my schedule, but it paid off now that I hit level 36 and am here. I'm assuming you've been watching my progress just like the Beholder demon said he'd been doing?"

She nodded, shifting her black eyes to glance over his body and ending at the amulet of the dragon on Riven's chest, the Chalgathi cultist amulet—and her eyes narrowed. "Yes, I've been watching you for a while now. We demons that don't want to enter the hells—which is probably about half of us—work very hard to find compatible and suitable summoners to bond to."

"You say the word *summoners* like it's different than just warlocks and cultists. How many other summoner types are there?"

Again she nodded, crossing her long bare legs and stretching out her wings while her tail flipped from side to side in anticipation. "Those with the class title of cultist, warlock, lich, black magic practitioner, soul-scarred, and more. There are a handful of different classes that can summon us. I'm glad I found you when I did, because you're quite the catch."

"Hmm." Riven rubbed his forehead and squinted to clear his thoughts, intentionally avoiding looking anywhere except her face to be respectful. "What's your name?"

"Oh! I'm sorry, that was rude." The young woman abruptly gave a sheepish smile of perfect white teeth, reached out a hand to shake, and awkwardly laughed with her head tilted to the side. "My name is Fay. It's very nice to meet you in person, Riven! I've been very excited for this moment."

They shook hands, though Riven could only faintly feel her touch in this ethereal form of his.

"Can you tell me why you've been excited?" Riven asked warmly as he took his hand back. "What makes you want to join me? And what can you provide for the team if I choose you instead of the others?"

Fay hummed, the sound equivalent to wind blowing through chimes on a midsummer's breeze while she smiled mischievously his way. Then she winked at him. "Other than satisfy your carnal desires?"

He immediately went a bright red, which was very obvious with his pale skin, to which she threw her head back and laughed.

"Uh . . . that's not really what I'm looking for," Riven stated bluntly, if a bit awkwardly, while he shuffled his feet.

"I'm just teasing you . . ." she said after another fit of giggling with her hand covering her mouth. "I actually picked you because you seem like a kind person, which is very rare in your line of work. You wouldn't believe how many summoners . . . Ugh, never mind. That's a story for another time. I thought I'd be a good fit because of your inability to blend in concerning human societies without a large social stigma attached to you. My Silvertongue trait would allow both you and I to speak with the humans you desire so much to be a part of. That in itself fascinates me . . . and perhaps we may even walk among the mortals of your old world for short periods of time without much problem if you expend enough mana. By the way, if you do choose me—I just want to point out that I have a clause in my contract regarding how I'm treated. My last and only master until this point was . . . violent. I don't want to have a repeat of that situation again."

Riven's mouth opened and shut as he mulled over how to reply to that last snippet of information, but he failed when she started up before he managed a proper sentence.

"I have three Unholy abilities and one Depravity ability. I am able to create a network of cursed sigils in the air, invisible to enemies without mana detection, creating a network of trapped explosive mana mines. I can set down a cursed mana zone that causes enemies to hallucinate while inside, and this goes very well with the first ability I mentioned. I can afflict enemies with curses that deal rot damage over time, building up a slowing effect that starts off small but increases exponentially. And lastly, I may charm or seduce a single enemy into a stupor if their Willpower is low enough, but this is a channeling ability, and I can't outright control them. Here, take a look."

[Curse Trap (Unholy)—Place invisible sigils of Unholy mana in the air or on objects around you. The act of placing a sigil emits cursed light for a brief moment before turning invisible, and these sigils will retain a mana signature that can be sensed by appropriate means. If enemies come within the sigil's radius of effect, the sphere detonates with Unholy damage. Radius of effect depends on Intelligence stat and amount of spent mana. Sigils lose energy over time and disappear if not activated. You may connect different sigils to create trip wires and chain reactions. Low cooldown.]

[Curse of the Dreamwalker (Unholy)—Create an Unholy mana zone that afflicts all the user deems as enemies. Causes enemies to hallucinate while in the zone. The more mana used to create the zone, and the smaller the zone is, the higher the potency of the hallucination effects. High cooldown.]

[Curse of Rot (Unholy)—Spray a cloud of Unholy miasma to afflict targets with a single Rot debuff before the cloud dissipates. A single cloud can disperse across multiple enemies. Rot debuff applies Unholy damage, slows the enemy, and can stack with other

Rot debuffs. This curse starts out weak but scales over time in both damage and slowing effect. Low cooldown.]

[Charm (Depravity)—Infatuate any enemies within range of sight that look upon you, causing them to lose focus. The farther away they are from you, the less effect this ability will have. The more Willpower the enemy has, the less effect this ability will have. Channeling ability that costs increasing amounts of mana over time.]

"Well, thank you for your honesty. Does your kind acquire any healing abilities later on?" Riven asked curiously.

Fay shrugged. "It is possible. The administrator works in strange ways . . . and within categories. Succubi certainly have been known to acquire healing abilities, so it is within our natural affinities to do such a thing, but it doesn't happen often. I saw you speaking to your other minions about this, actually . . . and you were saying you wanted a healing minion? This is a rare thing indeed for a demon. The Unholy foundational pillar and the magic of its subpillars often don't focus on healing, but your best bets for healing magics within these branches are found within the Blood subset of Unholy magic. Because of your vampiric heritage, you are much more likely than most of us to acquire healing abilities in the realm of blood magic. There are species of blood-type Unholy demons that do it and focus on the area of healing, but most other demons don't. If you wish to have a demon that focuses on that role, you are better off finding spell tomes or scrolls and teaching the spells you want them to learn—but again, finding those types of spells within your set of attributes will be hard. I could eventually acquire a class title if I played my cards right, and it COULD be one that focuses on healing . . . That way I would continue to have much higher odds of learning new abilities that revolve around what you want, though to get such a class would likely require I learn at least one healing spell of some sort, and then I'd be required to use it a lot first."

Riven snorted his understanding. "Gotcha. Do you have any questions for me, Fay?"

Fay paused, then shook her head. "No. My contract should be to your liking. It merely states that as long as I am not physically tortured by you, and as long as there are opportunities for me to progress and grow, the contract will remain in place. There are no other requirements."

Riven looked back at her, concerned. "Did you really think I was going to torture you?"

"No!" she replied happily with a clap of her hands as she wrapped her arms around her waist, drawing in her bat-like wings behind her. "But it did happen to me with my last contractor. One of my sisters is still under contract with a cultist who does exactly that, regularly carving pieces of my sister off to use for his alchemy before her body regenerates. She's also used in blood orgies quite often, and that never ends well. She doesn't die, but she desperately wants to be free of him and keeps coming up with schemes to get him killed—all of which have failed thus far. I feel bad for her."

Riven's jaw almost dropped. "How fucked."

"I know."

The two of them stood up, and Riven extended his hand again with a drawn-out sigh—still keeping his gaze focused on her face. "Hey. It was genuinely nice meeting you, Fay. You're not what I expected, and I'm glad we got to talk."

She nodded politely, hand still clasped in front of her, and then she gave a small bow. "It was great meeting you, too. How many other interviews do you have left?"

Riven paused as another hologram prompt for him to end the interview appeared in front of his face, his finger hovering over the prompt. "Just one more. It's with the Blood Fiend."

She made a grossed-out expression and stuck out her tongue. "A Blood Fiend? Disgusting alligators, those ones. Any chance I can get you to just accept my contract now and be done with it? I promise I will make a good teammate. I'm very low maintenance."

She winked, but he ignored her obvious attempt at flirting and shook his head with a polite smile. "You're definitely great, and you seem promising, but no. I want to finish all of these interviews before deciding."

She let out an exaggerated sigh of disappointment, then laughed heartily at his look of discomfort. "I'm just teasing you, Riven. Learn to relax. Go get the interview over with and then come back to me when you realize that I'm the best option."

Riven rubbed his forehead, gave her a final wave that she returned, then he disappeared out of the garden and back into the swirling purple mists.

"Typical Succubus," Athela stated flatly when he reappeared next to his two already-contracted familiars. "Always the flirtatious ones."

"I liked her," Azmoth stated in an even tone with his four arms crossed. "Her trait would come in handy for our master, too."

Athela bobbed her head left and then right. "Can't say I disagree. The trait is valuable to someone like Riven . . . She probably knows this. I'm surprised her contract wasn't more demanding. I actually looked it over while you two were talking, Riven. She wasn't lying—there are no hidden red flags to be wary of, and it's a good deal. Better than the one with the Beholder, certainly."

Azmoth nodded. "The Beholder wrote contract so that terms are vague. There are loopholes so can claim negligence on Riven's part and break it at any time. If you choose Beholder, Riven, you need him to rewrite contract—or you need to decline."

"Agreed." Athela nodded at the brutalisk in affirmation.

This was news to Riven. He'd not had time to look at the contracts in detail just yet, but he trusted both Azmoth and Athela with his life and would take their words at face value before diving deeper into the subject later on. "I liked them both, but I was definitely a little wary of how Jarmosh the Beholder wanted to experiment on animals or people. A little weird, if you ask me."

"It's probably for a craft he has," Athela replied as she tapped her eight blooded spider legs thoughtfully. "Now that I think about it . . . you should ask the Succubus whether or not she is into enchanting. Curses are a subcategory of Unholy-related enchanting and can be applied to items a lot like how she'd use them on whatever her targets had in combat. Makes for useful items if done right, but I don't know enough about it to tell you more than that."

Riven hummed, thinking back to his brief totem-making adventures when he'd read the manuscript that touched on the topic of enchanting. He'd have to pick that craft up again, eventually, when things settled down.

Coming up to the crocodilian Blood Fiend next, Riven reached out a hand and touched the ethereal image. In a swirl of light, Riven found himself on a floating pile of driftwood far out at sea from the closest land mass. Chunks of sea creatures lay half-eaten all around him, and he found the demon lazily basking in the dull light of the sun as it watched him from afar.

It was certainly large, about the height of Azmoth, though it didn't have as solid or thick of a frame. The long stinger at the end of its tail flipped back and forth lazily as its long snout lifted into the air, and it began to sniff in his direction.

"Greetings . . ." The hissing, serpentine voice came out as it opened its mouth to produce the sound from a voice box far in the back of its throat. It sounded like it was straining to speak at all, but it still managed to get the words out so Riven could understand it. "Have you come to beg of my assistance . . . ?"

Riven cocked an eyebrow. "Isn't this supposed to be an interview concerning your abilities, not mine?"

The demon snickered, making raspy gasping sounds when it laughed condescendingly. "No. I am a perfect hunter . . . You need to convince me that you are worth my time . . . otherwise I will not—"

Riven immediately clicked the prompt and willed the creature to disappear—ending the interview in an instant. He found himself back in the purple fogs of the nether realm a split second later. Orienting himself to the surroundings again, he quickly saw that the blood demon was beginning to fade away from the remaining three visages of interviewees, while yet another prompt lit up in front of his vision.

[Blood Fiend has declined the contract.]

He snorted. "Good fucking riddance. I lasted three seconds before it got high and mighty on me."

Azmoth gave an amused sneer in the direction of the fiend as the last remnants of the blood demon vanished with a hiss. "The puny alligator did not deserve the opportunity. I am glad you reacted that way. Let him find more desperate mortal to level off."

Athela let out a laugh and leaned on Azmoth's shoulder with her elbow. "The fiend likely didn't realize you had multiple offers, meaning he wasn't paying attention. Many summoners only get one or two offers in a single round unless they wait a long time, so it likely surprised him that you reacted the way you did."

Riven shrugged indifferently. "He can kiss my pale white ass. Now, which of these two to choose . . ."

At this point, there was only Fay the Succubus and Jarmosh the Beholder left. He liked both of them a lot and would have been happy to choose either of them.

Thus he was at a crossroads.

CHAPTER 35

On one hand, Jarmosh seemed a little less trustworthy, given that he'd put loopholes in his contract. Athela had outright told him he couldn't accept the contract in the way the Beholder had worded it, so he'd have to get Jarmosh to agree to rewrite it the way Riven wanted it done or he'd have to decline. He also didn't like the idea of Jarmosh experimenting with live and innocent creatures, though he could have some leeway if it came to people or monsters that had attacked them or posed a threat. Perhaps the experiments Jarmosh was planning could come in handy somehow? Especially if they really were related to a craft. His shielding, spotting, and identifying abilities and long-range attacks would be great in combination with Riven's ranged fighting, too.

On the other hand, there was the Succubus, with her Silvertongue trait that would transfer to Riven as a spell. It would give him some leeway when interacting with other races that didn't have negative Charisma orientation, especially as he grew more levels and accumulated more and more negative Charisma. It may be noticeable from time to time now, but what would it look like if he reached more than two thousand negative points? Or four thousand? Would they run screaming from him, collapse in fear, or would they outright hate and attack on sight?

Otherwise Fay's abilities were oriented toward crowd control with hidden mana mines, a hallucination field, a charm ability, and a damage-over-time curse that slowed enemies, too. The entire package would be great for keeping enemies off him while he sat back and let loose from relative safety, or at least that'd be the hope.

But what if Riven was ever going to date someone else? How could he explain having a Succubus with him?

They'd immediately think he was a dirty pervert.

That was certainly a concern, though one far off and not relevant to his current situation. Regardless, he was leaning more toward the Beholder demon.

They were both great options, but the identifying of enemies and spotting potential assassins alone was something that swayed things in favor of the demonic eyeball collection.

So with a minor amount of guilt concerning the fond interaction he'd had with Fay, he bypassed the Succubus and mentally bade her farewell as he went back to talk to the Beholder. He'd have to speak to Jarmosh about the loopholes in his contract and a complete rewrite of it before he'd agree, though—that was nonnegotiable. "Athela? Azmoth? Mind coming along and pointing out his loopholes so we can rewrite it? I'd like you in on this discussion."

"Oh! So you're choosing Jarmosh?" Athela said curiously as Azmoth gave him an affirmative nod. "Wow! You really AREN'T a simp!"

He rolled his eyes and gestured to the figure of the Beholder demon. "Oh, shut up. Fay was really nice, too, but I think the Beholder is likely a better pick in helping me survive."

"That Silvertongue trait, though!"

"Can only be used for short periods of time. Yes, otherwise it is amazing. Don't rub it in my face when I may be regretting this choice later. Now, hurry it up. We have work to do."

Unfortunately, the talk between Riven and Jarmosh did not go well. In fact, it was mostly Athela and Jarmosh going at it—with the arachnoid woman accusing him of manipulating the contract and pointing out said loopholes while Jarmosh, in his sophisticated British accent, denied all counts and refused to modify the contract.

"I refuse!" Jarmosh snarled as his large central eye and all the other ones surrounding him glared daggers at the hissing arachnid. "These are nothing but mere coincidences that line up with verbiage explicitly set there to protect myself from exploitation!"

"You're a damned liar!" Athela spat as her right-forward spider leg shook with anger. "You filthy little eyeball!"

"HOW DARE YOU CALL ME AN EYEBALL!"

"YOU'RE A PUTRID, VENOMOUS, UGLY EYEBALL AT THAT!"

Azmoth stared at the two bickering demons alongside Riven on the right side, folding his four armored, cindering arms with a grunt of disgust and scratching the back of his neck with one of his extra eel-like maws. The brutalisk then withdrew the two maws into his back, exchanged a glance with Riven, and sighed.

Riven didn't know what to make of it and began to whisper over at Azmoth as the other two other demons engaged one another. "So . . . Is Athela taking this out of context and being overprotective of me? Or is the observer demon really trying to pull one over on us?"

Azmoth turned his armored, eyeless head toward Riven. "Have you not read contract?"

"I did, but it's over sixty pages long."

"That . . . is true. Beholder likely did it on purpose to hide what Athela found. Anyways, yes, Athela correct. It obvious the loopholes are there. Two big ones that he's trying. The first would allow him break the contract without excuse or if he unhappy, and he could be unhappy for any reason and leave you in moment of need. Second loophole would allow him to force you to give up items that benefit him, even if you rather sell them or use them yourself."

Riven blinked, then turned his gaze back onto the Beholder with a new perspective. "Is it normal for demons to try and pull this stuff?"

"Depends."

The screeching and screaming were reaching new heights as Athela acted as Riven's lawyer.

"I BET YOU GET PINKEYE!!! YOU DIRTY, ASS-SNIFFING, FLOATING VAGABOND!"

"I'VE NEVER HAD PINKEYE ONCE IN MY ENTIRE LIFE, YOU OVERGROWN INSECT!"

"I'M A SPIDER! I EAT INSECTS FOR BREAKFAST, YOU UTTERLY HORRIFIC ABSCESS! I'D STOMP YOU LIKE A BABY IF WE WEREN'T IN THE NETHER REALMS!"

"YOU?! HA!!! YOUR KIND IS AS USELESS AS THE IMPS AND WOULDN'T EVEN BE ABLE TO TOUCH ME FROM DOWN ON THE GROUND!"

"YOU TAKE THAT BACK! I AM NOT COMPARABLE TO AN IMP! THEY'RE MERELY TINY FIRE-BELCHING MONKEYS, AND I HAVE PIZZAZZ!"

At this point, it was just becoming a ridiculous case of insulting one another. It wasn't getting anywhere at all, and despite Riven's original impression that Jarmosh would likely have been a slightly better asset to the team—he was now having second thoughts. Especially if the team mascot, Athela, wouldn't get along with him.

"You should choose Fay," Azmoth stated abruptly as he let out another exhausted sigh. "This getting nowhere. Succubus wouldn't be bad asset to have, but I warn you not to get involved with her."

"Involved? Do you mean romantically?"

"Yes. Don't do it if you do choose her. Succubi crazy."

Riven chuckled and folded his arms. "I'd had no intention of doing that if I did pick Fay. But yeah, she wouldn't be a bad choice, either."

Their conversation was interrupted as Jarmosh the observer demon huffed in anger and flew over to where Riven stood with a glowering expression at the arachnid behind him. "I refuse to change the contract, and I will not listen to any more of this spider woman's absurd ideas! Sign it and be done or leave me to find another!"

Athela was literally quivering with rage at this point, but she did not approach the eyeball demon again. Instead she folded her arms in front of her, snarled, and turned her back without another glance.

Riven cast a genuinely caring look over at the Arshakai. Athela didn't have to fight for him like this, and it wouldn't have hurt her cause much if another demon had gotten the better of Riven, but instead she was seriously angry.

For him.

[You have declined the contract.]

With a look of surprise, Jarmosh the Beholder demon began to fizzle out of existence as Riven and his two minions returned to the nether realms, where only one of the four demons who'd initially contacted him remained.

"You made the right choice," Athela confirmed with a satisfied sneer toward the last of Jarmosh's image before he fizzled out. "Stupid eyeball. The Succubus had a much better contract with absolutely nothing to worry about. Pick her."

Riven smiled slightly but didn't say another word. Team cohesiveness and trustworthiness were more important than whatever else the Beholder demon could have brought to their group. After the negotiations were through, that demon had neither.

"Come on Athela, Azmoth. Let's go talk to Fay."

[Your pact with Fay has been sealed under the watchful eye of the administrator. The demonic seal representing Fay will be etched into your flesh, and your body has been restored to perfect health. Congratulations on obtaining your new demonic minion.]

[You have inherited Fay's Unholy trait Silvertongue as a spell.]

[Silvertongue (Unholy): Soak your words with Unholy mana to briefly capture the minds of lesser beings, allowing only those with less Willpower than you to be affected and enabling you to persuade them more easily. This spell scales with both Willpower and negative Charisma, as well as the amount of mana you put into it. This spell may be developed into a better version of itself by acquiring the Depravity subpillar. Extremely high mana cost, low cooldown.]

In a flash he was standing back in the basement of the hospital, another red pentagram being drawn on his chest next to the ones containing the symbol of jaws for Azmoth and a spider for Athela. This one, however, was a set of succubus wings.

Riven took off his tattered cloak and draped it around Fay's shoulders, meeting her black eyes for a moment before stepping back. "Athela, go get some clothes for Fay. Some of the ones we picked out for you should fit her all right—you're about the same size."

"Clothes are stupid and should only be worn on special occasions," Athela stated flatly, folding her arms. "We're demons, and our bodies are great. Why hide them?"

Riven opened his mouth to speak, but then closed it and rubbed the bridge of his nose. "I'll let her decide. I'm not going to have this conversation with you again."

Fay was hesitantly looking around the small basement where the two elves, Senna and Ethel, as well as Dr. Brass remained motionless with raised eyebrows. Drawing her wings into her back and letting out a deep, relaxed sigh of contentment, Fay knelt and bowed.

"Thank you for choosing me, Master. You will not regret this decision."

"We're a team now; you don't need to do that." Riven smiled, motioning for her to get up as she brushed her long white hair behind one ear and took his hand to stand. "Glad to have you."

Fay stood up and gave a nod to the others, ignoring Dr. Brass's blatant staring. "Hello." She turned back to Riven. "If it makes you comfortable, I'll take your offer on clothes. It does not bother me either way, and it would probably draw less attention if I did wear something."

Riven nodded, intentionally keeping his eyes on her face. "Yup. Agreed, and thanks."

If he had to continue to try and look away for all eternity, that would have been a real problem. Clothes would certainly help.

Athela, on the other hand, threw up her hands and turned, muttering under her breath about stupid mortal customs before she fetched a crop top and short shorts from the bag of stuff, they'd raided from the clothing warehouse.

A pulsing sensation began to emanate from his bag and Riven raised an eyebrow before reaching inside and pulling out the communication orb he'd been gifted by Mara and Allie. "Hello?"

"Hey!" Allie's voice cut through the air like she was standing right next to him. "Have you started your trip yet?"

Riven glanced past the changing Succubus and over to the elves along the wall. "Unfortunately not. Hey, I know we talked about this a couple times already but are you really sure you're okay with me going? With Prophet building up forces, I've been rethinking things. Perhaps I should stay behind until that's settled."

"We have spies watching them, and we even have two in their own ranks. Human spies that want necromancer classes or a chance to join our faction. Jose wasn't the only one these new-age crusaders wronged . . ." Allie's voice trailed off, but she quickly cleared her throat and continued talking through the pulsing black orb. "The point is, we'll know when they're coming ahead of time. We have tough fortifications, and I'm stronger than anyone they have on their side. The problem is that relic Prophet keeps, the book, but in order to use its defensive capabilities, he has to set up a zone of influence. That's why this small war has dragged on for so long—it's harder fighting them on their own turf. Meanwhile, they lose advantage while leaving their own consecrated grounds."

"Consecrated? You didn't mention that."

"Yes, the relic is able to bless the areas they control; it severely weakens undead like us and does a whole lot of other things I'm not quite sure of yet. All I know is the rumors being pitched to me from our two insiders. Regardless, as long as we're not on their consecrated grounds, it'll be fine, and I have an army of my own in both minions and other sentient undead. You saw how tightly locked this place is, and we're only sending out assassination groups for now until we get a better picture of what their leadership is up to. I'm not taking risks."

Riven remembered the flesh golems, bone giant, and hundreds of ghouls, skeletons, and skresh walking around the skyscraper Allie was terraforming. He also remembered just how close Allie had come to kicking his ass in a one-on-one fight, and he felt confident she'd be okay while he was gone. "Well, I'd have to agree that it'd almost be suicide attacking that tower of yours—it is pretty much a fortress. Senna? Ethel? How long will this trip take again?"

Senna stuttered a response while Ethel's eyes hit the floor, massaging her stump arm. "I—I think it'll only take a few days . . . Maybe . . . but Ethel and I are injured, so it could take longer."

Riven nodded, giving Fay a polite smile and making room for her to pass as she and the other demoness, Athela, walked out of the room to start exploring outside. The two demonic women were already hitting it off nicely, speaking in hushed tones and laughing with one another mischievously before leaving. That was a good sign in Riven's book.

"Did you hear that?" Riven asked the bauble in his hands.

"I did," Allie replied. "Just be safe, Riven. No hero acts, okay? I'm going to be really, really mad at you if I have to come save you while you do a drop-off. You're not invincible, remember that."

"I know, I know."

"Promise me you won't do anything heroic and stupid? Even if it means other people get hurt?"

"I'll only take fights I know I can win."

"You have to promise."

Riven smirked. "I promise I'll try my best to do that."

"RIVEN! I fucking MEAN IT! You ALWAYS get hurt trying to help other people out, even when we were kids! Remember those bullies that dressed up in ninja suits and shoved your head in a toilet because you—"

"Fine! Fine. No embarrassing stories when other people are around." Riven grimaced at the memory and shook his head. "Hope I find those little bastards now that we're older. Anyways, I love you, Allie. I'll talk to you later, okay? And if you really need me, let me know. I'll drop everything and sprint back. I move pretty damn fast now."

She gave an amused grunt. "Okay. I'll have this orb on me at all times—call me if anything happens and I'll do the same. Love you, Riven."

The pulsing sensation cut off when the communication did, and he tucked the black bauble into the backpack again.

A wave of exhaustion hit him shortly after, and Azmoth caught him when Riven took a shaky step forward. He'd not realized he was this tired. Blinking a couple of times and yawning, he told the others he was going to take a nap. After all that fighting, it was finally time to get some rest before they headed out.

CHAPTER 36

When he woke up, Dr. Brass filled him in on what had happened with the other humans during the fight while Senna snored softly next to Ethel under a blanket.

Dr. Waters had been adamant that Dr. Brass leave with her, calling him a fool when she and all the nurses had taken the long hike down the underground sewers to find a way out. When Riven asked why Dr. Brass hadn't left to begin with, he'd just said that he'd taken a liking to Riven and Athela in the short time he'd known them. He didn't have any family and was too old to be scared of dying, so he'd put his chips on their success in the fight with the dream creatures.

Senna and Ethel hadn't had much of a choice of whether to stay given their injuries, though it was obvious that they were incredibly relieved that their side had won. Both elves had watched the entire fight from start to finish, and they were often caught staring at Riven and the demons who'd fought the monster with curious, fixated gazes.

As for planting the rod? He was likely going to use it near Allie's tower as a gift, and that was also where he'd probably put his guild hall, too. Though those things would have to wait until later.

They took turns sleeping, with the exception of Azmoth, who didn't sleep at all. Athela and Fay returned shortly after that, Fay with a giddy look on her face at being out of the nether realms for so long. The Succubus was incredibly polite in her interactions with everyone thus far. Even the elves, whom Athela had been very hot or cold with ever since meeting them. Even Dr. Brass, who ogled the Succubus regularly despite his poor attempts to hide it, was treated with a kind and brilliant smile whenever he spoke to Fay—which was often.

So all in all: Riven, Fay, Athela, Azmoth, Dr. Brass, Senna, and Ethel made for a total of seven that joked and laughed with one another through the remainder of the night between naps. The dream creatures were dead, Riven had found Allie safe and sound with an army surrounding her to keep her safe, and all seemed right with the world now that no immediate threats were present.

In fact, the mood was so good that most of them didn't get much sleep at all.

Riven was actually taking a break from all the banter, relieving himself in a bucket in an adjacent room, when Athela whipped around the corner in spider form and swatted him on the head a couple times with one hand.

"'Ello, chap!"

Riven glared at the demoness and grumbled something about privacy being ignored, pulled up his pants, and adjusted the new belt he'd taken from that clothing store. "What is it? And isn't your leg broken? You never rested in the nether realms after that fight—you shouldn't be walking around on it like that. I can't believe you went exploring alongside Fay without healing first."

"It's fine, see?!" Athela flexed and extended her knee but failed to hide her grimace when an audible snap was heard. "Bleh. I'll be fine for now, and I am able to get around using my arachnid limbs. I'll head back to the nether realm soon. Are you excited about your Elysium altar rod?! It looks so neat!"

Riven nodded, picked up the bucket, and took it over to the room's corner to set it down under a tarp of sorts. It wasn't like they were going to stay much longer anyways, with only Ethel capitalizing on the rest they likely all needed. Her forearm stump was bothering her a lot, and sleep helped the pain. "Yeah, it's pretty cool that we'll be able to utilize the system store. Now we just have to find a place to set up camp, so to speak. Somewhere safer, if possible."

"Agreed."

He glanced over his shoulder. "So, how's Fay doing? Did you get a chance to talk to her much?"

Athela's smile widened, and she knocked her knuckles against the door absentmindedly while leaning against the wall. "I really, really like her . . . She's very nice. Very different from most of the succubi I've met in the nether realms, but in a good way. I think you're going to like her, too."

"That's great to hear. In the meantime . . ." Riven paused, folding his arms and tapping his foot thoughtfully. "How big is that Elysium altar going to be when we set it up? It needed three square miles designated to plant the rod, didn't it?"

Athela held up hands out to either side, supporting most of her weight on the arachnid limbs coming out of her back to relieve some of the stress on her broken human leg. "Elysium altars are usually placed at random along the span of the newly integrated worlds. They'll be difficult to find at first, but as you'll find out when you plant that rod, they're usually pretty large and hard to hide. They're built like huge open-air temples, actually, or large monoliths. Once you know a general location, it'll be easy to see it, and that's also why you need three square miles of space. It's pretty big and will gain a lot of attention when you put it down."

The sound of a heartbeat growing closer and then a knock at the door alerted Riven to someone's presence. Out in the hallway, he saw Dr. Brass waiting for him.

"Hey. What's up?"

The graying old man stood leaning against the wall cleaning his glasses and adjusted them to put them back on hurriedly when Riven walked out of the room. "Oh, hey there. Are you busy? May we talk?"

"Does it look like I'm busy?" Riven replied with amusement. "Can I help you with something?"

The old man mulled over his thoughts while staring at the ground, then noticed the bloodstains on his white coat and grimaced. "Well . . . How do I approach this?" The doctor clicked his tongue, then motioned to his body and tugged at his wrinkling skin. "I'm pretty old."

Riven stared blankly back at him with Athela coming around to take a look, too, and laughed as he didn't know what the doctor was getting at. "Yeah, I suppose it's kinda obvious."

"Do vampires age?"

Oh.

So that's what this was about.

This was probably why Dr. Brass had stayed to begin with.

Riven shoved his hands into his pockets and thought about the prospect for a moment, then shook his head. "At the very least, my status page says I won't die of old age. So I'm assuming the body kinda resets to a certain stage of adulthood."

"I see. And . . . would you be willing to turn me? I heard you had a quest to grow and form a coven. I'd like to be part of it. This new world . . . it's brutal, but it's also magical. There's so much out there to explore, like an entirely new frontier. Like *Star Trek*! Go where no man has gone before kinda thing . . . and I want to be at the forefront of that exploration. The problem is, I won't last another two decades. I might not last even one more decade."

It'd been a while since Riven looked at his quests. He still had three active at the bottom of his status page, one being a notification that he'd actually been targeted by said quest and two of them guiding quests from the administrator.

[You have been made a target by a regional quest: **Crusade Against the Undead**—Benjamin, otherwise known as Prophet to his followers, has declared a holy war for the control of the city of Brightsville. Enacting a holy ritual and with his request being backed by a minor god, all humans within Brightsville will receive additional Elysium coins, XP toward leveling, and other undisclosed prizes based on performance when culling the undead in this area.]

[You have been offered a guiding system quest from the administrator: **Covens**—Either find a coven to join or grow your own coven to a minimum number of five vampires including yourself. To create new vampires, you must inject vampiric essence into your target via your fangs. Be wary of doing this too fast, as if you do not recharge your vampiric essence in between attempts to turn others, you will become sick, and in a worst-case scenario, die. Rewards: one portal ticket for an attempt to acquire another piece of Valgeshia's Item Set.]

[You have been offered a guiding system quest from the administrator: Acquire Cattle and Create a Thrall—As a newly born vampire, you will need to acquire cattle, or in other terms, people to feed on regularly. It does not matter if you do this through persuasion or force. Then after this, select one of these cattle to create a thrall. Thralls are mortals bent to a vampire's will and are essentially more subservient and powerful cattle, as many vampires like to say. Though they do retain their Intelligence, personality, and to some extent their own free will, their desires are instinctively and heavily oriented to align with your own. This places them in the minion category of your status page when acquired successfully. Thralls also acquire some vampiric strengths, while they are able to retain their own pillars and abilities outside of the vampiric influence. However: retained pillars and abilities will be corrupted— sometimes modifying them slightly for better or worse. Lastly, thralls are able to provide greater amounts of nourishing blood than normal mortal cattle do, and their bloodlines may be modified over time to evolve to your liking. To create a thrall, you must feed on them regularly for an extended period of time, and they must in turn feed on your blood numerous times throughout their initial evolutionary cycle. Reward upon acquiring thrall: one combat level, a stable food source, and a new avenue to acquire minions.]

Riven frowned at that last quest. He'd been feeding off the corpse of a dead nurse for the past day now, but he still needed a solid source of blood so he wouldn't go crazy. He looked up and met the man's hopeful eyes. Dr. Brass was nervously fidgeting with a pen between his hands. His gaze softened and he put a hand on the doctor's shoulder.

"I have no reason to say no. But let's wait awhile—I still need to figure out the feeding situation for myself. Having another vampire around would only amplify that problem. Just so you know, the transformation can be painful, and the notification talks about how some people may die in the process. I doubt that's a common phenomenon, from what Athela has told me, but she's a demon, not a vampire. She doesn't quite know for sure herself."

The doctor let out an audible sigh of relief, and his features brightened immediately. He stopped his nervous fidgeting and put his pen into a side pocket of his stained white coat. The man even looked happy. "Thank you, son. It quite literally means the world to me. I'll take the risk . . . and I'll leave the two of you to talk."

The elves were eager to get back home, and their excitement grew as the time approached. Neither of them got much sleep that night and stayed up late animatedly talking to Fay and Athela after Athela made it back from a break in the nether realms to heal. They talked about the merging of worlds, the Elysium system, Riven's sister and her horde of undead, as well as various backstories on their lives.

Ethel's left arm wound where it'd been cut off a couple inches above the wrist hadn't entirely healed yet, and one of her ankles was black and blue from a sprain, but the arm was doing far better and the infection was gone. Senna's collarbone was still touchy and likely would be for some time after this, and the infection was still present in the leg where that goblin had bitten her, but they were both doing significantly better, and Dr. Brass had given Senna some oral antibiotics to take with her along with instructions on how often to take them.

Regardless, the girls were happy to actually be going home and were excited to see their families again. Riven, Azmoth, and Dr. Brass eventually let them have their privacy through the end of that night and got to sleeping, and in the morning light of sunrise they set off.

Azmoth was tasked with carrying an old hospital laundry bin full of coins and supplies. They had an especially easy time hauling it on the roads leading out of the decimated city, and though they saw a few groups of other survivors, the humans in large part either ran or hid from the intimidating party at a moment's glance. Riven didn't dare leave the stash behind, and soon enough they reached the edge of the city and took to the plains. When they reached the forests not long after that, the trek became a bit harder.

Their pace was a bit slower than Riven would have liked, and he had to keep his hood pulled down so the sun didn't bother him. The two elves couldn't walk properly due to their wounds, so either Riven carried them or they sat in the bin Azmoth pushed and carried. Currently Riven was carrying Ethel while his unique weapon floated along behind him with occasional twists or turns as if it was curiously observing their environment. Which . . . it was, Riven came to find out. His staff still had memories of some sort relating to the old items he'd created it from. Both halves, the dagger and the staff, had essentially been locked in Dungeon Negrada's hellscape for millennia—making the experience of walking across the fields west of the city and into the forests in the foothills a rather scenic thing even for a semisentient weapon. He could literally feel the intent of the staff—its eagerness to explore was palpable. The flickering shadows flared along its black wood once in a while, the blood and flesh integrated into the wood pulsed whenever it got excited, and occasionally the blade at the tip would whip out to examine a flower or beetle as if it had eyes there.

Very curious.

[Vampire's Escort (Vampiric) (Unique Soul-Fused Weapon, Sorcerer's Staff): 104 average damage on strike with each physical strike dealing minor shadow-explosion knock back. Mana regeneration is increased by 102%. All Shadow and Blood spells cost 9% less mana while dealing 22% additional damage. This item has an abnormally high endurance and is hard to destroy. Requires vampiric heritage to wield.

- Sacrificial Kill: Killing strong opponents has a chance to imbue this weapon with additional attributes, stats, or bonuses.
- Scorpion's Sting: The blade at the tip of this staff can extend through flesh molding to cut down enemies. Enemies hit with the blade portion of this weapon do not experience shadow-explosion knock back like the rest of this staff, rather the blade portion of this weapon will imbue stacking bleeding damage to all biological enemies.
- Black Lightning: This staff can passively build up charges of Black Lightning. Power of Black Lightning depends on the amount of charge emitted.
- Portal Master: This weapon can sync to any stabilized portal you have permission to use by the maker and master. Current locations available for access: Dungeon Negrada.]

Dr. Brass was also a lot slower than the others due to his age and his mortal body. So it was something of a stroll, with Riven wondering from time to time if he should become nocturnal. He was continually adjusting his clothes, keeping himself cloaked and hooded to avoid the sun, while Fay flew overhead to spread her wings, her laughter chiming due to the freedom she finally had. The Succubus seemed genuinely happy, and this in turn solidified the mood of their trip even further despite the slow pace.

Hours passed, and Riven found that the closer they got to their destination, the more animated Ethel and Senna became. They began to laugh more, tell stories of their homes or families, make jokes, and interact with everyone else in good spirits. Leaves crunched underfoot and the oak trees of the forest grew in number, their shade giving Riven relief from the sunlight as the hours crept into afternoon.

"My mother always said I should practice alchemy and herbology, but I'd always wanted to be a hunter or scout instead." Ethel held up her bandaged arm and wiggled it, trying to make the best out of a bad situation as she laughed heartily at her own misfortune. "Looks like I'll be going back to alchemy after all!"

Senna snorted a laugh of her own from her position in the loot bin that Azmoth was carrying. "You could always get married and have some strapping lad take care of you! Elder Preen wants your hand in marriage—you'll just have to make sure it's your RIGHT hand he wants and not your left!"

"HEY! That guy is gross!" Ethel shot her friend a glare amid the surrounding laughter, then grumpily scowled at the ground as Riven princess-carried her across the forest. "Well, at least I can say that I'm alive. Thank you, Riven, for saving us that day."

Riven nodded silently, continuing to trot alongside Azmoth in front of the others while Athela scouted ahead for potential dangers. Dr. Brass took up the rear, injecting his own comments or questions about elvish culture along the way.

"There are many different cultures for elves, just like there are with humans," Ethel replied to a question from Dr. Brass. "There are a few dominant ones, though. There are the high elves, like my people. We stay in touch with nature and try to grow the forests. We worship the Forest pillar—a subpillar of the Fae foundational pillar—and some of the related gods or greater spirits. Before the integration, we still knew of the pillars—we just didn't have a leveling system yet. It was impossible to level up until now, actually. Aside from the woodland variant of high elves, there are other high elves from our old world, who often are distinguished by their mind-set rather than by race. They believe themselves to be the 'true' high elves, which is why they're usually what we refer to when speaking of 'high elves' rather than us 'woodland elves.' They have abandoned the old ways and think themselves better than us woodland elves, usually worshipping the Arcane powers due to their lineages granting many of their people affinity for such things. They think of themselves as . . ."

"As overly sophisticated." Senna called out from where she was being cradled by Azmoth.

Ethel nodded in agreement. "Yes, they think they're sophisticated. We don't get along most of the time because, well, our people can be rather pompous, too!"

Senna giggled in agreement.

Fay landed gracefully beside Riven and kept pace while observing the small rodents and other wildlife around them. "This is all so pretty . . . I'm glad you chose me, Riven. I know I said it before, but thank you."

She glanced over at him, folding her wings behind her back, and used her tail to tap the amulet of the dragon around his neck. "I can't get a read on that necklace you have, but I can tell it is cursed. What does it do?"

Riven blinked, shooting a look down at the piece of jewelry he wore, and looked back up. "Cursed? Seriously?"

"That doesn't mean it's a bad thing!" the blue-skinned Succubus quickly stated, raising her hands to keep him from worrying. "Curses are a subset of enchanting and can be very good for the wearer. They're just a specific type of magic. Enchantments are rather straight and narrow in their amplifications, while curses are more . . . complex. Usually there's a drawback to them when applied to items, but this can bring in better bonuses."

Riven raised an eyebrow while continuing to carry the young blonde woman in his arms. "Really. So, does using your curses outside of applying them to items cause any drawbacks? You use three curses, don't you?"

The Succubus nodded quickly, stepping over a large tree root and withdrawing her tail from where it'd been toying with the dragon amulet. "Oh, definitely. Every time I use my curses I experience pain. That's how most curses work, actually—the caster has to set down a sacrifice in order to use them. It's intrinsic to anything the system calls a curse, but what is paid depends on the caster. I could sacrifice many other things to use them instead, but pain is the one I choose regularly."

Riven nearly tripped. "Uh . . . and that's okay with you? Didn't you complain to me about how your last master tortured you? Seems kind of . . . rough, to have abilities like that."

Fay shrugged with a small grin. "A little bit of pain is actually pleasurable to me, believe it or not. The kind of pain that my old master dished out? That was another level entirely. That was torture. I can handle the abilities without any problems the way they are."

Riven took a moment to mull over this. "So what do you think the drawbacks of this amulet would be? How would I find out?"

"You'd need an identifier for that, or someone who is more in tune with curses than I am. I'm starting to specialize with curses now, but I have a long ways to go. I'm still only a beginner. All I can tell you is that whatever the curse is, its origin is the Unholy foundational pillar."

He cursed internally.

Fay laughed at the irritation plastered across Riven's features. "Don't worry about it—if you've been wearing it for a sustained amount of time, I'm sure the curse can't be that bad. If it was, you'd likely have noticed already. Keep wearing it—the bonuses you get are likely better than the drawbacks. That's how they usually work."

The singsong of birds chirping in the canopy intermixed with the babble of a slow-moving river to their right, and Riven fell back a bit to let Azmoth's larger frame push through the underbrush to create a path for him and the others while he shifted the bin on his back to his two additional maws. For a long while they trudged on in silence, enjoying the scenery around them and keeping it slow so that Dr. Brass was able to keep up. There was still no sign of Athela coming back to warn them of potential monsters, but they did occasionally pass by warg carcasses and even a warped version of a grizzly bear with two heads that'd been mutilated by the demoness. Fay was content- edly humming to herself while she walked beside him, his staff occasionally whipped from place to place as it inspected mushrooms or leaves, and Senna was beginning to fall asleep in the bin.

Riven eventually cleared his throat to break the silence shortly after crossing a small stream. "So what are the other types of elvish cultures?"

Ethel yawned, having temporarily forgotten she'd been telling a story, but she jumped at the opportunity to make conversation again. She still seemed slightly uneasy around Riven and the demons, but talking certainly helped her alleviate those remnant fears and she was quickly warming up to them. "Oh, yes, sorry. I got caught up in what Fay was saying. There are also blood elves, who originally started out as high elves but devoted themselves to the Unholy foundational pillar. The pillar warped their souls over the course of centuries, and they're often marked with Unholy blood sigils that naturally grow on their bodies. They looked like red enchantments, and different bloodlines have differ- ent inherent blood sigils that give the elves who own them power. They also have black eyes like Fay does, and they're shunned by the rest of the high elves that used to be their brethren many generations ago. Lastly there are the drow, but we don't really associate with them at all. The dark elves abandoned the surface elves long, long ago and are almost an entirely separate species now—they are also incredibly bloodthirsty, and they tend to lean toward the Unholy foundational pillar like the blood elves do and live in the underdark."

"And what exactly does your culture as a woodland elf entail? Do you have holidays you celebrate? What kinds of foods do you eat? Are there any weird customs that you have?"

Ethel let out a pure and singsong laugh with a smile that reached her ears. "Well, there's definitely one weird custom that even I think is rather pathetic! It's actually not a woodland elf tradition, though, rather it is a tradition to our village. Every year at the summer solstice, we dress up the two most troublesome elders and have them race one another. The one who loses gets pelted with food by the children while doing a ridiculous dance. Don't ask me how it got started; I don't really know."

Senna's voice carried over from where she was in the lead with Azmoth. "We celebrate a couple holidays! The most important one is the Ceremonies of Life, and it's my favorite. It's ten days where we give thanks to the Fae mothers for creating their pillar, as well as have light shows from elemental mages and parades or games revolving around nature. Lots of us get engaged during this time—it's kind of expected for at least a couple every year. We have lots of food, too! We do eat meat, but not a lot of it. We consider life sacred and only take it if needed to feed ourselves, otherwise we are primarily vegetarian."

"The opposite of you," Ethel said with a crooked smile.

Riven snorted in discomfort at the truth of that and then caught Ethel's expression next. Was she smirking at him? He felt a small smile coming on as he realized that Ethel was teasing him.

"I'm a sensitive new-age vampire. I only suck juice out of carrots now."

"Is that so?"

"It is. I'm a trendsetter."

She rolled her eyes with a silently laughing expression and gave him a tsk, tsk, along with a waggle of her fingers on her remaining right hand. "I don't believe it."

He opened his mouth to reject her statement but didn't get to start the sentence as he heard an uptick in a nearby heartbeat. He turned, barely looking in time to see a shadow passing through his peripheral vision. It immediately made him duck and whirl, and it was a very good thing he did. An enormous axe connected to an arm nearly as thick as his waist blurred past, barely missing him and making the forest floor shudder in a spray of dirt as Riven stumbled back while Ethel's shrieked in fright.

"AZMOTH!" Senna screamed as she was thrown from the bin. Coins sprayed all over the forest floor. The injured elf bounced off the ground with a shriek and watched as the demon who'd been carrying her fell to the ground, his head completely cleaved off his body at a point where his natural armor had been weakest. The others looked on, dumbfounded at the sight of one of their best fighters dead so instantaneously and without warning.

[**Your minion Azmoth has died. He will be returned to you twenty-four hours after you pay the blood price for your minion. To resurrect your level-30 infant Hellscape Brutalisk, you will be required to pay Elysium directly with a sum of thirty thousand Elysium coins. Simply will this transaction to happen and make sure you have the required payment to further this agenda.**]

CHAPTER 37

Senna tried to get up on her injured leg and tripped backward, hobbling toward the tree line to get away from the monster.

Riven was now staring at a huge, rotund cyclops. It was nearly as tall as some of the trees nearby, with a brown horn protruding above its single yellow eye. Each of its two hands had three sausage-like fingers, its nose looked like it'd only partially grown out with large slits in place of nostrils, and its ugly, toothy grin displayed many sharpened and crooked teeth.

It didn't wear any clothes and was about half as wide as it was tall—with rolls of fat that jiggled with each step it took forward as it leaned in and grinned at Riven and Ethel like it'd just found its next meal. Huge muscles rippled underneath its fat, and it'd obviously been lying in wait for them in order to get the drop on them. "SNACK!"

[Cyclops]

"NEFAJIA CRECUS BLOOD NOVA!"
SNAP-CRACK-BOOM
Riven dropped the elf, and the area around him exploded in all directions, the shock wave tearing up rock, dirt, and tree alike in a boom of crimson power that lit up the forest in an eerie glow and could be heard for miles. It rocked the very earth they stood upon, and the cyclops was thrown backward by the blast, going head over heels only to meet an enormous orb of condensed blood magic that expanded and tore out from Riven's cupped hands. The orb from Blood Nova broke the sound barrier and ripped into the monster like an atomic bomb, emitting a secondary thunderclap of power that shook the very ground Riven stood on. Fortunately the blood mana itself bypassed the bin of loot and the members of Riven's party on command, leaving them utterly unharmed other than wobbling slightly due to the radiating shock wave that tore through the

ground. A swarm of sharp crimson discs launched simultaneously along with a torrent of Black Lightning from his staff, which was floating behind him and acting of its own accord. The combination blow was utterly devastating, tearing through dirt and thick foliage along its path to slam into the cyclops head-on with brutal effect.

The ground was shaken and ripped from where the giant cyclops knelt and flung debris into the air, intermixing with pieces of the large cyclops's body when the magic ruptured its internal organs and tore through its limbs, spine, and head with deadly force. The spray of blood looked like an enormous popping water balloon. The effect was only heightened by each of the embedded discs as the power he'd stabilized them with erupted, sending explosive shrapnel tearing through the body and across the nearby forest like a grenade to follow up the initial torrent of overwhelming power, while Black Lightning ripped the remnant muscles right off sets of charred bone.

[Blood Nova's mandatory eight-hour cooldown has been triggered.]

It was certainly overkill, but Riven didn't take any chances after seeing Azmoth so easily killed like that. He paused and evaluated the wreckage: pieces of the cyclops were scattered across the scorched earth for over a hundred yards. A hand lay there, a portion of its skull farther ahead, a charred femur off to his right.

But the majority of the corpse lay as a disassembled and shattered skeleton, smoking in the sunlight where the trees had been uprooted or torn away not far off.

He coughed, grimacing due to the sunlight that was now hitting him full on after the shock wave had blown his hood back. He promptly pulled his hood back down, then made sure the others were okay.

They were in shock, but they were all fine.

A sack of coins appeared out of thin air, landing on the beast, but he didn't pay it much attention due to the severe headache he suddenly had after expending so much mana at once.

He walked ahead, came to a stop next to the fried cyclops, and kicked it once for his own satisfaction—only to notice that its yellow eye had not been entirely destroyed. In its place, within the majority of the skull that still remained after the attack, there was a small green orb.

He reached over, feeling the residual heat from his attack—and grasped the orb to pull it closer for examination.

[Cyclops Eye Stone: Ingredient for various crafts. Potential Effects: ???, ???, ???]

Huh. Interesting.

He tossed the green eye stone over to Senna, who was gaping at him in bewilderment, and it landed in the bin of loot not far off.

"Everyone okay?"

He looked around again. Even Fay was somewhat awestruck at the display of power, and she began to smile when she more thoroughly evaluated the devastation around them.

"Wow. You're improving really fast," the Succubus muttered slowly. "The time I spent watching you from the nether realms . . . I thought you were a fast learner, but this? This is an insane amount of growth in such a short time. I didn't even have a chance to do anything."

Ethel, Dr. Brass, and Senna were still just open-mouthed and gawking. Only a second later, Athela rushed into the clearing at blinding speed, swiftly stopping in front of the destruction with her chest heaving frantically. The demoness quickly caught sight of his injuries and ran over to him, inspecting his body for anything serious and laughing. "Sorry I'm late! Did Azmoth die?! Damn it! Resurrections are expensive!"

Riven sighed and scratched the back of his head, looking at the bin of shit he'd now have to lug around. "Yeah. And now we're going to need to wait for him to respawn so we can haul our stuff again. Even with my increased Strength, that thing is too heavy for me to carry."

They had to make camp in the forest at the base of the mountains. Ethel had come to check on Riven, hobbling over and clutching at her bandaged arm with a look of concern. After realizing the extent of Riven's exhaustion from that mana expenditure, and not having fully recovered from his previous fights with the dream creatures, it'd been a no-brainer.

"Is he going to be all right?" the elf asked Athela and Fay, coming back from relieving herself in the forest. Meanwhile Dr. Brass and Senna talked about varieties of elvish dishes native to Senna's home.

Athela had Riven's head in her lap, gently brushing her fingers through Riven's hair while he lightly let his chest rise and fall. He was so out of it that he was even drooling into her leg. She gave a soft smile, wiped the drool away without waking him, and bent over farther to adjust his shirt. "Riven's going to be all right. He's tough."

Ethel sat herself down on a log they'd dragged over, feeling comfortable in the warmth of the night with Athela's webs encircling their encampment for dozens of yards in any direction to alert the demoness if enemies were approaching. In this new world, there were far more monsters than her old one, and that wasn't even counting the goblins.

The young woman crossed her ankles and let her feet warm up next to the fire, wincing slightly when her left-arm stump brushed a little too hard against the ground while she tried to adjust her sitting position. Her sprained ankle still hurt, but it could be worse. She could be dead, being destined to become chopped liver for some disgusting goblin tribe to feed on. "You said there wasn't magic in Riven's world, right, Athela?"

The Arshakai demoness nodded absentmindedly, still playing with Riven's hair as he slept. "Why?"

"Are you sure?"

"Yes."

There was a long pause.

"Because that magic Riven demonstrated today, and back in the hospital: it was very powerful. The leveling system is new to me, to my people, but magic is not. I know it takes a very long time to develop that kind of power and cultivation of one's magical prowess."

Another long pause ensued, with Athela curiously staring the slender blonde elf down with a cool gaze as her red eyes locked onto her. The crackling of the fire continued to let plumes of smoke rise into the starry night sky, and Ethel adjusted uncomfortably again under the scrutiny of Riven's demon.

"We've only been here since the integration. It's been a little over two months, by my guess."

Ethel nodded slowly, shifting her gaze away from Athela to stare at the fire where it ate away at the branches and logs they'd piled up in the middle of their camp. She gave a glance to Fay, who was lounging lazily nearby and looking up at the stars, but the Succubus made no comment despite obviously listening in.

Ethel swallowed. "I just wanted to hear it again. It just doesn't make sense to me, even with the leveling system. Some of our more accomplished people went through tutorials or unique starter events of their own just like Riven did. Not many, but some. None of them came out like this . . . If I may ask, do you know what Riven's affinities are?"

Athela paused the brushing of Riven's hair and clasped her hands in front of her on Riven's rising chest. "I have no idea what you're talking about."

Ethel's blue-green eyes slowly shifted over to the arachnoid woman. Still slightly nervous in the demoness's presence, Ethel could tell that Athela likely knew exactly what she was talking about. "It must be high, and he must have at least two of them from what I've seen. Blood and Unholy, I think? Pretty common for a vampire."

A light and pure chuckle escaped Athela's lips with a brilliantly white smile that danced on the corners of her mouth amid the firelight. She grabbed something to her left, holding up some of the ash that Azmoth's body had turned into after his temporary death, and she let it flow out into the breeze when the winds picked up—carrying the ashes high up into the treetops. "Fine. Oh, I know what they are, all right. It's why I presented myself to Riven in the first place, during that odd little event he was a part of. I'm still curious about who or what Chalgathi is, but regardless—I am glad to have hit such a jackpot of a master."

"Agreed," Fay stated casually, clicking her tongue and swatting the ground with her long black tail.

Athela's smile grew wider at the looks of confusion or curiosity displayed not only on Ethel's countenance, but also on Senna's and Dr. Brass's. "And that was even before I realized he was a pureblood vampire."

Senna's eyes widened abruptly. "Pureblood? I thought they were extinct."

Athela shot the silver-haired elf a disdainful look. The demoness was constantly shifting between showing the two elves kindness and disgust—an internal battle waging between how she'd been raised as a demon, to despise mortals as lesser creatures, and the experiences she'd witnessed in the short time with her first and new master. Internally willing herself to draw in the repulsion she felt for the girl across the firepit for being a Fae creature of all things, she took in a deep breath and reminded herself that Riven had gone out of his way to save these pathetic women. "Pure-blooded vampires are certainly not extinct—they exist in rare quantities, though. Usually you'll find them in ancient families of vampire royalty within the core worlds . . . the worlds integrated earliest into Elysium's multiverse many millions of years ago."

"Then what's a pure-blooded vampire doing here? Is that why his eyes are different from the other vampires I've heard of?" Senna glanced curiously at Fay when the Succubus snickered. "What's so funny?"

The Succubus didn't answer.

Athela let out a long burp but covered her mouth when Riven started to stir. He didn't wake, and her body relaxed as she went back to playing with his hair. "Anyways . . . regarding your question, Ethel: I don't think it'd hurt to let you know. It isn't damaging information, and I suppose Riven would probably tell you on his own . . . but let me ask you this. What do your people have in terms of affinities?"

"What do we have?" Ethel queried.

"Yes. What types of magics and what do you think your average affinity would be as a percentage? In your village, or tribe, or whatever it is you mortals call it."

Ethel blinked, then proudly smiled and puffed her chest out. "Our clan is known for Forest and Storm affinities. Of course, in order to get those major subpillars, we have a large majority of our people having affinities to the Fae foundational pillar. Senna, what do you think the average affinity would be? Thirty-two or thirty-three percent?"

Senna also swelled with pride. "Yes, some people in our clan have affinities in the Forest pillar as high as forty-nine percent."

Dr. Brass curiously raised a hand. "Is that high?"

"Very high!" Ethel replied excitedly. "I myself have a Forest affinity of twenty-eight percent, which is pretty good! Below average for our clan, but overall suitable for a competent ranger, beast tamer, mage, or shaman. Otherwise I have a twelve percent Fae pillar affinity, which isn't great, but it could land me an ability if I took a decade to study with our elders. I haven't selected my class yet, but we did have classes back in our world, too. Back then it just helped orient your studies and gave flat bonuses, with the system guiding us in how we saw the world and experienced the Dao insights we happened upon. Classes seem to be more important now, though, because leveling exists now and they give stat points for every level. Better classes mean more progress for each level, therefore more power, so I'm hoping to get a better class option soon. Otherwise I might really become an alchemist like my mother has been telling me to do for years!"

Senna snorted with amusement while picking at a piece of granola bar they'd taken from the hospital, shoving it into her mouth and chewing in contemplation. "That'd certainly be something to see. You've been a rebel all your life, Ethel. I'd pay good money to see you ditch the adventuring life."

"Well, it isn't like I've got the odds on my side!" Ethel snapped back irritably, waving her stump around before sagging her shoulders apologetically. "Eh . . . Sorry, didn't mean to yell at you."

"It's fine, I'd be upset, too. So, Athela, you never did say what Riven's affinities were. Does he have pillars for all his affinities yet? I've been curious myself—it's way too early to be that strong if he just started cultivating his magic."

Athela shook her head and shared a look with the blue-skinned woman nearby, exchanging knowing smiles. "He hasn't collected all his pillars, not yet."

"Oh. Just some of them then. How high are they?"

Dr. Brass held up a hand to interject. "Why does it matter and what do affinities mean?"

CRASH

There was a flash of green light farther into the forest and the sound of splintering wood. They all turned to look past the layers of webbing Athela had set up across the trees. Out there, beyond the perimeter, one of Fay's sigils had been triggered. Out of the darkness, the front paw of a warg bounced along the ground, showing just what had come a little bit too close to the camp for its own good, and causing Fay to wordlessly get up and walk out of the camp to remake the sigil that'd been undone.

Athela raised an eyebrow at the departing blue Succubus—then turned to the old man, light from the fire dancing along her pitch-black skin. "Affinities directly affect the chance to receive ability cooldowns, the power output you can reach for every point of given energy spent on an ability, the speed at which you can use to enact those abilities, the manipulation of abilities to do things other than the rigid outline the system sets for you, and the ability at which you learn things under the umbrella of a given pillar. Essentially having a higher affinity for a pillar will allow you to control or learn magic, miracles, or martial arts in that pillar far better than if that affinity were lower. As for Riven's affinities . . ."

Athela, being Riven's minion, had access to his status page and scrolled down to where it described his pillar percentages.

[100% affinity to the Blood subpillar, 96% affinity to the Shadow subpillar, and 95% affinity to the Death subpillar. The Unholy pillar is unaffected by this change and remains at its original state of 80%. The Infernal subpillar is unaffected by this change and remains at its original state of 82%.]

Funnily enough, the subpillars of Chaos and Depravity were not listed to tell Athela what their affinity levels were. That was all right, though—perhaps he just didn't have them, but she doubted that was the case. His affinity for the foundational Unholy pillar was too high not to have them. Perhaps there was some other reason that she was missing, but in the end they'd find out regardless. Usually a status page didn't do this at all, and someone had to get an identifier to read off a percentage for them, but for some reason Riven's vampiric lineage actually informed them what these percentages were.

A smug smirk crept back over Athela's lips, and she just shook her head slightly. "Natural-born vampires usually have affinities for the Unholy, Death, Blood, and Shadow pillars. It is intrinsically part of what they are. Changed vampires, though, they can oftentimes lack the Unholy foundational pillar, as the vampiric transition only passes down the other three. Kind of an enigma, that one."

"So which ones does Riven have then? Obviously he has the Unholy pillar—everyone has at least one affinity, but does he have any of the subpillars?"

"He has all four of the typical vampiric affinities plus the Infernal subpillar. I also suspect he might have the Chaos and Depravity subpillars as well, though that is not confirmed yet."

Ethel raised her eyebrows in avid surprise. "Oh! Oh, wow. He seriously has five affinities? I've never even heard of that happening before . . . I don't think ever. I only have Fae and Forest."

"What are his percentages?" Senna asked, slightly more intrigued.

"Let's just say they're all above fifty percent."

Both elves stared blankly at Athela, then turned to look at where Riven was still exhausted and sleeping from the expenditure of mana earlier that day. In an instant, both elves started pelting Athela with questions and asking more about Riven's origins.

"You're telling us the truth?" Ethel questioned seriously, eyebrows furrowed and peering over half skeptically and half in awe. "That's incredible! That also explains why he's so strong after so little time . . ."

"He learned how to conjure those spinning discs of razor blades within two days of study," Athela chimed in, pride evident in the way she raised her chin. She held up two fingers. "Two days to learn his very first spell."

Ethel narrowed her eyes. "No, you're lying. That's impossible."

"She's not lying. I watched it happen," Fay's voice called out before the Succubus swayed her hips back and forth into the encampment again, coming to sit cross-legged next to Athela's position. She rested her head on her fists and leaned forward to better look at the fire. "Riven is, simply put, a genius when it comes to understanding magic. Perhaps not in other areas, but when it concerns mana, he's an absolute prodigy, surpassing anything I've ever seen before. Couple that with his insanely high affinities and this is what you've got. I've been watching him since the Chalgathi trials. What Athela says is true."

Dr. Brass scratched his chin, trying to make sense of all this new information. Meanwhile both elves exchanged glances with one another, not sure if they should believe the two demons, but it was Athela who spoke next.

"You're the Succubus that he could have picked in his trials." She turned her head to meet Fay's gaze. "Aren't you?"

Fay remained silent for a time but eventually nodded her confirmation. "They were the best Earth had to offer."

"You would have sacrificed all your levels to acquire one?" Athela asked curiously.

Fay nodded again. "Obviously. Just look at how much you've grown already, and it's been less than three months."

This very much confused Ethel, and the injured elf raised her arm and waved it around to get their attention. "Hey, um, what are these trials you're talking about, and who are you talking about when you say they were the best Earth had to offer?"

Fay let out a lighthearted laugh, then repositioned herself and kicked her long, sky-blue legs to the side, adjusting her clothes and brushing dirt from her exposed abdomen. "The unique event we talked to you about earlier concerning Earth's integration . . . Well, there were many unique events. But the one that I was interested in was Chalgathi's trials. They had all the people on Earth who inherited Unholy bloodlines present, and they were therefore the best candidates for acquiring new masters. I would have lost some of my abilities and all my acquired levels to participate, but obtaining a master with an Unholy bloodline would mean my potential for growth skyrocketed. Riven was one of the people I picked out early as a good candidate, but back then he chose Athela instead of me, so I decided to wait. I waited to try and get the next opening. Then Azmoth came along and I had to wait some more, but demons have very long lives and I am patient. The last and only master I had kept me as a plaything for over three hundred years. In that time I grew only twenty levels, but with Riven? I expect to far surpass that number in less than half a year . . . as long as he survives."

"He's going to survive," Athela stated flatly.

Fay could only smile. "That is my intent as well."

CHAPTER 38

Riven's recovery took a little longer than any of them had expected. He slept far into the midafternoon of the next day, and the others let him do it without interruption. Athela was able to hunt down and carry back a deer, and Fay went out to collect berries and nuts while Dr. Brass stayed with the two elf girls. If something was to attack them, they'd be sure to wake Riven, but the amount of power he'd expended over the past few days was enormous. There was even a huge scar left in the forest the next day that was still smoking with trails of remnant crimson mana a ways off where he'd blasted that cyclops, with many of them agreeing it was overkill.

Night was falling again in a brilliant array of orange hues on the horizon, and Riven finally woke up to the sound of laughter and joking from the others. Azmoth had reappeared as well after paying the blood price of thirty thousand Elysium coins for a resummoning, with a chunk of the coins they'd collected at the hospital disappearing into thin air, and Fay was teaching the huge demon how to play rock-paper-scissors. The Succubus had to correct him repeatedly, laughing at his joyous outbursts whenever he falsely thought he'd won. When Fay was asked where she'd learned the game herself, she stated that she'd had an opportunity to study Riven's culture upon integration just like Athela had. To an extent, anyway.

Riven rubbed his eyes with a yawn, stomach growling while he rolled over to watch the pair. He then lifted himself up off the pile of small blankets they'd taken from the hospital. He was beginning to get hungry again, and not just for blood this time, either. This didn't surprise him at all, considering he'd likely been asleep a long time if he was seeing another sunset—but despite this he was still a little concerned about a constant source of mortal blood. He didn't know where he was going to get it without basically kidnapping someone or creating a mind-slave thrall, and his appetite was voracious. Funnily enough, it was the first thing he thought of while sitting up, and those thoughts immediately centered on the people at the prison they'd scouted out with Jake's mapping ability in the basement of the hospital. If there were truly some bad people there that he could pick off and put into a cage of some sort to feed off regularly, that'd be far preferable to trying to suck the blood of random and innocent people for survival purposes.

He'd have to make this trip to the elf village a fast one.

"Hey!" Ethel's voice brought him out of his thoughts of hunger, and he blinked with a friendly smile when the elf hobbled over to sit next to him. "How are you feeling?!"

Her brilliant grin caught him off guard, and he couldn't help but stare for a second before rubbing his eyes and yawning. "Great! How's your arm?"

She flipped her long blond hair over to one side and held up the bandaged stump. "Not great, but I'll live. Thanks to you, anyways. Are you hungry? You've been sleeping for almost an entire day now."

She reached over to her side, producing a slab of cooked venison wrapped in a large leaf akin to pine needles, but with tiny ridges instead of a smooth edge.

Riven's stomach rumbled audibly, and he gave an apologetic glance over to Ethel before taking the slab of venison, at which she just smiled. Biting into the meat without any reservations, he groaned, feeling the medium-well texture and flavor of it coating his taste buds with warm deliciousness.

"My God. Thank you."

Ethel head-bobbed over to the arachnoid demoness, who was lounging in a hammock made from webbing. "Thank Athela! She's the one who caught it. I'm glad to see you're feeling better, though!"

"As am I!" Fay called out from next to Dr. Brass, who was drawing pictures in the dirt with a stick he'd found. She gave Riven a thumbs-up and a large grin, spreading her bat-like wings out to either side. "You ready to go soon?! The rest of us have been waiting FOREVER for you to get your beauty sleep!"

"Yeah, Fay, well, at least I don't snore like you do."

Fay's jaw dropped, and Athela burst into laughter. "I do not snore!"

"Athela, does Fay snore?"

"Like a big ol' hog squeal. Sounds a lot like *HRREEEEEEE* with each wheeze-snore she makes."

SMACK

"Owww!! Hey, hey—hey! Fay, you put that down right now!"

Riven rolled his eyes in amusement and continued to eat the venison, ignoring the two demons as Fay chased Athela around with a stick, whacking her repeatedly. Despite the shit-talking, they were obviously having a good time and laughing about the whole ordeal. It was good to see Fay getting along with Athela so easily and so quickly, because in Riven's opinion, Athela could use some girlfriends. Azmoth was great, but he wasn't much of a talker, and he was still a lot younger than anyone else here despite his size.

Ethel remained sitting nearby, occasionally smirking at the two demons and otherwise shooting Riven hesitant glances while he ate. It was obvious she wanted to talk about something with him, but her awkwardness didn't help things, and she was slowly starting to turn a shade of red while she fidgeted.

Well, she might be nervous. She'd come a long way from screaming in horror when first seeing him, and he knew his Charisma stat certainly didn't help things, either.

Riven raised an eyebrow, swallowed another bite, and cleared his throat. "Are you excited to get home soon?"

Ethel shot Senna a look and gestured her way, happy to continue the conversation instead of mull around in silence. "Senna is a bit more excited than I am, but yes. I'll be happy to be home, too."

Her words were a little less than convincing, and Riven was more than a bit confused by the way her facial expression and body language changed. She was wrapping her good arm around her knees and resting her jaw on top, looking at the ground with a suddenly faraway gaze of uncertainty.

He put the venison down, wrapping it up in the leaf to make sure it didn't get dirty. "So . . . is there something you want to talk about? You don't look convinced. Is everything okay?"

She let out a snort in response. "I love my family, and I want to see them. It's just that since the transition and merging of worlds, the leadership of the clan has been less than great to deal with."

"How so?"

"It's . . . personal stuff. I'd rather not talk about it."

It was obvious she wanted to talk about it.

Riven paused, then nodded. "Well, if you end up changing your mind, let me know."

They waited another half hour and then began to collect their belongings, with Senna being especially anxious to get back. Riven took time to call Allie through the communication orb to update her as the remnants of sunset fell below the horizon and night completely encompassed the sky. Dr. Brass, Senna, and Ethel couldn't see very well in the dark, but the moonlight and starlight did help illuminate the forest for them somewhat. It also made the snow-capped mountains to their right look rather majestic and made them all feel quite small. The demons and vampire in their group, on the other hand, had no problem at all, navigating the darkness without missing a single step. Dr. Brass occasionally stumbled, but the two elves were back to being carried like earlier due to their injuries.

"Should be able to see the village just over this next hill!" Senna exclaimed excitedly after seeing a wooden marking post and pointing to it. "That marks the outer boundary of our patrols!"

"Patrols? Are they going to attack us if they see us?"

"They'll see Ethel and me—it'll be fine!"

Riven was skeptical. ". . . I sure hope so. What's your home like?"

Ethel was the one to answer, exaggeratedly moving her arms about while Riven princess-carried the injured girl through the forest. "We set up next to a lake! It's a bit different than our old village—most of our belongings were lost in the merging, but we kept some of them. The clan is in the process of building a new home, and most of our people stuck together through the transition . . . thankfully. Some people never showed up after their tutorials, but a lot of the clan completed their tutorials or didn't have tutorials at all and were paired together. We used our shamans to grow homes right out of the trees with magic, or at least we've started the process . . . but haven't completely finished yet because our number of shamans is limited. A lot of us are still in tents or small, easy-to-make cabins."

Riven nodded thoughtfully without a reply. He only hoped they wouldn't attack on sight.

They traveled up a long slope for a couple miles after that. There were thicker trees in this area and scattered boulders dotting the forest, and they finally crested the next hill after passing another wooden stake marker. Finally coming to the top, they looked out to the southeast, where Senna had said her village would be. However, as they all gathered, Senna let out a gasp . . . and Ethel stifled a cry of her own.

Maybe a mile from where they were now was more or less a clearing. The trees were still present but were both larger in size and thinned in number. A glistening lake surrounded by forest at the base of the mountain shimmered in the light of a burning village, and even from here they could all see that there were figures moving about with magical blasts of light exchanging between combatants.

"*No!!!*" Ethel whispered in his arms, and Senna immediately began to cry.

God fucking damn it. What a load of horseshit—could he not catch a break?!

Riven didn't even think about it, turning to put Ethel down on the hilltop. "Looks like this is a tale of never-ending violence for me. You three wait here and hide—we don't know what's there, and frankly none of you are capable of fighting right now. My demons and I will handle this."

Azmoth pushed Senna into Dr. Brass's arms, who grunted at the exertion of holding the young woman.

Dr. Brass then began to protest. "I can help you! You might need me!"

Fay stifled a snort.

"You have no training and no magic," Athela stated simply with a flick of her hair out to the side, spear-like spider limbs ripping out of her back while she began to stretch. "You're pretty worthless. You shouldn't be itching for a fight until Riven changes you and trains you."

The comment stung the old man, but he grimaced and didn't reply.

Azmoth grunted his agreement, cinders beginning to light up across his obsidian plates and exposed fibrous muscles, and he pointed a long armored and clawed finger at the obviously anxious man. "You will just get in way. Stay safe here; we come back. You fight when strong one day."

Ethel and Senna both looked up to him with obvious emotional turmoil, and Senna managed to get out a hoarse, whispered request. "Please help them. My family is there."

Riven put his runic mask on, nodded once with crimson eyes flashing, and whirled around. Then, with a final wave, he sprinted off into the night—blurring ahead with speed none of the others except Athela could match. Fay took to the sky, blending in with the darkness above, but Riven could feel her presence there. He was curious about how she'd fit in with their combat style and was even a bit eager to find out. He just wished it was under other circumstances. Unsummoning Azmoth, he stored his larger demon in the nether realms so he could resummon him closer and picked up the pace.

The underbrush rose to meet him, and Riven plowed through it, taking out bushes or small trees that got in his way like they were nothing with a simple swing of his fleshy black staff. The weapon began to heat up in his hand and shimmered with shadow magic, sensing a battle to come.

His heart grew grim when he heard the sounds of battle in the distance. Part of him wondered why the village was being attacked, what reason they had for doing so, and if he was wrong for throwing himself into a pitched battle without realizing the stakes. What if he was joining the wrong side? What if Senna and Ethel's people were in the wrong somehow? What if they were all elves and he couldn't even tell the difference between the two groups?

This was stupid. But he continued on anyway, with the images of the distraught elves he'd left on the hillside flashing through his mind. He didn't know them well, but they'd asked for his help and he was going to give it.

The light of flames began to grow closer, and the screams of civilians and combatants alike echoed around him across the trees. Despite this, Athela began to cackle mischievously while the two of them rocketed forward through the dark—and Riven couldn't help but feel a flood of adrenaline and excitement coursing through him when he saw her looking like that. His feelings of uncertainty waned and faded, and his mind became a clean-cut razor as his shard of Gluttony began to howl within.

Despite the horrors that certainly awaited, he couldn't deny the stimulating emotions he got whenever he entered these life-and-death struggles. Not only that, but he was becoming damn good at winning them, too.

It wasn't much longer until they reached the village boundary. Thankfully when the two of them finally got there, it was easy to tell who was an enemy versus those who were defending their home.

They broke out of the forest's edge and into a clearing that extended another forty yards before another thicket of trees, tents, and small cabins, which were clustered along the edge of a large lake. Some of the unusually large trees had buildings built right into them as if the wood itself had been grown to someone's specifications—creating small or even large abodes where families or stores would have been. Many were burning, though, fires eating away at the wood or cloth of the tents, and numerous people lay dead on the ground or in chains.

The ones being dragged over to a central spot in the clearing were definitely elves, with heavy iron manacles around their ankles and wrists with chains connecting them to iron collars. Many of them were bruised, bloodied, and had various colors of silver, blond, blue, and red hair with pointed ears and fair, symmetrical features. The elves wore animal skins, furs, and clothes made of interwoven leaves with much of their skin being exposed even on the males. Many were also decorated with the same blue tribal paint that he'd first found on Senna and Ethel. The remaining defenders not in chains mostly wielded longbows, daggers, and thin swords that looked like a cross between a long sword and a curved scimitar. Some of them even wielded abilities, usually in the form of radiant green light that healed their allies, vines ripping out of the ground to entangle enemies, gusts of wind that billowed around their melee fighters to divert enemy attacks, or yellow elemental lightning that tore through numerous enemies at once. The defenders were desperately outnumbered, though, and a lot of those already captured were in obvious distress. They couldn't do much in the conditions they were in, either, resorting to sobbing or crying out to loved ones and begging them to win as the remaining fighters struggled against green-skinned intruders that came in two variants.

The first were the goblins Riven was already familiar with. There were probably about three hundred of them left. They were short, sniveling little creatures with sharp teeth and claws that stood about three or four feet tall at most. They held little regard for their own lives, with many of them already sprawled in death across the village and the remaining ones throwing themselves ravenously at the elvish defenders. Most carried small daggers or hatchets, and they tried to swarm their enemies with numbers—this method was effective to Riven's eyes but also resulted in many dead of their own.

The second variant of green-skinned enemies were less numerous but far larger, even larger than normal humans or the elves they were fighting. These were orcs. They were huge, muscular humanoids with bulging muscles and wore furs and hardened leather. They mostly carried axes, broader short swords akin to a gladius, thick wooden buckler shields, and short bows that they'd use for ranged weapons. The bigger or older the orc warrior, the more often they had tusks—and many of them had either black hair braided down the back of their heads or they didn't have any hair at all. Of note, there was also a trio of three casters in their raiding party—shamans, most likely, with painted wooden face masks adorned with feathers and the gnarled staffs they used. They, too, channeled healing spells, but instead of vines and lightning bolts they focused on keeping their dozens of warriors safe with buffs. Their magics shielded their front-liners with auras of earthy brown and orange hues, deflecting many of the lightning bolts or arrows thrown at the orc attackers.

Riven only stopped for a half second to take all this in, his mind easily sorting through it all in an instant—a feat he wouldn't have been able to do as a normal human before the integration. Perhaps this was because his Intelligence stat had increased, or perhaps it had something to do with his vampiric evolution. Possibly both. Regardless, he immediately settled on a plan with a wide and bloodthirsty smile on his lips underneath his black and red runic mask. Despite helping the elves he'd semi-befriended since arriving in Panu, this was also an excuse to kill. It was an excuse to gain levels.

But most of all, it was an excuse to feed.

CHAPTER 39

The predator inside screamed with excitement alongside Gluttony's core, but he kept his sanity and mentally tugged at Fay's contract. The Succubus landed beside him within seconds, standing with hands clasped eagerly in front of her.

"Azmoth will be the focal point. Athela, do your thing as soon as I start— assassinate the bigger threats first if you can. Fay, we're sticking to the shadows for a while. They can't see us as well as we can see them, and we're using that to our advantage due to the numbers difference. I want you to set up perimeters around me while I work, keep them quarantined with your explosive sigils."

Athela vanished in an instant, and Riven launched himself up into the branches of a very tall tree nearby. He landed lightly on his feet, the Succubus beside him already starting to create a pattern of explosive Unholy mana traps below where they now stood overlooking the battle. Five, then ten, then twenty, and then dozens of sigils flashed below them—drawing some attention from the battlefield but not enough to create any shift in the enemy movements just yet. Fay held her hands out in front of her, pointing to spots she wanted the traps to be placed, until she gave Riven a nod.

"I'm ready," Fay stated with a gulp and slight fidgeting. "Do you want me to set up a dreamwalker zone?"

Curse of the Dreamwalker was the ability she had to cause hallucinations for anyone she deemed an enemy. Riven nodded once, then glanced over his shoulder one last time as screams and the clash of battle continued to echo across the village. "Can you make it look like my magical attacks are coming from other angles?"

Fay cocked her head to the side, then nodded. "Yes."

"Good. Do that, then, and make it as big as possible. Don't be nervous— here we go."

He raised his staff, and the weapon shivered with excitement before exploding with a torrent of dark energy.

CRACK

The Black Lightning strike obliterated two of the unaware back-line orc shamans in a single go, shredding their bodies and peeling flesh off bone before they even had time to scream. The ground around them exploded, and Fay's magic sprang to life with a huge, expanding globe of green and black light. Suddenly the entire rear of the orc unit started scrambling and screaming, numbers of them dying as blood was ripped off the corpses of the battlefield and solidified into razors that tore through their ranks.

It was like all hell had suddenly broken loose. Fake magical attacks simulating Riven's own came out from all over, covering Riven's true location all along the outer village perimeter with hallucinations of Black Lightning, Crimson Ice, and Bloody Razors while the globe of Fay's magic grew to encompass the entire northern village edge before stopping. Athela was quick on the uptake, too, zipping through the scrambling orcs and ripping out throats or stabbing hearts at a rapid pace while focusing the orc archers first. Whenever she was spotted, she'd disappear again only to reappear elsewhere—using the prisoners, trees, or nearby buildings to fade in and out of enemy lines with her superior speed.

One of the orc shamans had managed to erect a defensive aura of brown and orange light around himself right before Riven's initial attack, though. His two comrades, the other shamans, went up in clouds of red mist amid the destructive torrent of obsidian energy—but he'd been thrown back through a small crowd of the orcs chaining prisoners to one another in a line.

"RRRRRAAAAAAAAAAHHHHHHHHHHHH!!!!"

Riven wasn't pulling any punches, and a good portion of the greenskins turned in shock, confusion, or anger to look toward the tree line, where most of the attacks were coming from.

Some of them started paling outright despite the tone of their skin when they saw Azmoth erupt, roaring, from a portal of flames to rip an orc warrior's head right off. Caught in vortex of flames, a crowd of goblins that'd rushed over to help withered in shrieking agony, and the absolute tank of a hellscape demon beat his chest with another earth-shattering roar. He dwarfed even the largest of the orc warriors and rushed like a freight train into the midst of battle, ignoring Riven's strikes and Fay's hallucinations. His extra maws writhed up over his back like snakes and started snatching up goblins to eat them alive while he continued tearing and stomping on other unfortunate victims that failed to get out of the way.

The shaman was visibly shaken as he stood up from where he was thrown, looked around to gain his bearings, and pointed his staff toward the tree line beyond the village—but then he saw the demon.

The shaman barely pulled up another barrier in time, only just avoiding a strike from Athela that would have taken off his head before blasting the demoness back—causing her to backpedal and dash into the shadows again. His voice was deep, gruff, and strained—but nevertheless had a commanding tone to it. "HE'S IN THE TREES SOMEWHERE! FIND THE SUMMONER! KILL HIM! KILL HIM NOW BEFORE THOSE DEMONS ARE UNLEASHED UPON US FURTHER!!!"

Instantly, Athela moved to intercept a group of braver enemies that'd responded to the shaman's call to charge the forest, cleaving through three of them in half a second with spear-like movements of her arachnid limbs and clawing out a fourth warrior's neck while Riven remained hidden in the treetops above.

He motioned to the right and then to the left, conjuring dozens more of the spinning crimson blood blades from combinations of his own mana and the bodies on the battlefield. The projectiles then blasted through an oncoming rush of orc and goblin warriors, spiraling into the mess of bodies all around the demoness like a meat grinder. She shrieked with gleeful laughter as they died, acrobatically ducking under a swing and flipping over another orc's axe before her shin slammed into a large warrior's tusk and broke it off completely—catapulting the poor orc into the ground as if she'd hit him with a war hammer rather than just kicked him.

The greenskin soldiers who'd been chaining up prisoners were closest to the forest when the shaman's command echoed through their ranks. Orc and goblin alike had taken up arms and charged recklessly ahead, confident in their numbers, only to be met with two obstacles.

The first were more hallucinations, causing them to become disoriented and fall over one another when they tried to dodge imaginary magic projectiles or making them swing at the shadows of enemies that weren't actually there.

The second obstacle was the layers of invisible, explosive traps that Fay had laid out below Riven's position all along the northern edge of the village.

BOOM-BOOM-SPLAT-BOOM-BOOM-BOOM-SPLAT-SPLAT-BOOM

It was like Riven had front-row tickets to a carpet-bombing show, with dozens of small, crooked-looking goblins going up in explosions of green mana that ripped apart their little bodies and flung them away. The orcs fared a bit better, usually being able to take out two or three of the traps before being killed, but even they were often maimed or severely injured on the first mana-made trip wire they came across.

"Fay . . ." Riven muttered, casting a red sheet of ice across the ground in front of their position with her hallucinations following suit across their left and right sides. "You never told me you were god-level valuable back in that interview. This is a goddamn slaughterhouse."

Wretched Snares bloomed around him on the treetops and were loaded with Blood Lances that he created one after the other, adding extra power and speed to the projectiles when the snares slingshotted them away.

Fay smiled widely at the praise and continued to create new trip wires, connecting her invisible traps one after the other as they were triggered over and over again. "Thank you, Master. I told you that you would not be disappointed!"

Though there were well over eighty enemies lying dead on the ground, with more of them dying by the second due to Athela's assassinations, Azmoth's rampaging, and Riven's magical barrage, they quickly stopped trying to push their luck against the invisible traps and mind-numbing hallucinations. Down below, more orc mages started coming from the front, where they'd been battling elves. They cast illuminating barriers of orange light to block Riven's strikes, two of them started to try and suppress Azmoth by creating a stone cage around the demon that was quickly ripped apart, and one of them threw out a spell that caused an eerie yellow mist to blow through the greenskin ranks.

The masked shaman was still screaming orders, trying to organize everyone else and setting up defensive lines of tusked warriors around the mages and ordering the more stupid goblins to charge the tree line again as cannon fodder. The goblins that hesitated were killed by the larger orcs, who were growing uneasy due to being pinched on two sides by this unknown assailant and the elves—but things soon changed. Yellow mist from the orc mage finally reached the village perimeter, and with it, all of Fay's traps started lighting up one after another. So, too, did the trip wires of mana connecting them, and the shaman barked another command to charge.

This time, the goblins were able to avoid her spells, and many of the sigils were outright destroyed by fireballs that set off chain reactions. The fireworks show was enhanced even more by explosions from Riven's Black Lightning and spiked walls of red ice that acted as a barrier to their progress.

Meanwhile, Fay started cursing the orc mages while grunting in frustration as her globe of Unholy mana took direct damage from some kind of light burst coming out of the greenskin ranks. Fay's hallucination shattered from an enemy spell a moment later, and she yelled out to warn her master. "I won't be able to set up the dreamwalker field for a while! The hallucinations are down!"

Then Riven heard a quickening heartbeat behind him.

His body erupted with red sparks, sending his muscles into a spasm, and he immediately ducked as an empowered arrow broke the sound barrier and whizzed by his head—grazing his ear and nearly taking his skull off his spine in the process.

"It looks like they've finally found our true location." He chuckled humorously and, having arced his fingers to charge up a Blood Lance, he sent it torpedoing into the orc archer in a tree not far off.

The torpedo blasted the archer's head right off in a movement so fast that the orc simply couldn't react even at such a distance, and the body slumped, falling off the branch he'd been positioned on to thud onto the forest floor twenty feet below.

"Move."

Fay jumped at his command, flapping her wings and soaring into the night sky above them while spraying a cursed black cloud of rot over the greenskin ranks.

[Curse of Rot (Unholy)—Spray a cloud of Unholy miasma to afflict targets with a single Rot debuff before the cloud dissipates. A single cloud can disperse across multiple enemies. Rot debuff applies Unholy damage, slows the enemy, and can stack with other Rot debuffs. This curse starts out weak but scales over time in both damage and slowing effect. Low cooldown.]

The orc raiding party erupted with a hail of arrows and fireballs in turn now that the vampire was within reach, and Riven launched himself off the side of his tree while barely avoiding incoming fire. The tree exploded behind him into splintered wooden shrapnel, starting to burn, while knives or tomahawks thrown by the incoming orcs came to intercept him.

His staff blurred with his empowered movement, the fleshy string connecting his blade whipping out and deflecting many of the oncoming projectiles in a single strike—but some of them hit true. He felt and heard the thuds of three daggers land, slamming into his chest and causing him to grunt before he dashed and rolled behind another large tree to avoid two more arrows.

The horrified screams from people around the village continued to come, with men, women, and children all dying around him in senseless violence that they'd no doubt never expected. But he had to push that out of his mind . . . because he couldn't save all of them. Instead he would focus on the fun he was having . . . that way he wouldn't get distracted and do something stupid that could get himself killed.

He yanked the daggers out of his chest, feeling his regeneration kick in, and snarled before kicking off and exposing himself to the carnage at a distance. "COME ON, THEN!"

A red torpedo blew through four goblins and smashed into an oncoming orc mage, discharging the fireball that the man had been summoning and causing the area to light up in flames. Azmoth then crashed into another group that'd come to charge Riven while others started to slow and wither under Fay's black cloud of curse magic—clawing at their faces while their bodies began to gradually rot away. The shaman and other orc healers desperately tried to contain the demons, with four rogues using movement abilities successfully keeping Athela at bay for the moment, but Riven's impact was more than just a little noticeable.

The scene was a shit show, and the attackers began to come after him in force when they saw how devastating his attacks had been in such a short time. The shaman exchanged a couple of earth-based projectiles with Riven's own Bloody

Razors while Riven dodged using his improved Agility, and the shaman or other orc mages used orange mana barriers to block the incoming attacks directed their way. The orcs were obviously confused as to why he was here after noticing he was a vampire, with shouts and exclamations directed at one another ordering them to engage the warlock. The imprisoned elves nearby obviously didn't know what to think about it, either, by the way they shot him fearful looks or screamed out warnings to the defenders that a new enemy had presented itself.

Perhaps the elves thought he was here to eat them?

That was utterly stupid, in his opinion, for obvious and numerous reasons. He had no backup and was here to help, but he'd deal with that when the time came—*if* the elvish defenders did actually attack him.

He pedaled backward, farther into the dark of the trees and drawing his pursuers onto a more favorable battleground. Riven ducked another arrow in the dark with his improved reflexes and created another Bloody Razor, vaulting over the head of an incoming tomahawk swing when a stealthed rogue got too close. While in the air he let loose the bloody disc of magic—sending it flying toward the archer.

He landed behind the rogue who'd tried to take him out and spun—slamming his staff into the side of the tusked man with a *crunch*. The enemy's head was entirely torn off by the brutal trauma, the shadow magic emitted by the staff flinging bloody debris across the battlefield directly in front of him. He also heard the archer who'd nearly hit Riven a second ago yelp in agony and drop his bow when the crimson disc slammed into him.

Feeling the connection to that disc, Riven imbued it with even more energy and caused it to burst—blowing a hole in the hooded orc's body and leaving entrails far behind the orc's hunkered position next to a charred cabin on the outer village edge. Immediately the man's blood condensed and rocketed toward three goblins who were screaming insults and charging his way—decapitating them in a fluid motion while the blood formed more projectiles.

Two other archers behind the first went down as well when Azmoth let loose another cone of fire breath, burning them alive with guttural shrieks of pain. A thrilling sense of satisfaction immediately overcame Riven, and he charged forward, forcing more mana into Blessing of the Crow to increase his speed boost with sparks of lightning fluctuating across his body more prominently—just as a cold arrow struck him in the chest.

WHUMPH

Screams of horror or rage continued to pelt his ears, battle cries from the incoming enemies and the sound of airborne projectiles centered on Riven's position tearing through what should have been a peaceful and quiet night. The first projectile that lodged itself in Riven's chest was imbued with some kind of ice mana. His right pectoral muscle started to freeze and he gasped, ripping the arrow out, only to have two more arrows slam into his left shoulder as he stumbled forward onto one knee. Pain and another deep cold sensation radiated across his body, and he let out an involuntary groan when his muscles began to freeze over, but that groan soon turned into amused laughter. His body's regeneration was incredible even during the daytime, but here in the dark? At night? The regeneration was just unfair and utterly absurd.

It hurt, yes. The cold certainly affected his regeneration a little bit, and the ice on his body remained, but it wasn't enough. More so, the ice actually sealed over his wounds. They'd have to hit him a whole lot more than that to get anywhere close to killing him.

Riven ripped the arrows right out of his shoulder and snarled at the orcs. Glowing red eyes glinting maniacally from underneath his hood as he threw the frozen arrows onto the ground, and explosions from more of Fay's Unholy traps blasted with green light, eliminating a group of goblins that'd tried to flank him.

Riven's staff blurred left, smacking a fireball straight out of the air with a collision of shadow that sent the blast into a nearby tree. The trunk exploded with flames, lighting up his position and revealing the wounds along his body in the otherwise dark surroundings of the forest at night.

Wide-eyed elves and orcs alike watched with mixed emotions of confusion, horror, and awe while his wounds sealed up in real time—the holes in his clothes showing them how easily he could shrug off their attacks. Even the arrowheads he'd snapped off and left in his body were pushed out and expelled by flesh that quickly sealed over, creating scabs and then new skin less than ten seconds later.

More fireballs slammed into Azmoth's huge frame when the tanky demon leaped to cover Riven's body in a renewed attack, with orc warriors bringing up large clubs and axes to beat back the huge demon in an attempt to protect the mages.

"KILL THAT GODSDAMNED SUMMONER!" the shaman shrieked, infusing the nearby warriors battling Azmoth with buff after buff until their bodies glowed, enabling them to take hits that would have otherwise killed them on the spot.

WHUMPH

Athela's blades dug through the heart of an orc mage nearby, drawing the shaman's attention as he flung another molten ball of metal her way. Fay flew overhead, dispensing clouds of black mist with each flyby that continued to settle down on the packed horde of greenskin enemies battling the elves at the other end of the village. Many of the goblins had already withered away because of the dark magic, piling up as rotting carcasses for their brethren to step over. Orc healers were simultaneously dispelling the rot afflictions, but most of them were single-target healing spells, while Fay's mist could target entire swaths of enemies.

BOOM

A huge bolt of elemental lightning crashed into Azmoth, bowling him over and briefly stunning him. The fiery monstrosity twitched on the ground, orc warriors jumping at the chance to hack away before Riven's own blood magic crashed into them in a wave of carnage. Riven looked up above with a frown, focusing on a red-robed orc mage that he hadn't noticed before now. The caster was positioned on the roof of a tree house in the center of the village and was beginning to conjure up yet another lightning bolt that condensed every couple seconds to empower the attack.

Riven pointed toward the caster, an obvious threat above most of the others while Azmoth picked himself up on shaky legs. "Athela, kill him!"

The screeching obsidian woman blurred forward, easily dragging a lightly armored fighter twice her size by his ankles using a tightened line of red silk. She jumped over the heads of a pack of goblins, whirling and flinging the warrior into the side of the building the red-robed mage was standing on with an audible crunch of bones.

The tree house shook violently and the tusked mage canceled his upcoming lightning bolt, frantically propelling himself backward with a clap of his hands that sent a short-range blast of storm energy Athela's way—barely saving him from her wicked claws and even shocking her by dealing moderate damage. But that didn't stop her, and she whipped out her long, sharp tongue that snaked its way like a black ribbon to pursue the mage. When that failed and he teleported farther into the village, she pursued with an eager scream and launched herself into the treetops high above like a true apex predator.

"I WILL FEAST ON YOUR BONES, LITTLE ORC!!!"

By now the orcs had thoroughly recognized Riven and his demons as the primary threats in the battle, even with a couple dozen of the elf defenders still remaining—and they began to focus on taking Riven down while the swarming smaller goblins kept the elves preoccupied.

Crystallized red ice spread rapidly along the ground in the direction of the incoming greenskins to slow their progress, and Riven dashed right into the crevice between a tree house and a cabin where one of the orcs who'd shot him earlier with an arrow was gurgling in a pool of his own blood. Riven leaped ahead, slamming his boot into the orc's neck with a sickening snapping sound and a gleeful cackle. "Like me now, bitch? DO YOU LIKE ME NOW?!"

The unknown assailant died there on the ground—forever ending his story.

CHAPTER 40

Azmoth's bellowing roar and Athela's gleeful screeches intertwined with one another as sounds of battle climbed higher, and Riven teleported through a black rift in space as an axe from another charging enemy rounding the corner sliced across his robe and nicked his shin.

CRUNCH

The back end of Riven's staff crushed the orc's skull with an explosion of shadow that radiated out upon impact—a relatively cost-free enchantment of the weapon whenever he struck a physical blow. The ice hadn't slowed the others down as much as he'd thought it would, though, and he was growing irritated because of the mana he was expending and the lack of time to rejuvenate it. However, he also couldn't count on close combat to relieve his mana expenditure for too long, as he honestly knew very little about handling a staff of this size other than the utter basics of *swing for the hills.*

But why was this so much different from back at the hospital? With this many bodies, he shouldn't be having mana concerns . . . there was plenty of blood to fuel his spells with a reduced cost. Yet here he was, resorting to physical combat and notably having sluggish mana regeneration.

That's when he noticed a little flashing icon in his peripheral vision. Focusing on it, he saw that he'd been hit with a debuff—likely from those frozen arrows.

[You have been afflicted with Frostbite. Mana, health, and stamina regeneration are all reduced by half for the next twenty-nine minutes.]

By half?

Jesus. Well, Riven didn't really use much stamina, and his health regeneration was insane. So it made sense in some regards that his mana loss would be most noticeable.

He whirled upon hearing a heartbeat come around the corner he'd just passed by, blocking a sword strike with the shaft of his weapon and knocking the man back with an on-contact explosion of shadow. Cursing and sending another spinning disc that ripped through the man's ankle, Riven's eyebrows shot up in surprise when his target's body glowed green for a split second before the orc was launched to safety in a blur of motion despite minor injury. The orc looked back, flinging his gladius to the ground in a panic and turned to hop as fast as he could in the opposite direction despite the useless right ankle just as another roar of challenge echoed from within the cabin.

Riven barely had time to dodge a huge battle-axe that tore through a wooden support beam of the cabin wall. Frantically conjuring a series of acidic snares around him and attaching them in layers from wall to wall of the short alley, Riven watched the new warrior bulldozing through the shoddy construct come to a standstill and glare his way.

"Vampire scum!" the tusked, heavily muscled orc brute spat as he hoisted his battle-axe with hatred in his eyes. "A GENOCIDE AGAINST YOUR KIND, UNHOLY CREATURE! I DO NOT KNOW WHY YOU ARE HERE FIGHTING TO HELP THE ELVES, BUT TODAY WILL BE YOUR LAST DAY IN THIS REALM!"

The enraged orc roared, his battle-axe shifting to a bright-red color as he brought it down and sent an arc of energy tearing through the snares and rupturing another piece of the opposite wall of the tree house in a spray of debris.

Riven shifted left to avoid the attack while laughing loudly at the attempt, enhanced by his electrified movement buff, and he began pouring mana into Crimson Ice. The red crystals of ice around his feet began spreading rapidly again, covering the entire alley, walls, barrels, and rooftops around him as the warrior roared and charged ahead—but was quickly set upon by concentrated flurries of red snowflakes that bloomed all around in the air to blind the orc.

It was instinctive and a very first. The blood magic had responded to Riven's will just as the idea popped into his mind, and as Riven focused the spell on a singular area in a way that he hadn't realized he'd be able to do before now, the magic obeyed. The command had just felt right . . . and his mana had reacted without him second-guessing at all. It wasn't a new spell; it was the same as the normal Crimson Ice he'd already acquired but utilized in a new way—and his chest swelled with pride at having found a unique use for it.

He could create snow with Crimson Ice, too, and could partially blind his opponents with it. That was something he'd have to continue utilizing if he made it through this fight.

Riven's opponent swore and cursed, waving his axe around and batting aside an iced-over barrel before slipping and screaming in rage when the blade of his own axe made a shallow cut into his right hand.

WHAM

The warrior's head was rocked back with a spartan kick to the face as the snow briefly cleared—stunning the man just as Riven's staff came crashing into him with a brutal horizontal swing that sent additional explosive shadow magic up through his weapon on contact.

CRUNCH

The orc's brains were immediately plastered against the side of the house, the entire front side of the orc's head caved in with nothing but his lower jaw remaining. This was pretty brutal. Even since he'd been engaged in close combat and needed to watch his mana reserves, even then, when his ability to kill masses of people dwindled to only a few at a time so he could regenerate, it was still a slaughter.

Fay's black mists continued to soak into orc and goblin alike from somewhere in the sky above, many of their withered bodies rotting with silent screams on their faces. Athela and Azmoth were still putting in work, too. Other bodies were cut in half, blown up, burned to death, heads lopped off, body parts strewn across the ground in mounds—the list went on.

Riven then looked around to all the dead elves, women and children alike. His heart grew cold, and his determination solidified. There was no excuse for killing people who couldn't fight back. What he was doing was right and just.

"ORC MAKES GOOD PUNCHING BAG!!!!"

Azmoth barreled through the adjacent building, sending it crumbling as he crushed two enemy fighters into the ground simultaneously. Flaming claws ripped and tore pieces of the flattened orcs off even as their broken bodies lay splattered against the ground, and the building around them fell to reveal Athela blurring across the ice with hit-and-run tactics: dancing up walls or trees, over rooftops and in between archers to leave headless corpses, venomous wounds afflicted with necrotic poison, or needles of hardened blood webbing that she was shooting from her fingers protruding from her targets. The red-robed orc mage she'd been sent after was also very dead, limp and impaled on a large broken tree branch far above them for all to see.

"KILL THE VAMPIRE, AND THE DEMONS WILL BE BANISHED!!" the remaining shaman screeched his encouragement over the clatter of battle while he accumulated a large ball of elemental lava overhead. He snarled and unleashed it a second later, tearing into Riven's position—but the shaman's hands were jerked left at the last moment.

Riven's body took the hit—sending him through the other adjacent building and tearing it down with a loud crash and explosion of wood when the condensed ball of molten metal struck. He was flung through the near wall, through a support beam, into a bed, and out the next wall before coming to a rolling stop as he twitched slightly from the attack. Broken bones quickly began to mend, and he let out a gasp when his crushed, burned lungs reorganized themselves—but although he was healing from the attack, he could tell that his regeneration had taken a big hit. He was healing more slowly now despite the darkness, still had the frostbite debuff plaguing him, and he seemed more prone to damage from that type of magic than any other attack he'd ever been hurt with before. If he had to guess, the shaman was using magic from the Volcano subpillar of Fae, though he didn't know why it would do extra damage to him when compared to other varieties he'd been hit with. His status page concerning his vampiric bloodline had never mentioned a weakness to volcanic-type spells or abilities, but it might just be that the spell he'd been hit with had some intrinsic properties that caused his healing to slow and wasn't an actual weakness concerning his race.

In fact he was pretty sure he might not have survived at all if he'd been hit a little higher up in the neck or head. Thankfully Athela had managed to throw the mage off with strings of webbing from her fingers, pulling the shaman's hands to the side at the last second and keeping his aim lower than it had been. Whatever that magic was, it was powerful.

He dismissed the pain from his mind and pushed himself up to a staggering stand, cursing as he saw a smaller orc rogue wielding daggers try to get the drop on him from behind. He responded in a split second, conjuring two more nets of acidic black needles.

The wiry rogue was sprinting ahead and threw a spinning dagger that embedded itself in Riven's right arm when he raised it to block, causing Riven to stagger back again just as the nets of Wretched Snare finished conjuring right in front of the rogue's trajectory.

The hooded orc, who was likely a little older than Riven, judging from his lack of tusks and well-trimmed crew cut, evaded the first net by blurring three feet to the left with some kind of ability Riven was unfamiliar with.

Fortunately Riven's second net had manifested itself slightly behind the first one, and the rogue's momentum took him tumbling face-first into the acidic black magic. It wrapped around the dagger-wielding man, puncturing his skin with innumerable tiny shifting needles as the snare dug in and began eating away at his flesh.

The rogue yelped and then began to scream and fall, begging for mercy while the black magic wrapped him up before finding his own dagger—the dagger he'd thrown at Riven's arm—brutally cutting across his neck.

Riven glared down at the orc, pushing the blade up farther into the carotid artery and then into the esophagus as sputtering and coughing replaced the screams with wide-eyed flailing.

"Nighty night!"

Riven sneered, yanking the dagger back out and plunging it into the rogue's left eye. He panted for just a moment, collecting the snare up in his hand.

The black net of Unholy magic was easily ripped off the dead rogue with his fingers—as easily as picking up a pebble off the ground—and Riven whipped it back over his head to send the snare crashing into yet another lightly armored fighter in studded leather who'd appeared on the other side of the ruined building. He watched the next man hit the ground in a panic while trying to tear the acidic black magic off him. It burned and sizzled, peeling away his skin rapidly as the needles dug into flesh and found muscles next.

The orc dropped his short sword with a pained grunt, fumbled for something in his pouch, and slammed whatever he had in his hand down on the ground right before Riven got to him with the gnarled head of his sharpened staff. Smoke billowed out from the scout's position, obscuring Riven's sight as he coughed and wheezed before retreating to a safe distance and sending a torrent of Black Lightning out of his weapon into the gray cloud.

When Riven heard another, higher-pitched grunt of pain, he smiled to himself and sent out a single Bloody Razor that ended its trajectory with a wet thud and a scream of agony. He then imbued the embedded shard with more magic. He might not be able to see the man he'd hit in the thick haze of the smoke bomb, but he could still sense the magic he'd thrown out.

The disc erupted in bloody shrapnel, turning the scream into an abrupt silence as pieces of the man in the smoke field flew around where Riven stood.

Azmoth was having a rather easy time with the melee fighters and archers, though not so much against the mages. He'd taken it upon himself to kill the shaman, one of the few casters Athela hadn't already assassinated, and was continually thrown back with blast after blast of molten metal. The heat certainly didn't hurt the Hellscape Brutalisk, but each impact was like a goddamned cannonball and hit just as hard. The demon was exhibiting wounds underneath the flames and dents in his armor, but he would still shake off the brutal attacks and charge in time after time. He was even slowly healing his own wounds to an extent due to the passive trait his hellfire gave him, though not nearly as fast as Riven's own vampiric regeneration could muster under a night sky.

Riven watched Azmoth get blown back three more times, admiring his defensive capabilities. Even though he wasn't getting close enough to take the caster out, the shaman was still panicking due to the constant pressure and was likely expending tons of mana trying to keep Azmoth at bay.

"KEEP YOUR MIND ON THE BATTLE, BOY!"

WHAM

Riven felt the front of his face take a heavy impact as a blurring object slammed into him, again sending him sprawling onto the ground and causing the world to spin. If the mask hadn't been there to take the hit, he would have had a much worse injury. He dizzily flailed back to his knees and gaped up at the large two-handed mace being wielded by a shirtless, bald hulk of an orc that grinned down at him from a short distance.

"I can't believe you survived that, vampire! The stories about your kind are truly accurate, though I hadn't believed them until now!" the hulking orc warrior said as he brought up his mace again, while another shirtless warrior with a braided ponytail wielding a large hatchet walked up beside him. "I'm sorry for your loss, boy, but don't take it personally! It's just part of the job!"

The mace swung down, crushing the spot Riven had just been in with an aftershock of martial power right after Fay yanked him out of the way, to the enraged bellows of Riven's two pursuers. She rapidly flapped her wings and swung Riven around the side of another cabin, gliding through the air between two burning tents, pulling him at breakneck speed up the side of a tree house like he was on a brutal roller-coaster ride until coming to an abrupt stop on top of a roof jutting from a tree.

The demoness dropped him, quickly inspecting his bleeding body and the wounds he'd accumulated that still hadn't healed completely yet due to his regeneration slowing down. Her nervous expression soon changed to that of relief when she saw he was okay.

Riven picked himself up, dusted his shoulders off, and gave Fay a head nod. "Thanks. Your hallucinations are still on cooldown, right?"

"Yes. I usually am able to use that ability once per battle, unless the battle goes on for more than a half hour." The Succubus gestured to the battle below them, where Athela was continuing to assassinate orcs at random while rapidly dashing in and out of the village terrain for cover.

"Okay. Stay with me and set up some defensive traps until I regain more mana and the ability to cast. My mana regeneration is being slowed down significantly." Riven glanced down at the ice still coating his chest and shoulder, grimacing when he touched the mana-infused wounds. His regeneration hadn't completely rid him of it, and the frostbite debuff was still in effect. "Who'd have thought those pain-in-the-ass arrows would be what cripples me this battle?"

Fay nodded eagerly, and her muscles relaxed, simultaneously withdrawing her long black wings to fold them behind her. "As you say, Master!"

She raised her hands and began to point. Unholy green runes flashed in the air around them and along the tree before becoming invisible again, with Fay's sky-blue hands twisting in front of her, starting to cover a large area before connecting different groups of them with mana-made trip wires for more of a punishing effect.

Meanwhile, the screams and roars of the battle a couple cabins down echoed across the village as Azmoth continued to tear through poor souls stupid enough to get close. The brutalisk was an absolute beast of a creature, and he was now keeping well over half of the enemy party occupied as he rampaged through their midst while breathing fire or tearing greenskins apart in a masterful display of violence. He'd moved on to chewing on goblins midfight now, swallowing bites off the tiny creatures while they gave out terrified shrieks and tried to get away and attack at range. The elves were still fighting on their own front, too, though they were regaining a foothold in the fight, pushing the greenskins back and simultaneously trying to make their way across the forest clearing toward their imprisoned loved ones.

"Fay . . ." Riven muttered under his breath, letting the seconds tick by and studying the absolute carnage of Azmoth's doing. "Is it normal for Hellscape Brutalisk infants to be this kill-hungry?"

Fay let out a laugh and came to stand beside him, finishing her network of defensive traps. "Yes . . . it is. Just wait until he gets bigger, though. Athela has already been talking about how she's going to make Azmoth her battle steed."

Riven snorted a laugh, shooting the grinning Succubus a smirk and letting out a long sigh. "Well, that sounds a lot like something Athela would say. Does Azmoth know of her master plan?"

"Not yet."

"Figures. Can't wait until the day she tries. I'd pay money to watch that episode unfold."

The sounds of multiple nearby heartbeats and rushing footsteps interrupted their idle chat midbattle and alerted Riven to an advancing enemy at the back. Before he could even turn, though, a series of explosions sent shock waves and debris along the tree house roof. Branches, body parts, and tiles blasted apart as two orc bodies were sent spiraling to the ground dozens of feet down, but he noticed the third attacker almost too late.

It was a rogue, a young orc woman with flowing raven hair who'd managed to avoid the traps. She had been stealthed somehow, making herself completely invisible until she'd gotten too close and the ability's influence broke. Her fur-clad body and tusked, sneering face shimmered into existence midsprint and only a couple feet away.

Riven was surprised, but he startled even more when a glass vial of purple liquid was thrown at his feet. It didn't hit him but exploded on impact to release a cloud of purple mist.

SPLASH

The potion quickly started absorbing into his skin, and his mana channels felt like they were on fire as he screamed and dropped to his knees. His veins felt like they had sludge moving through them, and he tried to summon magic to kill this new opponent with a rage—but quickly found out that he couldn't use the mana at all.

[You have been afflicted with Gulsh Lilly Toxin. Your mana and stamina channels are now blocked completely for the next three hours.]

Oh. Oh, fuck.

He looked up, wide-eyed, and brought his staff to bear. "THESE FUCKING ROGUES!"

Only a moment later, she leaped forward for his throat with a snarl and a dagger pointed directly at it. "FOR ANTHAS!"

CHAPTER 41

Fay tried to intercept with a hissing lunge of her own, but she was in no way a melee fighter and was easily slammed aside with a shoulder charge that left her gasping. The rogue vanished and reappeared two feet in front of her original position the same way the other rogues had sidestepped one of his snares earlier.

He stumbled and lifted an arm to block the incoming attack, unable to summon magic to aid him, and shouted a curse as the dagger intended for his throat impaled his left shoulder instead.

The two of them tumbled to the roof and struggled with one another, rolling off the multistory building and landing with a thud in the dirt far below. She was surprisingly strong—even giving him a run for his money, and he was dead certain that whatever level she was, it was far higher than the average of her group.

Riven headbutted the orc girl and grappled with her. She snarled, trying to knee him in the gut and get him off her with her free hand as his slightly superior strength and weight kept her pinned. He was quickly reaffirming the idea that although his abilities concerning magic were incredible, his physical combat prowess was subpar.

Fleshy strands shot out from his staff up above, connecting with Riven's hand and whipping downward to pierce the orc through her back.

She let out a pained gasp but managed to yank out yet another dagger strapped along her thigh. Not being able to bring it up farther because of how she was pinned, she let out a yell and sank it deep into Riven's right lung. Ice began to spread through the lung immediately, causing his ability to breathe to drastically lower—to the point that he was almost suffocating.

"See you in hell, bloodsucker!" She coughed up blood and grimaced when he twisted the staff impaled in her back, and then grunted in pain when he defiantly slammed his head into her own again.

"SHREEEEE!!!!"

Athela's screech was ear-piercing as the Arshakai vaulted forward, using some of her limbs to tear Riven away and her other limbs to push the rogue off at the same time.

As Riven came to a stop and continued to hyperventilate, feeling his lung fill up with blood, he watched the demoness and orc rogue face off with everything they had.

The injured woman was definitely far more skilled than any of the other orcs he'd seen, aside from maybe that shaman still fighting Azmoth. She was nimble, quick, and could reactivate movement abilities over and over again to great effect while also being ready with the numerous poisoned knives from her thighs and belt.

Athela was just as quick, though, blurring forward and side to side to match the rogue just off her base Agility despite not having any movement abilities.

Athela did have that trait Naturally Agile, though, something the rogue probably lacked.

The demoness lunged forward, using her arachnid limbs and jabbing out with them in a way Riven had seen her do many times before. It was as if she'd learned to turn her limbs into spears, pistoning them with lightning-fast speed and using her sharp, poison-coated tongue like a whip that flashed forward in strikes that a normal human wouldn't have been able to follow but were still blocked or dodged by the rogue.

The demon ducked and raced up a wall to launch herself at the rogue as the woman lunged left to avoid a spearing attack. The girl then counterattacked, flipping two knives on end and hurling them at the spider with tremendous speed—only to curse when Athela dodged them yet again.

Athela snarled, her claws extended and clacking together as she began firing needles of hardened blood from her spinnerets. "I'M GOING TO STOMP YOU, LITTLE GIRL! YOU'RE GOING TO CRY AND BEG FOR MEEEE!!!"

The needles caught the orc rogue off guard, and many of them found their mark, puncturing the woman's leather and skin as she screamed and held up her arms to cover her face. She ducked behind a burning crate, throwing a smoke bomb as Athela rushed her—and then vanished in the cover while activating the stealth ability again.

"CURSES!" Athela screeched, landing on the roof of the nearby building and frantically looking around. "YOU LITTLE BITCH!"

The glint of firelight from a throwing knife gave away the rogue's position, and Athela immediately reacted. She launched herself off the right side of the building with tremendous speed to avoid the blade and simultaneously attached herself to a nearby oak tree with her webbing, letting her body glide through the air before abruptly tightening and reeling herself backward while rotating over the ground.

The maneuver acted like a slingshot, launching the spider back through the air like a missile—directly at the stunned rogue. Athela's screech of victory intermixed with the woman's screams as four spear-like spider legs impaled the rogue's chest, skewering her heart and lungs just as Athela sank her tongue and then sharpening teeth into the woman's right breast. Poison, a tidal wave of black and necrosing venom, began spreading into the rogue.

Panicking, the screaming woman fell over, landing in the grass and frantically struggling to get the demoness off. But she needn't have bothered, as Athela had already dispensed fatal blows.

The spider-woman hybrid kicked back off her target, chittering angrily at the quickly dying orc while her necrotic venom spread through deep wounds—and leaving the rogue to shudder into death soon after that before rushing over to Riven.

"I'm fine," Riven muttered, gasping slightly while pushing himself to a standing position. His right lung was frozen solid, the frostbite debuffs were decreasing his regeneration, and the poison he'd been afflicted with stopped his use of mana completely. He was not fine, but he wasn't dead, either.

Fay landed beside him, embarrassed and wincing with an obviously broken collarbone. "Sorry, Master."

The Succubus looked defeated, and Riven spared her a glance now that most of the greenskins in their area were dead. He put a hand on her shoulder and squeezed reassuringly. "Hey, don't sweat it. You got two of those rogues before they even reached me—you're just not a melee fighter. And neither am I, as is very obvious."

Fay gave a small, amused smile, and she nodded to readjust her posture.

Athela, on the other hand, was rather angry, and she jabbed a finger into Fay's chest. "First fight on the job, don't fuck up again. Keep him safe while he heals or I'll find you in the nether realms."

Fay blanched slightly, nodded, and Athela took off to chase down some orcs running into the woods about fifty yards away.

Riven continued to gasp, took the remnants of his utterly ruined cloak off and threw it to the ground, then gestured for Fay to take them up again a second later. She nodded wordlessly and grabbed him before flapping her wings and launching them both into the branches above, landing on a tree house rooftop for a better viewpoint.

They both glanced back over to where Azmoth was still battling another small group. Over three dozen green corpses were strewn around Azmoth's immediate vicinity, and the flaming demon had five more enemies still alive. The shaman was firing off more cannonballs of molten metal to keep Azmoth at bay and downing potions at the same time, likely to keep his mana up. Meanwhile, an orc cleric was using some kind of slowing ability with white rings of light encircling Riven's demon—what he could only assume to be a kind of holy-type spell or miracle. Then there were three archers, all of whom were furiously firing at Azmoth as they kept their distance. One would occasionally score a hit in between the solid slabs of obsidian armor lacing the demon's body. Beyond that there was also a handful of goblins remaining—each of them throwing stones, debris, or daggers at the monstrous demon while maintaining a healthy distance.

The melee combatants were all dead, but Riven could see that even though Azmoth was doing his best, he was starting to wind down. No longer was Azmoth able to breathe flames, and the regeneration properties could only do so much with so many open wounds and projectiles sticking out of his body. He looked like a pincushion with bolts, hatchets, daggers, and burning arrows all lodged in the more fleshy areas of his muscles.

Then a man's voice called out, "FIRE!"

Both Fay and Riven turned, startled to see a group of elves lined up with bows and arrows aimed in Azmoth's direction.

Why were they aiming at Azmoth?

Were Riven and his minions really going to be attacked by these elves after all he'd done for them? A sneer of contempt was written onto a middle-aged elf's handsome features, and the bow in his hand was notched and pulled back just as he let out the order to the others.

Riven had been betrayed again. Just like Jalel back in Negrada, he'd tried to help someone and had received a dagger in the back for it.

The arrows, over two dozen of them and many of them empowered with yellow lightning, simultaneously fired toward Azmoth's location like a cloud of speedy death. They zipped over the bloodied, icy grounds and the ruins of their abandoned homes, past the burning buildings and trees—right into their intended targets.

Riven's eyes opened wide as the arrows didn't hit Azmoth at all. Instead, the arrows that hit true all landed to impale the orc archers, shaman, cleric—and the remaining goblins. One of the archers and the cleric immediately dropped dead, riddled with arrows, as a second archer caught one in the knee and went down screaming and cursing.

"I'VE TAKEN AN ARROW TO THE KNEE!!!"

The shaman took one to the ankle, tripping him and causing him to misfire as the cleric's slowing holy divinity became undone as well. The immediate result was a quick death from Azmoth's clawed foot as it came crashing into the scream-ing shaman's skull—splattering his brains along the ground while the demon beat his chest and roared triumphantly to the starlit heavens.

The last of the archers still able to flee immediately took off, vaulting over a nearby fence meant for livestock as another arrow nearly caught his shoulder before he turned a corner and raced out of sight.

[You have gained two levels. Congratulations!]

CHAPTER 42

[Riven Thane's Status Page:

- Level 38
- Pillar Orientations: Unholy Foundation, Blood Specialty, Infernal, Shadow
- Core of Original Sin—Gluttony: (Under Construction) (???)
- Traits: Race: Pure-blooded Vampire (Extreme Darkness Regeneration) (Sunlight Decay) (Extreme weakness to silver weapons, Sun pillar, and Light pillar attacks), Class: Warlock Adept, Adrenaline Junkie (Blood) (+15% to Agility)
- Abilities: Blessing of the Crow (Unholy), Wretched Snare (Unholy), Silvertongue (Unholy), Bloody Razors (Blood), Crimson Ice (Blood), Blood Lance (Blood) (Tier 2), Blood Nova (Blood) (Tier 3), Hell's Armor (Infernal), Riftwalk (Shadow)
- Stats: 70 Strength, 151 Sturdiness, 388 Intelligence, 178 Agility, 10 Luck, -368 Charisma, 184 Vampiric Perception, 116 Willpower, 9 Faith
- Free Stat Points: 0
- Minions: Athela, Level 30 Arshakai [36 Willpower Requirement]. Azmoth, Level 31 Hellscape Brutalisk [44 Willpower Requirement]. Fay, Level 23 Succubus [29 Willpower Required]
- Equipped Items: Crude Cultist's Robes (1 def), Vampire's Escort (104 dmg, 102% mana regen, Shadow and Blood dmg +22%, Black Lightning, Scorpion's Sting), Chalgathi Cultist Amulet (???), Leather Boots (1 def), Backpack of Supplies (Guild Hall: Stone Manor), Witch's Ring of Grand Casting (+26 Intelligence), Breath of Valgeshia (48 def, +13 dmg & +9% mana output dmg for blood dmg, 6% mana regen)]

For every level Riven gained, he got an additional +1 Strength, +2 Sturdiness, +4 Intelligence, +2 Willpower, +4 Agility, +1 Perception, +7 free stat points, and a whopping -3 Charisma. Smashing all the free stats into Willpower, Intelligence, and occasionally Sturdiness had become a habit at this point, and that's exactly what he'd done last night before going to bed. Battles could be tough, but the rewards they gave were always a pleasure to behold both by the way his body and mind felt afterward and by the power differential he saw whenever he cast spells the next time around.

Riven awoke in a dark room, yawning and covered in thick blankets. He stretched and huddled back into the soft feather bed that felt comfortable despite how tired he felt. Blurry vision met him as he opened his eyes, but his eyes eventually cleared amid the chirping of birds and low voices of men and women somewhere beyond the small, square room he was enclosed in. His items and clothes were all piled in a corner opposite the bed, just where he'd left them last night. One of the windows had intentionally been covered up with a thick sheet, and a pitcher of water was set out to the side . . .

No. It was blood.

Riven's eyes widened as the smell hit him and his ever-growing hunger gnawed at him. Despite his exhausted state, he clawed at the pitcher and sat up—putting the tin lip to his mouth and gulping like a man dying of thirst in the desert. He took it all, absolutely chugging it, and let out a long gasp before accidentally dropping the pitcher out of weakness.

He nearly fell out of his bed trying to get it back in his hands, but he was stubbornly able to grasp at it and place it back on the small bedside table. Despite this he had made some noise, and soon the sound of footsteps and heartbeats approached his doorway before a light knock reached his ears.

"Riven?"

The door creaked open, and Fay stepped in with Athela.

Senna was in the back, peering over their shoulders, and she waved when she saw Riven was up. "Good morning!"

He grunted his acknowledgment of the three women, noting Azmoth's large frame outside the adjacent room and near the front door, then turned his back to get some sleep again. "Morning. Now leave me alone, I need to catch up on my beauty sleep. Guy's gotta keep his complexion."

This earned him a snort of amusement from Fay and an eye roll from Athela.

"Get up, the elves want to talk to you, and you've been sleeping for the past eight hours." Athela came over and jabbed him ruthlessly in the side, and he swatted at her before hunkering down in the bedsheets even more.

"No! I refuse to leave this extra-comfy bed anytime soon!"

Senna giggled and dashed out of sight, yelling out a name Riven did not recognize—Genua—and soon she came back with another, older elf who was blonde and looked very similar to Ethel. That was because she, in fact, was Ethel's mother—he'd just never gotten her name last night when Ethel had volunteered their house. Riven had been quick to fall asleep, too, so introductions in large part had been put on hold.

Just like all the other elves he'd seen, this woman wore very little—just some fur shoes similar to moccasins and an outfit made of interwoven leaves that covered her breasts and lower region. She had similar blue paint adorning various parts of her as well, though not as much as he'd seen on some of the others. The woman was slender, blonde, and had familiar blue-green eyes, a gentle smile, and pretty features. She pulled a chair in from the other, better-lit room where the windows were open to the light and Riven could tell that it was likely midday based on how bright it was.

"Do you mind shutting that door?" Riven said, wincing. "It's awfully bright."

She stood up, whispered something to Senna, and closed the door behind her with Senna leaving again.

That's when Riven realized that Senna had looked completely fine. The break in her clavicle was obviously gone, and the infected bite wound was cleared up entirely. He blinked and shot another look at the door before a wave of nausea overcame him and he vomited into the nearest open container—a bucket that'd been placed at the edge of the bed.

"You'll be like that for quite a while," the older woman said, holding up a hand to his forehead and nodding to herself with furrowed brows. "I had to drain quite a lot of poison out of you—I'm surprised you were able to survive it. Then again, you are undead . . . so your body holds up a lot better to toxins than mine would."

He spit into the bucket again, wiped his lips, and looked up at the older woman. "Ethel's mom, right?"

The woman raised both eyebrows, then let out a melodic laugh while politely cupping her hands in front of her. "You are correct. My dear boy, you saved our village from destruction. You saved us from slavery and a likely brutal ending where we'd end up on dinner plates to those orcs and goblins. Not only that . . . but you saved my daughter and her friend before that as well. I was hoping to have words with you, to thank you personally. Let me express my deepest thanks to you now."

The woman bowed her head with a very genuine smile. "My name is Genua. I never thought those girls would be found alive again, much less traveling with a vampire and his three demons. Quite a positive turn of events, even if it does sadden me that my daughter lost her left hand. It also pains me to think the others of their hunting group who died that day, but I cannot express my gratitude enough for the things you did. I must say that I'm rather curious about the story she's told me. Perhaps when things settle down, we can speak on those events in further detail."

Riven's glowing red eyes shifted upward, scrutinizing her for a time. He rubbed his chin and lay back in the soft comfort of the pillow. "Okay, I've got to ask. Since you're her mother, you must be . . . forty? Just how old are you?"

She gave him a wink. "That's a secret. Here, chew this and swallow it."

Genua held out one hand, in which was a small capsule made up of plant matter. It wasn't a pill necessarily, but very much looked like one and had obviously been put together from mashed-up ingredients and then firmly pressed to stabilize it.

"What's this?" Riven asked while taking the item.

"Antidote."

Riven popped the item into his mouth without further questioning and sank back into the covers, chewing the medicine and swallowing it before giving his two minions who protectively hovered nearby a smile. "I'm all right, guys. It's pretty safe here."

"You're too trusting," Athela stated flatly. She gestured to the woman in front of her, who didn't turn to look back. "You're lucky I already checked that antidote out, otherwise I would have slapped it from your hands. Riven, be more proactive in keeping yourself alive. That regeneration of yours isn't something that can save you from everything."

"Agreed." Fay nodded sagely, cupping her hands in front of her with her long black tail flicking back and forth. "Much too trusting."

Riven scowled and was about to protest but stopped himself when the door was flung open, slamming against the wooden wall of the cabin to reveal Ethel and a similarly dressed elf man who was middle-aged and had a long blond ponytail in the back. The elvish girl was almost an exact replica of her mother, although a bit younger, now that he could evaluate both of them side by side.

Ethel quickly straightened up, caught her breath, and calmed herself after a glare from her mother, then walked in with a genuine smile of relief. It was obvious that she was sweating from recent exertion and had been doing something outside in the hot sun up until just a moment ago.

"I'm glad to see you're okay," Ethel stated, shutting the door behind her softly and glancing over to Genua apologetically. "I got excited when I heard he'd woken up, sorry."

Genua rolled her eyes, shot the man behind Ethel a glance, and regained her own composure seconds later. Turning back to Riven, she put a hand on his shoulder and pressed firmly. "I'll be checking on you regularly while you recover. I'm one of the healers and alchemists here in the village, so anything you need, just let me know. I'll usually be here in the house. And don't worry about the blood—we've kept a couple of the goblins alive for harvesting purposes."

Riven nodded in appreciation. He didn't necessarily need to be coddled like this, but it was nice to finally get some relaxation time after months of grinding. "Thank you."

The slender woman stood up, bowed slightly, and then exited the room while silently closing the door again to keep out the light.

Ethel stood there awkwardly in the unknown man's shadow, rubbing the stump of her left arm, which had now healed completely—likely by magical means—with her right hand. She opened her mouth to speak but blushed slightly and turned her eyes to the ground.

"I think it's time for me to go," Fay stated with a smirk. She grabbed Athela by the arm and began tugging the other demoness out of the room, despite Athela's protests. "We'll be back later! Get some rest, and get better! The elves are very nice, and they all want to meet you!"

Yet again, the door swung open and shut behind the departing girls, leaving only Ethel, the unknown man, and Riven in the room.

Riven felt as awkward in this situation as Ethel looked. He definitely smelled like vomit and was naked underneath the covers here, in the room with a girl he very much found attractive and a silent weirdo in the corner who was taking turns staring at the two younger people. Riven knew he looked terrible, disheveled, and waves of nausea repeatedly tried to undo his ability to see straight.

"I . . . did not expect such a warm welcome," Riven eventually said, letting himself fall farther into the feather bed and relaxing his muscles entirely. He was too weak to remain so tense for so long. "I'm very, very happy to realize I'm not being treated like a monster, like I thought I would be."

Ethel looked up from where she was staring at the ground between her feet, then took the liberty to sit in the chair her mother had occupied until recently. "Yes . . . Well, of course they wouldn't treat you like a monster. Not after what you did. Athela said you were concerned about that, and I even overheard you once in the hospital talking about your negative Charisma. Charisma can heavily influence first impressions, auras, a general feel for the person, and other less noticeable interactions with people. Though, at this point, it wouldn't even matter if you were a dragon or an ogre. To us—or at least to most of us—you are a hero. What you did . . . We are unable to ever repay you. I mean that, truly."

Riven let his gaze trail from the ceiling to rest on Ethel, who was shedding silent tears at the bedside and looking very vulnerable. He raised an eyebrow. "Ethel, are you okay? I'm not that scary—no need to cry."

"Oh, shut up!" Ethel pushed him teasingly and spread out a wide, bright smile. "I'm just happy."

"Ah . . . Well, that's a nice change. I'm glad you're happy, then." Riven didn't let his gaze drift away from Ethel, but he really didn't know what to say after that. "I am rather great, aren't I?"

"Oh, shut up!" Ethel repeated with a laugh almost identical to her mother's, and her cheeks flushed. She paused in her laughter when she caught the other man's blank stare, though, as if thinking about something, and then hesitantly leaned forward and gently kissed Riven on the cheek. Flushing an even deeper red with embarrassment, she quickly stood up. "Thank you for helping me. Thank you for helping all of us. I'll let you get some rest, but afterward I'd very much like to get to know you better . . . if you have time to spare for me."

Riven, still confused as ever at this very quick change of events and attitude, glanced curiously between the two other people in the room. "Uh . . . Sure?"

That was all she'd been wanting to hear, and beaming back at him, she exited the room. But before shutting the door, she turned halfway in the doorway. "Fay will be delivering your dinner later . . . Is it okay if I come along?"

Riven chuckled, a warm feeling growing in the pit of his otherwise cold stomach. This was kind of nice. "Absolutely. I'll see you later, Ethel."

With a quick nod and wiping some of the sweat from her brow, she turned to leave yet again, then slowly came to a stop near a window right outside in the hallway. Plants hung from the ceiling around her where the sunlight glinted off her bare shoulder, still wet with perspiration, and she turned around with her back to the wall—giving him a long, silent look he couldn't quite decipher, as if she wanted to say more before snapping out of it.

Then, after losing an internal battle against better judgment and with a final smile, she was gone, and the room had darkened once more. Sighing to himself after the door shut, and feeling rather smug despite the god-awful sickness he was experiencing, Riven began to daydream about the future. He'd been absolutely terrified of the idea that he'd get out into this new world and be shunned like some kind of outcast, but he was quickly proving himself wrong. Sure, he was a bit of a monster now, but that didn't define him. As long as he did good by the people around him, he could still carve out a little piece of happiness for himself after all.

With that thought, he bent over the side of the bed, puked again, and went back to curling up in the blankets before falling asleep.

A deep voice rang out from behind Riven's back. "I would like to have words with you."

"FUCK, MAN!" Riven whipped back up out of bed to meet the staring gaze of the weirdo in the corner again. He was still half-asleep, and though he could register the heartbeats of the people in the village around him, he had been getting used to phasing them out when he was relaxed. "JESUS! Who are you and why are you still here?"

The handsome older man gave him an unamused smile and crossed his muscular arms in front of his bare chest. "Mind if I have a short word with you?"

"Eh . . ." Riven looked the elf up and down. The blue warpaint was smeared in certain places, and his forearm and calf were bandaged. "Sure . . ."

The man nodded, sat down on the chair Genua had been on a minute ago, then steepled his fingers in thought. "To answer your question, I am Ethel's father and Genua's husband. I am the head of this household. My name is Farrod."

Riven blinked a couple times, waiting for him to continue. "All righty, Farrod, nice to meet you, then. To formally introduce myself, my name is Riven Thane."

Riven held out a hand, which Farrod only looked at and did not take.

"I just wanted to tell you that though you helped us, the price you are asking for is high. One that I barely accepted." Farrod leaned back in the chair, his blank expression growing cold. "Only barely, and at the request of the rest of the village. I find the entire idea . . . disgusting, frankly. And you are pushing your luck by asking it. Be very careful how you tread from here on out, vampire. I will be watching you."

Riven's face contorted with confusion. "Huh? What the bloody fuck are you talking about?"

Farrod only grimaced at his words, then stood up to slowly walk away. "We are past playing games with one another, Riven Thane. Far, far past that point."

A moment later, the door shut behind Ethel's father with a click, and the room became dark again. Riven rubbed at his chin, cocked his head to the side, shook his head, and shrugged. "For fuck's sake, he could have at least told me what he was talking about. Ungrateful prick."

CHAPTER 43

"You let him leave intentionally? To buy yourself time?" Mara asked, confusion written all over her face, her hands behind her back. She stood beside Allie on a rooftop under the starlight, watching their army of undead—minions and sentient creatures alike—march northward through the darkened streets.

Allie solemnly nodded, red eyes glowing, watching Vin and Nin pile up bodies of the civilians they'd just slaughtered to add to their undead ranks. "Riven . . . is too kind. You even heard him say it yourself—he wouldn't have allowed me to do what needs to be done. He wouldn't have allowed us to continue this war the way it needs to be finished. He would stop me from butchering the animals that need to be butchered."

"You know, I tend to agree with your brother on that one."

Allie shot her a glare, but Mara held up a hand. "No, don't give me that look, Allie. You know I'll do whatever you tell me to do. Beyond being friends, I owe you a life debt. However, don't you think this is a little bit cruel? I mean, they're children, Allie. Surely you're taking your revenge a bit far."

"They're being spared from a life of hardship and cruelty, " Allie cut back, an edge to her words, though she stiffened under Mara's scrutiny. Her right hand tightened around her bone brooch, and her eyes lingered on the bodies below while her people piled the materials onto wagons for future use. "Imagine what kind of life they'd lead if they followed in their parents' footsteps."

"That is not for you to decide, Allie."

"It is, though." Allie turned her entire body, fully confronting her friend with a glare. "Let me pose a question, one of morals, since you seem to be so keen on the subject this night. Do you think, for even a moment, that those children aren't going to grow up to hunt us down if we let them live?"

Allie waved over the piles of the dead as her undead soldiers continued to march past the wagons. "After everything that has happened? After their family members have died, their memories scarred, their loved ones hammering the ideas into them that their mortal enemies are the undead who scour this land? They are indoctrinated now. Prophet makes it so—he forces them to worship that holy book like some kind of new Bible. He force-feeds these children philosophical garbage so that one day they may become unquestioning soldiers like so many of the other religious fanatics of past generations have been. So tell me, Mara, do you really believe if we let them live, they'd grow up and just leave us alone?"

Mara frowned from underneath her hood. Her pale, dead eyes wandered over the carnage, and she winced at the gruesome sight.

"Well?" Allie pressed. "Go on. Tell me that I'm wrong. Tell me that they'd grow up to be loving neighbors, ones that could forgive and forget all the things they've been told or seen. Tell me that they would not grow into a new generation of hateful enemies that would breed even more of their kind. Tell me, Mara, that they would not cost us lives of our own in future decades to come."

Mara's frown deepened. "We could always bring them up ourselves. Allie, we could raise them as our own children—"

"HA!" Allie barked a cruel, cutting laugh and waved her hand in front of her to wipe away the idea. "MARA! Listen to yourself! Bring them in? Raise them as our own? Us? The people who killed their families?" Allie gave the other woman a grudging side-eye. "Do not be so foolish."

There was a long pause after that. Mara continued to watch their army trudge along. She listened to the screams in the distance of people their forces encountered along the way. Her gut felt heavy, and her gaze was downcast. "What if Riven finds out what you've done?"

"They'll all be dead before he gets back. There will be no witnesses, and I will mold a story that is believable," Allie stated with a shake of her head. Her long brown hair flowed about her in a midnight gust of wind when she pushed her fingers through it and downed her hood. She took in a deep breath, then exhaled and smiled underneath the bone mask she wore. "I love my brother. I love him enough to do the things that need to be done that I know he could never do. I will save him from himself, I will make the hard decisions that would break him, and I will carve out a piece of this world for ourselves. I hope you do not think me cruel, Mara, because I am doing this for us. For you, for me. For Vin and Nin. But especially for Riven. This may have started as a revenge story, but now it is something more. The rest of the world may not accept us unless we force them to do so . . . and I will be the hammer that drives that nail in."

The sound of singing woke Riven again a day later, and despite having a rather sore body, he was already feeling a lot better than he had even earlier that week. Ethel and Fay had come to try and wake him up multiple times, but they'd only succeeded once. Waking up had left his mind a little groggy, but the recovery from the poison had gone very well, and he drank another cup of blood that'd been left for him on the little nightstand next to the bed.

He went to dress himself with his hunger still mulling, pulling up his worn-out pants and the bloodstained shirt, now riddled with holes. His cloak had been utterly destroyed, though he'd been supplied with a new cloak of lesser quality by . . . someone. Nevertheless he put on the clothes and rummaged through his backpack and the bin of stuff Azmoth had carried to see if everything was still there.

None of it was missing. He still had all the coins he'd accumulated up until now, and he had the strange ivory amulet with those emerald eyes that he still didn't know the value of. He had the altar's planting rod, then he found the guild core. His mask was there, too, as was his staff.

Despite this weapon having the ability to move around and act on its own accord to a very small extent, it hadn't talked yet. *Could* it talk? It had part of his soul inside it, and that piece of him had merged with some weird-ass self-aware enchantments and another soul fragment to create it. Fifty bucks said this thing could talk. Unfortunately the staff usually just gave him compulsions, such as thoughts or feelings, and thus outright words weren't necessarily needed most of the time.

Riven reached for his weapon, but then hesitated. Withdrawing his hand and standing up, he sent the staff a mental image through their bond explaining why he was going to leave it here. He didn't want to look hostile or threatening any more than he already did, and after the way he'd been treated, there was no reason to bring it along while he was in the village. The gnarled object shuddered in response, and Riven got a confirmatory response back with a feeling of understanding.

Unfortunately the peaceful night was then interrupted by a new system notification.

[System-Wide Panu Announcement: World Quests have been initiated.

Hello, all participants. As your combined worlds have joined into one single world of Panu on the edge of integrated space, a new page is turned over in the history of the cosmos. All newly integrated beings chosen to undertake starter events and tutorials have finished their initiation events, and thus the World Quests can finally begin.

You have five years to complete all six World Quests as a planet. Failure to complete any of these World Quests will result in various

catastrophes, each catastrophe being independent and different from the others. Regardless of whether or not these catastrophes are avoided, at the end of fifty years, the integrated planet of Panu will then enter the Assimilation Phase—where other planets may interact directly with Panu without any restrictions. Currently, other factions within the multiverse are not allowed to visit Panu unless they have acquired invasion tokens or enter through other system-regulated measures, but the Assimilation Phase ends this era of safety.

Not participating in the World Quests is your prerogative, but you will be rewarded by the system based on your participation in each of these World Quests at hidden intervals. These prizes are nothing to scoff at and will sometimes be listed beforehand, with leaderboards for every World Quest on display for everyone to see. If you make the highlights section in your given leaderboard, video will be uploaded displaying your actions, and your reward will be drastically heightened. These leaderboards and prizes, along with forums regarding these quests, are heavily regulated by the Elysium administrator and will be available to you through Elysium's cortex.

With these leaderboards comes the Guild and Faction System function. Up to twenty people may be in a guild at one time. Guilds may be created with the Create Guild command, allowing you various options regarding the race toward these World Quests. The usefulness of guilds extends far beyond World Quests, however, with area quests or dungeons and raids being heavily focused on guild registrations. Prize distribution is particularly concerned with guild membership, and it will remain this way even off-world for those of you who live long enough to make it that far. A step beyond guilds is a faction, which can incorporate any number of guilds for war-coordination purposes but does not have the same unique benefits as a guild would have. Some examples of guild benefits that do not extend into the factions they belong to are: Blessings, Titles and Achievements, Raid Parties, Quest Rewards, Event Sharing, and XP Share.

For those of you from Earth, the Panu cortex is very similar to what your internet was. For those from the cybersword Drax faction, the Panu cortex is very similar to what your Neuralink was. This cortex is specifically set up so that you may complete the World Quests and invade against potential invaders by working together as a planetary society. For those of you who are not from Earth, it may be wise to explore the ins and outs of this system in more rigorous detail. There will be very limited forums, requests for video uploading options, communication centers, and limited map sharing. Let it be known again: These sections are all very heavily monitored and regulated by the administrator—and you will quickly find out what is and what is not allowed to be shared on the cortex. It may be on a situational basis, and it may be a long-term rule, but experimentation with what you may and may not post is heavily encouraged. You may create personalized forums for groups, countries, or guilds. Geographical areas are already set up and monitored by the administrator itself. You may also use the Search, Suggested, and Browse functions to see what you can find outside the system-given options.

Please visit the World Quests tab on your status page to see more information concerning these quests.

Please visit the Panu cortex tab on your status page to observe and participate in the cortex, as well as view leaderboards and video footage.

Please visit the Guild and Faction System tab on your status page in order to view your guild statistics.]

[World Quests are now active.]
[Panu cortex is now active.]
[Guild and Faction System is now active.]

The somber singing outside abruptly stopped amid a series of exclamations, and soon it became a mild uproar as people beyond Riven's cabin began talking with mixed emotions about the worldwide message.

Riven was equally vexed, excited, and a little bit intimidated as he reread the prompts—and his feelings were exaggerated even further when he pulled up the World Quests. He saw not one, but two World Quests that directly tied to him . . . and he really didn't know how to feel about it.

[World Quests (six of six remaining). You have five years to complete these quests as a worldwide team effort. Further details on each of these quests will be presented to you individually when you come into direct contact with the given quest. Only the basics are initially handed out otherwise. Current threat level is an indication of threat concerning the world at large, and not a direct representation of how it may or may not affect you individually. The World Quests are as follows:

- World Quest 1, The Lich King's Plague: In the far reaches of the northern Chaos Wastelands, an ancient lich begins to stir. Advanced details are locked until you come into contact with this quest.
- World Quest 2, The Apocalypse Beasts: ***ADVANCED DETAILS HAVE BEEN UNLOCKED*** Ah, this is one of my personal favorites. I present to you the apocalypse beasts! Your world has been cursed with three tyrannical creatures of astronomical power that are currently being incubated and grown into their adult forms. Each of these absolute monstrosities is able to turn the world on its head, demolishing countries in its path and tearing the very fabric of reality apart. Know that if these creatures are allowed to awaken, you will likely not live much longer than the five years' limit.

  Each of these monsters has cultist worshippers from your own planets, given knowledge of these creatures before the integration even begun. They will try to awaken the monsters' adult forms to destroy your world entirely, leading to astronomical amounts of power as a reward for the cultists in their success for when they leave the smoldering wreckage of Panu. Your goal is to stop and kill their cult worshippers and find out where these creatures are being incubated so that you will have a world to live on when the five years of time runs out.

  Current threat level: Extremely high; death toll in the billions. Catastrophe upon failure of completion when five years has passed: Nekra, the Skeletal Devourer, will be unleashed onto Panu. Chalgathi, the Plague Dragon, will be unleashed onto Panu. Chubin, the Glass Kraken, will be unleashed onto Panu. Other details: Upon completing this quest and finding the incubation chambers of any given apocalypse beast, you may either kill them before they're born for an item of immense power or claim their eggs for yourself. Killing them will bless you with a unique, currently unspecified item, while claiming their egg for yourself will link them to you as a minion. Claiming them as a minion will not produce them in their adult form, but rather they will begin as an infant version of themselves and must be cultivated to higher grades of power over time before coming into their true potential. You have already been in contact with Chalgathi's starter quests; thus you will soon receive an update on his particular quest line now that the World Quests have been distributed.

- World Quest 3, Invaders From Beyond: Other galactic civilizations greedily watch your fledgling world, wanting these lands for their own. Invasion tokens have been distributed. Advanced details are locked until you come into contact with this quest.
- World Quest 4, Blood of the Fallen God: An unnamed vampiric elder god has fallen from grace after having sinned against the Elysium administrator. The elder god has been trapped within a hidden, guarded labyrinth in the deepest levels of the underdark, and you must stop him from awakening. Advanced details are locked until you come into contact with this quest.
- World Quest 5, Realm of the Snow Giants: In the southern reaches of the glacial islands in the Numenor Sea, on the opposite end of the world from where the Lich King lies in wait, an ambitious king of the snow giants has united the warring tribes. Advanced details are locked until you come into contact with this quest.
- World Quest 6, Drums in the Deep: The merpeople and naga of this world have been given a choice . . . Advanced details are locked until you come into contact with this quest.]

CHAPTER 44

Despite the minor uproar after the system-wide announcement, the elves went back to singing solemn hymns somewhere outside the cabin a short while later. There was a lot to think about, and Riven sat there dwelling on it for a good amount of time before deciding to speak about this with Allie in detail later on. No doubt she'd have a lot to say about the whole "Chalgathi is an apocalypse beast" thing.

The main room of the large cabin was moderately sized, having a small circular table with an alchemy set atop it. Chairs carved from oak were nestled up against the table, and a basket of roots and fruit hung from the ceiling. Oddly enough, a lot of supplies hung from the ceiling in baskets, along with various herbs, which gave the cabin a thick smell of something akin to vanilla—but sweeter. There was also a fur rug, a couple bows lined up against one wall, and one other half-open bedroom door. The windows were all very large and open to the air without any glass, though they all had shutters that you could latch closed to keep the elements out.

"Are you Riven?" a small, soft voice called up to him from the left.

He'd noticed the little figure watching him since he'd entered and could hear her heart beating from the room over, but he'd pretended not to know in order to see what she did upon his arrival.

It was a tiny blonde girl, a child, wearing a dress made of reeds. She had two white flowers in her hair, which was braided back into pigtails, and she must have been somewhere between six and nine years old. She wore no shoes but hopped down off a stool where she was looking out one of the windows where other elves had gathered in the center of the village, circling a bonfire Riven couldn't make out very well from here as they sang, and she headed over to look up at the vampire.

She squinted suspiciously but nodded in affirmation only a second later. "Yep, yep! You're Riven! I've been watching you sleep today. You snore."

He looked down at her, snorted in amusement, and got down to one knee to eye level with the girl to kindly smile back. "I am indeed. Who might you be?"

"I'm Len. I'm Ethel's sister." The little girl fearlessly held out a hand to shake, expectantly glaring up at him with what he could only assume was a mischievous quirk to her lips. "Nice to meet you! I was told by Athela that this is how you greet people in your world?"

Raising an eyebrow at the fire in her eyes, Riven contained a laugh and took her hand in turn. He was surprised his Charisma didn't seem to affect this little girl at all, though maybe being accustomed to his presence in her cabin for the day had done enough to let his presence go without concern. "You'd be right. It's nice to meet you as well. Ethel never told me she had a sister."

"She didn't?! What?!" Len threw up her hands in dismay and let out a very exaggerated sigh. "It's probably because I'm the favorite. Can't blame her."

"Oh ho! Is that so?!"

"Yep! Don't tell her I said that, though—she'll eat all my cookies."

"Where'd you get cookies?!"

"I made them with Mother."

"Genua, right?"

"Yep, that's my mother's name."

"Can you tell me what's going on out there?" Riven hiked a thumb through the window toward the crowds of adults gathered maybe fifteen yards off in the center of the village. Firelight from the bonfire flickered across their scantily clothed bodies, men and women alike. Dirt and stone streets peeled off around bends between structures molded out of the trees themselves, many of the larger two-story buildings being of medieval design but growing flowers or vines straight out of the buildings. Much of the village had been destroyed, including most of the tents, but over half of it still stood tall and it had a very natural feel to it underneath the night sky.

Len's face fell, and her shoulders slumped slightly. "They're singing the hymns for the dead while they burn the bodies of our fallen."

Riven nodded, standing up straighter and staring out the window with the little girl. Shoving his hands into his pockets, he continued to listen to the melodic songs of a flightless bird finding its way back to heaven. They were definitely sad songs, but they delivered a message of hope and triumph at the end of each set of verses.

Len pulled up her stool, and with all the strength she could muster—grunting all the while—she dragged one of the larger chairs over from the table and set it next to the window so that her stool and the chair were next to each other.

She got up on her stool, pigtails bobbing, and patted the chair while looking up expectantly at Riven. "Whew! I'm getting stronger! Come sit."

Jesus, this kid was hilariously cute. Snorting a laugh, Riven shook his head. "I've been lying down this entire time, so I'll stand, but thank you so much for the thought."

"Nope! Mother says you're still weak from fighting off the bad orcs. You have to sit or I'll get in trouble for not letting Mother know you woke up."

"You were supposed to tell her?"

"Yep!"

"Why didn't you?"

"Because I don't want to go back out there. It's sad, and they're making all the other kids sing. I hate singing."

"I bet you're a great singer, though."

"I am, but I hate it."

Riven's lips twisted with amusement and then sadness before he sat in the chair as Len had asked. He put his hands on his knees and leaned back, watching the firelight flicker from the center of the gathering outside. There were hundreds of elves out there, all of whom on this near side had their backs turned to him—though he saw no trace of his minions or Dr. Brass. Nevertheless, the sound was soothing to his soul, despite the sad undertones.

"My dad made that chair before Avan died," Len abruptly stated out of nowhere, rubbing her hands together and staring out the large window with a far-away gaze that told of visiting memories from long ago. "I wish Avan was still here."

Riven remained silent for a long time after that, not knowing what to say at first. "Who is Avan?"

"He was my brother."

Riven's heart sank, and his fists tightened. "Did he pass away recently during the battle?"

"Last year," Len said with a frown, looking up to meet his gaze again with her hair blowing about when a strong breeze filtered through. "Before the worlds merged. He was killed protecting the village from raiders—that's what Mother says. Father and Ethel didn't take it well. I didn't, either, but I'm better than they are."

Riven's gaze fell to the wooden floor beneath his feet. "I'm sorry."

"It's okay. Father says he was a hero and that there are far worse ways to be remembered."

There was a long pause as Riven considered Len's words. He clasped his hands together in front of him and nodded his agreement. "I would certainly agree."

"I wish he was here now. He'd beat up Elder Preen for us, while Father won't."

The surprised look Len got from Riven was more than enough to prompt further explanation from the little girl, and she pursued this topic rather aggressively without even being asked. "Elder Preen comes to hit Mother and Ethel when Father is away. He's hit me, too, sometimes."

The fuck?

". . . I'm not sure I follow. Could you explain what you mean?"

The little elf girl with pigtails gave him a knowing look. "Because he is a man and he wants Mother and Ethel, of course."

Riven blinked. "I don't think I understand what you're trying to tell me. Who is Elder Preen and why would he hit you while your father is away? Does your father know someone is hitting you?"

Len's eyebrows rose; this time it was her turn to be surprised. "He's hitting us because our family owes him debts we can't pay. He owns all this stuff and ranks over Father. He sends Father away on dangerous hunts on purpose, is what Mother says. Father can't say no or we'll be kicked out of the village for not paying our debts, and while he's gone Elder Preen comes to visit us to spend time with Ethel and my mother. If they don't spend time with him while Father is gone, he'll take everything we have for our debts, or worse."

The actual fuck?

"But does your father, Farrod, know this?"

Len shrugged. "I think so. But he doesn't want to make it worse. That is what Mother says, but I'm not sure I believe her."

Riven's brows furrowed. "Why are you telling me all this?"

Ethel shot him a suspicious sideways glance, then shrugged. "I don't know. Reasons."

Riven glanced around, looking at all the belongings here and then back over to the little girl. "Isn't this house yours? Doesn't this chair belong to you, Ethel, and your mother?"

Len shook her head. "No, it belongs to the village Elder Preen. It used to be ours, but our debts weren't paid, so he took it all and let us live here. He's trying to get Father killed by monsters, to make Mother and Sister his next wives. But we can't leave—we wouldn't have anywhere to go. It got worse since the worlds merged, because now we need the village for protection. Father says we wouldn't be able to make it on our own."

The involuntary face-palm hit Riven square in the center of his forehead, startling Len and causing her eyes to go wide as she simultaneously flinched.

Riven apologetically dropped his hands immediately after that when he realized he'd surprised the little girl. "Sorry, I didn't mean to scare you."

The brief moment of fear passed over Len's face, and she adjusted herself in her seat once again to lecture him with a wagging finger, like her mother no doubt did to her. "Why'd you hit yourself? Are you a masochist? That's not good, Riven. Not good at all. That's how you get headaches."

There were many things Riven wanted to say to that. Among them were: How did she know what a masochist was? Why are people such scumbags? Why was he not surprised that some old guy would try to take advantage of their situation during a tumultuous time where Len's father was indebted and a transition of worlds had occurred? Was this Elder Preen trying to force Genua into an affair and have her daughter Ethel do something similar while Farrod was away? Farrod had been a prick in Riven's one interaction with him, but if what Len was telling him was accurate, he genuinely felt bad—if not angry that he hadn't stood up to what was going on.

This kind of exploitation of the weak was becoming a trend now that the equivalent of an apocalypse had begun: with similar situations happening in his tutorial, the groups in Brightsville, and now here.

Utterly ridiculous.

So he took in a deep breath, still wondering why the little girl had brought this up to *him*, of all people, and he asked Len a follow-up question. "Does this Elder Preen live here with all of you when Farrod is gone?"

"No. He visits a lot and spends the night with Mother sometimes, but she doesn't like it much and tries to make excuses so he'll leave. Sometimes they even argue in front of us, especially about Ethel or Father. Or his wives try to make me do chores for them, or they say mean things to me. I hate it when that happens."

Len humphed loudly and crossed her arms with a sullen frown.

"Why would his other wives say mean things to you? You're just a kid."

"I'm a BIG kid!" Len glared over at him with a humph full of venom and animatedly recrossed her arms in anger. "I can do lots of things for them, that's why! Because I'm bigger now. They think I'm not doing enough chores. They always try to get me to do their work, and I hate them. I hate them lots. Mother will tell them that I'm not there, and then they all yell at each other."

Boy, oh boy. This all sounded like a *Jerry Springer* episode with a twist of fantasy.

The little girl raised a finger. "You were really cool, by the way."

Huh?

Riven pointed to his chest in genuine surprise. "Me?"

Len nodded eagerly and grinned, turned fully to face him as her stool rocked back and forth momentarily under the sudden movement. "Yeah! Mother says I shouldn't like fighting, but you and your minions were, like, so fast! And evil-looking! I thought orcs were scary, but you made them pee themselves!"

Riven gave a frown of concern, not wanting to give off bad vibes after having just gotten here. "Surely I wasn't that scary."

"Yes, you were! You were even laughing! I even saw the orc man pee himself right in front of me when I was chained up!"

". . . Wait, I really made a guy piss his pants?"

"Yep! A big green musclehead! Then you beat him up and broke his teeth after that, after you stopped firing magic. Don't you remember?!"

There was a long pause, the palpable excitement from the little girl somewhat bothering him but also giving him a sense of strange pride. Should she really be that excited about what he'd done? Then again . . . why not?

"All right, that's actually a milestone for me, so I'll take it." Riven gave the little girl a playful wink and she laughed loudly, drawing the attention of some of the other elvish adults outside, who were about to scold her—but that changed when they saw Riven sitting next to her in the window.

Their expressions ranged between fear, relief, curiosity, and surprise. Thankfully the fear portion was far less than the other range of emotions shown, but their nearby comrades turned to see what they were looking at when they'd stopped singing.

It was like a wave effect, with one person after another all stopping the hymns until all eyes were on him.

He stared back evenly in the awkward silence, meeting many of their gazes and finding Senna, Ethel, and Genua in the crowd to his left waving his way—right before the crowd parted and two older elves stepped forward. They were both ancient, each of them graying with wrinkles, with one shorter with a hunched back and the other still rather tall. They each had on ceremonial robes of vibrant greens and blues, distinguishing them from the rest of the scantily clad men and women in nature-esque attire on the periphery of the central bonfire.

One of the two old men stepped forward to greet Riven while leaning on a wooden staff; it was the hunchback and likely the elder of the two. He fumbled with his hands to put them together in front of his chest, and bowed low, a lot like a Buddhist monk would do. "You've awakened. I hope you're feeling well, Riven Thane—the Hero of Greenstalk village. Do you mind stepping outside so that we can see you better?"

Riven stared blankly, then caught a jab in the side from the little girl, Len, who encouraged him into action with a whisper, and he stood up to step out of the window onto the grass outside. A lake shimmered in the moonlight off to his left over a hundred yards away, silent ripples wavering back and forth where he could barely make out Azmoth lighting up the shoreline around one of the tree-built houses. The majority of the village was still shaded from the night sky, even here before the surrounding clearing in the near distance formed a village perimeter and then continued on into forest and the base of the mountains.

The hunchbacked elder extended a gnarled hand in greeting, performing it uneasily as if it were the first time he'd ever done so—and Riven took his hand to shake. "I hope I am performing the greeting right, young man. Forgive me if I am not. We greet each other differently here."

Riven's red eyes traced the older man's wrinkled face for any signs of emotion and only found sincerity there. "You are doing just fine. If you'd be so kind as to teach me how to greet another with your own customs, I could adapt. I'd also like to thank you for your hospitality since I fell sick last night."

"Oh. So polite," the other elder, a taller man with good posture and a slightly crooked nose, said with a neutral expression. He clasped his hands behind his back. Long braided locks of white hair trailed past his shoulders on either side in the front and back. "Not very common for . . . *your* kind. In fact, this is the first time I've ever talked to a vampire face-to-face without wishing him or her an immediate and savage *death*."

"Indeed," the hunchback agreed with a chuckle, letting go of Riven's hand and taking in a deep breath. "This is truly an odd situation. Though, let it be known that you will never again have to thank any of us. We are in your debt forever for the things you did those few nights past, and we are all glad to see you have recovered. My name is Elder Bren. Ignore the jabs of Elder Preen; even though he does not like it, the village has spoken. I have spoken. You will forever be a friend and welcome here in our village. Though many of us have died in the recent attack, none of us would be here in this village today without you. As for our customs, we often greet each other by bowing with hands clasped in front of us."

Elder Bren demonstrated, bowing low at the waist with clasped hands in front of his chest—and to Riven's surprise, many of the others in the crowd did the same as a sign of respect. Riven evaluated the taller old man, who stared back at him with a forced smile that didn't even attempt to reach his ears. Based on the body language as well as the words Elder Bren had just spoken, the hunchbacked elder was the more dominant power in the village.

Turning his gaze back to Elder Bren, Riven bowed slightly to repeat the gesture in turn. "You have my deepest thanks."

Elder Bren nodded once, then motioned back to the bonfire. "We are finishing our hymns for the dead. Afterward, though, now that you are up, I'd like to have words with you. Have Ethel or Genua take you to my residence after the ceremony, and I will speak to you there. Or Farrod, though I believe he was sent out on patrol."

Riven raised an eyebrow at that last comment.

With the backstory the little girl Len had given him, Riven noticed the mild sneer on Elder Preen's countenance that shifted into a neutral stance just as fast as it'd come upon mention of Ethel and her mother. Making a mental note to keep an eye on this one, Riven watched the elders take their leave and position themselves in front of the bonfire, with the crowd closing back around them soon after.

Though he did continue to get occasional stares while he waited inside.

CHAPTER 45

Elder Bren's tree house was the largest in the village; Ethel explained that it had been formed from what she described as "tree shaping" to create rooms, balconies, and multiple floors all the way from the base of the trunk to about thirty feet up. The leaves, bark, and roots were all still intact, and the tree was actually still very much alive, unlike many of the smoking husks of the other buildings in the village after the greenskins attacked, but it'd been expanded and molded like clay to fit the needs of the people living in it.

"I'll be waiting outside!" Ethel whispered, urging him in and waving enthusiastically while Athela sighed in irritation in the background. "I'll talk to you after!"

The door to the first level closed behind him, leaving Riven staring at the hunchbacked old man and two redheaded women, one about his own age and the other middle-aged.

"Riven, let me introduce you to my two wives." Elder Bren gestured to the older woman first, an elf with a deep-purple dye coloring the front of her woven leaf vest. "This is Cherri."

The old man's staff moved to the younger, middle-aged woman next. "This is Nil."

Both women bowed politely, remaining silent and standing in the background behind a couch molded out of the tree itself that was adorned with furs and pillows.

The rest of the room was also a lot fancier than the house Ethel and her family lived in. It had a spiral staircase in the back leading to the next floor up, a long ovoid table and a kitchen to his right, a couple tapestries, a glowing yellow-orange stone in the ceiling that illuminated the main room, some open chests showing various items of clothing, and many open-air windows similar to the ones he'd seen in many of the cabins and tree houses here.

Elder Bren smoothed out his vibrant blue and green robes, sitting down with a huff, and motioned for Riven to join him on the opposite end of the couch. "Do you drink tea? I've never really asked a vampire whether or not they still enjoy . . . normal food."

"Tea would be great," Riven replied pleasantly, enjoying the smell from the herbs hanging from the ceiling in a similar manner to Ethel's home.

Nil, the younger wife, quickly went off to the kitchen and brought back a wooden tray with wooden cups that were filled with a warm and soothing liquid that ran down Riven's throat like a breath of fresh air.

He sipped casually in the warm light of Elder Bren's home, putting the drink down on the nearby equivalent to a coffee table, and turned his attention back to the old man who was silently evaluating him, tea in hand.

"So what did you bring me here to talk about?"

The old man took a sip of his own drink and placed it on the table next to Riven's. Hiccuping slightly and beating his chest with a gnarled fist, he cocked his head to one side and crossed his legs. A single pointed ear stuck out from the left side of his head, and Riven could now distinguish a long scar that he'd not seen before leading down from the ear to the old elf's neck.

The elder spoke. "First of all, I would like to reiterate that you are a welcome friend here in the village after the lives you saved. We were on the losing end of that battle until you arrived, and with the casualties you and your creatures inflicted, I doubt the orcs or goblins will mount any attack on us any time soon. That being said, after seeing you fight, I have a proposal for you."

There was hesitation in the old man's words, and Riven raised an eyebrow. "Go on."

"Ahem, yes. I was hoping you'd eradicate the rest of the greenskins for us."

The room became utterly silent, and Elder Bren's two wives stared just as intently at Riven as the elder did. Riven was a little taken aback by the brazen call to arms, especially after not having known them for more than half an hour now.

"And why would I do that?" Riven asked slowly, concern in his voice as he leaned back against one of the pillows on the couch. "Assuming there are a lot more of them than the group that attacked, what makes you think that I'm even capable of that?"

"Most of the fighting force of the orcs and goblins are already dead due to your actions. The problem is that goblins breed like rats, and the orcs still have a chieftain as well as a small war party of his elites that weren't here, based on our scouting reports. We know where they are—if you are able to take advantage of that knowledge for an ambush or surprise strike, you will certainly be able to kill them all."

Riven wasn't so convinced, but he didn't reply and motioned for the old man to continue the sales pitch with a wave of his hand.

"As for why you would do so . . ." Elder Bran continued while clearing his throat awkwardly. "They are a threat to the surrounding area as a whole. They would threaten you, as well as the people you care about."

Riven thought back to Allie, and he tried to hide his grin. "I doubt they'd be able to handle the people I care about."

"You speak of the other vampires?"

"Vampires as in plural?"

"Yes, your sister and whatever others follow her in the city to the north. Correct?"

"Wait. How did you know about her?"

To this, the old man looked confused. "Ethel and Senna informed us of her. They said there were more—were Ethel and Senna mistaken to assume you have a coven there?"

Riven opened his mouth to reply but hesitated momentarily. "That is somewhat accurate . . . though not entirely. I wouldn't really call it a coven."

"Then what would you call it?"

Riven thoughtfully tapped his fingers against the wooden table in front of him. "What would you call a large group of undead?"

"Undead that weren't just vampires?"

"Yeah."

Elder Bren furrowed his brows and crossed his hands. "You would call that a necropolis . . ."

There was an awkward silence between the two men, and then the older man cleared his throat with a dismissive wave of his right hand. "Regardless, I was also under the impression that you cared for Ethel. That is what she has been telling us. Senna confirmed this. They were saying that's the only reason you came to help, and that you expected recompense by taking in her as a . . . personal food source. As property."

Huh?

Riven stared blankly back at the old elf, trying not to give away any of his emotions, though he was definitely piecing things together now. The comments Senna had made about Elder Preen wanting Ethel's hand in marriage. About how Ethel didn't like the leadership, and her change in body language when talking about it on the trip here. The speech Ethel's little sister had given him concerning the problems Ethel and her mother, Genua, were having with Elder Preen's more-than-forward attempts to force himself on them whenever Farrod wasn't around.

Was Ethel using him as a scapegoat to get out of a forced marriage to some old guy? He didn't know whether or not to feel irritated about being tricked or not. Couldn't really blame her for wanting out of a situation like she'd been in, but at the very least she could have asked him first. She'd outright lied to the village elders, too, but perhaps that was a necessary evil to pull off her plan successfully. Apparently even her friend Senna had gone along with it, and this also explained why her father, Farrod, had been so hostile toward him when Riven had briefly talked to the man not long ago.

"I see . . ." Riven eventually said with an even, controlled tone despite the mild anger simmering up inside of him. "What if I said she was right in saying so?"

Riven lied through his teeth with that one, but the look of relief washing over Elder Bren made him even more confused.

"That would be good, very good." The old man leaned forward, picked up his cup, and took a long sip again. "Then it makes sense. I couldn't for the life of me figure out why else you'd come help us, being a vampire, but this does make sense, and it puts my mind at ease. You're wanting to turn her into your version of cattle—or a thrall, then. Or to take her as your wife alongside your female minions, like so many other warlocks do. I do not care. Well, I can tell you that Elder Preen is less than happy about this, because he'd wanted Ethel as his own third wife, but the village as a whole—including myself—has decided against his wishes if what Ethel has said is true. You may have Ethel as your own, and you may live or visit here in Greenstalk as a member of our community. We could even set up trade negotiations between your necropolis up north and this village. There is a stipulation, though."

"Being that I need to eradicate the remnants of the greenskins."

"Correct. Or at the very least, you need to drive them away from these lands. That was the concession that I made to Elder Preen—if you wish to live or travel openly among us, you'll have to do us this favor. You're more than capable, based on what we all witnessed already, and it appears you have backing from more of your undead brethren, too. You are far stronger than any of us, and many of our most experienced warriors are now lost to the earth and heavens."

Riven wanted to groan and rubbed his forehead with his fingers. This was not what he'd been expecting, nor what he wanted. He didn't have time to take responsibility for Ethel, because it was more than just that, and she likely knew it. If he accepted her as a thrall, he'd be committed to making sure she was safe—but he'd also in some ways be obligated to help her family out, too. Her mother, her father, and her little sister were also in a bad situation concerning this Elder Preen prick, and she'd likely try to drag him into the middle of it all. He also had a World Quest oriented directly at him, specifically concerning the apocalypse beast Chalgathi, and he had no doubt Allie would have a lot to say on the matter, because she'd been in his trials as well.

Speaking of which, he still couldn't believe Chalgathi had turned out to be a goddamned apocalypse beast, of all things.

Nor was Riven interested in creating any kind of harem, which apparently was a popular fad among the more prominent men of this village. But based on Elder Bren's comments on potentially taking Ethel as a wife along with his minions? Jesus, this guy had the wrong idea, and he could only imagine what kind of absolutely insane shenanigans having Athela as a wife would mean. Fay was attractive, he couldn't deny that, but he'd already promised himself that he'd never pursue anything of the kind with her due to their master-minion relationship. It felt gross to even think about those things.

In Riven's experience, even having a relationship with one woman was enough to drive him batshit crazy. In the dating world, women were essentially like aliens to him at times, always talking about their horoscope zodiac sign bullshit and whatnot whenever he got into a relationship long enough for them to get comfortable. Perhaps it'd just been bad luck, though, and he held hope that this would not be a continuing trend during his dating life in the future. But one thing was for certain: he didn't want to hear about Scorpio, Aquarius, or even goddamn asparagus even one more time, so help him God.

"Having a warlock of your caliber in the village would also be quite a protective boon against the local monsters . . ." Elder Bren stated after a thoughtful pause with a more upbeat and chipper demeanor now that he seemed to think Riven was on board. "So we'd be willing to overlook your more sinister attributes if you wished to move here. Perhaps the rest of your undead counterparts could move in nearby? I do not think having them in direct proximity with our own people would be wise . . . but having them as a close ally would be beneficial for us, given the frequent monster attacks."

Riven gave the old man a dubious look. It was very apparent that after this recent orc attack, the elves were very shaken. Perhaps they'd lost most of their fighting potential and wouldn't be able to ward off the local enemies, and given that Riven had seen a cyclops alongside numerous wargs and now greenskin invaders?

Riven was pretty sure Elder Bren, and the village, was desperate for protection. "You're willing to overlook my more sinister attributes, huh . . . I can see that. What makes you think that I can't just take Ethel right now? What's stopping me from doing it and keeping her as a thrall without your say-so?"

The hunchbacked man paused midsip and paled slightly. Slowly he put the tea down, coughed, and folded his hands over his knees while looking at the floor. "Ethel said you weren't that kind of person and wouldn't take her unwillingly. Was she wrong?"

Slowly, Riven let out a low groan and his head fell into his hands. "She's not wrong."

The old man beamed. "Very good."

"What about the other elf tribes in the area? Aren't there other groups of your kind that could help with this?"

Elder Bren's face fell almost immediately, and he shook his head. "They are all dealing with their own problems and are too far away to help. We are quite displaced from the rest, and even attempting to travel there by ourselves would make us easy targets for local predators or the greenskins again. Let it be known that this is one of the less dangerous areas of the wilderness, according to scouting reports . . ."

Riven pursed his lips while he thought this over. It was a lot to take in, and it'd all been thrown at him out of the blue. Well, at the very least, if he decided to go through with this . . . it did solve his problem of finding a thrall and someone to feed on. Perhaps it wasn't a bad idea after all, though he doubted he'd be moving here for good now that he'd finally found Allie again. No doubt he'd visit . . .

But that defeated the purpose of this proposal. Elder Bren obviously wanted him to stay. If he left to go back to his sister, where would that leave the elves? It would leave them defenseless, or close to it after most of their warriors had died. At least that's how it seemed. Perhaps they could come back with him to Allie's tower instead of staying here? Or perhaps Allie could have a host of undead guard this village as an outpost for their newly growing civilization, should the elves of Greenstalk swear loyalty?

[System Quest (triggered by Elder Bren), Eradicate the Greenskins: The orcs and goblins in this area have become a grave threat to the elves of Greenstalk village, having raided their hunting and scouting parties numerous times. Now they've even gone as far as to attack the village itself, nearly killing or capturing everyone there until your timely intervention. Elder Bren of Greenstalk village has offered the elf Ethel as private property in exchange for your help in killing or driving away the local orcs and goblins. You will also be given citizenship by completing this quest, free of persecution due to your race with all the rights of a fully-fledged village member. You will lastly be given an unspecified B-ranked prize for your level by the Elysium administrator upon completion of this quest.]

Riven reread the description and clarified a point. What was a B-rank prize? He'd never seen ranking on prizes before. "You want me to kill all the orc children and women, too?"

"They will grow up to become monsters just like the rest of them. So yes."

"But you'll be fine if I just drive them off?"

"Yes . . . though this will be hard to do without killing at least most of them. We'll also be sending one of our scouts to confirm your actions if you decide to take us up on this offer. I can see you're still not entirely sure of yourself on this decision, however, and the village wishes to know what your decision will be. If you need time to think on this . . ."

"The entire village knows about what you're pitching me?"

"Pitching?"

"Offering me."

"Oh. Yes, the entire village is aware. We discussed it publicly when Ethel and Senna revealed your original terms for helping us in the first place. Ethel's mother and little sister are in agreement with the terms as well, much to Elder Preen's disliking. And to Farrod's disliking as well, though for obviously different reasons."

"And you're all okay with having undead or vampires in your midst?"

At this, the old man hesitated. ". . . Yes, if it means that you offer us protection in return. You'll have Ethel to feed on. Along with some of the goblins we captured, it should be enough to sustain you. I would strongly advise against eating her, though . . . Even though Ethel would become your cattle, or a thrall to feed upon, she is still part of the village."

Riven had to hold back a snort of half disgust and half amusement. "I never intended to kill or eat any of you."

"That is what Ethel told us. She and Senna had some very kind things to say about you, which did a lot in convincing the others in our community. However . . . there are definitely naysayers who don't agree with you being here even after what you've done. Many of those same naysayers may have their doubts quelled if you do this great service for us."

Despite the obvious internal turmoil Riven was experiencing, he couldn't deny that having a constant food source was a very good thing to bargain with on the elves' parts. He'd had hunger pains regularly when not feeding on blood, and he'd been terrified he'd resort to the way he'd been back in Negrada when he'd killed that poor man from Earth in a fit of extreme hunger. He'd lost his sanity upon initial transition into a vampire, and his bloodline had informed him that vampires were very prone to this if they didn't stay fed, so he had to deal with the reality of it and find a consistent food source, which Ethel could provide. The goblins would suffice, too . . . but having fed on them already, he could safely say that they were a little less than tasty. Filling, but not good to the tongue.

His more primal side hoped that Ethel was more fulfilling in terms of the taste of her blood, despite his conscious desire to push those thoughts aside.

In the end, a cooperation of his hunger and the desire to help Ethel won out over his doubts and suspicions—despite his anger at how she and Senna had blindsided and tricked him. "All right. I'll do it. Let me know when and where, and I'll finish the job I started."

Elder Bren and his two wives were outwardly elated with Riven's words, and the old man stood up, brushing out his vibrant blue and green robes to clap Riven on the shoulder. "Very good, young man! I will see to it that we have a feast in your honor when the deed is done, and I will let everyone know! The sooner you can do this, the better, but we will not rush you out of the village just yet. Rest up and be sure that you are prepared for the battle at hand; we want you to succeed more than you know. If you fail, we will have to flee this part of the world in search of a new home . . . and who knows what awaits beyond the borders of this forest."

In the distance, a ruckus was building up. Angry shouts of men and women rose up in the dark of night, and the sound grew louder the closer the individuals got. Riven and the elves in the room fell silent, and one of Elder Bren's wives began to rub her temple, losing her smile with a frustrated groan.

Seconds later a rapid, angry knock sounded at the front door and a man's angry voice called out, "BREN! Bren, get out here, we need to talk!"

CHAPTER 46

Elder Bren let out a deep sigh, and one of his wives scurried over to the door, letting in a fuming Elder Preen. The old man was obviously disheveled from some kind of physical confrontation, with dirtied robes and a bleeding scratch along his right cheek. He stomped inside but quickly stopped upon seeing Riven sitting on the couch, flushing in anger and pointing an accusing finger Riven's way. "His BITCH Succubus attacked me! That DEMON attacked me! We cannot have these MONSTERS living among us! I will not stand for it!"

Behind him, Athela's barking laugh echoed among the trees, and Riven could see Fay standing defensively in front of Genua. The Succubus had her wings spread out, layers of Unholy mists radiating from her hands threateningly, shielding the elf woman from a trio of three men with Ethel holding her little sister Len's hand and yelling something at them in an obvious display of anger.

"They've got to go! NOW!" Elder Preen raged, shaking there in the doorway while Elder Bren eyed him with exhaustion and disappointment.

Elder Bren stood up, gripped his staff, and walked forward to meet the other village elder. He poked Elder Preen in the chest with the butt of his staff and frowned at him. "If the other elders were still alive to witness your pettiness, they'd be sincerely concerned about your mental state and abuse of power, Elder Preen."

"Abuse of power?!"

"That's right. You only want them to leave because you wish to take Ethel and Genua for your own—given your unhealthy obsession with them recently, I'd even say you've become rather unhinged in your attempts to force yourself on them. I can only imagine how Farrod feels about it, because he certainly knows." Elder Bren nodded solemnly, putting the staff back down against the hardwood floor with a light thud. "And don't try to deny it. I will not go into specifics about what you have been doing, but I am senior to you and have more of a say. This is final, and I have the support of the entire village in doing it. They support this vampire not only for what he did, but for what he is going to do."

Elder Preen snarled and wiped away a drop of blood that trickled down his cheek. "I have every right to take them! They are living in my house, and their patriarch owes me! I even paid them a dowry for their daughter!"

"A debt that has been paid many times over with the actions of this young man, or by the actions you so cruelly enforce on Genua because of her husband's gambling habits. It is true that they owe you a great deal, and that is the only reason I am allowing your behavior to continue as is," Elder Bren stated coolly. "As for their daughter, I will personally repay you for the dowry you placed on Ethel's behalf."

"You can't do that!"

"I can and I will. There will be no arguing about it further, unless you wish to go fight the greenskins yourself." Elder Bren cocked his head to one side speculatively. "Do you wish to go kill them yourself? If you can, I will seriously reconsider handing Genua's daughter over to Riven as a thrall. By all means, you may try."

The taller elf snarled again, showing his teeth and taking an aggressive step forward. "You are a traitor to our kind, Elder Bren, for allowing this to happen."

"Strong words from one who never joined the great hunt. I mean truly, are you daft? This vampire could kill you in an instant and you sit here harassing his property-to-be, along with one of his minions? You've lost your mind to jealousy. Bullying Farrod with your rank or followers is one thing—he cares little for the family he has, even if you do greatly insult him by pursuing his wife and daughter. But what you're doing now is madness."

At this, Elder Preen grew an even brighter red with anger. Despite his quivering rage, he did take a step back with a hesitant glare directed Riven's way. Then he shot a look over his shoulder at his three cronies, who were still harassing Fay, Ethel, and Genua—and took a moment to calm down. "All right, fine. But if the vampire dies trying to exterminate the greenskins, I keep the woman for my own."

Elder Bren shrugged. "That was the original plan regardless. If the vampire cannot hold up his end of the bargain, you may have her and even her mother for yourself. Genua has no husband who is willing to stand up for his own kin, so he is not a man worthy of the woman he is bound to. If this vampire fails, we will banish Farrod and allow you to indulge yourself with your pursuits of his family. This is a fair deal—is it not enough to keep you calm?"

Riven, in a state of shock, scratched his head, listening to the absurd exchange while these two old guys bargained over women like they were trading cards or collectible items. They were people, for God's sake, and they acted like Ethel and her family had no say in what would happen to them. It was disgusting. It didn't sit well with Riven at all.

"If I do this . . ." Riven cut in with a raised hand and a cleared throat, "you'll be forgiving Ethel's family of their debts entirely."

Elder Bren blinked and stared back at the younger man, while Elder Preen's face fell into a glowering, angry frown.

"I will not take no for an answer," Riven stated flatly, rising up to his full height to challenge the simmering old pervert who looked like he wanted to lunge at Riven's throat.

Riven could only wish he would.

"Done," Elder Bren stated with an abrupt wave of his hand. "I agree to your demand; if you do this, I will pay off all her family's debts, too."

The standoff didn't last much longer. Elder Preen didn't even acknowledge Riven when he made his exit and called out to whoever was harassing the women outside. The three men, all adult elves with blond or silver hair, joined him moments later while making rude remarks about Genua on their way out.

"Elder Bren," Riven calmly said while standing up to his full height and stretching.

The old man turned warily back to him with an exhausted sigh. "Yes, Riven?"

Riven gestured after the other elder, who was walking back through the village under the starlight. "I just wanted to say that I appreciate your hospitality, I truly do. I don't intend to cause any trouble and will do my very best to help you. However, I saw one of his henchmen almost strike my minion Fay while they argued out there. I don't know what was being said or why, but if that'd happened, I'd have laid his guts out on the grass without thinking twice or losing any sleep over it. And that's only if Fay didn't melt them into a necrotic pile of goo first. I'm surprised she didn't already, and it shows significant restraint on her part. Please relay that message to him and those buffoons so that there aren't any unfortunate deaths in the future. I may be calm now, but I wouldn't be if he or his people ever struck anyone I care about, and my familiars take a very keen liking to eating people."

Elder Bren paled slightly and gave a nervous laugh. "Of course!"

From the shadows of the room above and up the stairs, Athela's slim, pitch-black figure dropped down with absolute silence and trotted over to the old elf, nearly giving the elder and his two wives heart attacks when she made herself known.

"I'd been hoping he'd do something stupid," Athela pouted, frowning and folding her arms in front of her. "I've wanted to dismember something ever since our fight with the orcs. Oh, well! Off we go, Riven, come on!"

Athela's lithe form evaporated in a blur of motion, and she ran out the door. Riven was close on her heels, and soon Elder Bren was alone with his wives on the bottom floor of his house.

Genua's face was bruised where she'd been hit hard by Elder Preen's backhand slap. She'd been struck after finally telling him and his henchmen *no*, and that'd been all it'd taken for him to fly into a rage. He'd screamed at her and beaten her rather badly, leaving other bruises all over her body. Apparently Fay had stopped him when she'd come upon the scene. When she'd then struck him back, he'd almost tried to fight them before he realized the odds were significantly in Fay's favor. The Succubus might be utility oriented, but she could still kill. Azmoth had lost his temper and nearly ripped him apart right then, with Athela in the background watching silently at a distance to see whether she was needed.

Nevertheless, Elder Preen had followed Genua when she'd run off to find Ethel, harassing her the entire time while Fay followed, too, and requested that Azmoth stay behind to watch Len. Riven had literally just woken up earlier that night, and despite his half joke about this reminding him of a *Jerry Springer* episode, he could safely say that the situation in Greenstalk really was just as bad, or maybe even worse.

And what was all this talk about Farrod not standing up for his family? Riven had been under the impression that the man hadn't known. But he KNEW?! And he let it HAPPEN?! Riven was utterly baffled by the revelation. Just . . . just why? He had so many questions and so few answers.

Meanwhile, Ethel was in an absolute rage, swearing under her breath and cursing the old men while trying to simultaneously console her crying mother all the way to their house, where Len was curled up in a corner and whimpering after seeing her mother savagely beaten.

Fay opened the door for the two elf women and passed Azmoth, walking Ethel's family into Genua's room and ushering Len in before shutting the door behind them all.

Fay immediately whirled around, snarled and bared her fangs with rage evident in her expression. She clenched her fists and stomped over to Riven, black wings flaring, while pointing up a finger directly at his face as if to accuse him of something. "If that man EVER touches them again, I want you to slit his throat, okay?!"

"That's the plan," Riven confirmed with a nod, shooting a concerned look at the door to Genua's room, where he could hear Ethel's mother still sobbing. "I didn't realize what we were getting into here. Thanks for standing up for them, by the way. I'm proud of you."

Fay acknowledged his remark with a snort but otherwise remained outwardly livid.

"And what's that, exactly? That you thought you were getting into?" Athela asked while sitting in an oaken chair to the side of the room, steepling her fingers in front of her. "What's this all about? We just saw Genua get her ass beat by some old guy, and that's all we know."

Fay was still fuming, literally shaking while stomping back and forth across the front room of the small cabin. "We're gone for just a couple hours to explore, and THIS happens! Utterly ridiculous! If I'd been here earlier to see what she told me happened, I'd have fucking cut that guy's balls off! The prick and his friends were—"

Riven cut her off with a wave of his hand, putting it gently onto her shoulder with a soft but firm squeeze. He was genuinely surprised Fay seemed to care this much about people she didn't know, which he was pretty sure was very uncharacteristic of demons. Thus he was becoming more and more curious about her backstory.

"I know."

"THEN—"

"The situation is under control. He won't do it again, or else we really will kill him." Riven smiled softly, and Fay's fuming rage began to decline.

The blue Succubus nodded in agreement, then turned back to a chair and sat down. Her wings folded in, black eyes blinking rapidly, she pushed her hands up through her white hair and let out a shuddering, angry groan. "Fine. It's a deal, then. So, like Athela said—what exactly IS going on? What were you and Elder Bren talking about for so long?"

"I'd like to know, too," Dr. Brass stated firmly, adjusting his glasses over the white coat he still wore.

Riven gave them all a suspicious snort, then took a seat alongside Athela. "It's . . . an unexpected turn of events. How do I put this . . ."

"Master." Azmoth's deep, demonic voice cut through the laughter like a hot knife. "I do not mean interrupt. But what we do now? World quests . . . one pertain to you."

Immediately the room was filled with awkward silence at the abrupt change of subject, no one saying a word while Riven contemplated this.

Eventually Riven leaned forward to rest his chin on his hands. "Yeah. Chalgathi is apparently one of the apocalypse beasts the World Quest mentions, so that answers one of my curiosities. My log says I should be getting another quest update from it soon now that the World Quests are active. As for the other ones . . . who knows?"

Riven thoughtfully pondered these new developments, then rested his hands on the table between Athela and himself. "All right, sensei. You've been my guiding light this entire time. What do you think I should do about it?"

"What do you mean, what should you do about it? Idiot!" Athela karate chopped Riven on the dome of his head. "Get out there and get a new dragon pet or sacrifice it to get a new supercharged weapon! Seems pretty simple to me! AND YOU BETTER NOT FAIL! I'M NOT GOING BACK TO THE NETHER REALMS!"

Athela gave him another trio of karate chops for emphasis but leaned over with a cackle and blew into his ear. "I have faith in you, Riven. You'll be fine, and you have all of us to help you. Regardless, I think you should focus more on the quest to annihilate the orcs and goblins before you worry about these World Quests. Those can wait for a bit. Five years, to be precise."

"The goblins and orcs be good practice for Succubus, too," Azmoth said, his sentence structure becoming slightly better as time went on. He gestured over at Fay with one of his clawed, smoldering hands. "She need the experience and levels. Perhaps you could try teach her one of your abilities before end the greenskin menace?"

Riven straightened his posture. Teach Fay one of his skills? He looked the Succubus over, silently evaluating his options. "That's . . . actually a really good idea, Azmoth."

"If it works." Athela gave Azmoth a skeptical frown and sat on a nearby chair, crossing her long black legs. "I doubt I'll ever see anyone have as much success as you did, though Fay probably could work at it awhile and eventually get there. I have a hard time believing she or anyone else will actively teach themselves an ability without the help of the system as fast as you did, Riven."

To this, Riven frowned. "Well, we don't have an immediate time limit on this quest, so I think I'll at least begin to try and teach her something. And . . . oh, shit. Perhaps Fay should start teaching me her curse magic? That'd be interesting. I'll think on it for now. Maybe I can teach Fay one of my abilities from the Unholy pillar. What about you, Athela? Would you like to learn some spells? What about Riftwalk? It's a good movement ability to add to your already fast-paced fighting style."

The demoness frowned slightly and shook her head. She placed a hand on Riven's knee and gave a gratitude-filled squeeze. "I appreciate it, but I likely cannot. My affinity for Shadow is very poor, but any Blood and Unholy I'd be able to make use of. Demons are usually stuck in their assigned pillars from birth, unless we get racial evolutions or are incredibly lucky. Just as Azmoth has the Infernal and Unholy pillars as his baseline, I have Blood and Unholy pillars for mine. I doubt I'll be able to learn any abilities besides Blood and Unholy ones."

"Oh . . . Well, let's go over some Blood abilities later, then. Perhaps they'll be of use to you!"

"Perhaps, but most of your Blood abilities use mana. I am an assassin-type shape-shifter who hasn't even gotten ahold of her shape-shifting abilities yet. Shape-shifting requires stamina, as do my other abilities, which are martial arts, so my time would be better spent learning to perfect my shape-shifting instead of spells I wouldn't be able to use effectively because my Intelligence stat is so low. I fully intend to invest in a speed and dexterity build, too, so I don't intend to change it up just for a few skills. Thank you, though—it means a lot that you'd care enough to ask."

Athela gave him a blinding smile and leaned into his shoulder with a loud burp. "I appreciate it. By the way, if you're feeling hungry, the goblins are tethered in a makeshift cage on the opposite side of the village. They've had their hands and feet cut off with the stumps burned so they can't run. Just in case you need to feed."

Riven nodded in appreciation for the information, then went back to thinking on his abilities. The only Unholy spell he had was Wretched Snare. He already knew Azmoth wouldn't want it for the same reasons Athela gave for not wanting to use spells, but he thought he'd ask anyway. At the very least it was the polite thing to do, and he didn't want Azmoth thinking Riven wasn't considering him. "All right, Azmoth, Athela might not want spells, but do you? I have one that I could teach you—it's called Wretched Snare, and it's in the Unholy pillar category."

The large, armored demon flicked his tail to the right, apparently amused by the offer. "I'm all right. Magical aptitude is very low—even fire breath considered Infernal martial art, part of my body. If you find Unholy martial art instead, I take that. Thank you, Riven."

"Just making sure!"

The mood lifted over the next couple of minutes. Jokes and laughter were exchanged in small quantities, and Riven was tossed a piece of cooked warg meat Azmoth had harvested from a body earlier while out on the hunt. Azmoth went outside to watch the perimeter of the house in case anyone by the name of Elder Preen came by to bother them again, and all was well with the world until Riven had an epiphany.

"Oh, I just realized." Riven swallowed the last of his dried warg meat, stood and started for Genua's door. "I never told them that I'd agreed to Elder Bren's terms, or that I'd changed them up. They're about to be debt-free if I have a say in all this."

CHAPTER 47

He left the others to their chatting and came up to the door and rapped with his knuckles. He heard a muffled voice from inside telling him to come in and opened the door, shutting it quickly behind him.

There on the bed, Genua was holding Ethel in her arms with Len spooned between them. They had the covers drawn halfway up, and all three of them showed signs of recent crying, though they all looked his way when he made his appearance. Ethel's left arm was laid over her small sister, and the little girl's pigtails were disheveled. Meanwhile, Genua's bruised face had darkened and was just barely starting to swell.

Riven's eyes softened at the sight, and he felt a mixture of sadness for them while a flame of hatred sparked for Elder Preen. Riven still didn't know the situation revolving around Farrod in detail, but he was determined not to make any hasty judgments of the man—and he motioned to the nearby bedside. "May I sit?"

Genua sniffed, keeping the side of Ethel's face in one hand and Len's shoulder in the other—but nodded silently.

Riven plopped onto the edge of the bed, looking at the floor between his feet while figuring out what to say before turning back to the three of them with as kind a smile as he could muster. "Um, Elder Bren told me about your situation."

None of the three of them moved or replied but merely stared back at him.

"So, Ethel . . . I assume you were using me as a pawn to get out of marrying Elder Preen? Is that right?"

Genua spoke up immediately with a shaky voice. "That isn't true. She isn't using you, I—"

"That's true," Ethel stated unapologetically, fierce determination in her eyes and her hand clamping down over her mother's mouth. The young woman gave him a challenging glare. "Elder Preen is a terrible man, and my father refuses to stand up for me. For us. His gambling problems got us here, and now we are paying the price. Len told you the story, and although I did scheme some, none of what Len told you was a lie."

Genua shot her daughter a nervous glance, but Riven remained calm. The vampire rested his hands on his knees and nodded thoughtfully, looking out a small window at the top left-hand corner of the cabin room. "So Farrod actually does know about what's going on?"

There was an awkward silence.

"It depends on what you mean," Ethel stated, still trying to remain brave in the face of his confrontation. "My father knows about what Elder Preen is doing while he's sent out on these absurd scouting missions, but my father either doesn't care enough to act or he's letting it happen to buy time to repay the debt. Ever since . . . ever since my brother died, he hasn't been the same. He started drinking, gambling, and making risky trips into the wilderness for profit. He sells what he can from his hunts to try and regain what we lost, but it is a far-fetched plan at best."

Genua cut in, "Farrod isn't a bad man, Riven. He just . . . has lost himself. He's a shadow of the person he once was . . . and it pains me to see him like that."

"It's still no excuse," Ethel cut in sharply, obviously angry and having had this conversation before. "No husband would let another man do to you what Elder Preen is doing. Look at your swollen face, Mother! Father should be here protecting you, confronting that bastard and keeping you safe! Where is he now, though?! Where has he been the past twenty times?! What did he do when you finally admitted to him what was going on?! Absolutely nothing is what. You may accept what's happening, but I won't be subject to that old man's—"

"Stop it," Genua said in a cold, enraged voice, glaring at her daughter. Ethel cut her speech short but relaxed again when Genua took in a deep breath and closed her eyes.

Riven shifted a curious gaze on Genua. "Did you put Ethel up to this? To manipulate me for her own benefit? Or was this her decision?"

Ethel cleared her throat and hesitantly looked back over to Riven while stroking Len's hair. "My mother only found out that I was using you after Senna and I had already made up the story to tell our village, so it isn't Mother's fault. They were going to give Len away to another family and separate us if Farrod died on one of these trips; it is known in rumors around the village, but if I'm able to leave this family in name, I can take Len with me because the debt won't follow me. Please don't be mad at my mother. This is entirely my fault."

Riven's smile faltered slightly. "So you were doing this for your little sister, then . . . but you were intentionally manipulating me. Why didn't you just talk to me before we got here?"

The resulting silence was palpable.

He sighed and leaned back on his hands to stare up at the ceiling. "Well, this is slightly more awkward than I thought it'd be."

He didn't see it in their faces, but he could hear their heartbeats pick up like drums. Their pulses quickened, obviously anxious upon hearing his words.

"Awkward? You . . . so you said no, then," Ethel murmured, choking up at the last word. She blinked rapidly, trying to contain her emotions, and pulled her sister into her chest a little more fiercely. "I . . . I'm so s-sorry, Riven, I didn't m-mean to make you h-hate me . . . I was j-just trying to p-protect my f-family . . ."

"And you were protecting yourself," Riven corrected with a backward glance and a resigned expression. "But it's fine, I don't judge you for it. I said yes, so no need to get upset."

Genua's face dropped for a moment, then she sat up as if startled. "You said yes? You'll help my daughters leave the family name?"

"Wait . . ." Ethel said while quickly beginning to wipe her own tears away. "You said yes?! What did Elder Bren say to you?! Just, just to make sure we're thinking of the same thing . . ."

Riven shifted uncomfortably on the bed, feeling a little odd with all three of them staring at him so anxiously. "He basically said you told him and the other elves that I expected to be paid for my help. That I did what I did to acquire you as a thrall . . ."

". . . and?"

"And that I expect him to wipe out your family's debt entirely if I do this."

Genua's voice caught in her throat, and the middle-aged woman almost sobbed when she finally spoke the words. She repeated what she'd heard: "All of our debts, gone? You would expressly change Ethel's original terms just to help us?"

Riven slowly nodded. "I said I'd do it. Honestly, I don't like being tricked like this, but—"

He was interrupted when Ethel flung her arm around Riven's shoulders and began to sob loudly—extremely loudly. She shook violently, rocking Riven back and forth with the sheer violence of her crying, and her mother and little sister joined them. Riven quickly found himself in the center of a group hug, very wet with tears and very uncomfortable with two scantily clad elf women and a little girl in a reed dress hugging him for dear life.

"What's wrong?!" Athela burst into the room, black hair flowing in her wake, lasering her sight onto Riven with a growing scowl. "RIVEN! WHAT DID YOU DO?!"

"I DIDN'T DO ANYTHING. I—HEY! OW!"

WHACK

"Stop that!"

WHACK

"GODDAMN IT, ATHELA, GET YOUR SHIT TOGETHER. I DIDN'T DO ANYTHING WRONG!"

WHACK

"Oh, now you're just hitting me to be a turd! I SEE THAT SMIRK! AZMOTH! AZMOTH, COME SAVE ME FROM ATHELA! THAT'S AN ORDER!"

Azmoth's cackling, which had been rather loud up until now, briefly faltered and then resumed again when the large, lumbering demon entered the room. He quickly yanked Athela out of the room. There was a high-pitched squeal of surprise, and the door slammed behind them.

With a bruised skull and an irritated mumbling, Riven then found himself back at square one. The crying had gone from pure weeping to a mixture of laughing and sobbing, with Genua eventually being the first to let go. The woman wiped her eyes, pulled her two daughters off him, and bowed.

"Thank you, Riven," Ethel's mother stated in a quivering voice, happy tears sparkling in the moonlight while she held her two daughters close. "I cannot thank you enough. You will literally change all our lives if you do this, and it would not be the first time . . . since you saved Ethel once already. I will do my best to repay you for your kindness."

"As will I," Ethel said shakily with wide doe eyes and a sniffle.

Len raised a hand. "I won't. Since Sister is going to become your whatever it is, I'll be seeing you lots. You'll be baking me cookies regularly. That's what the deal with Ethel was when I participated in her evil plan to use you."

The other two women burst into melodic laughter, and Riven's growing smirk quickly washed away his irritation. At a loss for words and feeling somewhat like a willing idiot for accepting their scheme, he took this as an opportune moment to excuse himself.

He stood up, not sure what to think about any of this, and gave them a small bow. "It's been my pleasure to meet all of you, and I again thank you for nursing me back to health. I'll be seeing all of you in the morning, and I wish you a very good night."

"You're not staying with me?" Ethel asked, a mixture of teasing and genuine disappointment flittering over her face. "You should stay."

Riven opened his mouth to reply but quickly shut it and shook his head. "I shouldn't. You've been through a lot, and I don't want to take advantage of that. I'll talk to all of you tomorrow. Have a good night."

With a wave and another polite smile, Riven stepped out of the room to shut the door softly behind him.

"I wish Farrod would act like that. That he'd become the man he used to be. Riven reminds me of Farrod when he was younger and not so broken." Genua glanced over at her daughter Ethel, who was still staring at the shut door akin to the time she'd been a young girl and had first been stung by a bee. The older woman grinned. "Riven was quite scary at first, but after getting to know him . . . He's a real cutie, that one."

"Isn't he, though?!"

"And polite, too. I was not expecting him to go out of his way to wipe out our family's debt . . . does he know how much we owe? Riven really is a kind man. He doesn't fit the stereotype of vampires very well . . . it's too bad things have to play out the way they are. Just remember not to get too attached—you know what's coming."

Ethel hid her face when she felt a blush coming on, and she wiped her tears on her mother's shoulder. "You're embarrassing me, Mother! And don't act like this is any kind of romance; it isn't . . . I very clearly remember what happened to Grandmother. I'm just volunteering to be his regular meal for his help. Let's go to bed. This has been a traumatic experience for all of us."

A small voice called out from down below. "But you promised me we'd make cookies!"

Genua's fingers traced across her youngest daughter's back, scratching her child's skin lightly until she got an involuntary moan of contentment. "Another night, Len, another night."

"Can we make cookies for Riven in the morning, then?! He was telling me he liked cookies! I promise I'm not making it up—he really did say that!"

Her mother gave an amused laugh, then winced when the bruises along her face flared at a more sudden jerk of her head. "Yes . . . that'd be fine. We'll make cookies for all of them in the morning, now go to sleep. Your sister is right; tonight has been rather traumatic, and I'm in need of some good rest . . . and I wish to wake up early to see if I can find your father. I wish to talk to him, to try to bring my husband back home. I miss him."

Ethel grimaced in irritation but didn't say anything further on the matter when she saw her mother's yearning gaze out the window. She and Genua then ended up falling asleep in one another's arms—feeling far more safe and secure than they had in many years. As for the little girl, Len, in between them? She fell asleep thinking of what ingredients she was going to poison her sister's cookies with for making her participate in this ludicrous plan of hers. She'd been promised cookies tonight, and Ethel had fallen through. Ethel would therefore pay, no matter how many delicious, scrumptious cookies she helped Len make in the morning.

Revenge would be sweet, and revenge would be hers.

"This is disgusting! Oh, by the hells!" Fay puked over the side of the window and out onto the grass, letting Athela hold her hair for her as the other demoness cackled loudly at Fay's misfortune. Occasionally Athela would give Ethel an irritated glare, but fortunately for Riven there'd been little drama between the two despite Athela's confided misgivings on Ethel's manipulations. If anything, the demoness actually thought acquiring a thrall was in Riven's best interests— and this was a fast track to getting one without compromising Riven's morals.

Meanwhile, Genua was chiding Len for trying to poison her sister—with the cookies that Fay had eaten instead of Ethel, which the Succubus was now paying the price for. The cute little elvish girl pouted in the corner while she was lectured, staring at the floor and pooching her lips while humphing loudly every couple seconds, to the increasing irritation of her mother.

Len had zero regrets.

"I am so sorry, Fay . . ." Ethel said while coming around the side of the house, ignoring the stares of other people in the community as she cleaned up the mess the Succubus was making. "I'm so, so sorry . . . I think those cookies were for me."

Azmoth chortled in the back of the room while playing chess with Riven at a table far too small for a demon of his size, keeping himself hunkered down along- side Dr. Brass in order to not hit the ceiling with his head. "No, this is karma."

"Karma for WHAT?!" Fay screeched at the brutalisk without looking back just before projectile vomiting again. Her wings and tail went rigid, and she hiccup-gagged with another lurching noise.

"All evil deeds you've done! Succubus always more evil. They most evil of demons," Azmoth called back amid the laughter of Riven, Athela, and Dr. Brass.

Meanwhile, Dr. Brass raised an eyebrow and sipped water from a wooden cup. "I didn't realize you knew what karma was, Azmoth. Hey, Riven, would you mind talking to me sometime in private?"

"Yeah, sure. Later today. Is this about the vampiric change you want to undertake?"

Dr. Brass deflated upon Riven's out-in-the-open announcement, but the old man grudgingly nodded despite curious glances shot his way from Genua. Meanwhile, Azmoth just continued to laugh at the Succubus and her misfortune.

Fay spat out remnants of gastric juices and glared up with black eyes at Athela and Ethel, hissing through her teeth. "Remind me to kill that flaming, four-armed son of a bitch later."

Even Ethel had to keep her smile under wraps at the mocking laughter from all of Fay's companions, though she still definitely felt bad about her little sister's revenge prank.

Riven was doing a rather good job teaching Azmoth how to play chess, and the large, lumbering demon was gingerly moving piece by piece with his huge claws whenever Riven, still laughing, would instruct him on how a piece could move. To Riven's surprise, Genua actually was a solid chess player and even had a board with pieces stored away. He hadn't thought these elves would have chess on their planet but was very happy to see otherwise, and when he'd spotted the board, she'd taken it down out of one of the storage baskets hung from the ceiling alongside herbs to let him set it up.

"The queen can go in any direction—diagonal or straight—all the way until she hits another piece. It's the most powerful player, and you don't want to sacrifice it if you can help it." Riven touched the large central figure of the queen, then moved to the king with his pointer finger next. "This is the king. If he is threatened by another piece, he is placed in check, which means you must protect him by blocking the attack or eliminating the threat, or you must move him out of the way. This is an absolute rule, and if you can't do it then you're in what's called checkmate—this will lose you the game."

"This complicated," Azmoth stated with a huff. "It may take long memorize these pieces and what do."

"Nah, man, you're a fast learner. I can already tell you'll get it in no time!"

From within his robe's pocket, he started to feel the black orb Allie had given him pulse. He looked down, smiling widely at the thought of speaking with Allie again. She'd not picked up earlier that morning when he'd tried calling to update her on events, and he was very keen on talking about the Chalgathi revelation and World Quest.

He pulled the black communication orb out of his pocket, infused mana into it, and began to talk. "Hey, Allie! Goddamn, do I have a lot to tell you."

CHAPTER 48

Dawn's light had brought with it a flood of the undead, pouring over entrenched defenders like a tidal wave of death, bathing the northern city of Brightsville in blood when the two major factions present there clashed in the biggest battle yet.

And it had been short-lived.

Allie glared down at Prophet's second in command, a wiry old military veteran who'd managed to get a paladin class and cause grief for her forces numerous times. He now stood battered, beaten, broken, and bruised, with blood dripping down his forehead while he breathed out in ragged gasps. Her hand was through his chest, grasping his spine, and she gripped more tightly to hear the crunch of bone under her fingers.

The man screamed, and she yanked with a spray of gore to end him on the spot.

Tossing the vertebrae casually to the side and letting the man's twitching corpse fall onto the ground, she turned and gracefully stepped over the dozens of corpses between her and the burning cathedral Prophet had once called home. When she stopped not far off from Vin, the skeletal necromancer gave her a raspy chuckle and motioned for her to come closer.

"They never stood a chance!" Vin croaked, a crooked bone finger pointing to where thousands of fleeing refugees were frantically trying to escape the onslaught of their forces across the plains just outside Brightsville. Skeletons and zombies were in abundance, but there were occasional ghouls, blood golems, bone golems, skresh, and even a few ghosts that ran the crowd of screaming people down.

Allie watched her forces murder the families of the defenders with only a very small amount of guilt, but internally she knew this had to be done lest she endanger herself and the civilization she was going to build here. It was a great evil for a greater good.

"We didn't catch him, did we?" Allie asked impassively, gazing across the carnage and the fields of corpses.

Vin's smugness dropped, and he grunted an acknowledgment of her assessment. "Yeh, bastard got away with a couple hundred of his best fighters. They fled north across the plains to abandon these ones here."

The skresh waved a hand across the fields stained red. "They're long gone. But now this poses a question . . . What do you want to do with these ones?"

Allie's eyebrow raised, and she followed her lieutenant's gesture, seeing a couple hundred bound humans rounded up into an enclosure between buildings. Many of them were outright terrified. Some were young, some were old, while others were her own age. A couple of sentient ghouls had taken command of a group of minions and kept the humans in line while awaiting orders, and their dead eyes watched Allie with curious intent, waiting to see what she'd have them do.

"Why were they not killed already?" Allie asked flatly, shoving her hands and her wand into the pockets of her cloak.

Vin cleared his throat, or vertebrae, or whatever it was he did to make that sound happen. "They were not part of Prophet's forces. They were a negotiating group, one that was being blackmailed and coerced into joining Prophet before we struck. They'd not agreed to anything yet, and this is confirmed by our spies."

"Is that so?" Allie confidently strode through the crowds of Unholy creatures, the wave of them parting before her like the Red Sea. She came to a stop before one of the bound men nearby. He was a huge man, of Indian heritage, thickly muscled and built like a bear with a long black beard. He was very bruised but otherwise bore no wounds. "I hear you weren't part of the faction who declared war on us. What would your plans be, should I let you and your people go?"

The man hesitated, glancing back at the people behind him one by one in unspoken conversations.

Allie looked left to the ghoul soldiers standing nearby. One carried a sword, the other a rifle and a machete. "This is the leader of their group, correct?"

She got two nods, and in turn she stared back down at the man again with piercing red eyes through the bone mask on her face. "Speak. I do not have much patience for this."

The man gulped, then raised his face to the light. "I did not know you were the ones declared on—the man calling himself Prophet had told us that you'd gone out of your way to kill people just for being different from you."

"I have done terrible things, but that sin is not mine to bear. I did not start this war. I am merely finishing it."

Again the burly man hesitated, then he blinked a couple times and exhaled shakily. "We have no ties to the people you killed. Simply put, we will do whatever it takes to survive. The real question is, what would you have us do?"

Vin came to stop beside Allie, letting out a laugh when Allie hummed with contentment.

"That . . . that is the correct answer," Allie stated simply. Turning around and speaking to the ghoul soldiers, she gestured with a hand to the prisoners at her back. "Free them. Find Mara at the tower and have her integrate them into our society one way or the other. They'll be made useful, I'm sure."

Audible sighs or sobs of relief escaped numerous humans as the undead soldiers started to cut their bindings one by one, with many people crying or hugging one another after they'd been set free.

Allie continued to walk through the ruined compound, watching her forces dig through the remnants of Prophet's belongings to try and find whatever treasures could be salvaged. No doubt he'd taken the holy book with him, but there might be other things she could acquire that he'd not had time to collect in the panic of her surprise attack that morning.

Irreverently kicking aside a corpse and plopping down onto a wooden bench, Allie took her mask off and set it in her lap. Pulling out the communication orb she'd linked to Riven's, she let her mind wander for a time, wondering what he'd say if he saw what she was up to right now.

But she was doing this for him. Great evils for greater goods—that was what this was all about. There was a good chance he'd one day find out about the things she'd done here, but she'd face that when that time came. No matter what happened, they would always love one another. Riven and Allie had always been inseparable, and just as she would forever support him no matter what he did, he, too, would never abandon her for the things she was forced to do here. It still made her slightly sick to think about how disappointed he'd be in her, though, and she tried to push those thoughts away while wincing when the sunlight reached her eyes.

She pulled down her hood with a groan, and Vin took a seat next to her on the bench.

"I'm surprised you let them live, and even more surprised you're incorporating them into the community," Vin speculated while rubbing his bone chin. "Suddenly going soft, eh? You've probably been talking to Mara too much. We should have butchered them for parts like the ones running in the fields."

Allie gave him a frown, then shook her head, placing her communication orb in her lap but not activating it yet. "Do not think me evil for evil's sake, Vin. If you do, you'd be mistaken. I only kill those fleeing from us for reasons of practicality. I do not want to kill them, but they have to be killed. It is a matter of security for ourselves rather than one of cruelty."

"Truly?"

"Truly. Think about this, Vin. Would it not be wise to have a sect of our society based on mortals? Those that are not undead already?" Allie turned her entire body, shifting one leg to rest on the other knee to get a better look at the other necromancer. "There will been enemies to kill for more parts, to use as fuel to create more of our kin. However, it does not need to be a violent path all the time. What happens when mortals die? Their bodies go to waste. But we could collect those bodies when they die of old age and normal means and allow both of our people to grow under one umbrella."

"Under your umbrella."

"Correct." Allie shrugged. "It just makes sense. Yes, humans spurned us multiple times when we got here. But we are the ones in power now; we are the strongest faction in this city. They will fall in line because they have no choice, and when they realize that they are offered security and a path to a better life under my rule? It's a no-brainer."

She tapped the side of her head with a finger. "After we subdue the warring gangs of the suburbs and kill that man who's made a base out of the city prison, the rest of the city will be ours for the taking. Who else has the power to stand against us? No one. It is now simply a matter of time—and a matter of hunting down the rabbits that followed Prophet into the wilderness."

"They'll likely run far and fast," Vin stated flatly. "If we do not pursue them now, we may never find them again. Mara's assassins are pursuing their retreat, but we do not know if her minions are capable of catching them, staying hidden for surveillance, and finally relaying a message without problems."

Allie picked up the bauble in her lap again with an indifferent shrug. "Perhaps . . . perhaps not. We will see. I have a very strong feeling that this is not anything but a tactical retreat, however. Where would they go? None of us have any idea what lies beyond the borders of this small city, so unless they want to wander around aimlessly, I doubt they'd have a real trajectory to shoot for anyways. They have no true sanctuary any longer, but let's pause this conversation. I need to talk to my brother. Knowing him, he's gotten himself into some kind of trouble over the past twenty-four hours."

She rolled her eyes but grinned with amusement as she said it. Then, beginning to infuse mana into the black orb, she took her leave and began to walk aimlessly away from Vin and the other undead to maintain a semblance of privacy.

"You're being stupid. Why don't you just kill the old man causing you these problems and subjugate the village?" Allie's voice cut through the communication orb clear as day, garnering attention from the others in their cabin while Riven continued to play chess with Azmoth. "It sounds to me like these elves are just using you. A pretty face and a body to feed on are not something you need to negotiate for. You should simply tell them that you're in charge and take as many bodies to feed on as you want. Conquer the village and make it easy. How would they stop you?"

Riven grimaced at her words, but he was hesitant to leave the room for privacy's sake should Ethel's family think he was actually going to consider something like betrayal. He wanted them to hear the conversation back to front now that she'd openly told him to take the village by force. "I'm not going to just take over, Allie. That's essentially slavery. The idea to kill Elder Preen isn't a terrible one, but even that pushes a line I don't want to cross . . . yet. I'll deal with him if I need to, but I want the trust of these people. They just had a group of orcs and goblins come to murder their families two days ago—there's no way I'm going to come in and make them submit to me just because I can. Why would you even suggest that?"

"Didn't you just say that you were wanting them to join our new faction?"

"Well, yeah, it'd be nice. But not by force. I mean, what the fuck, Allie? Are you being serious?"

To this, Allie let out a long sigh. "Perhaps this is a conversation we would best have in person."

Riven let out an irritated grunt. "Yeah, it probably is."

"Huh. Well, I'm a bit busy. Was there anything else you wanted to talk about?" The way she said it was snarky at best.

Riven opened his mouth to reply but quickly shut it to give himself pause so he wouldn't lash out verbally. They were both obviously in bad moods. Talking more about anything right now would get them nowhere, and the topic of Chalgathi was pushed to the back burner because of it. "No. There's nothing else; we'll talk later."

"'Kay, 'bye."

The communication stone stopped pulsing, the connection to Allie disappeared, and Riven finally got up to exit the cabin, leaving his minions, Ethel, and her family awkwardly behind.

Athela plopped down beside the warlock and nudged Riven's rib cage with an elbow. "Yo. How you feeling? Any better?"

Riven didn't bother looking up but nodded his affirmation. "Yeah, I feel fine."

"You don't look fine. You look pissed off."

Riven gave Athela a half-hearted smile. "Yeah, a bit, but let's not talk about that now. I really am fine."

Athela crossed her arms skeptically, then abruptly shape-shifted into her spider form. Clambering onto his lap, she nuzzled under one arm and stayed there. "I'll pretend you're telling the truth. I suppose my next question is, do you feel good enough to get this greenskin deal over with?"

Riven's smile turned warmer, and he started scratching the spider's head like he would a dog's. His body became less stiff, more relaxed, and he felt his shoulders slump slightly with an exhale of air under the tree's shade. "Probably not that good. I want to be in top shape; apparently they still have their elites at the orc encampment—ones that didn't come with the raiding party. Give me one more day of rest from our last battle and I'll go."

"You know . . . there is one thing I agreed with your sister on." Athela blinked her red eyes from where she rested on his lap, looking up hesitantly. "Ethel is definitely using you. As long as you're aware of that, I'm fine with it. You can use her back and it'll be a fair trade, but I don't like how she was so manipulative."

Riven's expression soured, but he did give a grunt of acknowledgment. "Can't say I necessarily blame her, though. Imagine finding yourself in that situation. Wouldn't you do something similar if you could?"

"I sure would. I'm just trying to point out the obvious in case you weren't aware."

"Oh, I'm definitely aware."

"Want to play rock-paper-scissors?"

"What for?"

"Well, if you win, then I don't kill Elder Preen. If I do win, I go with your sister's plan to kill the old fart today. Then I'll eat him! That'll solve all our problems!!! Well, some of them, anyways."

Riven stifled a snort. "Rock-paper-scissors shouldn't be how we decide life-and-death events. Plus, I wouldn't get anything out of it if I won. We're already not killing Elder Preen."

"Yet. Not killing him—YET," Athela corrected with a spider leg waggling his way. "Five platinum says we kill him soon."

"I'd prefer not to come off as a murder-happy type of guy to the rest of the village, which is why I haven't seriously considered it—yet. I already look the part."

"Wah-wah, goo-goo, ga-ga! That's an impression of you, by the way. Let me bust out the sad violin music so Riven can wallow in his own misery!"

"Hey!" Riven cackled a laugh when Athela started rubbing two of her limbs together, no doubt referencing the act from back on Earth when people mimicked playing the world's smallest violin. How she'd known that reference, he didn't know, but he definitely found it amusing.

A strong gust of wind caused the trees of the village to shake and rustle. The chirping of birds was momentarily hushed, and the sun's rays glinted off the lake nearby.

Athela burped and readjusted herself on his lap. "Do we know where it is?"

"Where what is? The orc camp?"

"Yeah."

"No idea. I'll have to ask Elder Bren, but he said he'd send a scout with us to confirm our side of the bargain."

"Bargain? Oh, you're talking about citizenship and the . . ." Athela gave Riven another little nudge and a chittering smirk, head bobbing over to where

Ethel was kneeling below them on the ground, next to Len, and talking in hushed but stern tones. She, like many of the other elves in the village, was wearing only a thin two-piece garment of stitched leaves and furs that were quite revealing. "The hot babe!"

Riven's hand karate chopped hard into Athela's back, sending the spider into a laughing gasp. "Shut it."

Riven did manage to spare a glance at the woman, though, barely having enough time to reflect on her long, tanned legs before she swept her blond hair over her back to glance up his way. He immediately averted his gaze from Ethel to avoid detection and then went back to looking out at the lake. Now was not the time to get distracted with things like that—the world of Panu was literally in danger, and he was a key player in at least one of the six World Quests. He needed to get stronger, and he needed to do it fast. Five years might be a long way away in some aspects, but not in the realm of needing to finish world-spanning events. He had to assume Panu was at least three times the size of Earth if all those planets had been incorporated into one another, so there was little wiggle room in terms of a timeline.

"Have you looked at the Guild and Faction System, the cortex, and the leaderboards yet?" Athela's voice carried to question him while he stared off into space.

Riven immediately paused upon hearing the question. He'd nearly forgotten after all the things that'd happened concerning that jackass Elder Preen, or in his short bursts of craving directed toward Ethel. And by craving he didn't necessarily mean physically, but more in terms of blood. He was getting hungry again, and despite having had warg meat last night as well as some cookies that hilarious little she-devil Len had baked for him, he was wanting blood, too.

He'd already made a morning trip to where the goblins were tied down with stakes on the other side of the village. The goblins were stinking, disgusting creatures, and though he'd already feasted on one that day, it only satisfied his hunger and not his taste buds. Despite his disgust for the action that he'd performed in Dungeon Negrada, he still remembered what human tasted like compared to goblin . . . and it was a stark difference. The taste of it, the smell, the satisfaction of a human was far more enticing . . . even the corpse of the human back in the hospital had been incredibly appetizing, but each of the elves here gave off an even better aroma than humans did. It made his mouth water just thinking about it, and though he hadn't brought up feeding to Ethel just yet, he was certainly going to have that conversation sooner rather than later. She'd literally volunteered for it, so he didn't have many reservations holding him back. It wasn't like he was going to eat her—he'd never even consider it—he just wanted some of her blood, small amounts, really, from time to time so that the cravings would go away and he wouldn't go insane.

And he really, REALLY didn't like the taste of goblin.

He shook those thoughts off, then opened up his status page and scrolled, finding the three new options listed at the bottom.

[Guild and Faction System (Currently Delayed)
Panu Cortex
Panu World Quests]

CHAPTER 49

He clicked on Guild and Faction System first.

[You must create a guild with the Create Guild command prior to utilizing this page. You must have at least three people to create a guild. Guild functions are frozen until further notice.]

Riven frowned and dismissed the notification, deciding to move on to the cortex first. He'd talk to the others about guild creation later, when the system unfroze the guild functions, but that was definitely a team effort and not an individual one—decisions wouldn't be solely his. He didn't even know what they'd name their guild if he and the others created one, but the idea of having a group to go adventuring with in this new world was certainly likable. Clicking on the Panu cortex, he saw a very intricate display appear in front of him in the form of a perfectly square hologram three times as large as his status page. This one had the image of a world that he could only assume to be Panu slowly spinning in the background, with a headline along the front page: "Welcome to the Panu cortex!" An article underneath that listed options.

[Welcome to the Panu cortex!

This is the first week having the cortex intact. For this reason, the system administrator will be able to answer direct questions if you have them over the next seven days. Beyond that the system administrator will divert its attention to other more pressing matters regarding the world of Panu. Here you will find forum categories and branching categories; you can scroll through subjects, post your own topics, acquire or share video feeds, create enemies or alliances, and even bargain for goods like a marketplace. Be warned that each

has strict sets of rules, and you will receive a notification if your content is prohibited. Most prohibited material involves key events in the world of Panu or even in your local area, secrets of Panu that the Elysium administrator wishes to be found rather than publicly exploited, information released too early regarding worlds outside Panu, and spam content. Video feeds can only be uploaded by request. You must ask the administrator directly to upload content, and your request may or may not be recognized. Sometimes the administrator may also post video content even without an express request. In order to request video uploading, just mentally think of the time and place you want to upload and wait for a response.

Please note that restrained or imprisoned personnel may not access the forums of Panu's cortex. Forums extend only to places you have visited and guilds you have joined, with the exceptions of the main page discussion board and the World Quest message boards, both of which are world-spanning and more heavily moderated. No forums outside key areas visited and guilds can exist other than Global Forums.

Feel free to select from one of the already categorized subjects, or you may use the search function for more in-depth selections of guild forums. Your options are as follows:

Main Page and Announcements (Global)
Power Ladders, Guild and Individual (Global)
World Quests and World Quest Ladders (Global)
Greenstalk Village
The City of Brightsville]

Riven immediately clicked on The City of Brightsville, and an aerial view of the city popped up to replace the revolving globe. It was very much like the website Reddit from back on Earth, with various subcategories that he could select from and a feed of the most popular posts, with a number of quickly growing topics.

[In need of help, out of food and desperate]
[How do abilities work? Does anyone know how to get new ones?]
[My family was killed by little green men.]
[Forming a hunting group to level up. Taking applications, only class holders may apply.]

[Exchanging information on class types.]
[Repent! The apocalypse is God's will, and the sinners of these lands are to blame!]

There were a couple of interesting threads that got an insane amount of traction concerning the people of Earth still residing in Brightsville; others not as much. It was far more than Riven had expected, though, with thousands and then tens of thousands of people immediately blowing up the more popular forum topics with active and ongoing chatter. He also knew there were probably far more people just reading through the comments, like he was, instead of posting outright.

However, one forum topic caught his attention immediately. Frowning at it, he paused before selecting the following:

[Prophet's forces have been routed, undead are swarming the city.]

He clicked the link and began to scroll through dozens of comments. Talk about the surprise attack that morning was constantly being updated. Clicking one of the clips concerning the battle, Riven watched the attack with a mounting tide of conflicting emotions.

He was watching from the viewpoint of a man who stood along a makeshift wall surrounding a gated community, overlooking layers of barbed-wire fences and other brought-in barriers. The man had a rifle slung over his shoulder, wore a linen vest, and was yawning while gazing toward the sunrise beginning to peek over the horizon. Other guards also sporting rifles laughed and joked with one another while the man sipped his coffee, only to startle abruptly and drop to the floor when a bone lance blasted through the air and one of his companions exploded in a spray of viscera.

Unholy screeches rose up like thunder to meet his ears, and the man's body started to tremble as he beheld a wave of undead rushing across the broken city toward the compound. Hundreds and then thousands of the monsters swarmed over buildings, the broken rubble, streets, and trees in a mad dash that caused Riven to gasp. He began to scream out for help, only to have his vision go dark when a blur of motion collided with his head—ending the video instantly.

How a dead man's perspective was able to be obtained was beyond Riven's knowledge, but there was a sky-down view as well that showed the flood of Unholy creatures completely collapsing barricade after barricade while they scoured the northern reaches of the city. Was the system actually enabling these things to be shown from its own perspective rather than those of the people still alive?

Why had Allie not informed him of this? There was only one person in Brightsville with those kinds of forces, and the ones they were battling were those with holy abilities. It had to be Allie.

And the things he saw . . .

Riven turned off the video feed and shut it down. He shared a look with Athela. "I won't make any assumptions until I talk to her in person. Let's not talk about it until I do . . . okay?"

Athela didn't say a word, and he moved on, sheer determination not allowing him to jump to conclusions without speaking to Allie about what he'd seen. Yet he didn't call her immediately, either, for fear of what she would admit to.

The Greenstalk village forum was far less active. That being said, there were only a couple hundred elves in Greenstalk, so he wasn't too surprised—and it appeared to be more of a test run between the local fletcher and some of his friends to see just how the forums worked.

Then came the more interesting part. He clicked on Power Ladders, Guild and Individual, next. It turned out to be a categorized list, and it had an explanation pop up prior to scrolling. The guild sections were grayed out, with a little notification stating that the guild system would be released within the upcoming weeks.

[This is a onetime message: Power Ladders are categorized into Guild and Individual categories and only include natives of Panu; they do not include monsters or outworld invaders. They are ranked when combining and comparing raw fighting capabilities or military might, items, wealth, and ability to influence the world around you. Why do these lists matter? Rewards will be given out at random intervals based on your rank; the higher the rank, the better the rewards. World events will also take place and pit rival teams against one another or pair them up for cooperation based on power ranking. Lastly, certain world event invitations will only include people or guilds that are ranked high enough on World Panu's Power Ladder. It is usually in your best interest to be placed higher than not.]

[Thirty-two billion current participants have been analyzed. The ranking categories are as follows: Apex Rank (top 10), Paragon Rank (top 1,000), S Rank (top 0.0001%), A Rank (Top 1%), B Rank (Top 15%), C Rank (Top 30%), D Rank (Top 50%), E Rank (Bottom 50%)]

[Current Top 10 Native Participants:
1.   Judith Marcina, Level 82 Human, Apex Rank, Justicar
2.   Retesh Vorath, Level 91 Corpse Lord, Apex Rank, Elder Lich
3.   Aren Hrall, Level 69 Snow Giant, Apex Rank, Berserker
4.   Thofus Hrall, Level 84 Snow Giant, Apex Rank, Blizzard Mage

5. Cracius Mem, Level 85 Human, Apex Rank, Sword Emperor
6. Sinthil Tuk'tuk, Level 90 Lizardian, Apex Rank, Wind Blade
7. Thorman Bame, Level 90 Human, Apex Rank, Hammer of the Mountain
8. Esper Rite, Level 72 High Elf, Apex Rank, Glade Guardian
9. Toothly Rop, Level 60 Swamp Troll, Apex Rank, Man-eater
10. Chitter Teh-Sneaker, Level 61 Rat Man, Apex Rank, Dark-Blade Assassin

Your Status: Riven Thane, Level 38 Pure-blooded Vampire, Middle S Rank, Warlock Adept
Guild rankings currently not available. Guild functions are currently frozen.]

S rank wasn't too shabby. That meant he was in the top 0.0001 percent of participants on this planet that were fighting for its survival, though he certainly paled in comparison to any of the top ten. How they'd gotten that strong in such a short time when everyone here apparently started at level one upon initiation was beyond him, though he had a sneaking suspicion that they'd used various abilities already available from their original worlds to wipe out insane numbers of enemies in the short span of time Panu had been around. Riven also did some quick math and realized that although he was actually listed in S rank, this only placed him in the top 3.2 million participants—given that there were thirty-two billion people on Panu.

That was a lot of people to contend with. But it did say he was *middle* S rank, meaning he wasn't near the bottom of that bracket. So that was good.

"Nice!" Athela screeched, slapping Riven's shoulder excitedly with four of her legs and hopping up and down. "I knew it! I knew you were going to be highly rated! Ohhhhh, the opportunities that await us . . . I scored the jackpot!"

Kill the greenskins, visit the rat man Snagger at their predetermined meeting place in a few days, and have another long talk with Allie about both Chalgathi and the things he'd seen in the forums before returning to Greenstalk village to turn Ethel into a thrall. He also needed to figure out where he was going to plant his guild core and the Elysium altar he'd obtained. That was his list. That, and continue giving Fay lessons on the Wretched Snare spell. It was an Unholy foundational spell, which meant she could learn it, too, as she was a mana-user and not based in stamina or divinity.

Over the past day, he'd tried teaching Fay Wretched Snares, but the Succubus hadn't caught on to it at all. What had taken him a very short amount of time to learn the demoness was having a rather hard time grasping—and this was apparently the norm.

He also had the rod to plant the Elysium altar, but he still didn't know where he wanted to set it up. It was going to be very large and attract a lot of attention, especially when he'd not seen any altars before this, and it'd likely be a coveted resource if there were any other groups in the area.

Riven rubbed his forehead with his thumb while walking through the forest, his pointer finger and middle finger squeezing to relieve the tension building between his eyes. His three demons were close behind—the armored, four-armed Hellscape Brutalisk, Azmoth; the blue-skinned Succubus; and Athela, the Arshakai.

Ethel, her mother, Genua, and that cute little girl, Len, had bidden them a temporary farewell with emotional goodbyes for over an hour before letting them leave. With Elder Preen still a potential problem and Farrod nowhere to be seen, Riven was determined to finish this fast. He'd slaughter whoever he needed to and force the orcs out of the area—it was just that simple. If he could do it by sparing the innocent, all the better, but he'd not balk now.

Regardless, he was far busier than anyone in a postapocalyptic world should be, at least in his opinion. He just wanted some time to rest and reevaluate his life, not constantly be swamped with dumb shit like dealing with evil old perverts or carnivorous goblins and orcs that'd been having blood feuds with the elves of their planet for centuries pre-integration. Even now he was mentally fumbling over the logistics of traveling between Greenstalk village and the city of Brightsville to visit the underdark, trying to figure out how many of those captured goblins they should take with them for meal supplementation. Ethel could be turned into a thrall, but it wouldn't be an immediate change and before that she'd only be able to supply small amounts of blood before falling ill herself.

Being a vampire might have its perks, but it definitely was a pain in the ass concerning feeding. It was a primal urge that never completely went away, and it only got worse the longer he didn't do it. Would he stay in the underdark long when visiting that rat man Snagger, the one he'd met in the sewers? Who knew, but that wasn't really a priority right now. Allie was the priority right after this entire escapade with the elves was over with, and he was going to set things straight.

But he definitely wanted to check out Snagger's nest of other rat people. The rat man had seemed friendly, and it'd be as good a place as any to find someone with the Identifier class. None of the elves had any high-level identifiers, and from his conversations with Allie, he knew neither did her undead.

Meanwhile, Riven tried his best to keep the sun out of his eyes and off his skin. They would have traveled the entire way in the dark if it weren't that the elf guide leading them through the forests couldn't see in the dark.

"You look deep in thought," the voice of the elf scout called out from up front, causing Riven's gaze to shift from the grassy forest floor to the bare-chested man ahead. The elf was of a strong build with shorter hair than most his kind, though it was silver like many of the rest, and he wore tribal markings of blue paint along his arms, abdomen, and back. He also carried a longbow in his left hand and had two sets of quivers strung up behind him with a dagger in a sheath on his leg. "Something troubling you?"

Riven shook his head, using his vampiric artifact cane as a walking staff. "No, not really."

"You aren't nervous?"

"About the goblins and orcs? Perhaps this is overconfidence speaking, but no. Not after all I've been through."

The elf, an older man than Riven but still in middle age, grinned and nodded in approval. He slowed down slightly to let Riven catch up and began to walk beside him. "That's what I was hoping to hear. I have heard many good things about you, Riven, and though I was busy fighting the greenskins myself the night of the raid, I did get to see you in action briefly. What I saw was encouraging. My name is Ren. It is nice to meet you."

The elf put his hands together and bowed like most of his kind did when greeting one another for the first time, but then stuck out his hand to shake as well. Surprised, Riven took the man's hand in his own and firmly gripped it with a nod.

"So someone taught you our customs, then."

"Senna did. She's my daughter."

"Oh! That's why your name is so familiar!"

Ren laughed, ducking underneath one of the lower-hanging tree branches in their path and continuing uphill. "Yes, I never did get a chance to thank you with everything that has happened. I lost three sons in the fight with the orcs, and it has weighed heavily on me, but I must put on a brave face for my family. It just took me some time to get ahold of myself and sustain my rightness of mind, for I was in a dark place due to unbearable grief."

Riven's shock wasn't evident due to the hood and mask. He hadn't realized that Senna had lost family members—she'd never mentioned it. Then again, she hadn't really been around much and had stuck to her own family since getting back to the village.

"I'm sorry for your loss."

"Do not be," Ren stated absentmindedly, shaking himself out of his obvious inner turmoil and stepping over a fallen log with a grunt. "It would have been more of a loss if you hadn't acted—you have nothing to apologize for. Again, I just wanted to thank you. You brought my daughter back to me, and I won't ever forget the favor you've done my family. In fact, my wife is demanding that we invite you over for dinner after you get back. The elder might hold a small feast in your honor when this deed is done, but if that happens, we can merely have you over for drinks!"

"Drinks?!" Athela called out from the back of the line. "Like the alcoholic ones?!"

Ren nodded and waved back at the others. "Of course, you're all invited, in case you were wondering!"

"Way to invite yourself, Athela!" Fay stated with an eye roll. "Nice manners you've got there."

"We're demons! Since when are we supposed to have manners!?"

Dr. Brass began to laugh, but Ren assured them all that he'd been intending to invite the entire group over along with Riven.

Ren turned back to Riven while taking them onto a mildly worn dirt path running straight east. "I also wanted you to bring Ethel, Genua, and Len, of course. They've been family friends for many years—Genua, my wife, and I all grew up together. Thank you for helping her daughter."

Riven paused upon seeing a wild pair of wolves staring them down, but the animals hightailed it out of there once Riven launched a few well-placed Bloody Razors to scare them off. "So just wife, singular?"

"I'm not sure what you mean by that."

"You don't have multiple wives? It seems like a lot of the men in your village have more than one."

"Oh! That." Ren notched an arrow and casually pulled back, releasing it and infusing it with some sort of skill. The arrow glowed a light blue and crackled with lightning before slamming into a large snake farther up the path—the writhing creature quickly settled into death. A money pouch dropped on its corpse, and the elf bent down to pick it up while they walked past. "I only have one wife. She doesn't like to share, and she's a handful as it is."

"Got it. Why do so many people have multiple wives in your village, though? I've been meaning to ask. Don't the other young men run out of potential partners? Back on Earth, my original world, the polygamist groups in my country of origin would actually drop young boys off to fend for themselves in other territories so they couldn't compete with the older guys. They were called the lost boys, and they were completely abandoned because they were seen as a threat as they got older. They just didn't have enough girls to go around."

Ren raised his eyebrows in surprise and looked thoroughly taken aback. "That's horrible. No, we don't have that problem. Only the most prominent men, usually leaders, have more than one wife. Most of us only have just one."

Riven blinked, crushing a tree branch underfoot and batting away a large rock in the middle of the path with his morning star. "Oh. I guess I got the wrong impression, then."

Ren took the opportunity to explain further. "Elves live a very long time, hundreds of years, usually, but we're an infertile people compared to humans. When men acquire power or wealth, and given our patriarchal society, it is only natural for the most well-off of us to buy new wives. You were human once, yes?"

"Yes."

"That was what I thought. So although humans breed much more quickly and easily than elves, we make up for it with prolonged life spans and more time to conceive children. But elves aren't as fertile as humans and we all want to father children, or at least most of us do, and being rich allows one to acquire more wives for a better chance at acquiring a proper heir. Elder Preen worked very hard to have children of his own and only managed to acquire two sons despite having three wives and using fertility supplements. One of the reasons he wanted to take Genua was because she'd had two daughters in a very short span of time, so she is fertile and a higher prize than the wives he already had. Thus it is not that most of us have multiple wives—most of us don't, in fact. It is that the richest and most powerful of us can simply afford it. They can pay the extra dowry to the family of the woman and can support more people in their household. This is true not only for our village, but across many other elf societies. Probably even the drow."

"Drow being dark elves, right?"

"Yes, the ones who live in the underdark. Though that isn't confirmed by the elder I spoke to, because drow generally hate the elves of the surface. But back to the topic at hand: as for why I personally only took one wife, I just chose not to participate in the bad habits of my fellows despite my success because the woman I love wants me for herself. I respect her enough to abide by her wish and wouldn't have it any other way."

"That's so flippin' cute!" Fay called out, giving Ren a big thumbs-up and a wide, approving smile from underneath her hood. "Good for you! You have my official vote for next village mayor!"

Dr. Brass guffawed. "I would have taken five wives."

"That's because you're a dirty old pervert!" Fay shot back with a glare over her shoulder, pointing accusingly. "Old and perverted!"

"Guilty as charged! And that's rich coming from a Succubus."

"Don't stereotype me, you wrinkled old mummy!"

Riven smirked and turned to look ahead again. "We've had enough perverted old men for my liking recently."

CHAPTER 50

They made camp later that night and continued trudging along the next day. Riven tried calling Allie twice, but each time she'd confirm she was okay, then tell him she was busy and quickly hang up. It was like she was avoiding him, and he was getting the feeling that she'd figured out her videos had leaked on the cortex for him to see. It was highly likely, knowing her, that she was trying to figure out what she was going to say before being confronted.

Ren told them it'd likely be nightfall the day after that before they reached the place where the orcs had set up their own village. A three-day march in total. They'd had a lot of time to talk about various subjects that'd been on Riven's mind.

Fay continued to study Wretched Snares under Riven's tutelage. The vision, intent, understanding, and mana channeling were all pretty simple for Riven—but a lot less so for the demoness. Still, she was not deterred and told him outright she expected it to take her a couple weeks or even months to grasp it fully. In the meantime, the Succubus was just excited to learn something new, because knowledge like this was rarely traded between magical practitioners without a steep price. They often kept their knowledge close to the chest, which didn't really make much sense to Riven when it concerned minions. To him, Fay was an extension of himself in many ways, and making her great would only increase his own chances of survival. Perhaps other warlocks simply didn't trust their summoned minions? He'd have to ask whenever he met another one of his kind.

In between rest breaks, they continued their trek until the third night, when Ren began to make them slow down and be more vigilant in their approach. They were now coming toward a tree line where plains met the woods, and they were farther away from the mountains than Riven had ever been since arriving here on Panu. He could still see the towering, snow-capped mountains in the distance, but they were quite a ways away now.

The sun had already set, but despite not being able to see as well as them, Ren urged the group onward to take advantage of the cover of darkness. Coming along a slow-moving river that wound like a snake into the grasslands, Ren pointed to a large palisade wall along the northern edge of the river. It covered an area of maybe four square miles and had numerous huts and shoddy wooden buildings inside. Fires lit the perimeter with guards patrolling the area, though they were far and few between. Farther in, the settlement was lit up with even larger fires between buildings, and Riven couldn't help but think that was a bit risky considering their tents were all very flammable.

"This is it," Ren said solemnly, even angrily, while glaring across the hundred yards separating them from the greenskin village. "This is where I take a step back . . . I will support you with ranged shots from the safety of the darkness if it comes to a battle outside their gates, but otherwise I cannot get involved. This is on you now. If you really want to take Ethel as a thrall—see it done well."

Riven gave the man an irritated frown. As if he hadn't done enough for them already.

Standing there in the dark of night and barely visible to the naked human eye, Riven turned his red eyes toward Senna's father. "There will be children in there. I don't want to kill them if I don't have to. We will assess the situation first by sending Athela in, then, based on what she says, we will either try to negotiate or scare them off."

Ren grimaced, then nodded in confirmation. "Fine. As long as they're gone from these lands, that is all that matters to us. However, I must tell you that greenskins aren't known for negotiations. They're generally too stupid or violent to even attempt it. From a very young age, their children are taught to be cruel and bloodthirsty, and leaving them alive will only curse future generations of other races. You may think me evil for saying it, but I truly think killing them all would be doing the world a great service."

Riven considered the elf's words for a short time, then dismissed them. "Sorry, but I can't just murder a bunch of innocent kids."

Ren's lips curled, and if Riven hadn't been paying attention, he'd probably not have noticed the slight sneer—quickly hidden, but definitely there. "You're a vampire. Isn't that the kind of thing vampires do?"

This comment caused a flare of anger in Riven's chest, but he pushed it down forcefully. And the facial expressions? After all he'd done for them, these people still looked at him like he was a monster. It was definitely off-putting, especially after Ren had been so friendly along the way.

Riven shook his head. "Not this vampire. Athela?"

The demoness walked forward, utterly silent and grinning ear to ear with anticipation of the violence to come. "Yes, Master?"

She met Riven's eyes.

"Just like how we talked it over. Kill the chieftain and any of these so-called elites that Elder Bren warned us about. I want it done quietly and efficiently so you don't draw any reinforcements. Otherwise, I want you to assess the situation as best you can and report back. Let me know if you get any information that'd be useful in negotiations after we take off the head."

Athela nodded in satisfaction, bowing low and spreading her arms out wide. "Your will is my command, Master. It will be done!"

Athela gracefully slid over the palisade, bare feet touching the ground with such delicacy that not even the dirt underneath moved upon her touch. She silently cast aside the corpses of the three goblins she'd killed along the way and hid them under a loft of dirty hay, bodies sliding off the blades of her arachnid limbs like overcooked meat off a metal spit.

She licked her lips, her red eyes narrowed, her teeth began to sharpen, and she scanned the immediate area for any signs of potential enemies. She was standing in the middle of a penned storage area likely meant for herd animals, but it was currently completely empty. Thatched wooden huts were scattered about the immediate area in uneven rows, and bonfires lit up the streets every couple dozen yards. Despite this, it wasn't very well lit, and Athela quickly made her way toward the center of the greenskin village without much problem at all, her dark body blending with the shadows.

She passed numerous abodes on her way to the center. Rickety wooden furniture and dirt floors were the norm, with hay often stuffed into sacks made from animal skins for beds. The walls sometimes bore animal skulls as trophies, with a few of them even featuring human or elf skulls, too. Many of the huts had open windows where orc women were shepherding tiny orc children, many of them devoid of any tusks at this point but all with the same green skin and black hair. Others had an occasional goblin servant cleaning up after them, and fewer still contained orc men with the familiar large frames and hulking muscles of their kind.

Still, the lack of warriors was noticeable, and Athela felt a surge of satisfaction upon knowing that they'd helped quell the tribe's numbers and military might already. She was making quick time through the village and guessing at where the tribal leaders would be when she abruptly stopped at the sound of a call out from a nearby watchtower.

"Eh! Who's dat?! Show yaself!"

The watchtower was also made of wood, and it stood about four stories high with a long ladder going up to a boxy container the sentries could look out of. An orc archer was staring down at the dark alley she was in, and although she could tell he wasn't sure of what he'd seen, she'd definitely been spotted.

Before the orc could mutter another word, crimson threads ripped out of Athela's fingers and flew up toward the support beams of the tower. She didn't have sufficient control over the threads at that distance for a surefire hit, so instead she used them to yank and catapult herself from the ground all the way to where the orc's head was sticking out over the side.

A flash of black skin ripped silently through the air, blurring upward, and she tore the tusked man's head right off. Upon passing the tower and continuing up into the air with her momentum, she also saw another orc sitting with his back against one of the thin wooden walls of the tower's box.

Her arachnid limbs all turned in unison, locking on to her target with pinpoint accuracy, and now that she was close enough, she opened fire.

Threads solidified into needlelike red projectiles and broke off one by one, ripping out of the six limbs protruding from her back and lasering the startled orc in a barrage akin to that of a Gatling gun.

The attack was silent but brutally effective, skewering the sentry in over three dozen places and killing him instantly, leaving him looking like a bloody porcupine. Gracefully flipping her body midair, Athela then latched one of her threads onto the side of the box and casually swung around, landing on the edge of the tower's wall and stepping lightly onto the wooden floor without so much as a whisper of noise. Her long black tongue whipped out, licking blood off from the corpse she'd just created to savor the flavor, and she dropped the head she'd ripped off the other body with a thud onto the floor.

"By the hells, do I love this job!"

She sighed contentedly, turning and leaning over the tower's edge for a better view of the village. Wind whipped her dark hair all about her, giving her a majestic aura if anyone would have seen her, and with perfect posture she stood looking down at the greenskin settlement with a look of judging disdain. "Disgusting creatures. Truly, even among mortals they are vile to look upon."

Her eyes shifted, taking in a scene unsurprising to her considering what she knew of greenskin culture. Near the center of the village and a couple rows over from a large compound where she assumed the orc chieftain would reside, well-lit fighting pits had been constructed with various combinations of combatants in them. Most of them were animals and goblins, though a few orcs also participated in what was usually a one-sided fight.

Immediately adjacent to these busy, bustling pits were small crowds of orcs that cheered or booed and a butcher's market, also well lit. Greenskins did eat plant matter, but this group was apparently more carnivore than omnivore or herbivore. Things like this were likely the reason why elves and orcs back on Ethel's planet had such a long-standing blood feud and why the greenskins rarely if ever went to the negotiation table. The orcs saw elves, humans, and the like as mortal enemies, as physically weaker creatures and ones to be exploited. This place was a testament to that kind of mentality, with dozens of men and women—either elf or human—having already been butchered and put up for eating. Their bodies were often smoked and salted, alongside numerous bodies of wild boar or deer and other animals, with greenskins coming and going between the food stalls. That being said, there wasn't honestly that much food to go around for how many orcs there were, and the stalls selling food only gave out small portions. There were piles of bones where the aftermath of the feasting was collected, but Athela could still get a vaguely accurate number based on the heads.

Apparently orcs and goblins didn't eat the heads—the heads of humans and elves alike were piled on nearby wagons, mouths open in silent screams alongside those belonging to other types of animals. Whatever prisoners had once been here were now long dead, food to fuel the growing greenskin horde, and she hadn't seen any other captives on her way here despite her keen senses and vigilance in her mission.

She watched blank-faced while orc mothers encouraged their younglings in the smaller fighting pits, as little as even a couple years old, to kill one another for sport. She watched as the children obeyed, eagerly beating and hacking at one another until only one was left in what was probably a bloody childhood rite of passage. She saw pens where a couple dozen goblins were kept corralled in a thin layer of their own excrement, orc guards keeping them in line and occasionally throwing scraps of food over the walls for the goblins to feed on.

Athela's lips curled up in disgust. "They need to be purged. Even if it was a lowly elf who suggested it, that scout is right."

She hopped off the tower and landed on the ground without so much as a stirring of dust, her sharp arachnid legs taking the impact lightly and then lowering her humanoid feet to the ground before her spider limbs withdrew into her back.

Athela began to move with increased tempo, eager to find the chieftain and claim his head for her master. Her smile widened at the confidence he had in her to perform the job, and she wanted to make him proud. She'd gotten incredibly lucky to have such a spectacular summoner, and she would do whatever it took to keep her contract safe so she could remain in his service. Not only was he likely to be a powerful progenitor of this newly integrated planet, but he had an ancient vampiric bloodline. Both of those things would be immense boons and would translate into her own ascension with some variation or another and would present opportunities otherwise absolutely unattainable. Riven and his sister had no idea just what kind of luck they'd stumbled upon concerning their suppressed lineages, but Athela knew. She knew all too well the stories of that particular bloodline, what it meant, and what it labeled Riven and Allie as in the eyes of the vampiric empires in the multiverse. They were both a boon and a threat to the established and dominant vampiric factions, if they lived long enough, and Athela's primary goal beyond anything else was to make sure they got to see that future unfold.

Athela smiled, remembering when she first met Riven in that odd dimensional rift that'd been Chalgathi's starter trials. She'd just been minding her own business in the nether realms right before that, speaking to her sisters about how their grandfather was always too busy to give them the time of day while he conquered various sections of hell, when the system notified her of a summoner matching her specified qualifications. She'd excitedly accepted the system prompt and had watched, anxiety ridden, as Riven had gone through the potential lists of summons presenting themselves to him. When he'd picked her, she'd nearly done a backflip for obtaining her first-ever contract.

Or at least she would have done a backflip if she'd not been sucked right out of the nether realms with a final wave to her family and had been launched through the void into the pocket dimension to help Riven fight against that other mage and his undead dog.

The problem was that although the system had provided her with a contract meeting her specifications, the contract she'd been allowed to sign was open-ended. That meant that, unlike Azmoth, she hadn't been able to set her own ground rules before signing. At the time this had been outweighed by the very large sum of system money given to her by whoever this Chalgathi person had been, and she'd not known it to be an apocalypse beast back then—but even now that was irrelevant. She'd taken the money and had given it to her clan with her congratulations, as even demons could use Elysium coins for various and valuable perks, not realizing that the contract would be so important and so valuable. She'd not realized just how unique her master would be upon completing Chalgathi's starter dungeon in Negrada. None of her clan had known.

Nor had she realized just how much she'd grow to like Riven, either. She'd not cared much about him originally, though he'd been all right, but the day he'd gone out of his way to save her when she was still a Blood Weaver and hadn't evolved yet? That day in the cage when she was going to be fed to that monstrous lurker demon, destined to actually have her soul devoured because the system had temporarily nullified her contract? That was the day that she'd truly felt a bond form. It was the day she'd realized that, even though she was a spider with an overly sassy attitude, Riven still cared about her. He was a good man, and that was a rarity among both her own kind and the summoners that contracted with them. She wouldn't even consider herself an entity of good; rather she actually erred on the side of self-serving, thrill seeking, and even outright evil at times. She curbed those instincts to better serve him, though, because she owed him and knew that's what he wanted.

Usually when she wrote a contract, or what any of the demons in her clan would have done in most circumstances, she would add a series of clauses. These clauses were intended to give her more freedom, make sure that the contract wouldn't be broken unless she wanted it to be, would allow her to break the contract at will through a varied network of complex wording meant to confuse the summoner, and it would allow her to form a protective measure against any orders she really didn't want to obey. Just the standard stuff most demons tried to weasel their way into when contracting with mortals. She certainly had freedom now, but that was just because Riven allowed it. The open-ended contract she was bound to currently completely negated any free will she had if he wanted to pursue that route. If he wanted her to perform jumping jacks, he could tell her to do it and she'd have to obey as long as his command was given with meaning and not said while joking around. If he truly wanted her to run five miles every day on her hands, do a backflip, and then give him back rubs while burping the ABCs, he could literally force her to do it.

The usual protections of complex wording in her clan's contracts regarding her ability to negate or keep the contract also would have allowed her a measure of power over whatever summoner she'd been contracted to, forcing the summoner to keep her if she wanted it and nullifying the contract if she wasn't pleased. The open-ended contract Chalgathi had paid her a significant amount of cash to sign was quite the opposite of all that, though, with almost all the power in Riven's court. It meant that if he grew displeased with her actions, he could immediately snap his fingers and *poof*—she'd be gone, opening up a contract slot for him to find another minion to fill. With all the other demons in the nether realms awaiting potential masters, especially one of Riven's extreme potential, he would soon become a fan favorite of the nether realms. Demons awaiting new masters would no doubt take note of him soon, and he'd have no end to the applications he'd receive. If that were to happen, he might even end up acquiring a servant of amazing quality far beyond even her own ability. Her own clan was moderately sized, but it was nowhere near the top of the food chain in terms of demonic power, and she had no doubt that if she failed to retain her contract with him, one of the powerhouse clans of the outer realms would swoop in with an offering of one of their own younglings.

The case in point was Fay. That Succubus belonged to a very odd but very powerful demonic house, one that explained her unique upbringing and kindness. How they'd known of Riven even during the Chalgathi trial, though . . . that was still a mystery to Athela. They'd made Fay wait it out and apply again, despite other contract opportunities presented to her, and the Succubus had been delighted to sign her successful contract not long after.

But allowing herself to be replaced was not going to happen—Athela couldn't allow it to happen. Failure was doubly not an option after all the resources poured into Athela's new body and performance. She had a real opportunity to elevate herself and her clan, so messing it up would bring dire consequences. But she was in good standing with Riven right now, her own contract wasn't threatened, and their blooming friendship was only growing stronger—so thankfully she felt rather secure in her position.

Her thoughts regarding such matters came to an end as she came closer to the large central building of the village. It was poorly put together—circular, with two stories and a domed rooftop, all made of wood. There was a chimney made of clay billowing smoke in the very center of the domed roof, and a flag with a tusked skull flapped softly in the wind over the entrance. Two orc meatheads wielding spears and wearing metal cap helmets stood at the large double doors in front, looking bored and even beginning to doze off. One of them had an empty brown bottle of booze off to the side near his feet, probably from raiding nearby areas or having taken it from their old world via the integration.

Easy pickings.

RIP-SNAP

She activated her newest martial art, Flurry. Her claws and legs drastically increased speed and turned into a silent whirlwind of strikes, tearing through the two orcs in over two dozen places within a single second. Blood splattered across the wall, and their mangled corpses fell over, but she caught them so they wouldn't make any noise. The bodies gushed blood from their numerous lacerations, and she quietly dragged them over to a dark recess along a nearby wall to make sure it wasn't obvious she'd been there.

She gently tried the door.

It was locked.

Her eyes drifted up toward a gap in the roof, where the ones who'd built the building had left a hole small enough for someone like her to barely slide through, and her smile widened. Her fingers turned into claws again, and she passed the door like a shadow, noiselessly scaling the building at rapid speed. One of the perks she liked most about her new body was that it had an almost absolute sound-dampening effect when stimulated, as it made moving about for assassination purposes all the easier.

She poked her head inside, seeing a long hallway filled with various contraptions, chests, weapons, armor, and other items. They were no doubt the product of raiding the surrounding area to take whatever the local neighbors had after killing and eating them, because many of the items were far more intricate and delicate than what Athela would expect barbarian orc artisans to craft. Greenstalk village was probably just the most recent victim of these creatures, but it certainly wasn't the first.

Her bare feet landed on the second-story wooden floor, and she slid through the dark corridor, checking each room. Some of them were storage units filled with boxes and barrels, others trophy rooms with stuffed animal heads and liquor cabinets. There were also a few bedrooms, but every single one of them was empty.

This was a little odd. The chieftain could be downstairs . . . Maybe he was at the fighting pits watching the scuffles. But wouldn't there at least be more guards inside?

Finally she came to the largest door on this floor. It was thicker than the others, had a large iron handle, and was positioned right in front of the stairway leading up from the first floor. She glanced downstairs, noting it was dark down there as well, and observing no sign of life.

Curious.

She turned back to the larger door more warily when she heard the crackling of fire coming from the other side. There were no other ways in, thus she stepped back and attached a small string to the thick iron handle, then she backed even farther out of sight. Pulling on it, she realized it was a lot heavier than she'd originally thought. She had to yank just a little bit harder, but the door began to budge and creak ominously. Firelight poured into the dark hallway, but from her current position she could only see the left-hand side of the room—which was completely barren.

Then a deep, booming voice called out to her from inside, beckoning her to make herself known. "Come in, demon . . . I have felt your presence since you stepped foot in my village. I have been waiting for you, as we have much to talk about."

Athela only hesitated for a moment, somewhat surprised that she'd been found out, then carefully proceeded forward.

In front of her was a throne of furs and skulls, with a yellow linen tapestry of a tusked orc skull hanging in the background. Sitting on the large chair in front of a stone fire pit built into the floor was a large, hunched-over orc wearing a wooden mask painted yellow and blue. Probably the chieftain by the look of his shirtless, heavily tattooed chest—tattoos often identified orcs in positions of power—and he wore a number of feathered items that made him look like a peacock. He had burnt orange feather pauldrons and feathered bracelets and anklets to boot. Feathers adorned the mask along the top and sides, with leather straps keeping it securely fastened to the orc's head—and he held a long, wooden staff carved into the shape of a cobra's head. Two emeralds adorned the staff for the cobra's eyes, and a single green sigil that looked like some kind of hieroglyph was glowing brightly in front of the wooden cobra's flared hood.

He also wore many rings, some of them intricate gold and platinum, while others were plainer and had a sickly aura about them that Athela could even feel from here. A mixture of Forest and Swamp mana, if she had to guess. Beside him and on either side of the throne stood two heavily outfitted orc warriors, each as big as the chieftain himself. One carried a large claymore almost the size of a man and was decked out in heavy iron plate armor, having a large swath of horsehair creating a frill along a barbute-style helmet. The other one was adorned in thick studded leather and carried a large, basic war hammer with a round shield; he was absolutely bald and wore golden hoop earrings in his green ears.

Athela confirmed that there were no traps within the immediate vicinity of the doorway and stepped through, smiling venomously with sharpened teeth across the fire pit between them and letting her hands fall out to either side of her with palms facing outward. "Ah . . . So here you are at last . . . Tell me, how did you know I was here? I thought I was being rather elusive. The sentries outside never even saw me coming . . ."

The orc with the claymore let out a rumbling growl and took an aggressive step forward, but the chieftain stopped him with his cobra-shaped staff as it slammed against the other orc's metal breastplate with a clang.

The chieftain then laughed and leaned forward to get a better look at her. "And why would I tell you how I knew? You're a treacherous little snake, aren't you? Yes, I have heard about the Arshakai from that elfling village near the base of the mountains. You, the brutalisk, the Succubus, and that vampire master of yours. After our failed raid on the elf camp, we lost many of our seasoned warriors . . . but the few who managed to escape reported what they'd seen."

The chieftain settled back into his chair and stared at the wickedly smiling demoness, curiously tapping a finger along the armrest of his throne. "Tell me. Why would a vampire help high elves? Surely you cannot trust them—they would sooner kill a vampire than an orc."

Athela pondered whether to engage the chieftain further. It couldn't really hurt; her cover had been blown already. But just in case she failed to kill him now that she lacked the element of surprise, she decided to play Riven up in the minds of the greenskins here so they'd think twice about a countermove should the time come.

"Help them?" Athela let out a charming, ladylike laugh and let her right hand dangle as she raised that wrist over her mouth and fluttered her eyes seductively. "Oh, no . . . They're merely food for the coven! They don't know it yet, but they will submit eventually . . . You see, your warriors were trespassing on our claimed lands. The elves are ours to feed on; they belong to my master, not to you . . ."

At the word *coven*, the chieftain's eyes narrowed, and the warrior with the war hammer stiffened. Vampires had a very bad reputation even among the most hardened of warriors. They could regenerate extremely fast, they could see in the dark, turning night battles heavily in their favor, they had more speed and strength than most of the mortal races did on average, and all this made them very hard to kill. Usually vampires were territorial by nature, especially if other vampires encroached on their feeding grounds. This meant they tended to be solo hunters, so if there was a group of vampires instead of just one to deal with . . . it complicated things for the orcs in a very big way.

Athela could immediately recognize the realization of their situation in the chieftain's eyes, and her already big grin spread literally from ear to ear in a sickening display. The usually brilliant, humanlike white smile was gone, and instead was the look of a casual predator eyeing its next meal with a tinge of amusement.

The chieftain stopped tapping his finger and stood to his full height, anger apparent in his voice, but he kept it contained while gripping his wooden staff. "I wish to bargain with your master."

Athela blinked, and her smile began to fade as irritation welled up inside her. Her mission had originally been to kill the chieftain and scout out the orc village, but he was already wanting to negotiate the orcs leaving this land instead of Athela and the others brutally killing everything there. If she gave up this opportunity for an easy victory, she would never hear the end of it.

With a loud sigh and an obvious frown, she folded her arms and sneered across the fireplace while leaning against the door frame. "Unfortunately, I was told that negotiations are on the table . . . so if you have a deal that I think my master can agree to, I will hear you out. I suggest you not waste my time and spit it out, filthy creature, for I have better things to do than gawk at your unsightly features or smell the piss that lingers in the air here."

The chieftain growled angrily but reined in his temper despite her insults and nodded just once. "Very well. Let us discuss terms."

CHAPTER 51

The story Athela told had put a significant damper on the mood, and Riven was unsure of what to think regarding the orcs and their situation. On one hand, they'd killed and eaten many humans and elves in the area—they'd admitted raiding surrounding towns or villages that'd popped up after the integration. On the other hand, the orcs had claimed that they weren't entirely at fault here—but he was about to try and find that out.

The orc chieftain stood in front of his village gates with a dozen muscular orc warriors behind him, including the two elites of his village that had been in the room with Athela upon her initial talk. There were also thirty or so dagger-wielding goblins picking their noses, cackling to one another, or grumbling about being out this late. Orc women, elderly, and children stood up on the palisade platforms that'd been erected at intervals on the opposite side, some of them nervously holding bows while others simply stared.

On the opposite side and coming in from the darkness was Riven, and he was accompanied by their elf scout, Ren. His three demons and Dr. Brass were all there, too, standing on the perimeter just where the torchlight from the village walls was barely able to reach. It was enough to give the orcs the impression that there were indeed others out there, and that there might also be more farther back.

While Riven walked side by side with Ren, the orc chieftain and his two elites came out to meet them halfway between the two groups. Ren was obviously nervous, by the way Riven could hear his heart rate pick up, but that in turn was matched by many of the greenskins across from where Riven stopped fifty yards from the walls. It was a very, very tense situation—and the orc leaders stopped about ten paces away to keep a healthy distance while being close enough to comfortably talk.

"I've heard there are more of you," the chieftain said after surveying the others at the edge of the firelight—nodding to Athela in particular where her red eyes were easier to make out than the others. "For your sake, I hope your familiar wasn't lying."

The two elites beside the chieftain looked uncomfortable but tried to not let it show. However, their heartbeats escalated and betrayed their true emotions on the situation, even if they looked rather intimidating and fearsome up close.

Riven planted his staff into the ground, allowing Vampire's Escort to stand off its own power. Then he cocked his head to the side, evaluating each of the larger green men in front of him, and stuffed his hands into the pockets of his cloak. "Athela said you wanted to talk."

"To talk with you, bloodsucker," the orc with the hoop earrings and the war hammer snarled, growling at the silver-haired elf beside Riven. "Not with the pointy ears. They have done us nothing but harm for centuries when we wanted to only live in peace. They drive us from our lands, hunt our kind to the ends of the earth, and then act like it is they who are persecuted. Why is the elfling here?"

Ren flushed angrily at the accusation and his jaw clenched; he was visibly shaking and couldn't utter a response. It'd taken all his bravery just to come out here, let alone speak to the orcs.

"I see." Riven glanced at Ren, then turned his gaze back to the orc who'd addressed him. "That, specifically, is why I'm even standing here talking to you. You claim that you were attacked first and only responded in kind?"

The snarling orc hesitated, then nodded as the other two orcs joined him in unison.

"What about the humans Athela saw? Their heads decorate your feast at the fighting pits. Do they not?"

The orc chief coughed out a laugh from underneath his wooden tribal mask and nodded while planting his own cobra staff into the ground beside him. "They do. Our people are a warfaring people—I openly admit it. However we are not the cold-blooded killers you seem to believe us to be . . . We merely defend ourselves and actively attack those who have done us harm first. Which brings me to the same question that my comrade brought up—if you're not in league with the elves and merely using them for food, why is one of them guiding you to us?"

"Does it matter?" Riven shrugged casually, indifference written on his face as he removed the runic mask covering his nose and mouth. A toothy smile displayed his fangs, and he pocketed the mask. "Truth be told, I will be feeding on some of them, but they chose to do so willingly, for my help. What's your name, by the way? If we are going to be speaking, I'd rather not just think of you as 'meat.'"

The chieftain snorted with amusement and removed his own mask, revealing a bald man with a heavily scarred face; it looked like some kind of clawed creature had scratched him repeatedly. Whatever had attacked the orc had even taken off a portion of the tusked green man's upper lip in the process—giving Riven the impression that the chieftain was always snarling.

"So the elves pay for their protection with blood of their own. I suppose it does make sense. My name is Gurth'Rok, chieftain of the Yellow Skull Tribe. Who are you, vampire?"

"Riven. My name is Riven Thane, and I'd say it's a pleasure to meet you, but these are rather dire circumstances, and I'm not sure if we're all going to come out of this meeting alive."

"Truer words have never been spoken," Chieftain Gurth'Rok replied with a grimace. "What do you want from us? We have suffered many casualties already and only wish to be left alone."

"Well, that is all very good, but you actively attacked a village under my protection. I can't have you randomly slaughtering people in our claimed lands. And I'm not just talking about the elves in Greenstalk village." Riven continued to play the card Athela had already cast concerning the coven's feeding grounds, and in some ways, he wasn't lying. Allie's forces were less than a week away, though they weren't really a coven.

"Do you wish us to lie down and die then? Because that is what you are asking us to do. To have us lie down and die when the enemies come charging at our gates. We have only ever defended ourselves; never have we been the aggressors since arriving here in this newly merged world." The chieftain angrily snarled in frustration and waved a hand in front of his face as if to gesture to the surrounding lands. "There are too many enemies and too few allies for us to so blatantly go raiding. Yes, we have killed many of the humans here that sought to kill us first. We burned their homes, butchered them, and used them for food. My people are starving, and though we usually don't feed on humans and elves so frequently, I will not have my people suffer hunger if we have the bodies of our enemies to feast upon. The attacks on our people came first, and we responded in force each time. We have lost the great majority of our warriors, once numbering at eight hundred orcs and over a thousand goblin servants. We have been reduced to what you see here now after the many dozens of small battles across the frontier. Surely as a vampire you can empathize with us for the persecution you've endured yourself! Your kind is hated even more than my own by the races that call themselves enlightened, so it should not be a surprise to you that the elves of your claimed village struck at us first."

Riven considered the orc's words and slowly turned his gaze to the elf beside him. "What do you have to say about that, Ren?"

Ren's mild shaking had stopped; he'd calmed his nerves despite being in such close proximity to creatures he and his people had warred against for countless generations. He stared up at the larger chieftain for a good amount of time but eventually grimaced and nodded. "We struck first, it is true."

"The elf does not see fit to lie! That is a welcome surprise!" The armored orc laughed, and even the chieftain seemed a bit taken aback by the admission of guilt.

"We saw them searching the forest for food and panicked," Ren stated solemnly, casting a glance at the muscular orc in the iron plate. "It was weeks ago. They've been at war with us for so long now that it's usually shoot on sight and forego questions. We've tried negotiating with greenskins before, and it always ends in failure and our throats slit, so of course we attacked first."

"The same could be said on our end," Chieftain Gurth'Rok growled, but his appraising look at the elf did not exhibit hostility. "Though I want to thank you for your honesty, elfling. Perhaps if your people had tried speaking to us first before slaughtering our hunters this could have all been resolved. Are we not all strangers to this new world? These lands are alien, a tapestry redrawn in the eyes of the system, and we know not what awaits us beyond the plains. I had hoped to gain allies in my first days upon coming here so that we may trade and flourish as we did in the badlands of our ancestral home, but this . . ."

Gurth'Rok gestured back toward their village. "It has been nothing but death and misery for all of us. The fighting pits your demon saw, vampire? That is a way to quell our numbers so the rest of us do not starve. It may have looked like a feast to you, but not in the past twenty years have we resorted to eating enlightened races until now. We are completely out of food and have nothing else, and we do not know how we will get more, because we are constantly harassed by scouting parties sent from your elf village. Most of our hunters never return, and the woodlands were our best shot at finding more to eat. We had to act by striking at the elf village the same way we did with the humans who previously tried their hand. Yet here we are, reduced to almost nothing, with many of our best warriors slaughtered in our attempt to save ourselves."

Riven didn't know what to think about all this new information. At first he hadn't necessarily believed what he'd heard from Athela, but upon Ren's admission, he could only stare blankly at the ground in front of his feet. He felt guilty—guilty for slaughtering dozens of these orcs and goblins with his minions when they'd merely been trying to survive. He knew that if he hadn't acted the elves would certainly have died, but it seemed to him that they'd merely assumed the orcs were a threat and acted without trying to resolve things peacefully. It'd blown up in their faces in a big way, and they'd almost been completely wiped out for it.

"Do you believe us now?" Gurth'Rok asked with a tinge of hope in his voice. "I am no coward, and I am not afraid to die in battle. I even believe I have a chance to win if a battle does occur, but perhaps that is my pride speaking. Regardless, I do fear what would happen to my people if they don't have me to lead them. Surely even as a vampire you must have some empathy, as you otherwise wouldn't be speaking about who started the conflict to begin with. Do you see the women and children standing out there, watching us talk? All the old men who can no longer fight and rely on me for support?"

The chieftain raised his staff and pointed toward the wall, toward the hundreds of noncombatant orc villagers who fearfully watched the proceedings at a distance. He turned back to Riven with a wary shake of his head. "They will not live through the next winter if I pass. It is very likely that they will all be killed here and now if these negotiations fall through, and they know it."

Riven shook his head and drew his hands out of his pockets to fold his arms across his chest. "No . . . No, I wouldn't do that. I had no intention of killing the women and children."

Gurth'Rok's eyebrows raised in surprise. "Truly?"

"Truly. I only came here to eliminate the threat to Greenstalk. That meant either killing anyone who could pose a threat or driving you from these lands. It didn't mean slaughtering kids."

Gurth'Rok's mouth opened slightly in astonishment, taking Riven's words at face value. "You are not a normal vampire. Are you?"

"Excuse me?"

"Your eyes." Gurth'Rok motioned to Riven's glowing red pupils. "They are brighter than most vampires I have seen in the past. You are different. Are you a different breed of vampire? Are there different breeds?"

". . . No, I don't think there are different breeds."

"I see. Well, you certainly act differently. I was surprised your familiar even allowed negotiations at all. It'd been a slim hope at best, but when you began questioning us on who began the conflict to begin with, I became thoroughly convinced that you are unusual. Most of your kind would not care about who started the fight, they would not care about orc children, and they would not care enough to lie about why they chose to help a group of weak and relatively defenseless elves."

The chieftain smiled, and Riven had to laugh at the outright accusation.

"Fine," Riven stated with a grin. "It wasn't necessarily a lie—I really am going to feed on one of the elves, who has agreed to it, but you're mostly right. I helped because I thought it was the right thing to do."

The orc with the hoop earrings and the war hammer immediately gawked, and the other warrior in iron plate guffawed loudly and turned with his hands on his head.

"Never did I think I'd see the day," the heavily armored warrior said as he turned to walk away. "Now that negotiations seem to be improving, I'm going to go grab a drink. I think I'll need it. You okay with that, Chief?"

Gurth'Rok let out a laugh and waved his companion away, turning back to Riven with a slight but reserved smile. "So . . . a vampire with morals. That's a new one. Where do we go from here? If you wish us to leave these lands, we will do so. I do not wish to lose any more of my people. However, if you let us stay and allow us to hunt for meat in the forest and grow our crops in peace, I can promise you that we will put this conflict behind us. We have come prepared with tribute to help sway your mind on this matter, and if it settles the conflict between our people and the village of elves farther to the northwest, I will prepare a gift for them, too."

The orc with the war hammer stepped forward, producing a scroll from a pouch at his side. He handed it to Riven and stepped back, allowing Riven to unfurl it and get a better look at the document.

"It already has identification information attached to it by one of our village identifiers," Chieftain Gurth'Rok said slowly, hope riding along his words. "It may not be worth much to you because you're affiliated with the Unholy pillar, but it is still a valuable gift and was handcrafted by one of our elderly shamans. You may exchange or sell it to someone else who can use it for a great deal of money—of that I have no doubt."

[Spell Scroll: Nature's Winds (Forest) (Tier 2)—Select a target and deliver a small dose of healing potential in the form of a soft forest breeze, sealing the target's wounds and restoring HP. This spell also imbues an aftereffect of residual healing over time if the spell has leftover energy and thus can be used as a buff prior to battle. This spell can be stacked up to five times, with each additional stack beyond the first giving a minor boost to running speed. This spell does not rid targets of disease or debuffs. Very long range, short cooldown, short casting time, low mana cost.]

Riven's eyes took in the sight before him. On the actual parchment, what wasn't identification information was written in a language that he couldn't read, but the markings were nevertheless meticulously crafted and beautiful to look at. The system message was more than enough to tell him what he needed to know about it, too, so he didn't have any doubts about what it really was.

Meanwhile, the chieftain eyed Riven's expression uncertainly, trying to read whether the gift was enough to appease the vampire. "The shaman who created this scroll took nearly two years to do it, but he is very skilled and was actually the master who taught me my own trade. Most people take years to learn this kind of advanced magic, but with this scroll a person may learn it within a day as long as they have a high enough affinity."

The chieftain's worries were quenched when Riven put on a bright smile.

"I think this is more than enough," Riven stated while pocketing the scroll and turning to Ren. "If the orcs stay, are your people in Greenstalk willing to listen to me when I tell them to leave the orcs alone?"

Ren hesitated, shot the chieftain an uncertain look, then slowly shook his head. "No . . . I do not believe so. That was not part of our deal, Riven. Ethel will not be handed to you as a thrall unless you force them to leave these lands. We will not be safe until they are gone. That is not negotiable, as heard from the mouth of Elder Bren himself."

Riven's eyes narrowed slightly, and his grip around the scroll tightened. "Without me, none of you would even be alive right now."

Ren gave him an apologetic shrug. "It is not my order, I am sorry. A deal is a deal."

The two men stared at one another, and the orc chieftain curiously evaluated the brief exchange with a grimace. "I find it odd that they would not be accommodating to the one that saved all their lives, and even more so that they demand things of someone stronger. Riven, are you sure that you trust these people?"

Riven broke off his glare toward Ren with a sideways glance at the chieftain. "Yes. Why?"

"Because although you may be different, these elves are likely not." The large orc gestured to Ren, who scowled fiercely back at the orc but remained tight-lipped on the subject. "This elfling and his people are probably like all the others—they are likely using you to their own ends."

Ren let out a snort of derision, but that was the only reply the chieftain got.

There was a long, awkward silence after that, and then Riven's thoughts drifted back to Ethel and her family. To Len and Genua, whom he hadn't known very long but had developed a keen liking for. He shook his head and gripped the staff to his left. "I trust them, and I made them a promise. Take your people, orc, and leave these lands. I will not kill you, but I will not permit you to stay here, either."

Ren nodded. "Good."

Gurth'Rok remained silent for a time, scrutinizing the elf with a deep frown, but in time he nodded, too, and gave a gracious bow. "Very well. I will do as you ask, Riven Thane. I appreciate your mercy and the chance to leave this place without bloodshed. We will find somewhere else to live so that these elf friends of yours may find peace. My people will understand and thank you for what you have agreed to this day, for the freedom of passage you have granted us. Perhaps one day we will meet again as friends rather than as opponents."

With a conflicted smile, Riven held out a hand to shake. "Good luck with your rebuilding, and I wish you the best."

"And I wish the same to you. It was nice meeting you, Riven Thane. More than you know. May the gods watch over the path you tread on, and may the winds ever be in your favor."

Back in Greenstalk village, Farrod closed the door to Elder Preen's home with a click. Turning, he saw the old man sitting at his dining room table, sipping on tea and going over plans with Elder Bren on what would happen should Riven come back successful—or should he die instead.

"A brilliant plan. Either way, we win out," Farrod stated simply, nodding to Elder Preen, who smiled savagely while his first wife fetched a pot of hot water. "Are they coming now?"

"They are," Elder Preen stated matter-of-factly. "They'll be here soon. Given recent events, I'd say they're rather excited to exact justice. Has Riven caught on at all yet? Any inkling of an idea?"

Farrod shrugged.

"Surely you've checked on things?" Elder Preen gave the other man a skeptical, down-the-nose look.

Genua's husband rolled his eyes and shook his head. "Not much, you old fool. We have to keep up appearances, remember? Rather intricate but appropriate for the situation. This entire thing feels disgusting to me . . . I just want it to be over with so we can go back to our normal lives."

Elder Bren gave the middle-aged man a scolding look. "You know we have to do this to keep the village safe, Farrod. We don't have much of a choice, given our current circumstances. I'm sorry it was you that had to take the fall, but what's done is done. There is no turning back now."

CHAPTER 52

Riven's journey back was a quiet one while he contemplated the things Gurth'Rok the orc had said. Pondering the chieftain's words and feeling not just a little bit guilty about slaughtering so many of them to defend the elvish village, he wondered what the morally right choice would have been.

But he did not dwell on it for long. In this world, he could only do what he thought was right at the time. Thinking about how he *could* have done something differently would not change the past, and to mope on it would be nothing but pathetic.

So he chalked it up to a learning experience and would try not to make the mistake of assumptions again. He knew sometimes it couldn't be helped, but that was life, and he'd just do his best.

Firelight flickered and crackled where Ren had dug a small pit in the dirt. Azmoth had helped light the fire, while Fay and Athela had set up a defensive perimeter using webs and Unholy detonation traps.

"You're staring again," Riven stated flatly, gazing into the fire without looking up. "Is there something I can help you with? Anything you want to talk about? You seem nervous."

Ren was fidgeting with a knife and had been giving Riven side-eyes whenever he thought the vampire wasn't looking. Riven could also hear his heartbeat racing every time the elf talked about getting back to the village, and the man almost looked sick by the way he was occasionally caught sweating even at night.

Ren coughed, covering his mouth with one arm, and sank his knife into the dirt beside him. He pushed his legs out in front, closer to the fire, and shook his head. "Sorry, it's just odd traveling with a vampire, is all. Very strange—I never thought I'd be in a position like this."

Riven tucked the black communication bauble he'd been speaking to Allie with into a pocket of his robe, then took in a deep breath of fresh mountain air. "It's nice out here. Isn't it?"

Dr. Brass nodded wordlessly and adjusted his glasses, a content smile on his face. "It's peaceful."

Ren looked around, eyeing Azmoth while the brutalisk sat cross-legged and flipping his tail back and forth from side to side. "Um . . . yes, it's rather peaceful."

Riven smiled slowly and sadly. "Yes. Yes, it is. I wish it could always be this way."

The fire crackled and writhed, eating away at the wood while none of the men said a single word. Farther into the forest underneath the dark canopy of trees, the sounds of Fay and Athela chatting and bathing in a stream could be heard, too, in conjunction with occasional crickets or owls hooting under a starry night.

The silence was eventually interrupted minutes later when Riven cleared his throat and addressed the elf again. "So what has Ethel said about me recently? I'm a little nervous, making her my thrall. I don't want her to think I'm taking advantage of her."

Ren was happy to start up a new topic of conversation. "Oh! She and my daughter Senna both say great things about you."

"But what, exactly?" Riven pressed with a polite smile, arms folded and legs crossed with his back to a log.

Dr. Brass was curious, too, and he sat up a little straighter to listen in.

Ren scratched his head, then looked thoughtfully up to the stars in the sky. "Hmm. Well, they talked a lot about your battle prowess. How you were nice enough to help them when you could have let the goblins eat them. Ethel is a bit nervous to become your thrall, but she's also excited, or at least that's what she told me."

"Has she told you anything about Brightsville?" Riven asked, getting a frown of confusion from the other man.

"Is that the city where your sister is? The other vampire?"

"Yes, that's the one!" Riven gave a big, toothy smile. "I talked a lot about Allie. I hope she and Ethel will become good friends over time. I think they'll like one another."

Ren perked up at that. "Ah, yes! Ethel told us stories about her. She has another coven or something like that in a tower there, right?"

"Right. She's setting up an undead faction there—it's not really a coven per se, but it's full of other ghouls, skresh, some bone and blood golems, that kind of thing. I saw a couple other types of lesser, mindless minions, but those were mostly skeletons or zombies."

Riven hesitantly glanced to Ren from the corner of his eye and saw the man visibly trying not to react.

"Oh . . ." Ren stated, seemingly surprised. "A necropolis, then. It'll be good to have such strong allies nearby now that the world has turned upside down."

"Definitely. We'd be more than happy to help you out and protect the village—Allie has already said she would send a group down here to clear out any local monsters. But only if that's what you want."

Riven shot the man another quick glance and found Ren's expression was conflicted.

"I . . . We would appreciate that," Ren said with a nervous smile, scratching the back of his neck.

"Of course, that can only happen when the war with Prophet is over," Riven stated with a yawn. "Ah, excuse me. I'm rather tired. Did Ethel ever mention the war? I don't know too much about it, but apparently my sister is planning something big."

He let the comment hang there, still staring at the flames, while Ren contemplated his words.

Eventually, after much fidgeting with his knife, Ren glanced up. "So what's the big move? Ethel told me something of the war, but not a lot."

"Oh? What did she tell you? That way I can fill you in on the rest without wasting too much time." Riven grinned and motioned to where Athela and Fay were laughing loudly. "You know how girls are with their gossip. She probably told you most of the big details, but I just want to make sure I'm not glazing over unimportant stuff."

"Uh . . . Just the basics," Ren stated with a shrug. "Your sister has a tower, Prophet and her are fighting, those kind of details."

"Did she mention the recent battle?" Riven raised an eyebrow.

Ren slowly nodded. "Yes . . . Your sister routed Prophet and sent him to the north. Is that right?"

"Right."

"Well, that's about all I know. So what's this about a new plan your sister has? I'm curious." Ren held out his hands helplessly to either side. "I don't get out of the village much."

To this, Riven let on a low chuckle and nodded in understanding. He uncrossed and recrossed his legs, then snorted. "Hmm. Where to start?"

Riven intentionally set a slow pace, wanting to enjoy the scenic view of the mountains and wildlife around him. Ren went on ahead to talk to the village; a scouting party of elves had already gone on to inform the village of their impending and victorious arrival, and Riven sent Dr. Brass away with Athela and Fay to level the man up. The old man was determined to join Riven in the ranks as a vampire himself, mostly due to the fact that his old age would soon be the end of him, and Riven respected it. He wouldn't want to die of old age, either, and the vampiric curse was more of a blessing than anything else for Dr. Brass because of that.

A shrill wind, far colder than most days provided, rustled the treetops under a cloudy gray sky as Riven's boots crunched leaves underfoot. The beginnings of autumn were upon them, and speckles of orange and yellow dotted the oak trees in patches across the countryside. Taking a position on a hill, Riven couldn't help but wonder just how long he'd have gone missing out on this kind of hiking lifestyle if the system had never set in.

He'd spent far longer indoors than he'd realized back then, in his old life.

Unholy mana drifted on the currents around him, settling into the surroundings with only a light touch so that animals or people wouldn't be disturbed by it. His aura was a palpable thing now, and on command he could retract or press on the environment around him, influencing the shifting tides of power in ways that he'd never have guessed at prior to his revelations in the hospital basement.

"There." Azmoth pointed down the hill with a wicked black claw. His body flickered with cinder, and his rows of black teeth grinned in excitement. "We back to the elf home!"

Beyond the hill and across a flatter area of land at the base of the mountain was Greenstalk village.

"Indeed we are . . ." Riven muttered absentmindedly, gesturing for Azmoth to lead the way. "After you, my friend."

Azmoth carried four large barrels, one for each arm, each one a gift from the orcs and a tribute to the elvish people as a peace offering. They contained odds and ends, and an observer could see textiles, weapons, cutlery, and foodstuffs poking out of the tops. The large brutalisk proudly stomped down the hill just ahead of the smaller, cloaked man but kept the overall pace. The village was stirring, many of them already congregating on the periphery where a long stretch of flat ground devoid of many trees opened up within the forest. Many of the remnant elf warriors were present, along with Elder Bren, Elder Preen, Ethel, and Ethel's entire family with the exception of Len. Even Farrod and Senna were there.

The masked vampire, eyes glowing red underneath a hooded cloak, waved overhead to the happy group of men and women awaiting his arrival. As he got closer, he and Azmoth were greeted with shouts of celebration from the village periphery.

Azmoth trudged on, placing the barrels at the feet of Elder Bren with a proud humph. Each of the four large barrels caused the earth to shake slightly under its weight, and the elves gawked wide-eyed at the treasures.

"For you, from orcs," Azmoth stated with a grin, folding his four arms over his chest before scratching his neck with an extra maw—only to reel in the maw into his back again. "They peace offering."

"I see that!" Elder Preen cooed, stepping forward past the demon and running a hand over some of the textiles. "This is quality work. How did the orcs have such things with them? Had they raided these from other settlements?"

Riven halted a dozen feet away, hands in his pockets while he evaluated the crowd. "Yeah. That's what they said, anyways."

The vampire glanced over at the scouting party that had informed the village of his impending arrival, all of them along the sideline where the trees of the forest started growing thicker. They all gave him nods of appreciation, and he nodded back with a wave. "Did they tell you about the peace deal I brokered?"

"The orcs are leaving these lands, is what they told us," Elder Bren said stiffly, rubbing his chin and holding a beautiful gold and ruby necklace up before glancing over at Ethel. "For you, dear? It is your future master that did this for us."

The young woman blushed and shot Riven a look. "Well, would you mind, Riven?"

She couldn't see his facial expression underneath the mask he wore, but he nodded, and the elf smiled wide. "Thank you so much!"

She took the necklace from Elder Bren and placed it around her neck, her mother coming over to take a look.

"This is so nice! Very good job, Riven!" Genua laughed along with the merriment of the others, then shot Riven a wink and then turned back to the village. "Oh, I almost forgot! Len and I are supposed to pick mushrooms today. I'll meet up with all of you later!"

Ethel's mother waved over her shoulder and disappeared through the crowd.

Motioning for some of the younger warriors to take the barrels of goods, Elder Bren waved at Riven to come forward. "Come, lad! Let me have a look at you!"

People quickly started making room for Riven and the elder to speak with one another, and a large space where the elder stood became devoid of anyone else except for Riven, Azmoth, and the old man.

"Come on, don't be shy!" Elder Bren laughed while urging Riven to step up to him—opening up his arms in an embrace. He then gave Riven a confused scowl when the vampire continued to look around, shaking his head back and forth, before Elder Bren lowered his arms again. "Are you all right?"

Riven stared at the ground in front of him, right next to where Azmoth and the elder now stood. "Um . . . No. Not really."

There was a sudden silence, and an awkward pause between Riven and the group of elves.

"Do you wish to speak to me about something?" Elder Bren asked curiously, hunching even more than usual and grasping an amulet around his neck with furrowed brows. "Speak, boy! This is your victory celebration! Look there, Ethel is waiting for you!"

The pretty elf waved nervously from the sidelines and bobbed her head for Riven to continue toward the village leader. Riven stared back, then looked to the ground in front of Elder Bren's feet again while blinking rapidly.

Eventually Riven stepped forward, one foot in front of the other, until he came within just a few feet of the old man. Azmoth was to his left, and the old man's smile widened.

"Good . . . Good man." Elder Bren kept a hand on the amulet around his neck, and he patted Riven on the shoulder reassuringly while the vampire continued to get glares from Elder Preen not far off. "What's wrong? You seem . . . off. You should be happy! I mean, just look at all the goods you've brought us! This is a day for celebration and nothing less."

Riven noted the barrels in the crowd of elves behind where they stood, then slowly nodded just once. He cleared his throat and pulled the hood down slightly over his red eyes. When he spoke, his voice shook slightly. "Please. Please, don't do this."

There was a dead silence. Everyone immediately shut up, and Elder Bren's eyes widened.

In a flash of light, the old man ripped off his amulet and flung it on the ground, causing the earth around them to explode into hundreds of thick vines that whipped out of the ground. Thorns dug into Azmoth and Riven alike, pulling them tightly down as Azmoth roared, and predrawn runes of finely ground powder lit up a vibrant green and white for over a dozen yards around them—with Riven at its center.

But Riven remained stoic.

"Fire!"

CHAPTER 53

Harpoons launched from the trees, imbued with blinding white light of holy origins that slammed into the two being held down. Riven's body was easily pierced completely through, rupturing internal organs and sending his innards out the other side. Azmoth's own huge frame took even more of the harpoons, with over a dozen of them cratering into his solid body and five of them bouncing off. Over half of them sank in deep, though, either tearing off pieces of his armor or finding weak spots where the brutalisk was more vulnerable.

The huge demon screamed in rage, billowing into a cloud of flames and tearing apart the vines—only to have a sea of lightning-imbued arrows crash into him from where the elves stood on the perimeter with their bows drawn.

Riven's body lay mangled in the thicket of vines, unmoving, while Azmoth broke free and charged the line.

Out of the forest roared a series of battle cries, and dozens of men charged forward from hiding places in the trees. Some carried large axes, others carried swords, some even had machine guns, and all of them had their weapons imbued with holy white light.

RAT-TAT-TAT-TAT-TAT-TAT-TAT

A Gatling gun drilled holes through Azmoth's body, ripping pieces of his flesh and bone apart right before the first of the melee fighters closed in.

Azmoth ripped the man apart, stumbling slightly due to the green runes still producing vines that caught fire as they wrapped around his body's inferno. Snarling and crunching down onto yet another man wielding a sword, machine gun fire and then a large metal club to the knee caused Azmoth to trip.

The demon's extra sets of maws, like armored worms of death, ripped out of his back and started eating people alive while he swiped and roared in anger. He tried to get up, only to have yet another volley of arrows from the elves knock him back with another wave of lightning magic.

RAT-TAT-TAT-TAT-TAT-TAT-TAT

The Gatling gun homed in on him again, giving some of the holy warriors time to back up and regain their bearings.

Meanwhile, Riven continued to stay still in his bindings, grunting in pain whenever an arrow or bullet lodged itself in his mangled body.

A clap of thunder overhead saw a gigantic white bolt of lightning fall from the heavens, crashing into Azmoth and making the demon howl in pain until finally the brutalisk fell dead to the ground as a smoking cinder of the creature he'd once been.

[Your minion Azmoth has died. He will be returned to you twenty-four hours after you pay the blood price for your minion. To resurrect your level 31 infant Hellscape Brutalisk demon, you will be required to pay Elysium directly with a sum of thirty-one thousand Elysium coins. Simply will this transaction to happen and make sure you have the required payment to further this agenda.]

Silence overcame the clearing, with only the sounds of the wounded groaning or the smoldering corpse of the demon crackling.

Elder Bren had sweat dripping down his face, and he had to calm his breathing before steadying himself and walking forward to inspect the rune formation.

"Is he still alive?" one of the holy warriors called out, a human in Earth-made body armor that SWAT teams used to wear. Only he didn't have a gun; rather he carried a broadsword.

"The demon is dead; the vampire still lives," a husky voice called out from the woods, and the dozens of holy warriors that'd rushed forward to surround the captured target all got on one knee.

From beside a bush where the Gatling gun had been hidden stepped a handsome man who was easily seven feet tall. He had a thick, muscular build and a well-trimmed brown beard. His eyes were bright blue, and his hair was combed back with a thick gel. He wore plain brown robes, like those you'd see monks from medieval eras wear, and he carried nothing but a glowing white book.

"Prophet . . ." Elder Bren muttered before bowing in respect. "I—I didn't realize you'd come personally."

Prophet shot the old man a wary glance, then smirked. "Where else would we go? These monsters have driven us from our homes, just like they would do to you. I am glad you contacted us when you did—who knows what kinds of horrors they'd set upon you in time? Though we come from other worlds, I am glad we are of like minds on these Unholy abominations."

Elder Bren nodded eagerly, even enthusiastically. "The gods shun those who allow themselves to be corrupted by the dark. We would have dealt with it ourselves, but when we saw his might . . . we knew we couldn't do it alone.

Thankfully we were able to use him against another mutual enemy of ours, as the orcs should be spooked into leaving these lands shortly."

Prophet raised an eyebrow, then grinned. "Oh? How'd you end up doing that?"

"Manipulating this man's heart with a pretty face." Elder Bren gestured to Ethel, who stood staring in the background, and Prophet laughed loudly.

Approaching the spot where Riven was tied down and barely breathing, Prophet came to a smug stop and glared down at the bound man. Thorny vines still wriggled around the vampire, and his eyes were beginning to dull as blood poured out on the ground from numerous arrow or harpoon wounds. "Ah . . . the brother of the infamous bitch who ruined my life."

Prophet raised up his holy book and brought it back to smack Riven violently across the face. The clap of noise caused Ethel and many of the other elves to wince, yet none of them attempted to stop him.

The big man brought his hand back yet again, gesturing to the two elf elders. The old men both stepped forward to join Prophet at Riven's side, with Elder Preen cackling maliciously before he came to a stop.

"What an idiot. To think that you could take one of our own as a thrall? To think you could take my future wife as your thrall!" With a snarl, the lanky old elder brought his staff up and started viciously beating Riven across his face. The sound of bruising flesh and cracking bone could be heard over and over again, with Elder Preen's wide, bloodshot eyes glaring down amid huffs and puffs of exertion.

WHACK-SMACK-BAM

Elder Bren eventually held up a hand, motioning for Elder Preen to stop. "That is enough. He is nearly dead, and I would have words with him before Prophet takes his head as a trophy to send back to this Allie girl."

Prophet grunted with folded arms. "Meh. I think I was enjoying that as much as Preen was."

Elder Bren ignored the other two laughing men and sighed when he looked upon the beaten, bloodied features of the man who'd saved their village. Bren stepped forward, lifting up Riven's hood to reveal a fractured skull and dimming eyes. "My boy. I am sorry we had to do this."

Riven did not reply. He could not reply. He merely gave out ragged gasps for air.

Guilt surged in Bren's chest, and the old man gripped his cane more forcefully. He shot a glare at the other two leaders for their unnecessary cruelty, and then looked to the people around them. Both elves and humans alike had mixed emotions on the matter, but the vast majority of opinions were obvious—they were stares of approval. They approved of Riven's death; many of them had even enjoyed the show, and Elder Bren couldn't necessarily blame them.

The old man rubbed his temple and turned his attention back to the vampire. He cleared his throat and began to say his final words to the dying man bound to the earth. "You may be wondering why your regeneration isn't working, or why your mana isn't coming."

Riven only glared.

"It is because the runes of binding we have you tied down with sap your energy, my boy." Elder Bren tapped Riven's head, right next to the open fracture of his skull. "Again, I am sorry we had to do this. But you must understand, though you may be a good man yourself, any that you turn would likely not be. To even acquire the Unholy pillar is a feat in itself that speaks to a person's misgivings. It warps people, changes them for the worse. That aside, as a vampire, you are truly a monster. Whether or not you want to believe it, whether or not you see it that way, you survive on the blood of our people."

Bren turned around, calling out to Ethel. She, her father, Farrod, and her best friend, Senna, all approached from the crowd to gather around the dying vampire with looks of distaste and disgust.

The old man glanced down again with a fatherly smile. "Turning Ethel into a thrall would essentially kill her, Riven. You were willing to do that, to take her free will, to create a mind slave out of her to soothe your need to feed. A hunger that is justifiably needed to be sated, lest you go insane and kill everything around you. You and your entire species are an abomination, creation's mistake, and thus we could not simply allow you to leave. You are dangerous, like a cancer festering inside someone's body, and you must be surgically removed to mitigate any damage you could cause in the future. Do you understand?"

Riven's gasps had turned into incredibly shallow breaths, and his eyes barely stayed open any longer. The man was on the very brink of death, and Elder Bren shook his head before drawing out a long dagger made of silver. He handed it to Ethel, who was then urged forward by her father.

"This monster wanted to feed on you, to bed you, to make you his slave," Farrod stated coldly, pointing toward the bound man on his knees in front of them. "Kill him. It is your right."

"Do it," Senna agreed with an excited nod of her head. "Just imagine the stories about you! Vampire slayer—doesn't that sound neat? You're literally killing one of the most feared monsters of our childhood!"

"Let's get this over with. I have a carnivorous bitch to send his head to," Prophet stated with an annoyed growl. "Come on."

Ethel glared daggers back at the incredibly tall man, then grasped the silver blade in her hand. Resolve was set in her gaze, and she stepped forward, her stump arm pressing Riven's tilting head back in line so she could see eye to eye with him. Hesitation briefly flashed across her features, but she bit it back down when the others of her village stared at her expectantly.

Her nose wrinkled in forced disgust, and she managed to get out her words through clenched teeth. "I will never be anyone's slave. Especially not a bloodsucking monster like you. Did you actually think that I'd want to be seduced by something so gross? The mere thought of having you feed on me or use me in whatever other perverted ways you had in that gullible brain of yours is utterly revolting. You may be wondering about all those conversations you overheard when I thought I was all alone with my family or friends? All those looks of admiration? It was just a farce to get you to do what I needed you to do for my village. Thanks, by the way, for getting rid of those greenskin bastards. I can safely say I hate them a little more than vampires, but after one of your kind killed my grandmother so long ago, it's hard for me to compare accurately. See you in hell, creature."

The stunning young woman contorted her features with rage, and she plunged her dagger into Riven's neck. Yanking his head up by the hair, she began to saw and cut—removing soft tissue bit by bit in a bloody mess until she finally removed his entire head.

The body fell limp to the ground, and Ethel brought the head up over her head for the entire village to see. She smiled a perfect, white smile on beautiful features that any man would grow weak in the knees for. She waved the head around to the cheers of elf and human alike, until, all of a sudden, an audible gasp was heard.

"Father!" Senna screamed in horror, and she dropped to her knees while staring in disbelief at the head in Ethel's hands. "Ren!!!!"

Ethel dropped the head and immediately screamed in horror when she realized that the head she was holding wasn't Riven's at all, but rather that of her friend's father. The head rolled to a stop, and its red eyes opened wide with a sad and resigned smile on its lips.

Then it began to talk, and the voice coming out of Ren's head was Riven's own.

"I had thought better of you, Ethel. The same goes for all of you here in Greenstalk, really." Riven's breath shuddered one last time through a mere figment of Fay's magic still left in Ren's severed head before his words grew as cold as ice. The red eyes flickered to focus on Elder Bren last. "Old man . . . When I asked you not to do this, I was not begging for my life. I was begging for all of yours."

With those last words spoken through Fay's remnant hallucinations, Riven snapped his fingers—and the barrels nearby detonated in explosions of red shrapnel. Though he did not perish, he would forever remember this as the day his innocence died in his stead. It would forever mark the day that his life changed irrevocably, when ruthlessness overtook him. It was the day that he lost trust in others—and was the day he was born anew.

KABOOOM

On a hillside nearby that overlooked Greenstalk village, silent tears streamed down Riven's emotionless face. A cloud made from earth, stone, and body parts flew skyward when the barrels he'd packed halfway with Bloody Razors erupted. He'd injected insane amounts of mana into each of the razors, as much as he could muster without causing them to become unstable, and the result had been four massive shrapnel bombs that melted Prophet, the village elders, and anyone else in the explosion radius instantaneously.

He'd just killed over a hundred people in less than a second.

Including those he'd thought were friends. Ethel and Senna were dead, as were the village elders.

Perhaps Riven truly was a monster.

"You'll be okay," Fay said solemnly under her small black horns, grimacing at the sight below them. "You did what you had to do. My Curse of the Dreamwalker is ending now; the hallucinations will soon fail, so any survivors will probably be able to see us when that happens. There are still enough people down there to put up a solid fight."

Riven didn't look away. He merely watched. "I'm already okay, but thank you for your concern. They had it coming, and this is just a learning experience. A hard-won learning experience. Allie, send them in."

His sister nodded, raised a hand to ready the signal, and a series of feral roars echoed out around the village from multiple directions. "Find the book, kill the crusaders, enslave the elves. It's finally time to end this war. Oh, and bring me Prophet's head. I'm going to mount it on my wall."

Mara nodded and shot a beam of light into the air, signaling the attack. The thunderous charge of Allie's undead army burst through the trees toward the village, with people down below starting to scream and panic. The clash of battle was soon heard, and Allie turned to look at her brother with concern in her eyes.

"You are too good for this world, Riven. I'm sorry it ended like this . . . I told you that they wouldn't accept us, but you just wouldn't listen." Allie reached out to grip his hand, but he jerked it away and turned on her with a menacing glare.

"You lied to me," Riven said with venom in his words, glowering over her before spitting on the ground beside his own feet. "I thought you were better than that. I saw the things you did in Brightsville. You'd better hope that you keep your end of the promise this time—keep the kids safe, family units for the elves stay intact if at all possible. *That isn't a request.* Do what you want with the humans; I couldn't give a rat's ass."

Whirling in a rage, Riven turned heel on his sister and did not look back. He passed the orc chieftain Gurth'Rok and a small band of elite greenskin warriors, passed Athela and Dr. Brass, only to disappear into a rift in space he created with a swipe of his staff. The black portal blinked out with a clap of power, and Allie was left behind to blink tears away while clutching at her sides.

"He blames me, yet he was the one who figured this all out and decided on the plan. And I still don't even know how he did it!" Allie sniffed, taking off her skull mask to wipe off more tears. "Fucking stupid-head brother of mine."

Athela opened her mouth to make a rebuttal but decided better of it. If Allie couldn't see why lying to Riven about her actions in Brightsville was something that would piss him off, she doubted that she'd get through to the girl. Instead, Athela motioned for the orcs to head in alongside the wave of undead. "Well?! What are you waiting for, boys! If you're Riven's subordinates now, you've got to act the part. Stop being lazy and get down there!"

Chieftain Gurth'Rok abruptly nodded, and one of his soldiers blew a war horn. From up the mountain, a series of repeating horns sounded in kind, and the remaining fighting force of the Yellow Skull Tribe rushed toward their age-old enemies with glee.

"I hope you drilled into their heads that subduing the elves is a priority. No killing the elves unless it's absolutely needed," Athela warned with a waggling finger. "We're going to reeducate their brats and use the adults in other ways. They're Riven's cattle now, and you should know what happens when a vampire gets pissed off because his cattle are butchered prematurely."

Gurth'Rok chuckled with a nod and planted his cobra staff into the ground, kneeling before Athela in subordination. "Of course, my lady. They may rough the elves up a bit for fun, but there won't be any needless killing, just as Riven instructed. Your master will not regret taking us under your wing, and we look forward to serving a conqueror such as him. For the Thane coven!"

Mara shot a look over at the orcs with a sideways grin. "For the Thane Necropolis."

ABOUT THE AUTHOR

Ranyhin1 is the pen name of Trent Boehm, author of Elysium's Multiverse, an apocalypse LitRPG he originally released on Royal Road. A lifelong lover of fantasy, Boehm is also a science nerd, Dallas Cowboys fan, and wannabe gym rat. He hopes one day to pursue writing full-time.

DISCOVER
STORIES UNBOUND

PodiumAudio.com

Printed in the USA
CPSIA information can be obtained
at www.ICGtesting.com
JSHW022206140824
68134JS00018B/885